By the same author

RHANNA AT WAR
CHILDREN OF RHANNA
RETURN TO RHANNA
STORM OVER RHANNA
STRANGER ON RHANNA
A RHANNA MYSTERY

KINVARA
KINVARA WIVES

KING'S CROFT
KING'S ACRE
KING'S EXILE
KING'S CLOSE
KING'S FAREWELL

NOBLE BEGINNINGS
NOBLE DEEDS
NOBLE SEED

Non-fiction

BLUE ABOVE THE CHIMNEYS
ROSES ROUND THE DOOR
GREEN ARE MY MOUNTAINS

RHANNA

Christine Marion Fraser

coronet

CORONET BOOKS
Hodder & Stoughton

First published in 1978 by Blond and Briggs Ltd
First published in paperback in 1979 by Fontana
A division of HarperCollins*Publishers*
This edition published in 2000 by Hodder and Stoughton
A division of Hodder Headline

10 9 8 7 6 5 4

A CIP catalogue record for this title is available from the British Library

ISBN 0 340 76565 8

Typeset in 11/13pt Garamond by
Phoenix Typesetting, Ilkley, West Yorkshire

Printed and bound in Great Britain by
Mackays of Chatham plc, Chatham, Kent

Hodder and Stoughton
A division of Hodder Headline
338 Euston Road
London NW1 3BH

To Ken, Who Gave Rhanna Its Name

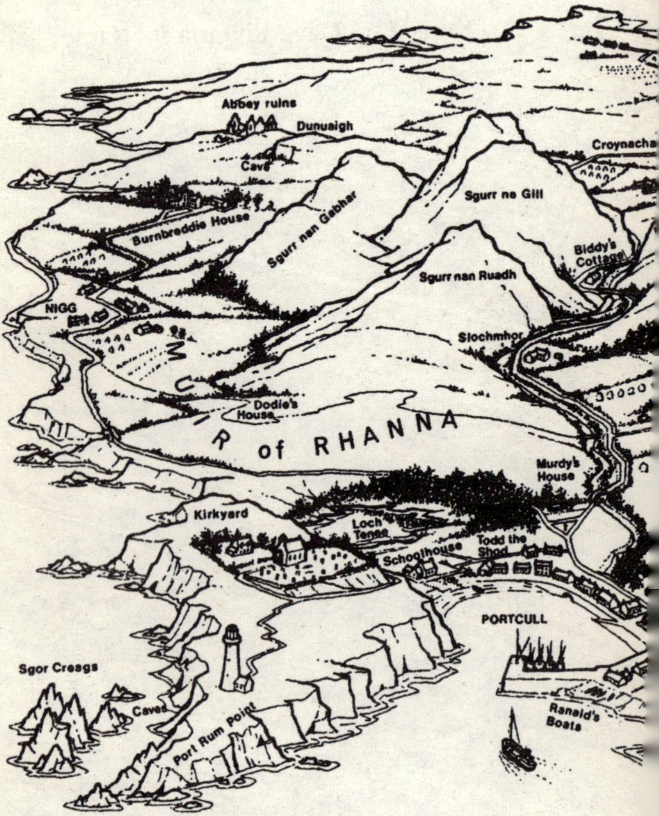
Abbey ruins
Dunuaigh
Cave
Croynacha
Burnbreddie House
Sgurr nan Gabhar
Sgurr na Gill
Biddy's Cottage
Sgurr nan Ruadh
NIGG
Slochmhor
Dodie's House
MUIR of RHANNA
Murdy's House
Kirkyard
Loch Tenee
Todd the Shod
Schoolhouse
PORTCULL
Sgor Creags
Caves
Port Rum Point
Ranald's Boats

Croft na Beinn
RUMHOR
Ben
Machrie
nish's/Mathew's
Cottage
Loch
Sliach
PORTVOYNACHAN
nhor
Bob's
Biggin
SOUND OF RHANNA

Part One

January 1923

Chapter One

The peat fire flickered in the hearth and the pale halo of light from the oil lamp cast long shadows on the camped ceiling of the room. A young woman lay in the big brass bed. Her face was pale, with beads of perspiration glistening on her forehead. Outside the warm shell of the big farmhouse a low moaning wind found its echo inside the cosy room as a soft groan broke from the lips of the young woman.

'Ach, there now, mo ghaoil,' soothed Biddy McMillan, bathing the fevered brow for the umpteenth time, and smoothing damp strands of red-gold hair from the pointed little face.

Wiry greying hair escaped Biddy's ancient felt hat. She felt tired and old, and her thirty years as midwife on Rhanna had stamped on her countenance the tenderness and toughness that went hand in hand with her calling. She sighed and turned to the young doctor at the foot of the bed.

'What do you think, Lachlan? There's no more strength in the lass. She was never fit to carry a bairn, never mind give birth!'

Dr Lachlan McLachlan shook his head, a dark curl falling over a forehead that was also soaked in sweat. He sighed wearily. 'I don't know, Biddy. She's not got the strength to push the bairn into the world. It looks like a forceps delivery. I didn't want it that way but if the infant isn't out soon it won't survive – the foetal heart is getting fainter by the minute. Go and fetch Mirabelle, we'll need all the help we can. Tell her to bring more hot water and some sheets. There's going to be much bleeding.'

Mirabelle, plump and homely, was in the kitchen. In anticipation of the doctor's needs she was boiling gallons of water on the range and clouds of steam rose from kettles and pans. She turned when Biddy came in and her round pink face was anxious.

'Well, how is the lass?' she asked curtly. 'I hope it won't be much longer for all our sakes. Fergus has been like a demon, with ants in his breeks since the start o' the pains. He won't keep from under my feet, asking endless questions about the time a bairn takes to be born. I could skelp his lugs so I could!'

Biddy ignored the sharp tones, knowing they were born of worry. Mirabelle had kept house at Laigmhor for twenty-six years but the title of housekeeper was a mere formality. She was the heart of the big rambling farmhouse. Without her, Fergus McKenzie and his younger brother Alick would have known a very different life. Since the premature death of their mother, Mirabelle had mothered them and cared for them. Hers was an ample heart out of which love flowed like a stream. It had flowed out to Helen, the girl who now lay upstairs in childbirth. Helen had come to Laigmhor three years before, a surprise to everyone. Fergus McKenzie had gone north on farming business and when he returned he brought Helen whom he had met and married in the short space of two months. Rhanna was amazed that strong-willed Fergus, who never did anything on impulse, should have behaved so untypically, and Malcolm McKenzie, Fergus's father, was angry and disappointed because he'd had hopes of a sturdy local lass becoming the mistress of Laigmhor.

Helen was eighteen years old, so small and slim that it seemed impossible that she could make a farmer's wife. But time proved everyone wrong. Her exuberance for life, coupled with her strength of character, oiled the cogs of Laigmhor so that life there ran more smoothly than ever before. She brought sunshine into the old house and even Malcolm, who had retained an air of dour, hurt silence for a time, eventually blossomed under her warm influence. She made him feel important and wanted, his cantankerous moods gave way to a new zest for life, and if the house was without her cheerful presence for any length of time he complained restlessly till she returned.

Laigmhor had been without a mistress for so many years that Mirabelle had come to accept the role as her own and she was wary about Helen. But though the girl was sweet and charming she was also discerning and wily. She discussed all household affairs with the old lady, and appeared to need advice about even the most trivial matter so that Mirabelle, flattered and secure of her position, remained sweetly oblivious to the fact that the girl got her own way without seeming to do so at all.

For Alick, Helen was a welcome addition to the household. He amused himself by flirting with her slyly and earned only gay peals of laughter from the girl who adored his brother with all her heart and took no bother to hide the fact.

Alick was the complete reverse of his strong, dominant brother. The farm and its running held no interest for him. He was flighty and perpetually in search of pleasures outside the demanding tasks of the farm. He was shy, yet glib, his greatest gift lying in the quick words of flattery he gave to the plainest of females. As a result, he was never short of women and at fifteen years of age had disgraced the family by making a local girl pregnant. His father, never very interested in his younger son's welfare because he regarded him as a weakling not fit to be a farmer's son, washed his hands of the matter and it was left to Fergus, barely eighteen, to sort out the affair as best he could. In the end the girl had miscarried and Alick had been sent to a school on the mainland. Well educated he returned to Rhanna with no real ambition for his life. He drifted around the farm, escaping as many of the manual tasks as he could and getting in the way of everyone. Finally he had left the island to seek his fortunes in Edinburgh. With the luck of his kind, he found a good job, married a girl as flighty as himself, and had only come back to Rhanna once in two years for the funeral of his father who had collapsed and died while helping with the harvest one ripe September morning.

Fergus now ran the farm, handling its affairs with the confidence of the born farmer. Those who had known him all his days said they didn't know him at all and were never likely to, for he was a man of few words and undemonstrative to boot, though this was not an uncommon trait in the dour demeanour of the Rhanna folk. But there was also a softness lurking beneath the surface of the main mass of the population and it was thought lacking in Fergus. He was labelled as hard and unyielding and had few close friends, but the more discerning of these knew that under the steel buffer beat a heart that was steadfast and fair despite his bouts of unreasoning temper.

Helen was his life now. The sight of her smiling could change anger to laughter. If, on rare occasions, she was displeased with him, he was like a little boy who had been naughty and wanted to make up. With every touch and glance she melted his façade and kindled in him fires of deep desire.

Now she was upstairs, struggling to bring his child into the world, her cries of agony searing into him till he could almost feel her pain himself. He had gone upstairs several times and she clung to him with hands that were cold and damp despite her fever. At times her body shook with uncontrollable tremors and she retched weakly, while he held a basin to her mouth.

'I'm sorry, Fergus,' she whispered as if the pain and sickness were her fault. 'I – I didn't think it would be so bad.'

You're sorry! You're sorry! his heart cried out and he thought, it was my doing! It's my fault you're going through this hell! But if desire was a fault, then they were equally guilty. Passion had engulfed them both with its eager searching for fulfilment, the warm lust they felt for each other coupling them in the dark intimacy of their bedroom as they lay together in the soft feather bed, the very bed she now occupied in her agony.

He sat by the peat fire in the parlour, the flickering flames outlining the bulk of his powerful body, his shock of black hair matching the coals in the hob, and his dark eyes bright with the unshed tears of anxiety. The springs of the old wooden rocking chair creaked protestingly as back and forth he rocked unable to still himself, the turmoil of his thoughts thrashing unceasingly till he felt he would go mad. He knew things were not going well upstairs. He had heard Mirabelle go into the kitchen and rattle pots and pans, filling them with yet more water that must be heated. Good God! What did they do with all that hot water? Biddy's voice floated through the door, requesting Mirabelle to go upstairs.

He bit into the stem of his unlit pipe then banged it back on the mantelpiece, finding no comfort in the familiar things of his life. He rose, and strode up and down like a caged wild thing, his stockinged feet making a soft padding sound on the hearth rug. All night long he had paced thus, hearing the low moan of the wind outside, feeling the chill of the fiendish snowstorm in the very marrow of his being. The blizzard was over now but the wind had gone raging on, piling the soft snow into every conceivable corner, humping it over windowledges and doorsteps. Several times he had left the warmth of the parlour to shovel snow from doorways, leaving paths clear for the morning when work must start no matter the weather. It was now 4.30 and another two hours would see the start of the farm tasks. Hamish Cameron, his grieve, had promised to come down for the milking. He would bring young Mathew, a local boy who had recently started work at Laigmhor. He, too, was a born farmer and tackled lowly jobs like byre-mucking and teat-washing with an enthusiasm that earned Fergus's approval. He took the milk cart on the morning rounds, filling milk cans from the big churns.

Fergus went to a frost-rimed window and peered out. The morning was eerily bright, the sky glittering with the farflung sparks of millions of stars. The snow reflected itself in strange haloes of light and it was quite possible to see the stretching white nothingness of the Muir of Rhanna and the sea a thread of silver in the distance.

Another cry came from upstairs and he stiffened. In a torment he cried aloud. 'Let the damned child be born soon. She can't stand any more, not my little Helen!'

He stared back into the cosy room and it looked so normal that for a moment he felt he was living alone in a world of unreality. Everything else was the same, but not he. He tried to think about the day before but could remember very little. Snatches came to him – small things, like taking Helen a cup of tea before he started his day. She had thrown her arms round his neck, laughing because the roundness of her body had prevented him getting too near.

'Can you believe you'll be a father soon?' she teased. 'I can't imagine it at all. The bairn will deeve you with its greetin' and you'll mump like an old man. Will you skelp your son's wee bum when you're in one of your moods?'

He had laughed with her. 'I'll leather yours now if you don't hold your tongue!'

He had pulled the sheet back to gaze at her, at her soft burnished hair spread over the pillows, and her blue eyes regarding him with the veiled fire of her vital attraction. It was a look he knew well and usually preluded sexual play. She knew she was desirable but she never used it as a weapon of control over him, rather she used it to make their love-making into something that took them both into a world of deepest intimacy and incredible sensual pleasure.

His hands had travelled over her rounded breasts to the hard swelling of her belly, feeling the warmth of her flesh through the soft flannel of her nightdress, and the contact started the familiar ache of longing in his groin. Sweat broke on his brow and he was ashamed of his hardness when she was lying there with his child almost ready to be born. It had been a long time since his cravings for her body had been satisfied. Really it had only been a few weeks but to him, lying beside her every night, with the perfume of her skin and hair in his nostrils, it had seemed an eternity.

Confused, he turned from her, but she had pulled him round and her hands caressed the hardness in his middle. Even through the thick material of his rough tweed trousers he felt the touch as though he were standing before her naked.

'My poor Fergus,' she said softly, 'you've been very patient but it won't be long now. Don't be ashamed of your feelings. You're a bull of a man but I'm not one to be complaining for I love every movement you make inside me. My belly won't always be this size, it's like a funny wee mountain and I'll be glad to be rid of it.'

He grinned, glad of the change of mood that allowed the heat to gradually go from his loins. 'I love your wee mountain because it has our child inside it. I hope it's a girl with your eyes and teeny button of a nose. But I hope she won't chase me round the kitchen table and clout me with the dishcloth the way you do when roused!'

She giggled. 'I want a boy, strong and dark like you and with eyes like coals burning in the grate. But he mustn't have your temper for I couldn't bear two going into tantrums.' She laughed in her abandoned way. 'I'll have to give you a few lessons on nappy-changing and the best way to break the winds, as Shelagh would say.'

An hour later, when the weak fingers of dawn were spreading out over the cold January sky, Mirabelle came panting up the slopes of the hill pastures to tell him that Helen's pains had started.

'I'll fetch Biddy at once!' he cried and ran to the byre where the horses were stabled. Mathew was hitching Mac the pony to the milk cart but Fergus stayed him with a quick order.

'The rounds can wait till later! I need Mac now!'

Mirabelle wheezed into the stables. 'There's no need to go right this meenit, Fergus! It will be a long whily before the bairn comes.'

'I'll go now,' he said and without another word led Mac outside.

Mirabelle shook her head in disgust and mumbled

under her breath, 'A real nipscart that one. As pig-headed as a mule!' She giggled, better humoured at having allowed herself the luxury of a quiet swear. It was a safety valve she used frequently, especially when she found herself harassed in the kitchen, often about Fergus because of his difficult ways, but mostly at the hens who clucked and strutted into the kitchen leaving droppings on her clean floor and poking into her pantry in a never-ending quest for food.

Fergus set out, excitement struggling with anxiety on the mile-long journey through Glen Fallan to the midwife's cottage.

At the sound of his imperative knock an upstairs window opened and Biddy looked out, her hair dishevelled and her face lined and yellow in the unkind light of winter. 'Ach! It's you!' she said indignantly. 'I thought it was thunder! What's wi' you? I've just had my breakfast and I'm not yet dressed so I can't come down.' She drew the folds of a thick wool dressing-gown round her neck and her eyes, small and tired without the aid of her glasses, peered at him in annoyance.

'We need you at Laigmhor,' he shouted, his breath condensing in the cold air from the moor. 'Helen's started!'

'How long since? Have her contractions been going on for a time?'

'Long enough!' came the short reply.

'Ach, away you go, Fergus! She'll keep for a few hours yet I'm thinkin'.'

'How do you know! She could be quick and no one there.'

'Not wi' a first! Never wi' a first!'

She fell to grumbling until Fergus exploded. 'Dammit, woman! Are you coming or not?'

'Och, haud your tongue, man, I'm comin'! Just give me time to put on my breeks if that's no' too much to ask!'

The window banged shut and Fergus was left to stamp his feet and swing his arms until the door opened and Biddy came out, calling a fond farewell to a big black cat which sat at the foot of the stairs mewing loudly.

'Bide a wee, my lamb. I'll try not to be too long. I've a nice bitty fish for your dinner!'

Fergus snorted and Biddy gave him a cold look before flouncing over to the trap. She grumbled at everything on the journey to Laigmhor. She told him he shouldn't have come for her so early. Babies didn't just pop out the minute a pain started. There would be a long wait ahead and she had heartburn from rushing about so soon after her breakfast. He remained silent throughout the tirade. He knew her so well; her bark was only a front. When she was with her patients her gentleness and patience were matchless. She had assisted most of the younger population of Rhanna into the world, and their own offspring. Everyone dreaded the day when age or death robbed them of the kenspeckle old figure who had devoted her life to her work. She was Rhanna-born as were her parents and grandparents, and had only left the island to take her training, returning to assist the existing midwife, then carrying on alone when 'Auld Murn' collapsed and died at the age of eighty.

Mirabelle had everything ready and Helen was curled in the chair by the bedroom fire looking very young in a blue nightdress. She giggled a little nervously when Fergus loomed big and speechless at her side. 'Don't look like that,' she chided. 'You'll make me more scary than I am already.'

'Pain bad?' he grunted gruffly.

'Getting worse now but I can thole it . . . och, c'mon now! We'll laugh at this later.'

Biddy intervened. 'Out, my lad.' She pushed him towards the door. 'Men are so feckless at times like these it just gets me angry!'

He tried to fill the gaps in his memory but it was useless. The day had passed in a blur with Mirabelle stolidly plodding up and down stairs, taking Biddy endless cups of tea and muttering under her breath.

Nancy McKinnon, the young daily help from Portcull, darted about from kitchen to yard to hang out wet dishtowels and feed the hens. she slopped soup into bowls and made thick sandwiches filled with dry mutton and told herself Fergus was lucky to get anything at all. He filled the weary hours with essential farm duties, his voice clipped and cold when he gave orders to the men. By the end of the day they were glad to be out of his sight.

Murdy McKinnon, a distant cousin of Nancy's mother, kicked dung from his wellingtons and chewed viciously at a plug of tobacco.

'He's a bugger o' a man is McKenzie,' he complained to Jock Simpson, the amiable ploughman, who was employed in no one place but gave his services to the widely scattered farms on Rhanna. 'My Cailleach just dropped our three lads like a ewe scatters its sharn.' He blew his nose on to the hard rutted road and rubbed the gob of mucus into the ground with his stoutly booted foot. 'McKenzie seems to think no one never had a bairn but his wife!'

Jock nodded placidly and was glad of the fact that he had never had the worry of a wife let alone a child. 'Ach, you canny compare Laighmhor to yoursel', Murdy. Yon wife o' yours is a real blossom o' a lass. Plenty o' meat to her bones you might say. The wee lass McKenzie wed's a nippet cratur – bonny, mind, but no' made for rearin' bairns.'

Murdy sniffed and plodded on, his mind on his cosy cottage by the Fallan river. A hot meal would be waiting and his three sturdy sons would clamour for his attention. Later, his wife would regale him with all the local gossip while he smoked his pipe with his feet on top of the warm oven in the range. The scent of snow was heavy in the freezing air and the men hurried on, the dim lights of Laigmhor already well behind them.

Teatime came and went, and Biddy decided it was time to call the doctor. She was getting anxious about Helen whose pains were violent but who was nowhere near giving birth.

Fergus, thankful for something to do, strode out of the warm kitchen and met the first flakes of snow from a leaden sky. Lachlan's house was but a short walk from the farm and later he remembered nothing of it. His memory was only of Phebie McLachlan, outlined in the dim light from the hall, her two-year-old son Niall clutched in her arms.

'Can Lachlan come?'

It wasn't so much a question as a demand, and Phebie's welcoming smile faded a little. She and her husband were incomers in Rhanna. Their four years there were a mere breath in time as far as the islanders were concerned and every move they made was watched warily by the natives. Lachlan was a Stornoway man and because he 'had the Gaelic' was more at an advantage than Phebie who hailed from Glasgow. They had met while he was at Glasgow University studying medicine, had literally 'fallen' for each other when he, late for a class, had bumped into her in the middle of Argyle Street and they had both landed in the gutter, he with a fractured wrist and she with bruises and a 'jelly nose'.

A year later they were married and moved to England where he had managed to get his first post as a doctor. But he pined for the Hebrides and when the post of Medical Officer became vacant on Rhanna he applied for the job and got it.

But being a doctor was one thing; earning the confidence of the canny crofters was another. They compared him continually with 'Auld McLure' who'd been Rhanna-born and bred and who knew every one of his patients and their ways. He had not been very well up on 'fancy modern cures' but that had not greatly mattered: he had healed with the wisdom of familiarity and age-old cures. Simply by spending an hour or so 'cracking' with a patient and having a dram or two had done more good than any medicine found in a bottle. 'Except for the stuff the tint o' an amber river,' the islanders joked with a glint in their eyes.

But Lachlan was making progress. His fluent Gaelic overcame a great many hurdles because the Rhanna folk were lazy, with the unhurried calmness of purpose passed down through generations, and they did not care to translate every thought or expression into English. Many of the older folk knew no other tongue than Gaelic. The young people had the English – they had to learn it before going to school or they didn't go at all – but even they found it more natural to use their native tongue and poor Phebie had been at a loss until she built up a reasonable Gaelic vocabulary.

'Auld McLure', now buried beside his wife and daughter in the Hillock Kirkyard, was still well remembered by his old cronies but his name was now less on their lips. Young McLachlan 'was a bright one and no mistake'. Lachlan, looking at bunions that ought never to have been, and administering to bronchial chests that could have been prevented with a little care, cursed 'Auld McLure' under his breath and set about righting the ails of the islanders. After four years of hard work they held him in respect and marvelled at his 'fancy ways' that really worked. His tall young figure and boyish smile, his kind yet firm way of dealing with even the most difficult of patients, had earned him a firm place in the hearts of the Rhanna folk. With patience and a good deal of understanding Phebie, too, had won her way into the affections of the islanders. Even so she'd been glad of the advent of Helen who was a 'foreigner' like herself but who didn't mind the tag in the least. With her vivacity and joy of living she drew people like a magnet and they came to her, the wary Rhannaites, because they could not help themselves. They spoke about her 'scrawny wee figure' and told each other she would 'never make a farmer's wife' but not a day passed without one of them seated cosily in the kitchen taking a Strupak and listening to her gay chatter, some of which they couldn't understand but which made them smile anyway it sounded so cheery. Ceilidhs were part and parcel of island life but the McKenzies had been a family who had kept themselves to themselves and Laigmhor had always been a quiet, dreaming place.

Now, with Helen it rang with gossip and song. Ceilidhs there were now a regular occurrence and Phebie was glad of Helen because she made life so precious a thing to be lived and passed the exuberance she felt to everyone she met.

The friendship between Fergus and Lachlan had developed with painstaking slowness. Fergus was a son of Rhanna, and caution and dourness had been his heritage. In his heart he admired the young doctor but it was not his way to let such feelings show. Enough it was that he could pass the time of day with Lachlan without feeling the impatience that others roused in him. With the exception of Hamish Cameron he had very little in common with his own kind. With them he experienced an anger because they squabbled like children over matters of little importance. With Lachlan he felt no need to indulge in silly superfluous chatter. Peaceable silences could fall between them and he didn't feel he had to search his mind for something to say to fill the time. He was at ease in Lachlan's company and Lachlan knew he was honoured by the friendship – the islanders were quick to tell him so.

'A real dour one that,' sniffed Behag Beag, the postmistress, when Lachlan went into her shop one day to buy stamps. 'Aye was – even as a bairn. Used to keek at me wi' thon queer brooding eyes o' his! Black as his moods they are. Alick was a different laddie altogether. A weak sort right enough but kindly in his ways. Fergus did all the fightin' for him at school for he couldny stick up for himself but he wasny to blame, he never got the chance to prove himself – it's no wonder he was aye in trouble when he grew older. That poor lass . . .' She shook her head sadly and let the words hang in the air before continuing. 'Fergus had to stick his nose into that affair as well. Always leadin' Alick's life for him – aye – you'll regret makin' friends wi' that man! Not a word o' cheer you'll get from him and that's a fact!'

Lachlan smiled to himself as Behag's mournful tones fell on his ears. She was the soul of doom with her down-turned mouth and jowls that hung from a wizened face. Thin wisps of hair escaped a threadbare headscarf and her whole demeanour reminded him of a doleful bloodhound. She complained incessantly about her rheumatism, her customers and her lot in general and if Lachlan had cause to cross her path he took care to always appear to be rushing off on some emergency.

James Balfour, the laird, and his sickly little wife were quite upset that Lachlan had made friends with one of their tenant farmers. They lived in Burnbreddie – a large gloomy house which stood on a rocky outcrop on the western side of Rhanna. The estate reached back for three miles and more and Robbie Beag, Behag's brother, was the ghillie. Away from his sister's watchful eye he spent his days browsing through the estate, swigging whisky from a hip flask and shooting hares and rabbits which he gave to his friends. He also landed fresh trout and salmon from the two rivers and these also found their way to the tables of the crofters. Behag, unaware of her brother's generosity, gave lavish Strupaks, sublimely believing that she and she alone was the sole benefactor of Burnbreddie spoils, and her neighbours came and partook of her fare with a great show of surprise at the treats offered and all the while they shared with round-faced, blue-eyed Robbie, the greatest secret on the island.

The laird, big and blustering with a red face and a bulbous nose that told of too much rich feeding and an unrestrained tippling from the fine brands of whisky in his cellar, came from a long line of Gaels and had earned his father's disapproval when he'd come home from college in England and announced his intention of marrying an Englishwoman. All manner of threats had no effect and he'd married the woman of his choice in the end. Despite his English education he spoke a strange mixture of Gaelic and English so that words burbled from him in waves of almost unintelligible sound, his voice thickly slurred by a lifetime of drinking. Madam Balfour was much more articulate and honeyed tones dripped from a small prim mouth. She had been pretty at one time and had small delicate features, but time had twisted them, time and the bitterness she'd harboured for years at being brought to live on a remote island among 'peasants and barbarians who knew nothing of civilization.'

The young James Balfour had seemed a good catch. But when he came into Burnbreddie and its estate and decided to live there, his wife was furious at first, then resigned, but her feelings manifested themselves in an open ear for malicious gossip and a barely concealed superiority towards the crofting community of Rhanna. She was slightly more tolerant of the people who had tenanted their farms for generations, but when she spoke of Fergus the honey in her voice was tinged with bitterness and her beady, pale grey eyes glinted with malice.

'I really don't know what you see in that man,' she sniffed to Lachlan. 'A good farmer, I grant you, but not the type one would have for dinner, if you see what I mean. He barely speaks to me – I don't know why because I was brought up to be civil to everyone – but these farming people have a rough streak, would you not say? Mind you, his mother was a fine woman, more genteel, but then of course she didn't really belong here. She was from the north, farming people but better quality than the McKenzies. Alick was like her, a bit more manners than his brother. What a pity he was such a weakling in other ways, but then his father's blood is in him. Fergus is like his father all over, no control of his emotions at all! Have you ever experienced his temper? Dear me, it's frightening! I wonder he ever found himself a wife and such a flighty little thing too. Pretty as a bluebell in her way but she'll never make a farmer's wife. I . . .'

She had stopped in mid-sentence as the doctor lanced the boil that had ripened on her neck. He dressed it but his touch was less gentle than usual and she looked at him in pained surprise, wondering if she'd said anything to upset him. He had found himself wishing that he could have stitched her tight little mouth so that she could never speak again. He found her a hypochondriac nuisance with too many airs and graces. He disliked her all the more for miscalling Fergus to whom he had grown very close. In the beginning he'd found it difficult to get underneath the man's steel exterior but patience had won and he admired Fergus for being his own man.

He was glad too that Phebie had found a friend in Helen. When Niall was born, Helen was at hand like a gay sunbeam, helping in every way she could. Now it was her turn to bring a child into the world and Phebie was worried because her friend looked too frail for such an ordeal.

'Don't worry,' Lachlan said one night when Helen had had a Strupak with them before departing for home. 'The skinny wee ones are sometimes the best in childbirth. It's the ones with too much meat to them we've to watch!'

'Lachy! You're getting at me, you – you whittrick that you are! I'll – I'll . . .'

His brown eyes had twinkled and he shouted with laughter, throwing his arms round her warm plump waist. 'I love you the way you are – like a bonny pink rose just waiting to be plucked!' He nuzzled her neck and caught the roundness of her breasts with eager hands.

'Lachy!' she had cried, but softly, her voice enticing and her fair hair falling over her face. 'Lachy! Niall's crying, I must go up to him.'

'Later,' he said, his tanned skin flushed. 'A bit of crying won't do him any harm but waiting won't be good for me at all. Just feel and see what you've done to me. Now, Phebie – here – by the fire!'

But things like these were far from Phebie's mind when she opened the door of Slochmhor and saw Fergus standing against the black background of moor. Snowflakes were whirling around his muscular coatless figure and a keening wind whipped the black hair from his brow, tossing it over eyes that were darkly intent with the urgency of his quest.

She heard his clipped question and her heart leaped strangely in her breast. Niall stirred in her arms and gurgled happily. 'Where Elly? Elly comin' soon?'

'Weesht,' said Phebie, shivering in the bite of the wind. 'Come in, Fergus, you must be frozen. Elspeth will make you a Strupak.'

'I'm not here for tea! I'm here for Lachlan! Dammit woman, are you deaf? Helen needs Lachlan!'

'B-but – he's not here,' faltered Phebie. 'He was called out to Glan Fallan. One of the Taylor bairns at Croft na Beinn has pneumonia. He left three hours ago and I'm getting worried. If this weather keeps up there'll be drifts. Oh, Fergus, what if he can't get back over the Glen? It gets blocked so quickly at Downie's Pass!'

Fergus exploded. 'What about Helen? He must come!'

Phebie shivered again. 'There's no need to shout, Fergus McKenzie! Lachlan can't be in two places at once – and on a night like this I fear for his safety too.'

Elspeth Morrison, Phebie's housekeeper, came bustling into the shaft of light. She was thin and angular, her bony features always strangely immobile no matter her mood. When she saw Fergus she gave a horselike snort.

'Humph! I might have known who was shoutin' like the de'il! Can you no' come into the house like other folk? The heat is just fleein' out the door.'

'Hold your tongue, you old yowe!' roared Fergus with a glare that would have quelled the bravest heart. 'If you were in my house you'd know your place all right!'

Elspeth stuck her sharp nose in the air. She was inclined to be annoyed with Laigmhor in general because the previous week she'd fallen out with Mirabelle over a recipe for tablet.

'Your house!' She sniffed. 'I wouldny be seen dead in it! As for anybody you can get to work for you – they must be gey weak in the head if you ask me!'

'That's enough, Elspeth!' ordered Phebie sharply. From the corner of her eye she had seen Fergus's fists bunching with rage and she couldn't blame him. Elspeth's tongue was sharp and bold. Many blamed her bitterness on her husband Hector who was a fisherman. When he was away her whole demeanour softened. When he came home and drank the cold of the sea from his bones till he was a sodden lump of cursing humanity, his wife bore the brunt of his fists and foul language and she in turn spat cynical words at her fellow creatures and was not popular even among the fisherwives on the harbour. She vowed a hatred for all men and prayed that her husband would be lost to sea. It was quite common knowledge that she went about saying, 'The sea's the best place for his carcase. He'd make a nice feast for the gulls but the craturs would likely die of alcoholic poisonin'.'

After such terrible utterances she would sit in her cottage with her bible on her lap and folk looking in could not tell if she was using the good book to strengthen her evil wishes or if she was in fear of her salvation because of them and was relying on the bible to resolve her difficulties.

She came out to the door and glared at Fergus before stretching out her arms for Niall. 'I'll take the bairn inside – poor wee mite's blue with cold. I'll be off in ten minutes so I'll just finish in the kitchen.' She glowered malevolently at the snow. 'What a night! There'll be a blizzard come midnight. I'd better hurry. *He'll* be home waitin' for his supper! Drifts a dozen feet high there could be but *he'd* sit with his feet up waitin' for me to fetch and carry for him!'

She went off muttering, bearing Niall into the warmth of the kitchen.

Phebie turned again to Fergus who was stamping with impatience. 'I'll send Lachy the minute he comes home, there's nothing else I can do . . . except . . . could I perhaps come over and help out? I'd love to be with Helen, she was so good to me.'

Her eyes were appealing but Fergus turned on his heel.

'There's nothing you can do! I've enough women

cluttering my house! I'll be waiting for Lachlan. If anything happens to Helen and he's not there, he'll surely be to blame!'

The wind carried away his muttered words so that Phebie did not hear them. She watched his hulking figure till it was lost in the whirling snowflakes, then she turned gladly into the warmth of the house, her thoughts centred on Helen and on her husband out in lonely Glen Fallan.

She shut the door and stood leaning against it.

'Oh God,' she whispered. 'Please bring Lachy safely through the storm – and – Helen . . . give her the strength for what's ahead. Please God!'

Chapter Two

By nine o'clock the wind had risen to a howling shriek and drifts were piling everywhere. Mirabelle and Biddy huddled over the fire and gave voice to their worries.

'Ach, poor lass,' sympathized Mirabelle glancing at the small figure in the bed. 'She's havin' a struggle and no mistake! I wonder will the doctor manage. What if he doesny, Biddy?'

'Ach well, I'm no' a midwife for nothing, Belle. It's the girl's first born. The wee buggers have had a cosy nine months o' it and are in no hurry to come out. As for Lachlan, he's as much chance as a fart in a constipated cow gettin' through the Glen in a night like this. I'm sure the de'il himself bides yonder at Downie's Pass.'

Mirabelle's frown deepened. 'Pray God he'll make it! Fergus is rampin' like a bairn wi' the skitters! Everything will have to be done proper for Helen or we'll never hear the end of it! I'm afeard for Lachlan roamin' aboot in weather like this. Hamish was down at Portcull and he came by to tell me the waves are washin' over the harbour wall. Some of Ranald's boats have been smashed to smithereens and them lyin' on the scaup too!'

Biddy took off her glasses and wiped her weary

eyes. 'Ach well, we can only wait. I'm thankful the lass has fallen asleep. Restless it may be but it will give her strength for the rest of the battle.' She sighed and spread her legs wide to the heat. 'My, it's been a long day so it has. I'd love a wee nap and I've got heart-burn again . . . no fault of your lovely broth, Belle, but my belly hasny given me peace since all the rushin' this mornin'. I'm all blown up like there was a wheen o' wind caught in my bowel. You wouldny have a wee touch o' bakin' soda, Belle?'

Mirabelle sighed too. All day long she had been on her feet tending to the needs of the household. She longed to put her feet up and sleep for hours. She'd missed her usual nap that evening. The kitchen was her kingdom at the day's end. With a long day behind her she could nap in the peaceful warmth with Lass the old sheepdog on her ample knee and Ben the spaniel making cosy little grunts of contentment on the rug. Three cats usually occupied the warm depths of the inglenook and Mirabelle drifted dreamily, enjoying the drone of talk and laughter from the parlour where Helen and Fergus sat together before a glowing peat fire.

But tonight was not like any other night and wearily she rose to fetch Biddy's soda.

Fergus, unable to settle himself in the house, was in the byre with Hamish who had come over from his little cottage to see if there was anything he could do. He knew only too well the havoc created by gale-force winds. Laigmhor, though well protected by trees, was nonetheless vulnerable. The winter before, a gust of wind had brought down one of the trees, crashing straight through the byre roof, killing three cows and injuring one of the horses so badly he had to be shot. A new roof had been built but door and windows could be blown in by the terrible winter storms that swept Rhanna, so Hamish was busy piling bales of hay against the windows and Fergus was nailing planks of wood over the doors in the milking shed.

The two worked well together for Hamish was as silent and purposeful as his young employer. He had been grieve at Laigmhor when Fergus and Alick were infants and knew every trick there was to know about farming on an island lashed by Atlantic gales. He was a big man with powerful shoulders. A shock of red hair matched a bushy beard and fair eyebrows beetled thickly over pale blue eyes. Dressed in a hairy tweed jacket and plus fours he was a fine figure of a man. Clad in a glengarry, lovat tweed jacket and the Cameron kilt he was not to be missed in a crowd. In his younger days he had carried off numerous honours at Highland gatherings all over Scotland and for years had tossed the caber as if it were a piece of driftwood. Women gazed at his tall sturdy figure and wondered why he never married, and his attentions were still sought by eager young maidens who could well picture themselves in his cosy cottage by the tumbling burn that flowed from Ben Machrie. It was a comfortable homely place with an ever open door, but Hamish seemed quite content to retain the freedom of his bachelorhood. Animals seemed to bring him more satisfaction than humans and he shared his home with two sheepdogs, three cats and several wild rabbits he had rescued from predators.

He worked quickly and efficiently at the windows and talked in soothing tones to the beasts who moved uneasily in their stalls as the sough of the wind whined round corners and rattled at doors. He finished tying ropes and went through to the stable to caress and calm Heather and Thistle, the two huge Clydesdales used for the plough. Mac snorted and Hamish pushed a piece of carrot into his mouth and whispered into ears that were twitching nervously.

Fergus came in, stamping snow from his wellingtons. Hamish saw that he was in a sorry state. Worry, impatience and nerves had made his face drawn and grey and it came as no surprise when he said thickly, 'We've done all we can here, Hamish. You get along home before the drifts get worse. I'm going up the Glen for the doctor!'

Hamish stared at him. 'I'm not one for interfering, man, but you'd be a fool to venture out tonight. Mac would never make the drifts at Downie's Pass!'

A small muscle in Fergus's jaw worked furiously. 'I'm walking!' he stated shortly.

Hamish bit back an angry retort – he knew his argument would be lost. Both men moved into the bitter night. Footsteps crunched somewhere in the dark and Hamish held up the lamp. Lachlan came into view, his greatcoat plastered in snow and his steps dragging.

'Lachlan!' The cry broke from Fergus in a great wave of sound that defied the wind. 'Thank God, man!'

'I just got back from Croft na Beinn,' said Lachlan through frozen lips. 'Phebie gave me the message and I came straight over.'

'Good God, man!' bellowed Hamish. 'How did ye get through the Glen? No pony and trap could have managed the Pass on such a night!'

'I left Benjie at Croynachan and came the rest of the way on foot. The Taylors wanted me to stop with them but I didn't want Phebie and the bairn to be alone and I knew Phebie would worry if I didn't come home.'

Lachlan's voice was breathless with exhaustion and his shoulders sagged. The struggle over the Glen had been a nightmare of whirling white spicules that stung his face till it felt raw. He had got stuck several times and bitter air froze in his lungs and numbed his hands and feet. He had cursed himself for not taking the Taylors' offer but he hadn't realised the severity of the weather. His administrations to little Fiona Taylor had made him oblivious to all else. The struggle to break the child's fever had been a hard one but he had won the battle, and, triumph making him jubilant, he had taken no need of Donald Taylor's pleas to wait till morning. It was only when he was going through the Glen with the great masses of Sgurr na Gill and Ben Machrie looming on either side did he realise how stupid he'd been. The mountains channelled the howling winds till it seemed all the forces of the terrible night were against him, and the blizzard hurled curtains of snow with such an intensity that Benjie reared and whinnied with fear.

Croynachan loomed out of the darkness and Tom Johnston, astonished at the sight of Lachlan, ushered him into the wonderful warmth of his kitchen and led Benjie to the stable where he had a meal of hay and a brisk rub-down. Mamie Johnston had wanted him to stay, her round kindly face dismayed at the idea of him going out again but Slochmhor was but a mile from Downie's Pass and stopping only for a cup of tea he'd ventured out again, little dreaming that the last part of the journey would be the worst of all, with drifts ten feet high at the Pass. Frozen to the marrow and at the end of his strength he'd decided to stop and rest awhile at Biddy's cottage but her house was in darkness and he'd battled on, his mouth covered by his scarf in an effort to keep out the icy snow-filled winds. After what seemed an eternity Slochmhor appeared like a beacon, a little haven sitting in the middle of a smothering world. Thoughts of a hot meal and bed hurried his steps and he almost fell into Phebie's arms at the door. She cried with thankfulness into his snow-caked collar and rumpled his wet hair with hands that trembled.

'Lachy! Oh, my Lachy! I'm so glad! I was nearly coming out to look for you but then I thought you might spend the night at Croft na Beinn! One half of me hoped you would and the other half wanted you home so badly. Come inside quickly. There's a pot of broth, salt mutton and boiled potatoes and . . .' she giggled with relief '. . . if you're good I'll make you a hot toddy to warm you while I get the meal.'

He collapsed into a chair by the fire and stretched every aching limb. 'Ach, it's good to be at my ain fireside,' he said shutting his eyes. 'I feel I've been away for years. Any calls while I was gone?'

'Y-es – but you must rest and eat first.'

'Are they that important?'

She knew it was wrong but she was reluctant to tell

him about Helen. Her love for him was strong and she knew his body was crying out for rest but the doctor in him would not let him do so if a patient needed him.

'Helen's been in labour since morning, but Biddy's with her, Lachy! You must stop in for a while! Please, Lachy! You're exhausted!'

But he was already in the hall struggling back into his wet coat. 'I must go to her, Phebie, I'll get a bite to eat there. Don't wait up for me, it might be a long night.' He gave a wry smile. 'To think I battled through the Pass so that I could be here with you and you will be on your own after all.'

'Och Lachy,' she whispered tenderly, 'I'll be fine but you – how weary you must be, my darling.'

He took her face in his hands and kissed her mouth gently, then turned into the bite of the storm once more.

Mirabelle gave a cry of consternation when he was ushered through the kitchen door. She stood with Biddy's soda in her plump hand but laid it on the table to rush over to help him out of his sopping coat.

She looked at his thin tired face and her kind heart turned over. 'My poor laddie! You're frozen and done in by the look o' you! Will you take a sup of hot broth? It won't take a minute.'

'Later!' interrupted Fergus. He looked at his friend with something near to pleading. '*Please*, Lachlan,' he added with unusual humility.

Lachlan put his hand on Fergus's shoulder. 'I'll go up at once. Don't worry, man, she'll be fine.'

Biddy jumped up at sight of him. 'Gracious laddie! You're like a spook but thank heaven you're here. I've just had a wee look and think the waters haven't broken just right.'

Lachlan strode quickly to the bed and touched Helen's hot brow. She looked at him with a smile lighting her tired eyes.

'Lachlan, how tired you look. I'm sorry I couldn't wait for better weather. I can hear the storm, whining and wailing like myself.' A flash of humour touched her mouth but another pain made her bite her lip and she reached for her husband's hand. 'Fergus, how are you managing . . . and poor Mirabelle? She must be scunnered running after us all.'

'Nonsense, lass,' said Mirabelle and turned away to hide a glimmer of tears. Helen looked so young in the big bed and delicate with the pallor of her skin showing the blue veins at her temples.

Fergus crushed her hand and she winced at the strength of him. It was as if he was trying to convey some of his power to her by his very touch.

'Sorry, my lamb,' he apologized. It was his pet name for her but he never used it unless they were alone. Now he was uncaring of the others in the room. 'You're going to be safe now, Lachlan will see to it.'

Lachlan looked up and a strange look of uncertainty shadowed his brown eyes. Fergus was laying so much store on him that the burden of his responsibility felt like a weight on his back.

'I'll do everything I can, but go now. I want to examine Helen.'

Without a backward glance Fergus left the room and

the doctor washed his hands and rolled up his sleeves. He checked his patient quickly, then went to Biddy and said, 'You were right, Biddy, the membranes haven't ruptured properly. Bring a bowl over, we can speed things up a little.'

At a little past six Hamish arrived with young Mathew. Fergus could hear them in the byre but he sat on in the rocking chair by the dying fire in the parlour. An immobility had gripped him so that his muscles, tense and stiff, were unable to obey the commands of his brain. The cold of the bitter morning stole through the cracks in doors and windows, seeping into his bones. Sounds came to him as from a great distance. The soft lowing of the cows, a gentle snicker from a horse, the clucking of hens, Peg and Molly barking happily at Hamish, the desolated bleat of sheep in the fields. Later he would have to go with his men and dig out the ewes on the high ground. In such conditions they could be lost in snow-filled corries and trapped in drifts. The bleak baa'ing came to him again and he thought how much it sounded like a baby's cry. A baby's cry! He leapt to his feet. A thin threading wail came from upstairs and his heart pounded into his throat.

'Helen!'

His body surged with life and he bounded upstairs, exploding into the room. In a split moment he saw Lachlan holding a red scrawny infant. It was fresh from the womb, its body glistening, a shock of jet hair plastered thickly over a tiny head. It was upside down, and Lachlan was slapping it, forcing it to cry that it might gulp the air of life into its lungs. Mirabelle was bustling with a tray containing cotton wool and olive oil. Biddy was bending over the bed working with Helen. In the dim light from the lamp Fergus saw her removing sheets that were red with blood, so much blood that Fergus felt his own draining from his face.

'Helen!'

He strode over to her but her eyes were closed, her head turned sideways on the pillow with her lovely red-gold hair spread out like a fiery halo round her white face.

'Helen.' His voice was a dull whisper. 'Helen, my lamb.'

Her eyes opened slowly and even in the dim light were a deep gentian blue. A smile of quiet radiance lit her pointed face. 'Fergus, we have a baby . . . is it a boy?'

Fergus looked at Lachlan who was washing his hands in a bowl, the baby now transferred to Mirabelle.

'A girl,' said Lachlan briefly.

Fergus took Helen's hands and gathered them to his lips. 'We have a daughter, Helen. A wee lass who's going to look like you.'

She smiled. 'A girl, och I'm so happy. A wee girl can be dressed in such bonny clothes . . .' Her voice trailed away and lids of softest purple closed over her eyes.

A hand fell on Fergus's shoulder. 'Leave us now, Fergus,' said Lachlan. 'There's a lot yet to be done. Helen's bleeding badly, complications with the placenta. We'll call you the minute we can.'

Fergus began to protest, but Lachlan and Biddy

were already busy and he went from the room, his feelings of joy already fading, leaving a new dread in his heart.

He paced the hall, the tick of the grandmother clock keeping time with his footsteps.

Hamish came stamping in. 'We're off now, Fergus. I don't know how far we'll get but we'll do our best. I thought it best I should go with Mathew. Murdy and Johnnie are away with Bob to the sheep. You take it easy, man . . . any news yet? Has the babe arrived safely?'

Fergus swallowed hard. 'It's here – a girl.'

'Och, man, that's grand! A wee lass, eh? We'll have a dram later to celebrate. How's the new mother? Proud as a piebroch I'll ken.'

Fergus merely nodded and went into the kitchen on some pretext. Hamish shook his head sadly. He knew that something was far wrong. A man newly made a father didn't behave the way Fergus was doing. Above him a door opened and Mirabelle stood looking down. Her plump face looked thin and old and her voice, low and shaky, barely reached down to Hamish.

'Bring Fergus,' she said dully, 'the lass has but a few minutes.'

Hamish took a deep breath. 'No! It can't be!'

'Hurry!' urged Mirabelle and turned away.

Hamish found himself bursting towards the kitchen where Fergus was gazing from the window. Hamish felt his throat go dry, making the utterance of his message harsh. 'Go quickly upstairs, man . . . Helen – she's – she needs you!'

When Fergus reached the bedroom it was empty but for Lachlan. He was by the fire and flickering flames found every hollow in his tired face. 'I'm sorry, Fergus,' he said tonelessly. 'We did all we could. It's a miracle we saved the baby but Helen . . .' He spread his hands in despair. 'It was too much for her, we couldn't stop the bleeding.'

He left the room quickly and Fergus turned to look at his dying wife. The bed was clean now, the whiteness of the sheets matching the small face on the pillow, a face from which life's blood was flowing quickly. The shadows round her eyes had deepened to blue and her lips were as pale as her face, emphasizing the vivid burnished gleam of her hair which surrounded her face like a delicate painting.

'Oh God, no!' The words were torn from him in an agony of grief.

Her eyes opened and the blueness of them pierced the depths of his crying soul. Her lips moved and he gathered her into his arms.

'The baby,' she whispered, 'call her Shona – it's a gentle name, don't you think, Fergie? And . . .' Her chest heaved as she gathered breath from her failing lungs. 'I love you, my darling – I wish I could have had more of you – I've been so happy. Don't be too hard on the little one – you haven't a lot of patience, Fergus. If she's like you she'll need . . . a lot of handling.'

He gathered her closer and the familiar warm smell of her filled his nostrils so that he felt he must cry out, scream his feelings to the world. Instead he murmured, 'We'll all manage between us. Mirabelle will help you to keep us in hand.'

But she seemed not to hear him. She had turned her head towards the window. 'Och, look, Fergus, it's a bonny morning. What a lovely day for our wee girl's birthday.' He had to strain to hear the whispered words. 'So clean,' she continued, 'with the sky all wet like a mountain burn. It's funny . . . the way it's always so calm after a storm . . .'

Her hands came up and stroked the dark tumbled curls on his head, then a long sigh came from her and her hands fell back to her sides.

'Helen, don't leave me,' he whimpered. Then he screamed aloud in his grief and crushed her body, his whole being burning with pain, an ache inside him so raw and deep it cried for some salve to ease it but the tears of release would not come. 'Oh God, why, why?' he said bitterly and rocked the slender body back and forth, feeling he could never let go of the lovely creature who owned his very being. A memory came unbidden to his mind, one he had thought forgotten.

He remembered himself, a small boy gazing at the dead face of his mother. He had loved his mother with a passion unusual in a child so young. But he hadn't thought it strange, the strange thing was that his mother didn't return his demonstrations of love. But she loved Alick for sure, she was always kissing him, making all his little ills better with a kiss, giving him her attention all the time. Alick was the one who got everyone's attention because he had a gay friendly smile and perfect manners, yet he could change so quickly to a little devil, mocking the people who made so much of him. Fergus didn't mind the other people, all he had wanted was the love of his mother. She treated him differently from Alick, almost as if he were grown up. He'd had to take the responsibility of the elder brother all his childhood. He protected Alick from bullies and fought battles for him because he knew it was expected of him and would earn words of praise from his mother. Sometimes he'd felt the burden of Alick too heavy a load to bear but in his child's way he knew his mother relied on him to keep Alick in order because their father had no time to spare for his younger son.

Yet, despite everything, Fergus had gone on loving his mother though he had learned to hide it behind a façade of indifference. But he never forgot her whispered words to him on the day she died.

She had clasped his small hand and he'd gazed at her dying face with eyes that ached with unshed tears and a heart full to bursting.

'Fergus, my lovely strong laddie,' she said clasping his hand till it hurt, 'you're the child of my heart. Poor Alick, he's not strong like you and his father can't understand him. You've been a wee man these years and I'm sorry but Alick needed you Fergus. Try to see it that way, my dear proud laddie.'

Fergus's heart had known no real feelings of love after his mother's death, not until Helen came into his life. Everything in him that had lain dormant for years had burst forth in a tide of love. She had captured his very spirit and had roused him to feelings that he hadn't known himself capable of.

He had had flirtations with girls since his school-days, fine buxom girls with big breasts and berry-brown skin. He had lain with them on the warm summer moors, ran with them over sun-kissed fields till laughter and the pretence of play had ended with rough kisses and caresses. Hidden by swaying stalks of golden corn he had enjoyed the feel of soft naked breasts, and love-play had satisfied his physical desires without actually possessing any of the girls, sometimes to their annoyance that the bounties of their bodies could not entice him further.

Helen had been his first complete union. Her delicate, enticing beauty had made him burn with a longing never before experienced because, mixed with his need for her body, was the deep and lasting emotion of his love for her.

Now she was gone from him. For the second time in his life he had lost someone who had captured his heart.

He sat holding her in his arms till a footstep behind made him turn. It was Lachlan, his eyes dark with sympathy.

'C'mon, Fergus,' he said softly. 'Come downstairs and have a drop of whisky. It will do you good. Try to think that Helen is at peace now.'

Fergus stood up, his face chalky white in the dawn light filtering through the window. He looked at the doctor and a new feeling took the place of grief in his heart. A cold anger slowly boiled in him. He could feel it churning in his belly and knew he was going to say things he might later regret. He'd had the feeling before but never so intense, so pressing as now. He fought to keep the words from coming and pressed a bunched fist to his mouth, all the time staring at Lachlan with an intensity that was almost tangible. But the bubbling rage kept on inside and finally exploded to the surface.

'You!' he whispered in a tight tense voice more commanding than the loudest cry. 'You let my Helen die! You ought to have known there would be complications but you did nothing till it was too late! She bled to death because you are incompetent! Why did it have to be her? Why not the bairn? Why save it and not Helen?'

Lachlan felt his heart beat strangely. He was exhausted, so tired that his legs felt weak beneath him. He hadn't slept or eaten properly in twenty-four hours. The day-long battle to save little Fiona Taylor had been bad enough, the struggle through the storm a waking nightmare, but worst of all had been the fight to save Helen and her child. Fatigue had lain like an old man on his shoulders yet he had given of himself all there was to give. He had felt a triumph in bringing the child live into the world. Complications that no one could have foreseen had taken Helen, and his heart was heavy. It was always bad to lose a patient and when that patient was also a personal friend, the loss, the feeling of failure at being powerless to save a life, was even harder to bear.

But despite his fatigue his voice was strong when he spoke. 'You don't know what you're saying, man! I tried everything to save Helen and it wasn't a choice between her and the bairn! I nearly lost the two of them! Dammit, Fergus! Can't you see you're lucky the little one survived? My heart's sore about Helen. I'm more sorry than I can say but at least be glad you've got one of them!'

He spread his hands in appeal but Fergus took no notice.

'Get out!' he said, his voice rising menacingly. 'Get out, McLachlan! I never want to see you in this house again!'

Mirabelle appeared at the door with the baby in her arms. Her face grew scarlet at Fergus's words and she looked at him in disbelief. 'You canny be serious, Fergus! I was here most of the night, remember! I saw the way this laddie worked and he so weary too! He fought like a Trojan to save poor Helen. If she could hear your bitter words, how do you think she would feel? We're all in the presence of her dear soul this meenit, let it rest in peace and be thankful you have her bairn – a bairn ye havny even set eyes on yet. Look at her! She's the bonniest wee thing. Look at her, Fergus and thank Lachlan for her life!'

But he turned away, everything in him so spent that his strong shoulders were stooped and his head sunk on to his chest. 'Get out,' he murmured dully, 'get out and leave me in peace.'

Lachlan was already running downstairs and Mirabelle went out leaving him alone in the room. He went over to the bed and touched his wife's smooth brow. It was already growing cold and he covered his face with his hands. A ray of winter sun stole into the room and turned the small figure in the bed into a pale golden statue. He looked towards the window, out to fields and hills unbelievably beautiful in a mantle of purest white, but his eyes saw none of the beauty. An abyss loomed ahead of him, one filled with incredible loneliness where he felt the sunlight would never penetrate again. Above the bed a calendar told him that it was the twenty-ninth of January, 1923. He shuddered and tried not to let his thoughts crystallize but it was no use. It was a day never to be forgotten because it was the day his dearly loved wife had left him behind and the day his daughter had taken her first breath of life. A life for a life that had no meaning for him. He shuddered again and banged his head with his fists in an effort to stop such thoughts, but they were etching themselves into his brain. He would have given anything, everything, to have his wife back and if he could have had one wish it would have been for the baby to be taken and Helen brought back in its place.

He could hear the child crying in the next room, the room he and Helen had prepared with such joyful anticipation. She had made the curtains, golden yellow like the sun, he had distempered the walls a fresh white and revarnished the old family cradle till it gleamed, waiting for the day it would be filled with the child of their love. Now it didn't matter any more. The child of their love had become the child of his sorrow and he put his hands over his ears to shut out the thin wailing of the newborn infant.

Rhanna was a jewel of beauty on the day of the funeral. The tattered peaks of Sgurr na Gill gleamed in a brilliance of white against a cornflower sky. The snow had melted from the lower slopes and churning burns frothed down from the mountains. The Sound of Rhanna was a rippling mass of liquid silver that hurt the eyes so that it was easier to look at the shoreline where soft little wavelets kissed the white sands that encircled the bay. The long finger of Port Rum Point enticed the water round its rocky length and there the sea spumed in frothing sprays.

The Hillock Kirkyard sprawled untidily on top of a wooded slope. Ancient stones, that looked as if they had been thrown by some giant hand to land where they would, surrounded the church which stood outlined against the sky, its fine old stone battered by the wind but withstanding the wiles of the weather like a sturdy old sailor.

Fergus looked down into the yawning black hole that awaited Helen's coffin and he felt sick. The mourners stood round the grave with bowed heads, waiting for the minister to speak. He was a tall, grey-haired man with piercing eyes and a compelling voice. He had come from Dundee seven years before and was an incomer who had never been quite accepted because he gave all his sermons in English and showed no intention of trying to learn even the odd Gaelic word. Because of this he always remained on the fringe, never quite understanding and never being fully understood. Nevertheless his congregation listened, or appeared to listen, when his powerful voice reverberated through the church.

The Reverend John Grey could see the blue smoke from the manse chimneys climbing into the sky and he followed the spiral upwards and looked for a long moment heavenwards before he started to speak. His mouth felt dry and he licked his thin lips nervously. He hated the island funerals because he never knew quite what to say. Confidence oozed from him on the

Sabbath when he had prepared his sermons so carefully and when he spoke from the pulpit he could be quite impersonal towards the parishioners. But a funeral involved so many personal feelings of grief and loss and he found it difficult to commune wholeheartedly with the tight-knit community of Gaels who made it so plain he would never be one of them. Help me, God, to say the right things, he thought wistfully and began his opening words, his voice drifting sonorously in the frozen air of morning.

Helen's two brothers moved restlessly, their feet crunching the blades of frosty grass and her father took out a large white handkerchief and blew his nose loudly, drowning the end of the minister's sentence.

He began the Lord's Prayer and the men joined in, their voices a drab monotone, blowing steam with the utterance of each word. A bird chirped sweetly from a nearby tree and the bleating of sheep came from the slopes. Alick gave a loud sniff and Fergus heard it like an explosion. He glowered at his brother's bowed head, momentarily hating him because of his display of tears. He could not show his emotions to the world. He watched Helen's coffin being lowered into the dark cold cavern of her last resting place and he wanted to reach out and enclose with his arms the hard wooden box that encased the body so dear to him. Instead he closed his eyes so that he wouldn't see the first scatterings of earth thrown over the coffin.

Numbly he sensed that the mourners were moving slowly away. An arm was thrown round his shoulders and Alick's voice murmured futile words of sympathy into his ears.

Fergus opened his eyes and looked into his brother's face. He saw the blue-grey eyes, red-rimmed but eager for an acknowledgement that his presence was of some use. He noted the handsome features, finely drawn, but the drooping lips too thin under the dark wiry moustache, and the prominent bulge of the Adam's apple working desperately to swallow his tears.

Automatically Fergus assumed the role that had been expected of him for as long as he could remember. He put a strong arm round his brother and led him out of the kirkyard back to Laigmhor where the parlour was crowded with black-clad women and sombre sniffing relatives. This was the time Fergus dreaded most of all. The condolences, the weeping, all the formalities he had to go through before his house was his own again.

He could hardly bear to look at Helen's mother. He'd never liked her but had put up with her for Helen's sake. She was a small fussy woman. She'd fussed because he'd wanted Helen buried on Rhanna and she'd fussed about every little detail since her arrival on the island till he'd felt like hitting her. Three years before she'd been delighted because her daughter was making a 'good marriage' to a fairly prosperous young man, but now she realised it had all been a mistake and Helen should never have married a farmer because she had been too unsuited for such a 'rough' life.

She sat in a corner dabbing her eyes with a lace handkerchief while her husband, a short balding little man, red-faced and uncomfortable in the hot stuffy room, patted her ineffectually on the shoulder. Alick's wife, Mary, a slim blonde, frivolously pretty even in her dark clothing, sat by the window primly enjoying the attention of several menfolk. Alick appeared not to mind in the least and after a time he followed his wife's example and began flirting with Tom Johnston's eldest daughter.

Hamish sat apart from everyone, quietly sipping at a glass of whisky and Fergus went to sit by him, appreciating the strong unassuming companionship that could be felt without words.

'Fergus!' Mary's high light voice floated clearly above the general murmur of voices. 'Aren't the doctor and his wife coming? I understood they were good friends of yours!'

It was difficult to know if her question was entirely innocent. She and Alick had arrived only that morning but gossip ran quickly on Rhanna. Fergus glowered at her and she giggled but turned red. The room had grown quiet and everyone was looking at Fergus. He grew warm with embarrassment and thought, Not a questioning! Not now when everything in me longs to have Helen at my side instead of in a cold grave on the Muir of Rhanna. A sick icy feeling gripped him and he longed to run from the room like a small inarticulate boy.

But before he could say anything Helen's mother fired another question at him.

'What's to happen to the bairn? Have you considered it at all? The wee mite will need a woman's care. Donald and I have talked about it and think it only right we should bring up the child. The Lord knows it won't be easy. You know yourself, Fergus, I don't keep good health but I think my grandchild deserves a good upbringing. We owe it to our own lass too. We have our boys but they have their lives to lead. The wee girl will make up for . . .'

She began to sob quietly into her handkerchief and Mr McDonald grew redder and patted her awkwardly.

The room was agog for Fergus's answer. He could feel the hush of the curious who had been wondering about his daughter and who would take care of her.

But now Alick broke the silence. He turned away from Tammy Johnston whose face fell because she'd been enjoying the surreptitious pleasures of having Alick's hand halfway up her skirt. He'd forgotten her now, his handsome face animated as he spoke.

'Mary and I have talked too. We're young and no doubt will have bairns of our own but we'd still like Shona to come and live with us. Isn't that right, Mary?'

She nodded with a distinct lack of enthusiasm. She didn't like the idea one bit. She and Alick hadn't talked about taking the baby, they'd argued. She didn't particularly care for children – if one of their own came along it would be different, but someone else's child, especially one that belonged to a man she had never understood, didn't appeal to her at all. She prided herself on her looks and these would soon go with the strain of continual washing, sleepless nights and all the other attentions a child demanded.

Fergus looked at her and saw her vanity. He looked at Mrs McDonald, fragile like Helen, but with none of her daughter's vivacity or zest for life. She was prim and prudish, with a hypocrisy that belied her religious beliefs. He couldn't imagine her bringing up a child, its spirit would be stifled from the beginning. He couldn't even begin to consider Mary. He could find no desirable quality in her that would render her fit to bring up Helen's child.

His thoughts were a surprise to him because he hadn't till then cared very much about his daughter's future. He had barely looked at her since her birth but he hadn't been able to avoid thinking about one picture that repeated itself continually in his mind. It was of Mirabelle feeding the child from a bottle that looked enormous beside a tiny elfin face. Wide blue eyes were open, gazing unseeingly at the ceiling, yet they held a world of wisdom as yet out of reach, undeveloped beneath the smooth bloom of the high forehead, waiting for time to ripen each impression till the miracle of memory and learning blossomed from each living cell. And there was something else, something so poignant that a needle of pain pierced the shell round his heart and hurt deeply. Helen stared out of those eyes. A glimmer of life-loving mischief lurked in the periwinkle depths and the mouth was Helen's, full and soft with upturned corners giving the impression of a permanent smile.

His voice lanced the expectant silence in the room. 'I think the child will stay at Laigmhor, it's her home after all. It's good of you to offer, Alick, I know you really mean what you say but Mary doesn't . . . do you, Mary?'

He looked her full in the eyes and she turned away guiltily. Then he swivelled to face Mrs McDonald. 'I thank you too – for wanting to do your duty by Helen but as you say yourself you're not really able to care for a young child. She will be far happier on Rhanna where she belongs.'

'How dare you!' She trembled and the hanky was in evidence once more.

'I dare because the child is mine.'

'But a child needs a woman to care for it! How can you, a man . . .'

She was interrupted by Mirabelle who appeared from the kitchen, the baby snugly asleep in her arms. Mirabelle was feeling harassed. The house had been in a turmoil all day and even with Nancy's help she was hot and tired. They had cleaned from top to bottom and aired and fired the spare rooms because several people were staying till the return of the ferry. It all meant a lot of extra work for her and some of the guests she didn't care for, in particular Mrs McDonald who had complained too much. On top of everything she had the baby to see to, but already she loved the tiny mite with all her kindly heart and enjoyed the wonderful trusting feel of the downy head against her bosom. She'd been having a rest in the kitchen when the heated voices drifted through from the parlour. She knew it wasn't her place to interfere but she hadn't been able to stop herself and she stood in the doorway and stuck out her chin proudly.

'And am I not a woman? I'll look after the little one and see she gets all the love that is her due. So long as there is life in me she'll get all the care it is possible for a bairn to get!'

Mrs McDonald blew her nose indignantly. 'Even the servants don't know their place in *this* house, it would seem. I can see I don't have a say about my grandchild at all. I'll be glad to get away from this place I can tell you!'

'Serves you right, you auld Cailleach,' said Jock under his breath and Fergus looked at Mirabelle with gratitude.

'Thank you, Belle,' he said quietly. 'The matter's settled.'

When dinner was over he made an excuse and went outside. Lass and Ben padded at his heels, sniffing the frosty air with silent joy.

Fergus found his steps taking him away from the farm over the road in the direction of the Kirkyard. He climbed the frost-rimed Hillock and saw a figure coming out of the rustic wooden gate, a plump familiar figure wrapped up tightly against the cold. It stopped and looked towards him and he saw clearly Phebie's bonny face, her skin whipped to a deep rose by the frost. For a long moment she looked at him then turned away, wrapping her shawl closer round her shoulders before hurrying down the hill.

Something tightened round his heart and he sighed, a sigh that told of all the sorrow in his heart and the regret he felt at having lost the friendship of two of the finest people on Rhanna. He knew that he was too proud to go cap in hand and admit his sorrow for his hasty words on the morning of Helen's death. He also knew that he would want to apologize a thousand times in the months to come but that he wouldn't do so because of his pride, the terrible pride that bound him in a lonely prison of body and soul.

Slowly he went to Helen's grave and saw on the

fresh earth a bunch of snowdrops, the petals tightly shut, lying on the hard ground like drops of exquisite purity.

'Phebie!' he murmured. The wrong that he had done tore afresh the caverns of his mind. He had denied the McLachlans the right to see Helen laid to her rest and the enormity of his feelings forced him to his knees. The setting sun had turned the Sound of Rhanna into a sheet of flame and Portcull thrust its peacefully smoking chimneys into the fiery sky. Sheep bleated mournfully on the moor and the shouts of children from the village were borne over the Glen to be lost in the corries of Sgurr na Gill.

Lass made little whining noises and buried her nose in his arm. He caressed her ears gently.

'You feel it too don't you, lass?' he whispered. 'The loneliness. It's all so lost . . . or is it just me?'

He shut his eyes and Helen came to him, laughing, her mane of hair blowing in the wind, her blue eyes crinkled with the joy of living and of gazing into a thousand suns of happiness. They had known it together, that happiness, but each memory was a locked door in his mind. Later – later, he would remember the happy times but just now he was too numb, too tired to think very much about anything.

'Goodnight, Helen, my lamb,' he whispered, so low it was like a sigh of the wind.

Part Two

1928

Chapter Three

Shona opened her eyes and lay very still under the warm blankets. The curtains of sleep still lay heavy over her eyes and she blinked long lashes in an effort to get them to stay open.

She liked to lie still when she woke, letting her eyes travel over her neat little room with its sloping ceiling. Her bed was in an alcove and there she felt safe. Sometimes she imagined it was a cosy cave, or that her bed was a boat tied in a hollow on the shore. The rag doll made by Mirabelle lay beside her. The floor was polished and shiny with a mat near her bed. A family of dolls and woolly dogs flopped lazily on a shelf and on the dressing-table was the china bowl in which she washed each morning.

The light of the January morning filtered through the gold curtains and she wondered what sort of day it was. There was something special about today but she couldn't quite remember what it was. Then it came to her – it was her birthday. Today she was five years old and grown up because being five meant that she would soon be going to school and would enter a new phase of her life.

Excitement churned in her at the prospect. Birthdays were exciting things altogether but today's birthday would have a special flavour because she was going to feel grown up and very proud. But somewhere at the back of her mind a cloud hovered. It had something to do with her father because while all the people she loved celebrated their birthdays he withdrew into himself and became very strange and short-tempered.

She sighed at the thought of her father. He was so big and strong and she loved him with all her heart even though he was often brusque and impatient with her. Every day she longed to throw her arms round his neck and smother him with her love. Sometimes he let her kiss him and call him pet names. Sometimes he even swept her up in his big arms and crushed her till it hurt but she didn't mind because the feel of his strength made the hurt worth it because it meant that deep inside he loved her too.

She pursed her small mouth and said out loud, 'Today I am five! I am five years old today!'

The feeling of wanting to snuggle in bed left her and she padded over the cold floor to open the curtains. The wind whistled in from the sea making the rusty grasses cringe against the earth. The ocean was grey in the distance and white horses leapt and pranced to the shore. It was the kind of day she loved because inside everything was warm and cosy but outdoors the breeze would ruffle her hair and make her face tingle. On the breath of the wind would be all the smells she loved, the tang of the sea and peat smoke, the clean smell of tossing heather and the rich warm odour of the dung midden mixed with the scent of hay from the two big sheds.

She heard Mirabelle plodding upstairs with the jug

of hot water for her face and hands and she raced back to her bed and pulled the blankets over her head pretending to be asleep. Her heart beat faster and she waited, smothering her giggles. The door opened and the hot water gurgled into the basin.

'Ach mo ghaoil,' said Mirabelle slightly breathless. 'I know you're pretendin'. It's up wi' you this meenit. Your father will be in from the fields and wantin' his breakfast and you keepin' us all back wi' your mischief.'

Shona slowly peeped from the blankets and Mirabelle looked at her with an exaggerated frown on her round face. She had changed little in five years. The hair that escaped her mutch was a shade whiter and her shoulders stooped slightly, but otherwise she was the same Mirabelle who had undertaken the upbringing of Fergus's child. It had not been easy. Shona had been a lively, demanding infant, crawling at seven months, walking at a year and speaking fluently at two. Mirabelle often felt more tired than she would ever admit but the little girl's affection and love made up for everything, even the determination of will that had earned her many a spanking on her plump little bottom. But she never sulked and took the spankings and scoldings in her stride knowing she had earned them.

'Mirabelle?'

'Yes, my wee lamb?'

'You've forgotten what day it is so you have!'

'Indeed you might be right. I am always so busy I never know if it's Monday or Friday.'

'Mirabelle! You really have forgotten.'

A glimmer of tears shone in the big blue eyes and laughing, Mirabelle rushed forward to fold the child to her bosom.

'Ach, you're too quick by far to take offence. You're like your father in that queer wee way of yours. Happy birthday, my lamb. You're a big girl today and you must learn to behave like one. Now get your face washed, take your goonie off and put on your blue dress. We'll go down to Portcull after breakfast.'

'Truly, Mirabelle? Can we go to Merry Mary's and buy sweeties? I have a penny that Hamish gave me.'

'We'll see, but weesht now. Stop your blethers and get dressed.'

Shona hurried through her toilet and flew downstairs to the kitchen. Fergus was already at the table supping his porridge.

'Good morning, Father. Good morning, Ben.' She stooped to hug the old spaniel which rose stiffly from the hearth to greet her. Lass was gone now – she had died in her basket one night at the ripe age of fourteen. Mirabelle had cried for days and vowed no other would take her place but sheepdogs were a necessity on the farm. There was too much work for Peg and Molly who were now growing past their best so Kerrie came, a fine young dog who had learned fast but was a man's dog and preferred to stay with Bob the shepherd in his steading half a mile up Ben Machrie.

'Good morning, Father.' Shona repeated her greeting quietly but with a hint of stubbornness in her voice.

Fergus looked up slowly, reluctant to speak on a day that held so much joy for his daughter but none at all for him. He seldom looked properly at his little girl because the sight of her turned his heart to jelly. When he looked at her he saw Helen in every smile and glance, the way she turned her head, the glimmer of mischief always bubbling just under the surface.

But now he did look and saw his growing child, the blue dress matching her eyes, the deep auburn hair tied with a big blue ribbon to keep it from tumbling over the small pointed face. Something caught at his throat and he tried to turn away but her glance, powerful and compelling in such a small being, held his and unable to stop himself he rose and swept her into his arms.

Shona held her breath in delight, the hurt of his crushing arms only serving to heighten her happiness and she buried her face deep in his hair.

'Happy birthday, my wee chookie!' he breathed. 'Oh, God help me! You're so like her!'

Her happiness suddenly fled. The pain was there again in his voice and she didn't understand it. It puzzled her and frightened her. There was so much depth in his voice, such a force of longing that she felt him tremble. Something caught in his throat that sounded like a tear but which couldn't possibly be because he was so big and strong and never cried. For a moment she didn't want to be five. She wanted to be a baby again and to cry on his shoulder because she felt so sad. But he was putting her down and her sadness turned to hurt when he ordered her curtly to eat her breakfast.

She went to her place despondently but smiled when she saw the small pile of parcels by her plate.

'Oh Father, look! Please can I open them before I eat my porridge? I don't care if it gets cold. And please, Father, will you read the writing for me so's I'll know who they're from!'

He smiled despite himself and helped her open her gifts, losing himself for precious moments in her child's world.

'Look, father – a whirligiggy . . . from Mirabelle! Och, look at this bonny wee purse . . . with a whole shilling inside! Who is it from?'

'It's from me,' said Fergus gruffly.

'Och Father!' She flew round the table and kissed him on the end of his nose. Another parcel was opened and proved to be a roughly sewn pink apron from Nancy. The last parcel was a puzzle. It was large and soft and she enjoyed guessing what it was before opening it. Out fell a long black pair of woollen stockings and a pair of navy blue knickers. She held up the stockings, her face a study.

'Father! who are they from?'

'Mirabelle!' he supplied.

'Och Father, look at them! They're like long tubes of liquorice. You don't think she expects me to *wear* them do you?'

She stared at him in consternation and he burst out laughing.

Mirabelle stood amazed at the kitchen door. 'What's a' the skirlin' for? Mercy child, have ye not started breakfast yet? And what's so funny I'd like fine to know? Fergus! Have ye taken leave o' yer senses?'

Shona held up the stockings. 'It's these, Mirabelle! They're so funny!'

'Funny!' exploded Mirabelle. 'I'll have ye know I near blinded myself knittin' the damt things. My een havny been the same since! They're for school, madam, that's what and I'll have none o' yer cheek. Would ye rather have frostbite than wear these lovely warm stockings I've sweated over for weeks?'

'Yes, Mirabelle, I would rather have frostbite,' giggled Shona, her heart aglow with joy because she had made her father laugh.

Hamish put his head round the door. 'Can I come in and wish my wee lass a happy birthday?'

Shona clapped with happiness. She adored the big red-bearded man. He was always spoiling her with sweets and pennies but more than these she loved his hearty laugh and unstinted affection, and a visit to his cottage was a highlight of her life.

'I've a wee surprise,' he said, his eyes twinkling. 'Shut yer eyes a minute.'

She screwed her eyes up tightly. There was a murmur and a scuffle then something soft and warm was placed on her lap.

'Och, it's a wee puppy,' she said softly, tears springing quickly at sight of a tiny golden spaniel. She lifted the furry bundle to her face and a pink tongue licked her nose and snuffled into her ears. Animals were the delight of her life. The big ones held no fear for her and she sat on Heather or Thistle while they stood quietly in the stable. She was already an expert at driving the cows and it was a laughable sight to see her small figure wielding a stick at a large stubborn bull.

She ran to Hamish and hugged him. 'Och Hamish,

I'll love you all my life so I will. What a dear wee puppy!'

'See you look after her well,' he ordered, his voice muffled in her hair. 'You've to walk her and train her. Remember she's just a wee baby and needs a lot o' care.'

'I'll do everything for her, I love her so much already. I think you're the most wonderful man on earth.'

Fergus watched the scene and a strange feeling came over him. He didn't recognize it at once, then he knew it was jealousy. He was jealous that another man had given his daughter a present that pleased her enough to single him out as her most favoured person. The violence of his feelings swamped him and he couldn't think clearly. He'd had the feeling before but it had been vague and he hadn't been able to place it. He'd kept thinking of her as a baby, an infant who toddled about asking tiresome questions. At times he had felt like striking her, so much did she disturb him with thoughts of what might have been if she had never been born. Lately she disturbed him even more because a real person was emerging, one who could form her own ideas and opinions with a determination that he knew she'd inherited from him. Also there were these other feelings, the ones he experienced on holding her close, when love for her swamped him so that he had to push her away, drive the love back into his heart because it claimed too much of him and he never wanted to belong to anyone again.

Now this other feeling annoyed him so much that he stood up and spoke sharply to Hamish. 'C'mon, man, there's work to do. We've got to drive the bull over to Croynachan. Johnston has some cows coming on!'

Hamish raised a bushy eyebrow but said nothing. Shona was too busy playing with her new puppy to notice her father's displeasure. She screamed with laughter when Ben rose with a grunt and waddled over to examine the newcomer. They snuffled for a while then the pup made a lunge and caught one of Ben's long ears, holding on with sharp little teeth till the old dog groaned protestingly.

Shona bent and smacked the newcomer hard on the bottom and the golden bundle looked up at her with surprise in its blue-brown eyes.

'Naughty!' reprimanded the little girl severely. 'You mustn't plague Ben, he's an old Bodach and you treat him with respect. Now – I wonder what I'll call you. Tot would be a good name, you're such a teeny wee thing!'

Mirabelle grunted. 'Aye, and ye'd better fetch a cloot for that lochy on the floor. She's your doggy and that means you must train her. I'm too auld for such capers!'

An hour later Shona was skipping beside Mirabelle on the narrow track to Portcull.

'A whole shilling,' she sang. 'Can I spend sixpence, Mirabelle, and buy lots of sweeties? I'll get you some Granny sookers if you like. Och, isn't it a lovely day? I feel so clean in the wind!'

But Mirabelle didn't agree and pulled her coat closer to keep out the biting wind.

Merry Mary's shop was a place beloved by all the island children. It smelled of apples and boot polish and everything from bootlaces to bobbins of thread could be had there. But it was the jars and jars of colourful sweets that interested Shona and she spent a lovely time pondering over her purchases while Merry Mary and Mirabelle gossiped. The shopkeeper's real name was Mary Merry but the islanders had repeatedly got it back to front and she eventually stopped correcting them knowing it to be a fruitless task. She was an Englishwoman; but she had spent thirty of her sixty years on Rhanna and instead of being a 'new incomer' she was now honoured as an 'old incomer' and, because she spoke Gaelic like a native, the younger generation could hardly believe she was an Englishwoman and loved her dearly because her nature suited her name. She was a quaint little creature with limp ginger hair, a big happy smile and a large wart on the end of her nose. The children were fascinated by the wart. Its hold seemed so precarious on the large square nose it had become a challenge as to who would be the first to see it fall off. The child to witness its demise would receive a halfpenny from every child on the island, so Merry Mary's shop was very popular indeed. Though she sometimes wondered why her door would open to admit a solemn-eyed youngster who merely stared at her briefly before turning out of her shop without a purchase.

'Did you hear about Dodie?' she asked Mirabelle eagerly. 'He's gone and got himself a cow so he has.'

'Ach, away wi' you! Dodie will never manage a cow. He canny look after himself!'

'Well, he's got one right enough! It's a queer looking beast and its udder so big it near has to leap over the damt thing! But Dodie says it will give him plenty milk. He's that sick of trekking to the bottom of the hill where Mathew leaves his can and sometimes it's been knocked over by a damt yowe and nothing in it but grass and sharn!'

'And where did he get the cow is what I'm thinking? Poor Dodie hasny twa farthings to rub together and these beasts cost money so they do.'

'The laird gave it to him for doing wee jobs about the estate. Aye, and it was a dear cow sure enough for the laird doesn't give anything for nothing and Dodie has worked most of the winter to get the damt cow.'

'Aye, well he'll be lucky if he doesny have to go further than the end of the track to work the udder. These hill beasts just roam where the will takes them.'

'Ach well, he has a wee hut to keep the beast in but he'll have to comb the hill every evening to get her in for the night so that he'll get his morning milk.'

The two shook their heads sadly and murmured 'Aye' by way of sympathy for Dodie, the island's eccentric. He was what was quaintly referred to as 'a wee ways wrong in the mind' yet everyone knew by experience he was by no means lacking in intelligence and was not to be cheated out of a farthing. He lived alone in a tiny remote cottage in a treacherous hill track between Glen Fallan and Nigg, the minute Clachan perched on the cliffs near Burnbreddie. His real name was Joseph, conjured from the bible by his mother who had borne him out of wedlock and who had died when he was thirteen leaving him to fend for himself. He had never been able to pronounce the name and his childish pronunciation was so familiar to everyone his real name had been forgotten with the passing of time.

'Ach well,' sighed Merry Mary, 'it's good luck to him for he'll have a job getting milk from the damt thing at all with thon great hands of his. Ten thumbs he was born with and no mistake!'

Shona had made her choice and proudly brought out her new purse.

'My, what a fine purse,' commented Merry Mary. 'And a whole shilling to spend too. Have you been saving your pennies then?'

'It's my birthday and Father gave me the purse and the shilling.'

Merry Mary had argued with Fergus the day before over the price of tobacco and she wasn't feeling kindly disposed to him. Her lips pursed till they were almost touching her wart.

'Things are looking up indeed! He must have been in a good mood right enough for he'd fight over a half-penny like a bull over a cow when he has a mind!'

'Aye, we'll get going now,' said Mirabelle and hastily bustled her charge away.

Behag Beag looked up when the bell over her door jangled to admit Mirabelle and Shona, and a gleam of blatant interest showed in her beady eyes. Phebie and Niall were in the shop too and it was always vaguely exciting when Laigmhor and Slochmhor met.

'Ach, it's yoursel', Phebie!' Mirabelle's greeting was cheery for she was extremely fond of the doctor's wife. 'And Niall! What a big loon! Dodging school, is it?'

Phebie smiled. 'He's got a bit of a cold but feeling better today and driving me crazy so I thought to come out for a message or two. Hello, Shona.' She stooped and looked into the little girl's blue eyes. 'What a bright bonny lass you are this morning.'

'It's my birthday,' explained Shona.

'Y-es . . . I know.' Phebie stood up and Behag stopped rustling papers to listen better. A silence fell over the shop and Mirabelle glared at the postmistress.

'I'll have some stamps please, Behag . . . and you'd best pay attention to what you're doing! The last time I got stamps from you they were covered in blotches from your inky fingers!'

Behag stuck her nose in the air and went to get the stamps.

Shona and Niall stood beside the high wooden counter and regarded each other shyly. Niall, now a sturdy seven-year-old, was tall for his age with a mop of corn-coloured curls and his father's deep brown eyes and quick smile. Shona had seen him often, kicking stones on the road on his way to and from school, a whistle never far from his lips. It was his gay whistling that alerted her to the fact that he was passing Laigmhor and she would leave whatever she was doing to race to the gate and watch him in the distance. Sometimes he saw her and waved and she waved back wistfully, longing for the day when she too would be going to school. Now that day was drawing near.

'I'm going to school soon,' she volunteered.

'You'll be in the infants' section,' said Niall in slightly superior tones. 'In amongst the rest of the babies!'

Shona's eyes blazed. 'I'm *not* a baby! I'm five and you're cheeky for saying such things! Anyway, Mirabelle's been teaching me things. I can count to twenty and I can do the alphabet and – and I'm sure I can do a lot more than you!'

Niall's young face darkened. 'And you're nothing but a right wee crabbit baby and spoiled too! Why don't you ever come out to play instead of keekin' at folk on the road?'

Shona stamped her foot and tears of anger gleamed in her eyes. 'Because I was too little before! But I'm big now and I will be out to play! And I've got a new puppy who'll come with me everywhere but you won't because you're a nasty cheeky boy and I don't like you!'

'Wee baby!' he taunted but his eyes showed a regret at the turn of things because he had noticed Shona McKenzie often and in his toddler days had longed to play with her, but, for some reason, he wasn't allowed to visit Laigmhor and it had puzzled him because on Rhanna people Ceilidhed all the time. Eventually he had come to the conclusion that the McKenzies thought themselves above other people, so aloof that their little girl wasn't allowed to play with a doctor's son. Yet he admired the strapping figure of Fergus McKenzie and always shouted a cheery greeting when they passed, even though the big man's reply was hardly more than a grunt.

Phebie and Mirabelle had been having a quiet chat

at the other end of the counter but turned at the sound of shrill childish voices.

'Bairns!' cried Mirabelle. 'What on earth are you mumpin' about?'

Phebie came over to her son, 'Niall, I heard you call Shona a baby! Say you're sorry at once!'

Behag lurked in the little cubbyhole she proudly called her 'back shop' and listened gleefully. It seemed that even the children of Laigmhor and Slochmhor couldn't agree.

Niall shuffled his feet. His head dropped on to his chest and his words were low. 'I won't! She called me cheeky and I'm not! I'm not!'

Phebie grasped his hand and pulled him out of the post office, rushing him angrily away. Mirabelle grabbed Shona by the back of her collar and bull-dozed her outside away from Behag's long ears. It was seldom that Mirabelle got really annoyed but now her eyes shone with rage. She hurled Shona round a corner and whirled her round.

'You wee bitch that you are! Causin' a rumpus in that Cailleach's shop! It's a good skelpin' you're gettin' this very meenit, birthday or no'.'

And there, in the middle of Portcull, Shona found her knickers at her ankles and her bottom soundly spanked. The sharp sting of Mirabelle's heavy hand made her want to cry, but humiliation and determination would not allow a single protest to escape. Two Portcull children passed and shouted, 'Baldy bum!' and her face grew red with shame.

Mirabelle hastily pulled up the knickers and yanked her charge away. The two walked home in dejected silence but at the bottom of the track to Laigmhor Shona looked up at Mirabelle with a gleam of mischief in her eyes.

'Och, I'm sorry, Mirabelle! Don't look so angry, because your face was made for smiling and you look awful funny with your mouth all twisted like Behag's. I'm not sorry about that Niall though. He *is* cheeky and I'm *not* a baby!'

Mirabelle took a large hanky out of the folds of her voluminous attire and blew her nose soundly. She looked down at the child's upturned face. 'Ach well, I'm sorry too for skelpin' you on your birthday. We'll not mention a word to a soul for I shouldny have bared your wee bum and you shouldny have been so cheeky. It would be nice if you made friends wi' Niall so mind your manners in future.'

Nancy turned a rosy face from the stove at their entrance and the puppy pranced to meet them, leaving a pool in its wake.

'That doggy!' exclaimed Nancy in exasperation. 'I've had my feet chewed all mornin' and slipped on a great platter o' shit! I dropped all the spoons and they got covered in skitter. Poor auld Ben stood in it and I had to wash his feets, clean the pup and wash my stockin's for they were reekin' and me meetin' Archie tonight for the Ceilidh at Croft na Beinn.'

Nancy was very down to earth and never used dainty words no matter who she was addressing. Her entire family had the same indelicate use of language but were not less liked for it.

It had been rather difficult for Mirabelle when Shona first started to speak because Nancy's colourful expressions were the ones the toddler could pronounce perfectly. For a time the housekeeper had dreaded when someone dropped in for a Strupak and the day Madam Balfour came to discuss some business had been the worst of all.

Mirabelle had completed the delicate intricate embroidery of the chairback covers that had been given to her from Burnbreddie and the laird's wife had called to collect them. In raptures over the faultless work, with Mirabelle intent on explaining how a certain stitch was executed, neither noticed the small figure stagger unsteadily into the parlour till gleeful ecstatic baby tones announced, 'Vat bloody dog's farted! Vat bloody dog's farted. Fink he's shit the floor!'

Madam Balfour's mouth had dropped open and Mirabelle had scooped Shona under an arm and borne her hastily away.

Now Shona knew better than to repeat Nancy's words though she still giggled on hearing them. The young woman's language was more earthy than ever of late and there was a sparkle in her. She was 'walking out' with young Archie Taylor, eldest son of Croft na Beinn and a summer wedding was in the offing.

'I'm sorry about the mess,' apologized Shona, grinning. 'I'll train her as quick as I can, Nancy. And thank you for the apron. Now I can help Mirabelle make scones without getting in a mess.'

Mirabelle groaned at the thought of her charge making merry with flour and currants and Nancy sniggered wickedly. Fergus came in and they all sat down to stovies with cold meat followed by apple tart and fresh cream. Later, when Nancy was clattering busily with the dishes, Shona went with Mirabelle to scatter meal for the hens.

'Greedy creatures!' said Mirabelle mildly, watching while the hens squabbled and pecked.

But Shona's thoughts were far away. 'I'm a big girl now!' she said almost to herself.

'Aye, you are that,' agreed Mirabelle.

'And I'll have a lot more freedom now, won't I?'

'That's up to your father, mo ghaoil.'

'Och, but he's away with Hamish to Rhumhor to buy some piglets and I want to do something very badly.'

'Well, you know where to go. Is it a wee pup you are that knows not how to control itself?'

'Mirabelle! You're laughing at me! I want to go away up on the moor with Tot. All by myself . . . without you, Mirabelle.'

The old lady looked thoughtful. She was thinking of the scene in the post office and knew the time had come for the child to learn some independence. In a few weeks she would be off to school which was a very competitive world full of little humans who could be cruel to sheltered and inexperienced children. She patted Shona's head.

'Aye, my wee lamb, away you go.'

The reply was so unexpected that for a moment Shona was nonplussed, for she had expected an argument. She had been allowed to certain places on her own, like Hamish's cottage, and she had often gone on an errand to Portcull, but the wide open spaces of the island had demanded an adult escort because there were many hazards inland that were a challenge even to the experienced.

'I won't go far,' she promised breathlessly and ran indoors for Tot, then raced down the track and on to the road. She was like a wild thing that had been caged up for too long. She sped on to the moor and kept on running. The sound of a burbling burn was music in her ears, the cold sharp air streamed into her lungs and wakened every cell to pulsing life. Her hair streamed in the wind and the ribbon came undone to fall unnoticed in the rusty bracken. Eventually she rolled over in the heather, panting and laughing. The pup rolled too, barking and biting, and the child giggled, spreading her arms wide and looking at the racing grey clouds above, feeling herself riding with them in a great surge of freedom. Heather tangled in her hair and she buried her face in the sweet smell of the straggling shoots. Raising herself on one elbow she looked at the scenery spread below. Laigmhor sprawled untidily, tiny from this distance. She strained her eyes for a sign of life and saw Mirabelle, a tiny doll figure hanging out clothes. Suddenly she felt queer and sad. She loved Mirabelle, she loved her father, she loved Laigmhor, but she knew now that it wasn't enough. Now there had to be more loves, more people and places in her life and she felt a traitor to the people who had surrounded her for as long as she could remember. There were so many new feelings inside herself she didn't understand and she felt she wasn't ready for them because there was a lot of old feelings she didn't understand either. One of them was about her mother. She knew she ought to have a mother because Mirabelle read her stories and they always had mothers in them. She had asked Mirabelle where her own mother was and had been told she was in heaven. That was another mystery because no one seemed to know where heaven was though it was mentioned all the time in the bible and when Reverend John Grey came to visit her father she had heard him talking about this place called heaven but it hadn't made any sense because he'd used so many big words.

She knew her mother was buried in the kirkyard so she really couldn't see how she could be in heaven and in the kirkyard at the same time. How could something that grown-ups called a soul be with God, when the body belonging to that soul was deep under the ground?

Tears sprang to her eyes at the idea of her mother being in a wooden box buried in the earth. It must be terrible because beetles and worms and all sorts of creepies were in the soil.

She knew her mother had been beautiful because there was a photo of her in the parlour but she seldom saw it because the parlour was hardly used now. But Mirabelle had shown her another one that she kept in a little cardboard box in her room. It was a nicer one than the parlour photo because it was more natural and the delicate cameo face was smiling, the eyes alight with some secret joke. But to her it was only a photograph and she felt nothing except a great pride that her mother had been so beautiful.

It was very strange that her father never spoke of her mother because Mirabelle had said he loved her very much. How could you love someone and not speak of them even if they were dead?

Mirabelle spoke of her own mother and two sisters who were dead yet could be recalled by just talking about them.

It was all very mysterious and sad and difficult to understand.

She sighed and wrapped her arms round Tot who was sound asleep on her chest. It was lovely to feel the warm trusting bundle against her and she wished she had been able to let Niall see her puppy. She was sorry she had argued with him. It was the last thing she had wanted to do but her quick temper had let her down again and she vowed to try and keep it in better control. She chuckled. A temper was a funny thing because you could lose it yet still have it. Other things were easy to lose but difficult to find. She hoped he would never get to hear about her being spanked outside Behag Beag's shop. Just thinking about it made her face grow red.

Something flapped on the road far below and she looked down to see Niall's mother hurrying along in the direction of the woods near the Hillock. Shona wondered where she was going and wished she had been near the woods to talk to Phebie whom she liked very much. Next to Mirabelle, Phebie was her favourite woman person. Next to her father and Hamish, she loved Lachlan. He was like a big boy, he was so eager about everything. Once he had given Shona and Mirabelle a lift to Burnbreddie in his trap. Mirabelle had been going to see the laird's wife about cushion covers she had been asked to do for the sitting-room. Mirabelle hadn't been keen on the task because she had so little time, but she was an expert needle-woman and Madam Balfour insisted she was the only person fit for the job. There was going to be another house party soon with London people coming and new chair covers were a must.

Dr McLachlan had joked all the way to Burnbreddie and it had been a lovely ride over the high cliff road. When they arrived at the house he had gone to seek out the laird who was having trouble with something Mirabelle called 'piles'.

Going home Shona had sat silent thinking about the laird's piles till she could contain herself no longer and had asked the doctor to explain. Mirabelle's face had reddened but Lachlan roared with laughter and for the rest of the journey explained with great delicacy about haemorrhoids. Shona was delighted that another discovery was adding to her growing list and announced her intention of telling her father but Lachlan's face had clouded.

'Better not mention it, lass. In fact don't mention me at all.'

He had gone off quickly and Shona turned to Mirabelle. 'Why can't I talk to Father about the doctor? He's so kind and nice. I'm scunnered with all these secrets you big folk have!'

'Ach, don't worry your wee head,' Mirabelle counselled. 'You know your father's a bit ramstam and he and the doctor don't see eye to eye. Anyway – what a nice secret we have! We've had a ride in the doctor's trap and not a soul knows but us.'

Shona felt like a conspirator and her eyes gleamed.

'Ach, you're right, Mirabelle, we won't tell a soul. The doctor's our cronie even if he and Father don't get along. But Father will find out anyway because that Madam Balfour will tell him. I don't like her, do you, Mirabelle? She's got wee beady eyes that take off your skin and tries to look into your mind and her mouth goes all tight and thin like a wee red dash made by a crayon. I don't know why she bothers with lipstick because she has no mouth to put it on!'

'Weesht wi' you!' said Mirabelle sternly but hid a smile because she shared the child's sentiments. Sitting in the big formal parlour at Burnbreddie it had taken all her willpower to hold her tongue when told: 'Make a good job of the covers, Mirabelle. My friends from England must see that we're not all uncivilized on the Islands. I'll pay you well for your trouble, of course. If you were my housekeeper you would get a handsome salary. At Laigmhor you are . . . let me see . . . cook, housekeeper and nurse and no doubt only get paid for housekeeping. Yes, my dear, you're wasted and no mistake.'

Mirabelle straightened, stuck out her bosom majestically and said in her dourest tones, 'Money is not everything, my leddy, for there are those who are none too happy with the aid of it. I'll bid you good day and see you get your covers in good time for your English friends to rest their backsides on. We must let the gentry see that we aren't *all* peasants . . . eh, my leddy? There's some can put to use the hands that God gave them.'

Out she had flounced pulling Shona with her and an indignant 'Well!' had floated into the empty room.

In due course Fergus heard about his housekeeper's 'impertinence' and he had looked at the laird's wife with contempt when she also mentioned that the doctor had brought Shona and Mirabelle in his trap. He had put his face very close to hers, and his black eyes were like steel.

'And what is wrong with that? It's a fair trek from Laigmhor. The doctor must have saved my housekeeper a hard walk over the hill for no doubt you would not have thought to send your groom to collect her.' He had turned to go and, whitefaced, she had scurried off to her husband to inform him that 'something must be done about Fergus McKenzie'. But the laird had looked at her with bleary eyes and told her, 'McKenzie's a damned good farmer and you talk too much.'

Shona knew about this because she'd heard Annie McKinnon who 'worked to Burnbreddie', telling Mirabelle and she hugged herself with glee at the thought of her father scaring the wits out of Madam Balfour.

Her thoughts were interrupted by a scrunch of heather and Dodie loomed big and dark on the skyline. He was well over six feet, though a pronounced stoop belied the fact. Everyone said the stoop had something to do with the years he had walked Rhanna with his quick loping gait, his eyes glued to the ground and his neck thrust forward as if he expected to encounter some rare find at any moment. His skin was nutbrown, weatherbeaten by years of wind and sun. His grey-green eyes had an odd dreaming expression and his large mournful mouth rarely smiled. Brown broken teeth were stained forever by the juice of the tobacco he chewed continually. His most startling feature was his nose or rather the huge carbuncle that sprouted from its side. It was almost like a second nose, but nobbly, and shook with the movements of his head. Long arms hung down at his sides, useless-looking with short stubby fingers calloused from years of hard work, for he excelled in manual tasks and had worked on every croft and farm on Rhanna. Nobody knew if he had hair because his head was perpetually covered by a green frayed cap and his long lean body was draped in a threadbare raincoat that looked an impossibly inadequate garment to combat rain and wind, yet he refused kind offers of warmer outerwear. Enormous feet were encased in stout wellingtons worn winter and summer and the smell that emanated from them had incurred many a comment.

'He breeah!' Dodie greeted Shona mournfully but his eyes were alight with pleasure at seeing her. No matter the weather his greeting was always the same and even if it was pouring from the heavens people returned the greeting in kind because he was hurt as easily as a small boy and so inoffensive, but for his peculiar smell, that everyone liked him.

'He breeah!' said Shona. 'Look at my new puppy, Dodie. Do you like her?'

'Ach, but she is lovely just!' He gathered the puppy tenderly in his big awkward hands and it sniffed eagerly, obviously enjoying the smells so offensive to humans. His love for animals had endeared him to Shona and when he worked at Laigmhor she followed him about asking questions that he answered with unending patience. The pup nibbled at one of his long ears and his eyes gleamed delightedly when a wet nose was poked into his neck. Shona smiled when she saw that the portion of skin that had been licked was decidedly paler than before.

'I'm going home now, Dodie,' she said, taking Tot before she disappeared inside the greasy raincoat.

'I'll just walk with you. I was coming over to ask your father if he was needin' odd jobs done for I'm wantin' to bring Ealasaid when she comes to season.'

His candid way of speaking was no surprise to Shona. No matter the age of his listener he spoke freely about the facts of life with beguiling innocence. But Shona knew all about animals and their 'seasons'. Most of the children on Rhanna did – one could not live on croft or farm without witnessing animals mating and giving birth.

'Who's Ealasaid?' giggled Shona. 'Are you courting then, Dodie?'

Dodie's face reddened, for while he could talk freely about the habits of animals with complete candour, he grew embarrassed if anyone hinted that he had an interest in the human female. As a result he was always being teased.

'Ach Shona, my lassie,' he chided gently. 'Ealasaid is my cow. Did you not know I had a cow? A right bonny beast too.'

'Yes, Dodie, I heard you had a cow and what a fine name I'm thinking. The fanciest I've heard for a cow.'

'Well she's a real fancy cow but a bugger for all that. I've to trek miles with her hay and there I sits in the middle of the damt moor milkin' her and sometimes she kicks the pail away till there's nothing in it and her udder dried out. So I've to bring her home and wait till she's full again before I can get anything, but my . . . it's worth it! Damt fine milk it is, the cream to it inches thick and lovely spread over my tatties for dinner.'

'Och Dodie! You don't spread cream over tatties, it's for porridge.'

'Well mine's for tatties! Nothing finer wi' plenty salt and bread.'

'Och well, we'd best hurry now. Mirabelle might give you a Strupak. She was baking cake and scones this afternoon because it's my birthday.'

Mirabelle greeted Dodie with some reserve. She'd had a busy day and wasn't in the mood for a crack but, with her usual hospitality, she ushered him to a seat near the door in the hope that the draughts might carry some of his odours away. He munched scones and drank tea with relish, while Tot and Ben watched with dribbling muzzles. Fergus came in and was treated to a long list of reasons why Dodie wanted his Ealasaid to be mated with Fergus's bull, the main one being that it was a prize bull and in return for its services Dodie would do all the spare jobs till his debt was paid.

'It's to keep the cow in milk you see, Mr McKenzie,' he explained earnestly. 'She's a fine cow and if she and your bull came together they would produce a fine calf. Ach! It would be a fine day for us both, would it not?'

Fergus had to smile. He had seen Dodie earlier that

day, milk pail in one hand and a bundle of hay in the other, standing on the moor talking lovingly into the ear of a rather dejected looking cow. The beast was past its best and Fergus felt sorry that guileless Dodie had been cheated by the laird. He knew he should have refused the services of his bull because the cow looked unfit to bear a calf but he couldn't resist the appeal in Dodie's eyes. He had a soft spot for the old eccentric and admired the way he worked so willingly to provide the bare necessities for his simple life. Dodie had received less rebukes than any man to cross Fergus's path and the islanders told each other that McKenzie had a heart after all. Dodie was always quick to defend him.

'Aye, and a big heart just! He is a fine man, the best there is. A lot better than some o' you lazy lot!'

'Ach, maybe it's because you're a cheap way o' labour,' they'd counter.

'Mr McKenzie never gives me more than I'm paid for. It's that sly Bodach at Burnbreddie who would work your fingers to the bone and hardly a reek o' his dung in return.'

Fergus considered Dodie's proposal for a long moment. He opened his mouth to refuse but the pleading in Dodie's eyes made him say instead, 'Very well, Dodie, when your cow is ready, drive her over to Croynachan and put her in with the rest of the kie. My bull will be there for a while yet.'

'Ach you're a good man just! She should be comin' on soon for she was jumpin' on some o' the beasts up on the hill.'

The matter was settled and Dodie took himself off

well pleased. Mirabelle quickly cut an onion and tied it to the chair on which he had been sitting.

'That will clear the reek in no time,' she told Nancy. 'Now, mo ghaoil, I know you're champin' to be off. You've worked well today so away you go and have a nice time at the Ceilidh.'

Nancy's dark eyes lit up. 'Ach, you're good so you are, Belle. It will give me a chance to get home and put some scent on these stockings for they still reek a bit and I wouldny like Archie to think I had a natural smell o' shit off me. It might put him off the weddin'.'

Shona was out of earshot and Mirabelle chuckled. 'Aye, but keep a finger on your halfpenny just the same. If you had a bairn out of wedlock he still might not wed you. Men can be gey queer that way!'

'Och Belle! As if I would!' Nancy's smile was innocent but her memory delighted in recalling her last outing when Archie had walked her home to Portcull. He had pulled her into a boatshed and kisses had led to his hand creeping into her blouse while his whispers tickled her ear.

'You have the finest breasts on Rhanna,' he mumbled. 'I like them big with fine nipples like cherries that a man can get his lips over. Let me play with them, Nan!'

He had played and worked himself to a nice frenzy but even though her body wanted more, her quick mind warned her against it.

'Och, please, Nan!' he pleaded. 'We're as good as wed! I'll be careful, I promise.'

But Nancy had seen too many of her mother's pregnancies and knew how easy it was to get that way and she wasn't going to the altar looking like a Christmas pudding.

'No, Archie,' she told him firmly. 'Bide your time, it will come soon enough and think how nice it will be to have your first night with a real virgin!'

Further begging had got him nowhere and he had crossed his legs in agony and smoked two cigarettes while she tidied her clothes before going home. On the way they had passed her sister Annie who was also having a tussle with a young fisherman in old Shelagh's peat shed.

Nancy hurried off and Mirabelle went upstairs to tuck Shona into bed. The little girl lay with her rag doll in one arm and Tot in the other.

'And what way is that pup doin' here?' asked Mirabelle sternly. 'She'll have pools all over the floor come mornin' and I'm not going to clean them up.'

'Och Mirabelle, she's such a wee thing and would cry all night and Ben might clout her 'cos he's too old to bother with noise. Let me have her beside me, Mirabelle. I get lonely sometimes.'

Mirabelle's softening glance told her she had won and she reached up to pull the old lady close.

'I love you, Mirabelle! You'll never be a Cailleach with that nice face you have!'

'Is it trying to get round me you are?'

'Maybe just a wee bit. Has it not been a lovely day . . . except for that Niall McLachlan! It was grand on the moor all by myself. Father was nice today as well, he hugged me close and laughed. Do you think he loves me a wee bit?'

'Of course he does, my wee lamb. It's just he canny show his feelings easy.'

Mirabelle's voice was gruff because of the tears in her throat. She always felt unhappy when the child asked her such questions. Things would have been so different if Helen had lived. Oh, how happy a place Laigmhor then, and Fergus a completely contented being.

While they talked he was at that moment out on the dark windy moors, his steps taking him on a pilgrimage he made often but especially on this day of all days. The bare trees crackled in the Kirkyard and he could barely make out the dim lines of Helen's stone. Even dimmer was the mossy ground beneath but he knew without seeing them that the snowdrops would be there. He felt for them and picked them up, crushing the cool pale drops to his chest.

'Helen, my dearest lamb,' he murmured. 'I loved you – I love you with all my heart but she – Phebie – loved you too and I'm too proud to tell her I'm sorry.'

Chapter Four

The shrill cries of newborn lambs echoed over the fields. March was moving into April but to the uninitiated there seemed no sign of spring in the bare trees. But the expert eye saw the tiny swollen buds on the stark branches and the sharp new green of tender heather shoots through the tangle of rusty bracken and bramble on the moor. The air was still raw but there was a softness hidden in the rough caress, a hint of the glorious summers that could bathe the Hebrides in long days of golden sunlight.

Shona skipped through the lambing fields but stopped to watch twins running to their mother, tails wagging as they nudged her belly with no regard for her swollen milk glands.

Bob and her father were moving amongst the flock with Kerrie dancing in their wake. A trio of carrion crows rose from a hedge, their shrieks telling of their rage at being disturbed from a feast of a dead lamb dropped from the talons of a golden eagle.

'I'll shoot that damt bird yet!' said Bob, wiping his nose with the back of a brown hand on which a pattern of knotted veins told of a lifetime of hard work. 'The brute has its eyrie on Ben Machrie for I've seen it fleein' abouts there.'

A ewe, heavy and awkward, was in the last stages

of labour and the men went to help her.

'This one's in trouble,' said Bob, examining the swollen vagina with expert hands. Several moments later an unformed embryo was expelled on to the grass.

Shona watched with quiet interest. She had seen it all before but each lambing season brought renewed excitement. It was so lovely to see the newborn lambs taking their first wobbling steps, the legs shaking but miraculously supporting a perfect little body. Each year brought its casualties like the lamb now feeding the carrion and there were always orphan lambs needing care. Shona delighted in feeding the motherless babies and now that she was five her father had allowed her to go to the fields with him though he had forbidden her to bring Tot and she sulked because the pup went everywhere with her. But she soon got over her mood and watched fascinated while Bob worked with the ewe who was lying on her side with her eyes closed.

'There's a live one in there yet,' he said. 'The contractions are weak but wi' luck we'll have a lamb, though there's no' much chance for the poor auld yowe.'

The ewe was dying even as a tiny head appeared under her tail. For a minute the head hung helplessly for there was no more help to be had from its mother who had taken her last shuddering breath. Bob's hand disappeared into the birth canal and grasping the lamb gently but firmly delivered it from its mother's body. Shona's eyes filled with tears for the dead sheep but she gazed at the new lamb with tenderness. Bob had removed the delicate skin bag which encased the lamb and skinny ribs heaved to draw in life-giving oxygen.

Fergus turned to Shona urgently. 'Can you be trusted to run to Mirabelle with this wee lamb? It's a weak one and needs heat. I can't come but she'll know what to do, she's done it often enough.'

Shona gazed at her father in disbelief. The enormity of the trust he was placing on her took her breath away and her heart raced with pride.

Bob placed the fragile warm body in her arms and she turned to go.

'I'll take care, Father,' she promised. 'The wee lamb will be safe for I'll keep her warm with my jacket.'

Her feet barely touched the turf. She had two fields to cross going the shortest way but it meant crossing the burn and climbing over a stile.

The stepping stones were slippery and she held her breath when her boots slithered on slimy moss. The stile was more difficult because she couldn't use her hands to cling to the fence. Her heart jumped when she almost fell from her precarious perch but she steadied herself with an elbow and flew over the last field. The lamb bleated weakly from her jacket. The sound made her afraid, it was so faint, and her whole being urged her legs to go faster. If the lamb died, she would blame herself and her father would never ask her to do anything important again. The cobbles in the yard threatened to trip her tiring feet but in seconds she was in the kitchen, her heart light with the knowledge that the burden of saving the lamb would now rest with someone else.

She stood in the warmth looking expectantly round the room but it was empty but for a wildly ecstatic Tot, and Ben in his usual place by the range.

'Mirabelle!' The cry was torn from her in a torment of anxiety. She ran to the parlour, then to the hall where the ticking of the grandfather clock echoed in her ears. She had often noticed that the tick of a clock was so much louder in an empty house and it was then she remembered that Mirabelle had mentioned going to Portcull to visit Morag the spinner and wouldn't be back till teatime.

Shona's mind raced. Nancy! She would get Nancy to help! She was an expert at dealing with the new-born, both animal and human. But it was Nancy's day off and she and her mother were going to start work on the wedding dress, a grand ensemble which Mirabelle had promised to finish with embroidered white flowers on the bodice.

Shona suddenly felt small and very young, not at all like the big girl she had felt on her birthday. The lamb bleated again and the sound stung her into frantic action. The lamb was very weak and its small body, still wet with amniotic fluid, was cold and trembling. She ran to the linen cupboard and found a blanket and a rough towel then holding the lamb on her knee she rubbed briskly with the towel till the soft wool curled and the small body grew warm. She wrapped it in the blanket and laid it on the rug beside Ben who began licking the small white face with his warm tongue.

Food was the next thing and Shona rummaged in the pantry till she found the feeding bottle kept specially for weak lambs. She mixed cream with water and poured it into the bottle.

'But it's got to be warm!' she said in despair because all Mirabelle's pans were on a shelf out of her reach. But she spotted Tot's tin ashet in a corner and hurriedly washed it and poured the mixture into it and with the aid of the clothes tongs held it over the glow of the range. Panic made her try to pour it directly from ashet to bottle but it spilled and she uttered a frustrated curse and rushed once more for the jug.

A moment later the lamb was on her knee sucking slowly but firmly from the bottle. She held her breath in delight and felt like a mother with a new little baby. Milk dribbled from the small inexperienced mouth and she wiped it gently with the towel, helped by Tot who was entranced by the whole proceeding.

When Mirabelle came home she found Shona fast asleep in the cosy inglenook, the lamb clasped firmly in her arms, contented burping pops coming from its milky lips.

'Well! I'm blessed!' Mirabelle folded her arms over her stomach and chuckled. 'Two wee lambs snoring like thunder!'

Shona opened her eyes and her smile was triumphant. 'I saved the wee cratur, Mirabelle, all by myself. Look, it's warm and fed.'

Mirabelle removed her voluminous coat and bent to take both lamb and child into her arms. 'I'm proud o' you, so I am, and your father will be too. So proud he'll feel like burstin' the way I am!'

At teatime Fergus was greeted by his excited daughter.

'Look at the wee lamb, Father! Mirabelle wasn't here but I warmed and fed it. It's going to live!'

He looked at the fluffy lamb, now on wobbly legs, its tail wagging with pleasure as Ben licked it and Tot jumped around with the unrestrained antics of the very young, and a feeling of pride glowed in him.

'You're a daughter of the farm right enough,' he said briefly but it was enough for Shona.

'It's what I want to be, Father. I'm glad I can help you now. It's a lovely feeling to save a wee thing's life. It was a shame about its mother but at least her baby is alive.'

He looked at her, a long considering look, the strangeness back in him again.

Tears sprang to her eyes. 'Och Father, what is it that bothers you so? Did I say something wrong?'

'Shona!' He knelt beside her and looked into her blue eyes. 'You haven't said anything wrong. You just have a queer wee way of hitting at the truth. And I do like . . . love you but don't expect me to fuss about it. There's so much you don't know and so much I can't talk about.'

She folded her arms around his neck and nuzzled his rugged weatherbeaten skin. 'My poor father! Talk to me about the things that bother you. I'll understand.'

He unclasped her arms and stood up, a look of weariness in his eyes.

'Go and wash your hands, tea will be ready in a while.'

She turned dejectedly but his voice stayed her. 'You're a clever wee lass – I'm – proud of you.'

She didn't look at him but ran to her room, her heart singing. Living with her father was like sailing the sea forever. One minute it was calm and the next so stormy that each of her senses reeled till she didn't know where she was. But the squalls made the times of calm like lovely bounties of treasure, precious jewels that she could hoard in the caskets of her memory.

Saturday came and Mirabelle bustled about in Shona's room, laying out her best clothes because the next day she was going to church for the first time. She had mixed feelings about it. She had heard so much about the Reverend John Grey's sermons. Nancy had told her that he could see into a person's soul and Shona wasn't sure she would enjoy that. This soul that people spoke about must be a very important part of a person and she felt that it ought to be a strictly private piece of property.

'There we are!' Mirabelle laid the black knitted stockings over the back of a chair.

The child stared aghast. 'Och no, Mirabelle! I can't go to kirk in these!'

'These you are wearin' and no' another word. There's a bite in the wind still!'

'But . . .' Shona searched desperately for an excuse. 'What if I rip them and won't have them for school next week?'

'Rip them and your bum will be warmer than a hot toddy. What's the matter wi' them anyway? Are they not fine enough for madam?'

Shona didn't reply. She had put the 'liquorice tubes' to the very back of her drawer hoping that Mirabelle would forget about them till she had outgrown them. The thought of everyone looking at her 'liquorice' legs filled her with horror and when she got into bed she racked her brains for a way to escape wearing them but could think of none.

The Sabbath was a very pious day on Rhanna. Saturday evening was spent in preparation. Zinc tubs were brought to the fire and filled with hot water for the weekly bath. The less fussy 'steeped' their feet in a basin. All over the island people bathed and steeped. The latter was favoured by solitary old men who, safe from watchful eyes, kept their socks on and thus accomplished two tasks at one time all the while alleviating any twinges of guilt with the thought that economy was a saving grace and they were saving both soap and water. Old Bob, safe in his lonely biggin on Ben Machrie, simply bared his feet to Kerrie who, with ecstatic expertise, slapped his tongue in and around toes while his master lay back blissfully by his cosy peat fire. The women busied themselves preparing meals so that there was nothing to do but heat them and lay them on the Sunday table. Clothes must never be seen hanging to dry on the Sabbath though many of the womenfolk cursed the fact and surreptitiously hung sheets in the big airy hay sheds consoling themselves that 'cleanliness was next to godliness'.

The bell was pealing its rather mournful notes when Mirabelle patted her best hat and took Shona firmly by the hand. The little girl wriggled.

'Mirabelle, these stockings itch something terrible. I'll scratch all the time in kirk. Can't I wear my brown ones?'

'I'll skelp your lugs if you don't be quiet. Now – have you got your collection?'

'Yes, Father gave me threepence.'

'Come on then. Carry your bible like a real wee lady and put this nice clean hanky in your pouch. Remember, you mustny cough too loudly in kirk and don't keep squirming like an eel or folks will think you've worms.'

They met Hamish on the road, his beard smooth and tidy and his kilt flying proudly in the breeze. No one mentioned Fergus. He hadn't attended church since Helen's death though the Reverend Grey visited him regularly and never gave up trying to persuade the young farmer that his soul would find no rest till he came back to the Lord's house. But Fergus was not easily dissuaded and told the minister, 'God and myself understand each other all right. I'll be no better going to kirk just to listen to old wifies sucking mints and criticizing each other's hats.'

The trio wandered past the cold green waters of Loch Tenee but known better to everyone as Loch Wee. Scurrying figures were coming from all directions, something in their bearing suggesting the discomfiture they felt being rigged in stiff Sunday best. Shona skipped between Hamish and Mirabelle till she earned a sharp rebuke from the latter. 'Bide still ye wee weasel! You're like a hen on a hot girdle!'

Hamish grinned indulgently. 'Ach the bairn's excited. It's no' every day we get goin' to kirk . . . thanks be to the Lord!'

Mirabelle pursed her lips. 'The de'il will get you, Hamish Cameron! You're a blasphemer and should know better than to say such things in front o' the bairn!'

Voices hailed them and they were joined by the McLachlans and Biddy, her best hat slightly askew.

'It's a queer way the Lord has o' givin' us a day o' rest,' she said with slight regret. 'Every other day I'm called to a confinement but no one seems to have bairns on Sundays. The very day I could put my feet up I've to drag myself to kirk!'

'You don't *have* to go, Biddy!' twinkled Phebie.

'What! And have that blessed meenister comin' to my door threatenin' my soul wi' a' sorts o' things! No thanks! I'd rather hae a snooze in kirk than risk that!'

Lachlan smiled at Shona. 'Our little lass is looking very smart today. Going to meet the minister in all her Sunday best, is it?'

Shona wriggled and tried to hide behind Mirabelle, her whole being concentrating on hiding the awful black stockings from Niall who was eyeing her with covert amusement.

A black speck was coming towards them from the hill track to Nigg. In front of the speck was a larger one with four legs that turned out to be Ealasaid mooing protestingly with every step because Dodie was driving her at a pace which didn't suit her in the least.

'Bless me!'exclaimed Mirabelle. 'It's Dodie wi' thon queer cow!'

'He's no' bringin' it to kirk, surely!'

Dodie came nearer and his mouth cracked into a mournful grimace which was the nearest he ever got to a smile.

'He breeah!' he cried with something akin to elation in his tone. 'I'm just drivin' Ealasaid over to Croynachan!'

'Bless me, what for?' asked Mirabelle, eyeing the cow who had seized the chance to nibble heather shoots at the roadside.

'She has just come on real strong and I'm wantin' to get her to the bull while she's in the mood.'

He nodded his head enthusiastically causing his carbuncle to wobble alarmingly.

Mirabelle was shocked. 'Not on the Sabbath, Dodie! She can't go to the bull on the Sabbath. Anyways, the Johnstons passed in the trap a whily back. They'll be in kirk now. You'll get no help wi' the beast!'

'Ach, Angus will be there. If Ealasaid's ready we'll get the bull on her between us.'

'I'm sure the Lord won't mind this once,' twinkled Lachlan.

Dodie nodded earnestly. 'Aye, you're right, doctor. I had a wee word wi' Him last night and I got the feelin' He was not annoyed at all.'

Biddy smiled dourly. 'I'm sure there's not just the beasts that go matin' on a Sunday. I've a funny wee feelin' half the bairns on Rhanna are started on the Lord's day.' Her smile changed to one of mischief. 'Folks have got to pass the time some way and there's not a lot to keep the hands occupied on the Sabbath, is there now?'

Mirabelle gave her friend a prim glance and pulled Shona hastily up the Hillock to kirk leaving Dodie to shout abuse at the cow who had wandered to a small green patch and now stubbornly refused to move.

Inside the kirk it was dim and musty. Light filtered through the ruby glass of the window above the pulpit and the colour splashed on to the floor. Shona stared at the rows of bowed heads all round her and was amazed that they were the same warm-hearted lively creatures who peopled the crofts and cottages in Portcull. Elspeth was near the front, almost unrecognizable in a black coat and bowler type hat, her sharp nose sticking out resolutely in the direction of the pulpit as if she expected to see her salvation at any moment. Hector was by her side, his hair plastered down with oil, his red nose tamed to a duller hue in the dim mists of the kirk.

Near them was old Joe who had spent all his life at sea, retired now and beloved by the village children whom he entertained with amazing stories hoarded from his many voyages. His white hair curled over his dark collar and his sea-green eyes were closed in prayer. Shona wondered if he was really praying because a smile hovered at the corners of his large mouth and she wondered if he was reliving his past adventures. Idly she asked herself if some of his stories were really true. That one about the mermaid sitting on the rocks near Mingulay was lovely. He had described her as having long golden tresses, a fish tail and 'never a stitch to cover her birthday suit'.

The Taylors of Croft na Beinn sat in a neat row. Little Fiona, small for ten, thirteen-year-old Donald awkwardly trying to arrange his gangling form on the hard pew, and strong thick-set Archie meekly staring at his shoes but every so often sneaking a glance at Nancy who sat with her family in an opposite pew.

Behag Beag sat with her brother, her headscarf exchanged for a blue felt hat with a discreet feather sticking out at one side. It looked like a grouse feather and Shona grinned to herself.

Merry Mary was staring trance-like at the window, her wart outlined in the ruby glow. Beside her sat deaf old Shelagh McKinnon, Mr McKinnon's aunt and old Joe's cousin. She too wore a long black coat and a round black hat trimmed with faded green felt daisies. Old Joe had described the hat as looking like 'an upturned chanty wi' the bile' but Shelagh, deafly oblivious, was very proud of her hat. She was a quaint figure altogether with a small inquisitive face, sloping shoulders and broad hips giving her the appearance of a walking pear. At seventy-two she was surprisingly agile yet it was a practice of hers to haunt Dr McLachlan in a never ending quest for a magical cure for 'the winds that make my belly rumble and causes me to fart all the time'. She sucked Pan Drops continually, her deafness making her sweetly oblivious to the loud satisfying belches she emitted at regular intervals. At the age of sixty-five she had acquired a set of false teeth, and had, for the first time in her life, taken a trip to the mainland to have them fitted, but after months of half-hearted effort she gave up trying to eat with them saying, 'They're nothin' but a damt nuisance and I'm chewin' the buggers wi' my dinner half the time!' Nevertheless the teeth were carefully wrapped and placed in a drawer to be brought out and worn on the Sabbath so that she could sing to the Lord with proper 'prenounshun.'

She was humming untunefully, singularly content

and oblivious to the frowns thrown at her by red-haired Morag Ruadh, the nimble-fingered spinner who was very proud that she was also the church organist. It took a lot of patient persuasion to get any sort of tune from the ancient harmonium and she had to pedal furiously to get the bellows inflated before the instrument wheezed into life. Prior to the minister's appearance she liked to play quietly to get the congregation in a properly sober mood and Shelagh, humming an entirely different tune to the one being played, was an annoying diversion.

The McLachlans sat in the pew opposite Mirabelle and Shona. Niall's golden head was bowed in his clasped hands but one eye was open and he was grinning over to Shona. Hastily she tucked her legs under the hard seat and peeped at him over the generous swell of Mirabelle's bosom. She smiled back and brown eyes met blue in a shared moment of suppressed mischief.

A door opened and the minister came in. Morag pedalled harder and managed to coax some enthusiasm from the harmonium. The coughing and rustling died down and the Reverend John Grey climbed to the pulpit, pausing for a moment to bow his head in prayer.

He raised his hand and everyone rose to sing *Rock of Ages* while Shelagh remained seated and sang one of her favourite Gaelic hymns. A small girl from Nigg shuffled to the front and read a passage from the bible and the old Gaels, not understanding a word, rustled in their pockets for a mint or a handkerchief, and wished it was dinner-time. But when the minister started his sermon, everyone paid attention, whether they understood or not. The church reverberated with his booming voice and Shona sat with her mouth agape, her expression of wonder a copy of every other child there.

Shelagh, conditioned to years of church-going, kept dropping off to sleep, only to be brought back by a sharp nudge from Merry Mary. Each time she woke she muttered, 'Eh? Ach leave me be! I canny understand a word he's sayin' anyways!'

Psalms were sung and another passage from the bible read by Lachlan. He returned to his seat and the minister held up his hand again. It was his habit to divide his sermon so that he could begin by gaining the attention of his parishioners and end by giving them something that would keep them going for the rest of the week. Today he excelled himself and extolled about the virtues of clean and sinless living.

'The day will come,' he boomed, 'when we must all come to the threshold of our existence. We must prepare ourselves for that day for when it comes, according to the way we have lived our earthly lives, so will we live our eternal lives. If we have tried to be truly good, chaste of mind and body, the angels of heaven will be there to meet us. Trumpets will sound! The gift of everlasting life will take us to the gardens of heaven where the gentle winds of purity will bear the scents of sweetness that we may breathe the clean good air we have earned. Will you feel those winds, dear friends . . . will you?'

He paused and looked round his congregation. It was a habit of his to stop at a vital question and fix his flock with his piercing eyes so that the full effect of his words would have time to sink into their minds.

Shelagh stirred and grunted, smacking her lips on the sliver of mint that had stuck to her top plate. She had been enjoying a nap but the minister's deep boom had penetrated both sleep and deafness. She was confused for a moment and was quite unable to stop the great surge of wind that burst from beneath her in a triumph of sound. One after the other the farts tripped merrily like a roll of drums, the hard wood of the pew only serving to heighten the boisterous echoes. Shelagh sat quite still and upright, her look of supreme innocence confusing everyone for a moment. The acoustics in the kirk made sounds difficult to pinpoint and those in the back pews looked at each other accusingly. But there was no confusing those who sat at the front. Merry Mary made a surreptitious but noticeable movement away from Shelagh while everyone choked to keep back their laughter.

Morag Ruadh's face, red from her fight with the harmonium, grew redder still and her fingers fluttered over the keyboard as if she were debating whether or not to take the huge responsibility of playing the congregation out of the kirk before the end of the sermon.

'God help us all,' muttered Maggie Taylor and dug her youngest son in the ribs before he burst out laughing.

Elspeth's face remained like a poker and she glued her eyes to the pulpit, ignoring Hector's hissed remark about Shelagh being even ruder than she was.

Shona sat rigid in her seat and fought to keep back

the bubbles of mirth but a glance at Niall, whose face was crimson with suppressed merriment, caused one of the bubbles to escape in a strangled snort. Mirabelle was very aloof and upright but Shona glanced at her and knew that if she were to allow one muscle to move she would shame herself for the rest of her life because the laughter was sparking out of her eyes. Old Joe had turned a strange shade of blue and Lachlan had his head in both hands while his shoulders shook like a jelly. He had heard Shelagh's 'winds' many times but today she had surpassed herself. The minister coughed discreetly then, with admirable calm, went on with his sermon. When it was over, the congregation poured hurriedly from the kirk. Shelagh bid everyone a reserved 'good day' and went calmly down the slope emitting a small belch in her wake.

'Ach, but that was the best laugh I've had in weeks!' said Tom Johnston. 'My God it was the trumpet voluntary right enough!'

Old Joe nodded. 'Ach! It's shamed I am just that she is a relative of mine but it was the best turn I've heard yet in kirk! It was heaven "scent" right enough!'

Merry Mary sniffed disdainfully. 'It's all very well to laugh but I was the one sitting next the old scunner. The minister gave me a gey suspicious look. As if *I'd* do a thing like that! The smell near killed me!'

Lachlan threw back his head and roared. 'Ach, don't worry, Mary,' he consoled, 'just think we'd *all* be dead if we couldn't do what old Shelagh did, only we might not make ours so public.'

'*Really*, doctor!' said a shocked Merry Mary and walked stiffly away.

Tom Johnston turned to Biddy who having laughed herself to exhaustion was sitting on a stone fanning herself with her hat. 'Can I give you a lift home, Biddy? The bairns can sit on each other's knees and leave a wee space for you.'

Biddy's face lit up, but Mirabelle, who was very fond of the midwife and liked her company, said quickly, 'Och, but I was going to ask you over for a bite of dinner. There's more than enough.'

'Och, that would be nice now,' acquiesced Biddy. 'I was only having cold mutton so it will keep till tomorrow.'

'I'll away then,' said Tom and went over to his trap where his family were waiting impatiently.

Shona and Niall followed in the wake of the grown-ups.

'Did you like the kirk?' asked Niall gruffly.

Shona, clasping her bible and walking like 'a real little lady', tried to sound polite. 'It was very nice. I liked your father reading, he has a nice voice so he has. But . . .' Her dimples deepened. 'Shelagh was the best of all.'

'I heard a cow do that once!' exploded Niall. 'But not so loud as Shelagh!'

They were still giggling when they came upon Dodie at the roadside at the same spot they had left him more than an hour before. Ealasaid, imperious to all his coaxings, was standing, sublimely chewing a mouthful of cud.

'God, man!' cried Hamish. 'Have you not got her over to Croynachan yet or are you on the way back?'

Dodie looked like a soulful bloodhound. 'She won't

come, no matter how much I calls her. I've tried pushing and pulling but the damt beast is like a consumed bowel! She just won't move!'

Phebie looked thoughtful. 'Dodie, it's maybe because she doesn't recognize your new name for her. What was she called before?'

'Buttercup,' he said disdainfully. 'I wanted her to be fancy-like and thought Ealasaid would be lovely just!'

'Why not call her by the name she's used to . . . just this once!' Phebie hastened to add as Dodie's eyes brimmed with tears.

'Ach, c'mon, man,' coaxed Hamish. 'Phebie's right. You can call her anything you like when you've got her safely to Croynachan.'

'Just this once,' agreed Dodie with a watery sniff.

'Buttercup! Buttercup!' they all shouted together but the cow lifted a bleary eyelid, bellowed disdainfully and remained where she was. A flock of gulls rose from a nearby field and flew to the sea that shimmered in a blink of sun peeping unwillingly from behind deep grey clouds.

'We'll *all* push her!' decided Hamish and strode purposefully forward. The others joined him, their shoulders against the massive hairy backside. Biddy pulled off her best hat and set it carefully on the heather before going into the fray.

'Damt cow!' she puffed. 'I'm too old for this! Get going, you auld Cailleach!'

But instead of going forward the cow took several paces backwards pushing everyone aside. Her tail flicked then curved into an arch and manure poured from her like thick porridge. There seemed no end to it and all the while the cow stood with a look of pure relief on her face.

'My hat!' screamed Biddy but it had disappeared under the deluge.

'My God!' Dodie's tobacco-stained teeth showed for a moment. 'It's maybe she was consumed after all!'

Without further coaxing the cow turned and lumbered gently in the direction of Glen Fallan and Dodie loped hastily after her.

Biddy stared aghast at the sea of dung that covered her hat. 'Damt cow! The dirty bugger has ruined my best hat! I'll never be able to wear it again!'

'Tut, tut!' admonished Hamish with a twinkle. 'Swearin' on a Sunday, is it?'

'Away wi' Sunday!' cried Biddy, outraged, and flounced away home despite Mirabelle's reminder that she was invited to dinner.

'And how did you enjoy your first kirk service?' Fergus asked Shona when they were seated at the table.

She looked up, a piece of chicken halfway to her mouth.

'Oh, Father! It was the best laugh I've had for a long time!'

He raised his brows and Mirabelle threw Shona a warning look but it was too late, she was already relating all that had happened and great gusts of laughter roared from her father.

Mirabelle's frown disappeared. Fergus was laughing more often of late and it was his daughter who could draw the laughter from him in such abandon. He wiped his eyes, eyes that were still alight with fun.

'And did you learn anything at all about God?'

'Oh yes,' Shona assured him, 'but mostly I learned about Shelagh's winds and Dodie's consumed cow! Ach, poor Biddy! She was very upset about her hat. Maybe God will see to it she gets another because the minister says He works to give us what we want and I think Biddy wants a new hat most of all.'

That evening Shona was so excited she could barely sit still while Mirabelle read from the bible. She was starting school the following day and it seemed a whole new world was opening up for her.

'You'd best behave yourself tomorrow,' Mirabelle warned. 'I hear there's a fine new teacher come from Oban. Old Roddy has retired and gone to live with his sister in Mull. He was aye too soft wi' the bairns but this one's a real tartar from all I hear and stands no nonsense.'

'Can I wear my brown stockings now that it's spring? My legs were terribly itchy and warm with these wool ones you made me.'

'The black ones it is, madam! It's still gey bleak and cold. Now into bed, say your prayers, and don't ask God for anything for yourself.'

Shona snuggled under the blankets and asked God to bless all the people on Rhanna especially her father and Mirabelle.

'And God,' she whispered. 'Mirabelle says not to ask anything for myself but there are one or two wee things that bother me. I want my father to love me all the time, not just sometimes, and I'd like Biddy to get a new hat because she's old and doesn't have a lot of money, so maybe you could arrange a miracle. Also

Mirabelle's the best there is but she's making me wear those black stockings tomorrow and I'll have to do it, but please God don't let any of the children notice them. They're cosy and warm but they're *black* and make my legs look like spurtles so be a good boy, God and I'll try always to be a good girl, Amen.'

She turned on her back and gazed at the ceiling. There was a little damp patch shaped like a man's head. A nice kind head and she knew it was Jesus's head because it had a little beard exactly like the picture on her bible marker.

'Goodnight, Jesus,' she said, and, hugging her rag doll, she cuddled into Tot who was snoring.

Next morning she choked over her porridge, left her boiled egg and got so excited that Mirabelle became exasperated and her father impatient and finally bad-tempered. She was ready long before Mirabelle who, because it was her first day, was seeing her into school.

Niall whistled past them on the road and children were streaming from all directions, some still with their breakfast 'pieces' in their hands. The school faced the sea. Waves thundered to the shore and the tang of salt was thick in the air. There were three new children to be enrolled and Mirabelle waited till it was Shona's turn before she turned away, her shoulders humped and a suspicion of tears in her eyes. Up till then Shona had felt very happy but when she watched Mirabelle walk away a lump came to her throat and she suddenly felt very small and deserted.

'Shona McKenzie?'

'Y-yes.'

'Come along with me, Shona. I'm new too so I think we're both feeling a wee bit strange, is that right?'

The new teacher was tall and slim with fair hair and blue eyes. Shona thought she was utterly beautiful and didn't know why Mirabelle had called her a 'tartar'.

The classroom was big and smelled of chalk and musty books. A sea of faces turned to look at Shona and the other new children. Fresh from the Easter holidays, and not liking being back at school one bit, the older children were ready to seize at any distraction and tittered when the newcomers were placed in a little section on their own. Shona went hot and cold and thought everyone was looking at her stockings. She tucked her legs under her seat till they hurt and concentrated her attention on a pale shaft of sunlight that danced through the window.

It was soon evident that the new teacher was a disciplinarian. The children, used to 'Old Roddy', sprawled untidily over their desks till a sharp reprimand brought them upright.

'Straighter! Straighter!' commanded Miss Fraser. 'Pretend you have each got a ruler up your jumper.'

The dumbfounded class sat like pokers and clasped their hands sedately on their desks. One boy sniffed loudly and drew his sleeve across his nose.

'What's your name?' asked Miss Fraser, fixing him with her clear blue eyes.

'Er – Wullie McKinnon, miss. It's the cold I've got so I have! The snotters are just trippin' me so they are.'

He was Nancy's youngest brother, the one she had delivered into the world, and his language was even more indelicate than the rest of his family. The class tittered but one look from Miss Fraser quelled them.

'Bring a handkerchief tomorrow, William,' she said and turned towards the blackboard.

Wullie gulped and wondered if the tail from one of his father's old shirts would pass muster as a hanky. He was bothered continually with a runny nose and his mother 'skelped' him regularly on the ear and said she could go for a slide on his sleeves. He was plied with bits of old sheets and bits of old shirts but more often than not used them to clean excessive mud from his shoes in case his father skelped his ear too.

The class was given a number of sums and a dejected silence fell while Miss Fraser turned her attention to the newcomers. She was delighted to discover that Shona could do the alphabet and asked her if she could write the letters down and show them to the other two little ones. Shona glowed with pride and spent a happy hour printing big coloured letters. But at playtime she was surrounded by a jeering group and she stopped gnawing at the big rosy apple Mirabelle had given her and stared at the chanting children.

'Teacher's pet, awful wet! Liquorice legs like wee black pegs!'

'Och, away you go,' she cried, angry tears filling her eyes.

'Will you give us a bite of your apple?' asked a freckle-faced boy whose hair stuck up in red spikes.

Niall suddenly burst into the group, his fists bunched. 'Leave her alone! he cried menacingly, 'or

I'll punch you all on the nose. You're just jealous because she's cleverer than you!'

'Stickin' up for a lassie!' yelled Wullie disgustedly. 'What's wi' you, Niall? She's a wee baby!'

Like a flash Shona darted forward and grabbed Wullie by the hair. His nose frothed and tears poured down his face but the hold on his hair grew stronger.

'Take that back,' warned Shona, 'or – or I'll pull all your hair out and leave you like a baldy old man!'

The other children screamed in delight and Wullie screamed in agony. 'I'm sorry! I'll no' say you're a baby again!' he promised in terror.

Miss Fraser came running. 'What on earth is happening?' she demanded. 'I thought someone was being killed!'

The children shuffled sheepishly and Wullie drew his sleeve across his streaming nose. 'We were just playin', miss.'

'Well, play quieter in future . . . and for goodness' sake bring a hanky tomorrow, William. You should be ashamed – a big boy like you.'

The children filtered slowly away and Shona was left to look triumphantly at Niall.

'Can you skim stones?' he asked gruffly.

'Not yet.'

'Well, I'll show you – at dinner-time.'

Shona smiled. She knew she would never be called a baby again.

Chapter Five

The summer of Shona's sixth year was spent roaming the glens and moors of Rhanna. She and Niall were inseparable. Sometimes they were accompanied by other children; more often they were alone, finding in each other an appreciation for the wide open spaces and the small creatures of nature. They were both sensitive and intelligent and felt a certain impatience with others of their own age whose boisterous presence chased away the wild life they so eagerly looked for. Birds' nests abounded on the long stretches of open moor. Trout flashed in the clear brown rivers and they spent hours lying on dappled banks, silently intent on a pastime enjoyed by many of the island children, that of guddling. Niall was well practised in the art and could easily bring an arching silver fish from the water, much to Shona's frustration because to her the whole thing seemed an impossible difficulty she would never learn.

On really hot days, when the world outside beckoned and the classroom was a hot stuffy prison, Miss Fraser took the school swimming. The shallow waters at the edge of Loch Tenee were ideal for beginners. Nothing was more delicious than easing hot feet into the cool water and the first breathtaking sensations were hailed with screams of ecstatic agony.

Miss Fraser's 'modern ways' and extreme good looks had already caused her to be the subject of much speculation. Local crofters and fishermen suddenly had very pressing tasks that took them suspiciously close to Loch Tenee where, through the cover of summer green, they could furtively inspect Miss Fraser's lithesome body in a swimsuit, comparing her mournfully to their 'Cailleachs'.

Some children had no bathing suits but splashed happily in underpants and knickers. Mirabelle had hastily sewn a piece of material into something resembling a costume and Shona proudly splashed in her bright red attire.

Dogs came and joined in the fun. Tot had grown into the habit of going off to school each afternoon to await her young mistress and naturally, if swimming was to be in the curriculum, it meant a welcome break from long afternoons waiting for school to finish.

Each day dawned blue and cloudless. Bees droned lazily in the heather. Dunlins called out with their peculiar buzzing whistle on the marshes and oystercatchers probed unhurriedly with their long red bills for molluscs. The haze of heat caused strange effects and from a distance the white shimmering sands looked like burning snow. Old men sat on harbour walls smoking their pipes and dreaming of younger days when more than the mind could wander at will.

Yet though the island droned with the lazy sounds of summer the people themselves bustled about with great purpose. Summer was a time of preparation. Peats were lifted and turned, fields planted and the damage wrought by winter gales put to rights. But

Rhanna folk never hurried. A simple job like repairing a lobster pot could take a long time amidst agreeable companionship. Tar and salt titillated the sense of smell. The screaming of gulls, the wavelets slapping green barnacled stilts, made time a thing to hold on to rather than pass.

On such a day Fergus strode out to the fields to meet Bob and young Mathew. He braced his strong shoulders and took a deep breath of air heavy with fragrant scents. It was one of his good days. Everything had gone well and the sight of his corn fields already knee-high added to his sense of well-being. Memories of Helen still tormented him but time was gradually taking away the bitterness he had felt on losing her. At first he felt he hated God, hated the circumstances that had taken her young life. Utter loneliness engulfed him and his very soul pined for her. His dreams were filled with visions of her and he would reach out to take her in his arms only to wake up and find the reality of the empty room. He knew he called her name in his sleep because several times Shona appeared at his door, her eyes round and frightened.

'Father you were calling *her* again!' she said once, a sob catching her throat. The small white figure looked so forlorn and afraid he wanted to take her in his arms and snuggle her down in bed beside him but something held him back. He no longer thought of his little girl as the usurper who lived in place of his wife because when he looked at her he knew that Helen had been reborn in every glance, every dimpled grin. But he was afraid to love again. He knew his attitude was cowardly but the black shadow of death had already robbed him of his two loves and he couldn't risk giving of a heart that was already badly scarred by grief.

He looked at the field of corn and remembered the day he had coaxed Helen into the field on some pretext and then made love to her on the bed of sweet grasses. Passion had engulfed him and his senses reeled. Green corn and blue sky had merged into one. But she had escaped him and ran laughing, tantalizing him, her auburn hair glinting like fire in the sun and her breath coming fast when he had caught her and tussled with her, the struggle making the final conquering of her lithe body all the more satisfying. Perhaps that day of hot sun and warm bodies joining, had been the day their child was conceived.

Bob's harsh shout broke in on his thoughts. 'Have you seen Kerrie?'

'No, he's usually with you, man!'

Bob's walnut brown face showed impatience. 'Ach, the damt bugger has likely got wind of McDonald's bitch. I was needin' him to help old Peg to bring down the lambs and yowes from the top field.'

'I saw him at Loch Wee,' volunteered Mathew, now a strapping youth of nineteen. 'A lot of the dogs were in the water wi' the bairns and that new teacher.' His eyes gleamed. 'She's a bonny woman so she is, nice shaped without bein' skinny. I could see her bosoms peepin' out from the top o' her suit. It brought me out in a sweat just to look at her.'

'Damned woman and her swimming!' Fergus exploded. He had heard all about Miss Fraser – Shona was full of her, the men made eager remarks about her looks and the women also made remarks but none of them favourable. He turned on his heel. 'I'll go down to the loch! There's too much nonsense in that young teacher's mind. If Kerrie's there I'll get him back but not before I've given Miss Fraser a piece of my mind. Distracting everything from what I hear!' He strode away and Bob spat in disgust.

'See what you've done, you young upstart!' he told a shamefaced Mathew. 'From all I hear the lass is a real lady but a wee firework for a' that. If she and McKenzie has words the woods will be afire wi' a' the sparks fleein' abouts!'

Fergus reached the road and crossed over to take a short cut through the woods. Shafts of sun dappled the covering of pine needles at his feet and a squirrel scolded him angrily from a high, hidden place. The woods were cool and peaceful and his burst of temper was evaporating as quickly as it had come. A little burn tumbled nearby, the water sliding smoothly over green stones. He stopped to splash his face in the bracing mountain water and lifted his head to see a rabbit washing its whiskers in a patch of sunlight. He held his breath, keeping still till the little creature completed its toilet and ambled slowly away. The sight of the wild rabbit brought a strange thought to him. He was always so purposefully busy he seldom had time for any of the things that had once been so precious to him and he walked on slowly, thinking deeply. Shouts of laughter came to him from Loch Tenee and he pictured Shona, bronzed by the sun, splashing and screeching with joy. He knew her companion would be Niall McLachlan and he wondered if it would be through the innocence of the children that he could make his peace with Lachlan. The thought of a reconciliation had occupied a good deal of his mind of late for he knew the black cloud of guilt and shame would remain in him till he had made his peace. But he didn't know how to go about it. Mirabelle always took Shona to be treated for childhood complaints. When she'd had measles and Lachlan had had to come to the house to treat her he had been at a cattle sale in Oban and by the time he got home Shona was up and about. He himself had never had the need of a doctor since his boyhood so there was no excuse for their paths to cross. He had often passed Phebie or Lachlan but they were either accompanied by friends or Lachlan was trotting by in his trap and he had never been able to pluck up enough courage to shout a greeting, not after so many years of silence. He knew Shona was often at Slochmhor and he had pondered about going on some pretext to fetch her but somehow he was either too busy or she was home before he'd made up his mind.

He approached the thickly wooded slopes above the loch and paused to relight his pipe. It was very quiet except for the scurrying of small creatures among the ferns and he heard the audible gasp of dismay as clearly as if the sound was at his elbow. Less than four yards away stood Miss Fraser. He had seen her quite often at a distance, her tall slim figure not to be mistaken for any other. He couldn't mistake it now although she stood before him quite naked, her blue eyes round with shock and a red flush spreading over her neck and face. She had come into the woods to dry herself and dress, never suspecting that she would encounter anyone in the quiet sleeping glade among the trees. The swim had been good and her body glowed with the exhilaration of the freezing water. The children were getting dressed behind various bushes skirting the loch and she had come to her usual place, well away from prying eyes. Her costume lay at her feet where she had just dropped it and she was reaching for a towel when the twig had snapped nearby.

For a brief moment man and woman regarded each other, neither of them having the will to move. It was a fleeting tableau when all time seemed to stand still. The forest rustled with small sounds but the warm wind that had caressed the treetops seconds before now held its breath. A gull screeched overhead and a tiny vole scampered for cover in the moss but all else waited.

Fergus stared at the utter beauty of her slim body fresh from the water. He was unable to stop his eyes from travelling over every part of her. Her lithesome brown legs were long and shapely. Belly and hips curved to a narrow waist and her breasts were small but perfect, standing up young and firm, heaving because she was breathing rapidly. Her neck was slender and the bones of her face fine and sensitive. Her hair glinted like corn in the sun with crisp small tendrils drying round ears that were pink with embarrassment. His heart pounded into his throat and a sound like the sea on a stormy day rushed through his ears. Passions that he hadn't felt for years gripped his body and his loins churned. Every fibre in him cried out and he felt the blood pulsing till every cell seemed to rush downwards and he felt a hardness rising up against his belly. He knew that she could see what was happening but he was powerless to stop it. He wanted to rush forward and crush her lovely body in his arms. He wanted to feel her naked breasts in his hands, to throw her down on the moss and take her there in the middle of the silent wood, and he wanted to hear her cry out in pain and ecstasy because he knew he would be brutal and rough in his overwhelming desire. Sweat broke from him and his legs felt weak so that he had to lean against the bole of a tree to steady himself. His heart raced while he fought to gain control over the pulsing heat at the pit of his stomach and his mouth felt dry.

She stared at his tall lean figure and her first impulse was to run. She had heard all about Fergus McKenzie. The Rhanna folk were wily with newcomers. They dropped hints and innuendoes and pretended that they didn't want to gossip but all the time the gossip went on and she had gradually learned that Fergus had lost his beloved wife in childbirth and had blamed Dr McLachlan for what had happened. It was the story of a bitter lonely man and Kirsteen Fraser had watched him from a distance and felt sorry for him. She also felt sorry for little Shona McKenzie, who was spirited and brave, clever and quick yet somehow forlorn and lost.

But the man that she had heard about was not the same one she was facing now, his deep dark eyes looking at her with an intensity that shook her. She looked at his bronzed arms and strong hands, clenched till the veins had knotted and she thought he would break the bowl of his pipe. His tightly muscled body strained against his thin shirt. The collar lay open and she saw quite plainly the pulse beating swiftly in his neck. His face was handsome with rugged strong features and his hair was so black it glinted blue in the light. She saw with a sudden catch of tenderness the damp tendrils clinging to the sweat on his brow. She no longer wanted to run but felt she could stay in that wood forever just looking at him. She let her eyes traverse every bit of his body and saw that her nakedness had roused desires in the strong rugged creature who was supposed to be without feeling and who was said to be ill-tempered and unapproachable.

She forgot her embarrassment and became aware of a strange feeling in the pit of her stomach. A pulse beat rapidly in her groin and her body became warm with an excitement she hadn't known since Donald. Donald! How sweet the name was to her. He had died of a cerebral haemorrhage only a month after they were engaged to be married. She hadn't wanted to live without him and after a time knew she had to make a complete break away from her home and her family, especially her mother who wouldn't let her try to forget Donald for a moment. She had mourned and cried over the loss, not letting go of the past, and constantly grieving about the future that her daughter would never have with a young man who had met with her approval in almost every respect.

In Rhanna Kirsteen was slowly picking up the pieces of her life and already she loved the green island. She had discovered that Rhanna people were furtive and secretive about many aspects of life yet the intricacies of human relationships were so intriguing to them they were always ready with a hinted account of unsavoury gossip, some of them so outlandish she had found them hard to believe.

People like Behag Beag and Morag the spinner were certainly too good to be true both in manner and prim speech, others like the McKinnons open and frank to the point of embarrassment, yet so likeable it was easy to feel natural in their company. She would always remember her first visit to the McKinnon home. She had wanted to have a word with Mrs McKinnon about Wullie's continual sniffing and had been ushered in by Nancy who immediately made her a Strupak and settled down eagerly for a talk. Nancy's wedding was imminent and she regaled Kirsteen for a full hour with tales of Archie whose strong desires for her body had made 'the buttons o' his fly fairly go poppin' every time they were alone together'.

'Ach, but I'm lookin' forward to my wedding so I am,' she had continued. 'It's taken me all my time to wait, so it has, for all my family are that way inclined. My two big brothers are wed now but they had poor old Roddy near off his head in school for they used to be puttin' their hands up the lassies' skirts in the classroom and Wullie's only going on ten and already he lets the girls see his rooster!'

Kirsteen cleared her throat. 'It's your little brother I

came about, Nancy. When will your mother be back? I can't wait too long.'

'Ach, she'll be awhily. She's taken my dress up to Laigmhor and will crack wi' Mirabelle for ages. Mirabelle's doing wee flowers all over the top of my dress. Och, I'll be just lovely in it so I will and because I've kept myself a virgin, though God knows how, I'll not be like some o' they hypocrites who go to the altar in white and are droppin' bairns like elephants seven months later and sayin' they've come afore time.'

'Nancy, I'll have to go but I wonder – I know you'll be leaving home soon but meantime, could you try and teach your little brother not to swear quite so much and could you ask your mother to take him to Dr McLachlan. He's got a continual runny nose and, as well as being annoying, there must be a reason for it.'

Nancy had stared at the earnest face of the pretty young teacher and burst out laughing.

'Ach Miss Fraser, it's funny you are. We could all swear before we could talk properly! You mustny mind it for we canna help it. I'll have a word wi' Mither about taking Wullie to the doctor but I'm sure that it won't do a bit of good. Wullie was born wi' a dreep at his nose! I should know that for I delivered him and he snottered from the start. But it's kind you are to think of him and I'll tell the wee bugger to watch his tongue in future!'

Kirsteen escaped the warm dim kitchen and hurried round a corner where she burst out laughing, then, composing herself, she went up a grassy lane to the Morrisons' cottage because she had wanted Elspeth to take a message to Phebie with whom she was very friendly.

Hector came home and Kirsteen heard the raised voices even before she reached the open door. Elspeth was baking and in her floury hand she held a rolling pin which she was brandishing at Hector who was steeping his feet in a basin by the fire into which he stared with glazed eyes. Neither of them noticed Kirsteen and she tiptoed hastily away from the scene, not knowing that Elspeth would not have been offended because her argument with Hector had been overheard. Hers was an open hostility and she didn't care who knew it and Hector, conditioned to years of nagging, was hardly aware that any other way of life existed.

But swearing or nagging, gossiping and laughing, the islanders were refreshingly different from any other people Kirsteen had met and she was growing to love their way of life. The gentry at Burnbreddie were a different story. Kirsteen had been invited to Burnbreddie for tea. It was Madam Balfour's habit to invite all newcomers to her home so that she could look them over. Kirsteen had hated every minute of it and had sat on the edge of a huge chintz sofa and been cross-examined to the point of rudeness, all the while aware that Madam Balfour's beady little eyes were taking in every detail of her. Afterwards the laird had taken her to his study to show her his collection of butterflies. He had pressed himself hard against her on various pretences and leered into her face with watery lustful eyes. When one big hairy paw came out and openly fondled her breasts she had slapped him hard on the face and asked to be taken home immediately. 'Pretty young woman,' Madam Balfour commented, watching the carriage drive away. 'Nicely mannered but nothing much of interest in the way of family. I wonder why she left so quickly. It was very rude, yet she *seemed* to have been well brought up.'

'Spirited little lass,' mumbled the laird, his bloodshot eyes gleaming at the memory of Miss Fraser's firm young breasts in his hands.

Kirsteen had settled well to her new way of life. The schoolhouse was cosy with its big fireplaces and exciting little neuks and crannies. Slowly her heart was healing and she felt a peace stealing into her. Now here she was, in the heart of a pine wood, her whole being tingling with the feelings Fergus McKenzie roused in her. Somehow she knew that even after the moment was over she would never again know peace of mind, not so long as the strong vital force of the man was in her thoughts.

He was breathing easier now though he still surged with a passion he thought had died with Helen. But anger slowly took the place of longing and he was unable to find a reason for it. Perhaps it was guilt, or shame that he could experience such a tide of excitement for a woman who wasn't Helen, he didn't know, but he was in control of himself again and with a slight nod of his head dismissed the incident as if it had been of no import whatsoever.

'Miss Fraser.' His voice was clipped and cold. 'Begging your pardon I will bid you good day!'

She watched him disappear into the greenery and her face flushed with shame and embarrassment. In a few words he had humiliated her, made her feel cheap and degraded. The power of the man, his virility, had touched cords she had never felt before, not even with Donald. She knew he had desired her but the tone of his voice, the elusive quality of his departing figure, made her wonder if she had only imagined his attraction to her. The fact that she was naked had played a big part she knew but there was something else, something that had burst out from each of them to meet in burning streaks of electric magnetism, a silent force that each of them had been aware of. She couldn't have mistaken it and it would be a long time before she forgot the dark passion glazing his eyes and his almost tangible depth of longing. She dressed slowly allowing her hot cheeks to cool and her hands to stop trembling.

The children were growing impatient but knew better than to wander. Shona plopped stones into the water and Niall sat on a mossy boulder, his hands clasping his knees and his brown eyes contemplative.

'Shona!'

She turned to look at him. His brown skin was glowing and his tumbled corn curls ruffling in a faint breeze. She was only five and he seven yet already she thought him the finest boy in the class. He was protective towards her and though they often had rough games and angry words he always knew when she had had enough.

'Yes, Niall?'

'Why does your father hate mine?'

She stared. 'He doesn't, does he?'

'I heard Father and Mother talking. It was at night

and I couldn't sleep I was so hot. Their room is next to mine and I heard my mother asking Father why they couldn't have another baby and he said no, not after what happened to Helen.'

Shona examined a piece of heather. 'That's a strange thing. My father cries out in his sleep for a lady called Helen!'

Niall frowned, his child's mind trying to grasp a mystery. 'But Helen was your mother's name. Didn't you *know* that?'

'N-no, I always just call her mother. It's a strange thing about her because I don't know very much at all. I ask Mirabelle and she tells me quite a lot but she's so busy she often tells me to be quiet. My father tells me nothing at all – well almost nothing. Hamish says she was a lovely lady with hair and eyes like mine.'

Niall glanced at Shona's deep blue eyes and auburn locks but he was not yet of an age to appreciate feminine beauty.

'Anyway,' he continued, 'my mother said, "Damn Fergus McKenzie! He knows he's been wrong all these years but not man enough to apologize."'

Shona's eyes flashed. 'My father's a fine big man! Say you're sorry, Niall McLachlan!'

He remained calm and plopped a stone into the glassy surface of Loch Tenee.

'Wasn't me that said it so I can't say I'm sorry. Anyway, it's true, your father never talks to mine and it's nasty of him because my father's the best in the world.'

Shona's eyes filled with angry tears. 'He's not – mine is! He is – he is – and he loves me the most in the world!'

Niall looked at her fierce, sad, little face and knew he had gone too far. He jumped from the boulder and put an arm round her with an unconscious gesture of affection.

'Look, Shona – over there by the bushes! Wullie McKinnon's showing off again! He's letting the lassies see how high he can pee!'

She wiped her eyes and saw Wullie, his body arched forward, and a thin spurting stream rising into the air. Several girls watched avidly from behind coyly raised hands and, thus encouraged, other boys joined Wullie till a row of fountains arched at varying heights.

Niall squeezed Shona's hand and they collapsed in a giggling heap till Miss Fraser appeared and gathered her little flock together.

Summer passed. The days were long and golden interspersed by fierce electric storms that threw rain on to the parched earth with such force that the grasses cringed under the onslaught.

But the crofters and farmers welcomed the rain and it was a good harvest with everyone reaping till last light. Carts were piled high with sweet hay and children and adults rode home in the gloaming, the lilting sound of Gaelic tunes filling the evening till melody and summer, birdsong and laughter, all mingled and became one.

It was the habit at harvest time for one farm or croft to help the other. Croynachan had been gathered and now it was Laigmhor. Heather and Thistle plodded up and down with the reapers and the air was thick with the warm fragrant smell of freshly cut corn.

Shona loved this time of year and had looked forward to Laigmhor's harvest. She raced home from school each day with Tot scampering at her heels and had a slice of freshly baked bread thick with jam and a drink of creamy milk before she went off to the fields. She knew her father would be there, big and strong, stripped to the waist while he worked. She loved to be near him, to watch his rippling muscles under his bronzed skin, and to smell him, the warm afternoon smell of him. His smells varied according to different times of day. There was his morning smell of shaving soap and freshness, his afternoon smell of earth and horses, hay and honest sweat, and his night smell of carbolic soap and wet hair, fresh breath and tingling skin. She wondered if he attached different smells to her and hoped they were mostly nice. She tried to stay clean but it was difficult. She loved to roll in the hayshed and get cobwebs and dust in her hair that made Mirabelle snort with disgust and bring out the bath tub.

It was nice to be working beside the men and she was quite useful with the rake. She looked at Hamish on top of the cart, his red beard glowing in the sun. Mathew raked with Bob and Murdy, and Dodie, who enjoyed harvest time because he was never out of work, was turning and lifting. There was a quiet elation about him these days. The dearest thing to his heart was Ealasaid and she was at last expecting a calf. She had not been ready for the bull when Dodie thought she was and he had walked her back and forth through the Glen till both man and beast were footsore and disgusted. The laird of Burnbreddie heard of Dodie's efforts to mate his broken-down cow with McKenzie's bull and he sent word that Ealasaid had always calved in spring and June was her month for mating. Dodie had fumed and waited till the great day finally came and the bull had joined with Ealasaid.

Dodie was now at the zenith of an excitement he had never known before. He owned a cow who was going to have a calf and for the first time in his life he really felt somebody. He was also in love with Ealasaid and spoke into her flicking ears in a mournful whisper which she seemed to understand because she bellowed in response. Certain other little riches had come his way. His greasy raincoat had been replaced by a smart navy macintosh and he had been able to solve a certain matter that had been on his conscience for some time.

Biddy was touched and pleased when he appeared in Glen Fallan one peaceful summer morning and presented her with a surprisingly attractive hat. She had watched him coming up the Glen and wondered where he was going at such an early hour though it wasn't unusual to see him at any time of day or night because he seemed to roam perpetually. The linnets were soaring and the wrens singing loudly and Biddy was enjoying her porridge when she saw the figure on the road. When it stopped at her gate and looked soulfully up at the stream tumbling down from Ben Madoch she knew the visitor was for her. Dodie never went straight to anyone's door but hung about dolefully at gate or doorway till he was asked in. The islanders knew his ways and never offended him by letting him stand about too long.

Biddy gave him the remainder of the porridge from the pan on the fire and he had supped, drank tea, and lingered till Biddy grew exasperated. She had been called to the other side of the island and was less able to hurry now. Sometimes a cart was sent for her or she met a trap going in her direction but on occasion she had to walk all the way and her varicose veins were getting no better.

Dodie was acting suspiciously, clutching at something under his coat, opening his mouth to speak then shutting it again without saying a word.

'What's wi' you, man?' burst out Biddy finally. 'Are you knowin' someone with child and wantin' my advice?'

He blushed to the peak of his cap and his brown teeth showed nervously. Suddenly he pulled a bundle from inside his coat and pushed it at Biddy, overturning his cup with excitement.

'It's a wee thing for you,' he gulped, his words almost unintelligible. 'To make up for the one Ealasaid shat on! She couldny help it bein' consumed but I was ay thinkin' how she ruined your hat. It will be fine on you, sit nice it will! I know leddies like hats to sit nice. Not like the other in colour but nice, nice it is, ay nice just!'

Biddy didn't hear the rather confused explanation. She was already trying on the hat, preening in front of the mirror on a shelf. It was a fine velvet hat with a nice trimming and she was so pleased she stooped and kissed Dodie on the cheek. He blushed again and rising quickly, almost knocked over the table. He opened the door and loped hastily over the winding road till he was lost to view. Never, never in all the years he could remember had anyone kissed him and he put up his large fingers to touch the favoured spot on his cheek, his mouth opening wide with pleasure. Biddy hadn't asked where he got the hat and he wasn't going to tell her or anyone else. There had been so many hats in the attics at Burnbreddie. Trunks of them and clothes too. He shouldn't have looked really because he had been sent up to clear out accumulated rubbish. But he had peeped and there were so many clothes – enough to keep the folk on Rhanna warm for years – the temptation had proved too much. The laird didn't pay him well for all the work he did, so the hat and the navy macintosh were a sort of bonus. He had worn the coat with a certain trepidation, savouring the warmth of it compared to his old one, yet dreading that it would be recognized by the laird and his leddy. But they hadn't given him a second glance and he knew Biddy's hat would go unrecognized too.

So he worked and dreamed of Ealasaid and her calf, his dreams taking him into realms of fantasy where Ealasaid would provide him with enough offspring to have a herd of his own, one that would be the talk of Rhanna so grand it would be.

Shona grew tired of raking after a time and Murdy helped her scramble on to the cart beside Hamish. She sank into the warm sweet hay and shaded her eyes to look at Slochmhor nestling in the hollow. She had wanted Niall to come to her father's harvest but he had refused. He could be stubborn when he liked and had set his chin, adamant about the matter. He dearly loved his father and couldn't understand anyone who didn't. Shona too had her own brand of determination and she too adored her father though she was hurt and puzzled that he couldn't show his affection the way Lachlan did to his child.

'I go to your house but you never come to mine,' she accused, trying to swing the argument in her favour.

'Your father must say he's sorry first!'

'But what for? Och, I'm fed up so I am! Do *you* know what he should be sorry about?'

'No and I can't ask Mother because I wasn't supposed to hear. Anyway, it's a grown-up thing and they can be gey queer if you ask questions.'

'Oh Niall, come to our harvest! We've been to all the rest together and I saw you working with my father quite contented. Mirabelle makes a grand harvest supper, she bakes piles of bannocks and fancy wee cakes and we have chicken and ham on new-baked bread. You'd fairly love Mirabelle. She's big and cosy with a nice smell of baking off her and though she cuddles a lot she doesn't do it *too* much!'

'I do like Mirabelle. She's grand! I wish we had her instead of Elspeth but I'm still not coming to your harvest!'

'Don't you like my father even a wee bit?'

'I've hardly spoken to him and when I did he sounded girny. He's fine and strong and I like the way he strides like a giant but he's still girny!'

Shona's face grew red because she couldn't deny this and she knew she had lost the argument as she always seemed to when she was discussing her father with Niall. Harvesting wasn't the same without Niall's presence. Other boys and girls laughed and tumbled but they weren't the same and she looked down at Slochmhor wistfully. Clothes were flapping lazily on the line and the tiny dot that was Niall ran in the garden. Two bigger dots were Phebie and Miss Fraser who was a regular visitor to the doctor's house. Shona sighed. She wished Miss Fraser would visit Laigmhor. The only people who ever came were for Mirabelle; no one seemed to visit her father. She looked at him, unaware that she wasn't the only one to sigh for things out of reach. Fergus worked purposefully but one eye looked towards Lachlan's house and Miss Fraser. She had occupied his mind many times during the long weeks of summer. In bed at night his thoughts whirled till sometimes he felt like one demented. There was so much he wanted to do. One of them was to apologize to Lachlan. He needed the friendship of the man he had wronged so badly. He knew he was a man apart from others but he had been in tune with Lachlan the way he was with Hamish. They both enjoyed the same things and they could be happily silent in each other's company. Yet Lachlan was so different in many respects. He was outgoing and friendly, everyone liked and respected him. Fergus was treated with respect by most people but only a handful liked him and he was a lonely man. He was glad of Hamish and often sought solace in the cosy friendly cottage. There was an atmosphere of peace there. He could enjoy a dram and relax like the animals lying everywhere. Farm affairs could be discussed with unhurried demeanour and he could forget his loneliness. But Hamish had been rather preoccupied of late. It was rumoured he was 'courtin' steady' but like most rumours on the island it had been lacking in concrete evidence. Word was passed from croft to clachan till original beginnings were lost in a sea of speculation and exaggeration. But this time fantasy turned to fact when Hamish was seen several times arm in arm with a lady, mature of years but attractive nonetheless. She was a widow who had come to Rhanna two years before for reasons of health. The hopefuls who had eyed Hamish for years fumed inwardly but smiled at Maggie McBain with admirable composure and hoped the affair wouldn't last long. When it was rumoured that Hamish was making marriage plans, Mairi McDonald, the blacksmith's daughter, cried for a week. She had adored Hamish for years and when he had reason to visit her father she stared at his red beard and fine figure with open longing in her rather vacant eyes. She was a plain young woman with none of the buxom quality the Rhanna men liked in their women but she had never cared for any other man but Hamish. She paid regular visits to his cottage when she knew he would be out and cleaned and tidied much to his annoyance because after one of her visits he could never find anything in its proper place. But more than Mairi were disappointed when it became known that Hamish had every intention of abandoning his long years of bachelorhood for Maggie McBain and those females who saw their years on the shelf becoming a near certainty sniffed and remarked disdainfully, 'And she an incomer too. Why could he not have chosen a nice local girl?'

Fergus was pleased for Hamish but while the big

red-bearded man pursued his courtship, he had nowhere to go in the evenings and he had a lot of time for contemplation. He longed for a change in his way of life. He wanted to open his heart to his little girl who gave so much love which he found hard to return because the years of locking his love away made it difficult to turn the key of release. And he wanted Kirsteen Fraser so badly that at times it took all of his willpower not to go blundering down to the schoolhouse and take her in his arms. His evening strolls took him to Portcull, there to walk along the lonely stretches of shore past her house in the hope he might get a glimpse of her. He saw her several times but she was always with someone else, though she had glanced at him and smiled – a quick, shy smile that belied her racing pulses.

He did not know of the nights she lay dreaming of him, her body tortured by longing and her mind throbbing with the remembrance of the meeting in the woods so many weeks ago. She visited Phebie more often than was necessary knowing she would have to pass Laigmhor and he might be about. Just to see him fed the love in her heart for one brief moment but knowing she had to pass him by made her ache for days. She went back to Loch Tenee where first they had met and relived each second of their few minutes there. The memory of his strong tawny limbs went with her everywhere but most of all the intense burning passion in his black eyes haunted her every hour of the day and night.

Part Three

1929

Chapter Six

The wind battered against Rhanna. Frothing white spume hurled on to the shore and the schoolhouse garden was awash with salt water and rain.

Kirsteen looked in dismay at her daffodils and wondered how long they could survive the gale. She sat at her window eating a boiled egg laid by one of the hens she had been coaxed to keep by various islanders.

'Nothing finer than an egg fresh frae the erse o' one o' your own hens,' nodded old Shelagh wisely. 'They give myself the winds but good they are for young folks ay just! I'm readin' in one o' they wimmen's papers Mistress Behag orders from the mainland that eggs are a fine source o' nourishment. If that's the case then I should be well nourished just for my mither gave me eggs till they were droppin' out my ears and I'm blamin' too much o' them in my young days for the farts I have now!'

'I didn't know you could read English, Shelagh,' said Kirsteen, smiling at the wily old lady.

'Ach well, just a wee bit. I picked it up when I worked to Burnbreddie though they never knew. It's handy when folks are gabblin' away and thinkin' that you only have the Gaelic. You can find out a lot. After I could speak it I learned to read it. But you won't tell a soul, I'm sure. You have the two tongues yourself and you and I could have a lot o' fine wee secrets, eh?'

She nudged Kirsteen and twisted her wizened little face into a conspiratorial grimace.

'The magazines are rubbish mostly,' she continued with asperity. 'I would never buy them but Mistress Behag gives them to me thinking I'll like the pictures. I *know* what she reads in them . . .' She lowered her voice a note below its usually boisterous bellow. 'Prim is Behag on the surface but underneath she'll be sensual they calls it and there's a lot o' that in they magazines but then . . . there's some will read anything in place o' a man!'

Kirsteen had no time to answer because Shelagh confounded her still further in the next few minutes. She came closer and spoke in a confiding bass whisper.

'There was a wee bit once on the doctor's page. Someone wrote in about having a lot of winds and he gave a recipe for relief. I tried it and was worse than ever . . . skitters for a week and farts for a month. You've never heard the likes! I was never away from Auld McLure till he came back to my house and asked me to show him the recipe. Do you know what he discovered, Miss Fraser?'

Kirsteen struggled to keep back her laughter and looked suitably interested.

'I had put in liquorice powder instead o' bakin' soda and I was more generous than the recipe said. It said a teaspoonful and I just put in a tablespoonful for good measure. I just ignore the doctor's page now and tear it up for the wee hoosie. It's fine if you're in a long time and nothing to hold your interest, you can read wee bits so you can, while you're waitin' for a miracle.'

Kirsteen knew by now that the 'wee hoosie' was the name the islanders gave to the dry lavatories situated discreetly at the backs of houses amongst the bushes. Running water and indoor plumbing were unheard of on Rhanna. Except for Burnbreddie and the bigger farms with hand-cranked generators, it was a case of carrying water and suffering the 'wee hoosies'.

Kirsteen, after a year of sharing her own 'wee hoosie' with midges and horseflies, had become quite accustomed to it and she didn't mind bathing in a zinc tub before the fire.

She had bought a clutch of chickens and they were now fine big birds thanks to the 'hen's pot' that Phebie had shown her how to make. She was grateful for the huge eggs with which the hens rewarded her. She liked to hear the hens clucking about and it was not unusual for them to come strutting into the classroom if the door lay open.

Spring had started early and she was looking forward to it. Now, in the second day of April, winter seemed to have come back, with the storm rattling doors and windows. She glanced towards the road and saw the first of the children battling their way to school. Little Shona McKenzie was with Niall as usual. His curls danced in the wind and Shona's auburn tresses escaped her woollen hat. Kirsteen wondered if Shona resembled her mother. If so, Helen must have been beautiful because her daughter was like a glowing cameo with her peach skin and pointed face, her huge blue eyes and that hair tumbling down her back in thick fiery waves and curls.

Kirsteen had asked Phebie about Helen but had been careful to make the question sound like an afterthought. Phebie had spoken with tenderness, a little smile of wistfulness lurking at the corners of her mouth, but she had seemed reluctant to discuss her personal feelings and Kirsteen understood that the matter was a sore point at Slochmhor and didn't pursue the subject further.

She sighed and rose to make her way to the schoolroom. If Helen had been beautiful like her daughter, if, as Phebie said, Helen had been vivacious and gay, charming and loving, then Fergus must have loved her deeply, so deeply and devotedly that no one could possibly take her place.

Fergus was alarmed by the force of the wind and hurried through his breakfast. Shona came into the kitchen dressed for school and she came round the table to give her father the usual peck on his cheek. She was growing more restrained in her displays of affection and with a start he tried to remember when last she had thrown her arms round his neck and called him 'my big boy'.

She was only six, yet in many ways grown up for her years. She was still puckish and gay, moody and bad tempered on occasion, but there was a growing dignity in her, and looking at her pointed little face and deep eyes that withheld her innermost thoughts he suddenly wished she would hurl herself at him and cover him with kisses the way she used to. He studied her for a long moment and tried to fathom the look in her periwinkle gaze. There was a sadness there. He caught a fleeting glimpse of it as she matched his stare with hers and something tore at his heartstrings. It was the way Helen had looked when she was forlorn but with Helen he had been able to discuss the reasons for her sadness and between them they had been able to dispel it.

He knew he couldn't communicate with his own child. When had he ever spoken to her about her hopes and dreams? Had he ever asked her about her childish pastimes? He couldn't even remember when, if ever, he had taken her on his knee to cuddle her and let her know she was loved and wanted. He hadn't loved or wanted her at the beginning. Now that he did he was unable to know how to go about letting her know. How many of her lovely child's years had he missed because he was so wrapped up in himself? Six! Already six! He had missed all her baby years, they were gone from him and he would never know what they had been like because he had been blind to all but his own sorrow. She had sat on Hamish's knee hundreds of times and tugged at his red beard because he always hid a penny there for her to find. She had laughed with Hamish, a happy child's laugh, when he grasped her in his arms and gave her bear hugs, all the things her own father should have done.

Impulsively he put out his arms to hug her to him but she was turning away, kissing Tot goodbye and throwing her arms round Mirabelle before opening the door.

He went to the window and watched her battling against the wind to meet Niall who was waiting impatiently at the gate. He cursed under his breath at the sight of the two of them bending their young bodies into the gale. They were animated. Shona's laughter was tossed back by the wind, making Fergus scowl harder. That boy, with his sturdy good looks, his strong handsome little face, his openly resentful gaze when he met Fergus, he could make Shona laugh. He could talk to her and play with her and do all the things that her own father couldn't. They were an intimate pair in their child's way and Fergus felt shut out and very alone seeing Niall take his daughter's hand in an effort to hold her upright on windswept Rhanna.

Mirabelle was clattering the things off the breakfast table and he took his resentment out on her.

'Oh, woman! Stop your rattling!' His dark eyes snapped with temper and he nodded towards the window. 'That two! What's with you that they're always together? Can't you speak to Shona and tell her to find another bairn to play with? A wee lass would be better!'

Mirabelle stood with her hands full of dishes.

'Fergus! Fergus!' Her voice was weary. 'If you weren't so proud you'd make your peace wi' Lachlan! He's a fine lad and his son's a fine bairn. He knows there's something wrong between you and his own father and he knows it's you that should put it right. I've heard things, Fergus . . . about Lachlan and Phebie . . . things are no' right wi' them and I've heard tell it's because you accused poor Lachlan about Helen!' She shook her grey head wearily and sighed deeply.

He was about to hurl abuse at her but something in the stoop of her shoulders stayed him. He realised that Mirabelle had grown into an old woman under his very eyes and he hadn't noticed. She had always been in his life. Hers were the arms he had tumbled to for comfort in his troubled boyhood. She had scolded and loved, cared for and comforted people all her life. She was part of Laigmhor, she held it together in a hundred ways that had nothing to do with bricks and mortar. Hers was a life of utter self-denial. Half of it was spent in the kitchen, the other half devoted to bringing up his daughter. In a way Mirabelle *was* Laigmhor because she had been there even before he was born. The thought was strangely disquieting. She had come to Laigmhor in 1897, two years before he was born. She must have come in young womanhood, now she was old, the hair that escaped her mutch was white, her plump face was still smooth but her kindly eyes were tired. But it was her hands he noticed most of all. Years of washing, cooking, scrubbing had left their mark. The veins were knotted, the skin crêped and dry, the fingers slightly disfigured by rheumatism.

She stood at the table and saw the anger go out of him. Suddenly he crumpled and looked like the lost lonely little boy who had come to her with his troubles long years ago.

'Belle!' he whispered. 'I'm sorry . . . if it wasn't for you, my dear old friend, none of us would be here. What am I to do, tell me? For God's sake I don't even know my own bairn. Och! If only Helen had lived! I loved her, Belle. The very marrow went out of me when she died but I've fed on memories too long now and there's so much I have to put right!'

It was a cry from the heart and tears sprang to Mirabelle's eyes. She went quickly to take the dark head to her bosom, a thing she hadn't done for many a year. 'Fergus! My laddie! I know how you've suffered! Bless me, I know only too well!' She rocked his head gently. 'There, there, my poor laddie, auld Mirabelle's here. I know your hert is sair but Helen wouldny want you to grieve so. You've held on to memories too long now. You don't know your own wee bairn because you tried to shut her out. You've kept poor Helen a prisoner o' your hert for too long. Tell the bairn about her lovely mother, you'll both be the better for it, believe me.'

Fergus felt the gentle old hands stroking his hair and a strange peace stole over him. A feeling of release came to his whole being as the lilting Highland voice soothed him.

'Make your peace wi' Lachy,' she crooned softly. 'Rid your hert o' its burden o' guilt . . . och yes, you know it's true. You'll not be a happy man till you do as I tell you.'

He raised his head and looked deep into her wise old eyes. 'Aye, you are right, Belle . . . about everything. I'll do as you say, I must or I feel I'll go mad. I've to see to the yowes, I told Bob I'd be up at the field early, but when I'm done I'll go straight to Slochmhor and hope they'll want my apology after all this time.'

'Ach they will, they will,' beamed Mirabelle. 'Och, I'm so pleased and this will be a happier place I'm sure.'

A flapping movement in the garden caught her eye and she saw Dodie loping along, his navy raincoat ballooning in the wind. This time he didn't wait to be invited but came straight to the door and rapped imperiously.

'I'll be blessed!' exclaimed Mirabelle. 'There must be an emergency or Dodie wouldny be chappin' the door!'

Dodie opened the door with a quick gesture and the frenzied wind ushered him through without ceremony so that his ungainly wellingtons caught on the doormat and down he went.

'Ach it's glad I am just to have caught you, Mr McKenzie!' he panted, struggling to regain his feet. 'It's Ealasaid calving and me not knowing right what I'm doin'. She's a wheen overdue but she's been labouring all night and me up with her holding her and rubbing her belly! Now she's just lyin' down and bellowin' and I think she's dyin'. Och, Mr McKenzie! Will you come and help? I'm feart o' losin' my Ealasaid and you're the only man I'd trust with her!'

Fergus thought about all the work waiting for him but, as always, the simple faith of hardworking guileless Dodie touched his heart. Tears of weariness and anxiety had stained his coarse brown cheeks and his usually faraway dreaming eyes held a frightened urgency. The thought that he might lose his beloved cow had brought him out of the simple innocent world in which he lived and tossed him into one of harsh reality.

Fergus placed a firm hand on his bent shoulder. 'Don't worry, man, I'll come with you! Come with me to the byre, we'll need one or two things. Belle!' He raised his voice. 'I'm away with Dodie to help with the calf! I don't know when I'll be back!'

'Right, laddie!' Mirabelle's voice was jubilant. Things were going to be happier soon at Laigmhor. Fergus would apologize to Lachlan and there would be an easier atmosphere all round. Singing an old Highland love lilt she went as usual to halve an onion in the kitchen to dispel the smell of Dodie.

Ealasaid lay in a bed of fresh hay in the little shed behind Dodie's cottage. Fergus saw immediately that she was in difficulties. Her breathing was rapid, her bloodshot eyes half-shut with pain and weakness.

He examined her quickly. 'It's just as I thought, Dodie, it's going to be a breech and the cow hasn't the strength for it. Go and get the ropes. When the back legs come out we'll have a pull between us. The old beast won't be able to give much help.'

Half-sobbing, Dodie galloped away for the ropes. The morning passed slowly. Ealasaid was unable to stand. Dodie sat sprawled in the hay beside her and held her huge head tenderly in his lap. He stroked her and whispered in her ears and every so often sobbed out, 'Ach, my Ealasaid! I shouldny have let this happen. It's my fault! Dodie's to blame!'

At one o'clock Fergus was outside smoking his pipe when he saw a distant speck toiling up the track. It came nearer and proved to be Mirabelle wrapped in a thick tweed cloak, a basket over her arm. Her face was red with exertion and she was unable to speak for a few moments. Fergus made her sit down on a rickety wooden bench and scolded her thoroughly for coming so far.

'Ach weesht, laddie,' she gasped. 'I know you wouldny get anything to sup here so I brought a bite for the pair o' you. There's cold chicken and ham and a loaf fresh from the oven.'

She nodded towards the shed. 'What's doin'? Has the beast calved yet?'

'No, she's not got the strength for it and it's going to be a breech into the bargain.'

She shook her grey head sadly. 'Ach, poor Dodie. She's all he has and not for long I'm thinkin'. That old goat Burnbreddie needs his lugs skelped . . . givin' a poor simple man a cow like that!'

A sudden flash of lightning lit the lowering purple-grey sky followed by a rumbling growl of thunder. Mirabelle rose. 'I'm away before that blessed sky opens again! What weather – in spring too!'

Fergus watched her flapping tent-like shape till it was out of sight. He felt his hands trembling. He was in the role of the deliverer and the thought made him feel sick because he knew Ealasaid would not survive.

Dodie, tearstained and exhausted, refused to eat and went back to the shed to be with his cow leaving Fergus to peck half-heartedly at the piece of chicken.

'Mr McKenzie, she's pushin'! She's started to push!'

The wind hurled Dodie's urgent cries to Fergus and he ran to the shed. The cow was straining, using every last ounce of her strength. Fergus knelt and massaged her massive belly. He had delivered many calves in his day and was used to seeing the agony that went with birth but somehow, watching the dying old cow using all the life that remained in her to bring forth her calf, he was filled with admiration.

An hour passed. The world outside the little shed became a raging, wind-battered torrent. Ealasaid had been moaning softly but now her eyes opened wide and she began to struggle to her feet. The men helped to pull her up and she sagged against them as the hind quarters of her calf were expelled.

'Hold her till I tie the ropes!' ordered Fergus.

He secured the ropes to the calf and began pulling with all his might. Ealasaid cried softly and Dodie wept into her neck.

'Help me, man!' panted Fergus. 'Grab that other rope!'

Ealasaid sank to her knees and the men pulled and sweated. The calf came surging out in a sudden burst and both men fell on their backs.

Fergus quickly cut the birth cord. It was a lovely black and white calf, amazingly sturdy, and he carried it to where its mother had once again sunk into the hay. She licked the warm wet little face and her long-lashed eyes regarded it lovingly. Her breath was coming very fast and she was moaning quietly at the back of her throat.

'Will she live, Mr McKenzie!' asked Dodie, dropping on his knees. He was staring at Fergus, willing with all the might of his simple brain that the man he held in such faith would give him the answer he so desperately wanted.

Fergus stopped in the act of wrapping the calf in a blanket.

'No, Dodie, she'll die.' Pity and a feeling of inadequacy made the words sound blunt and callous. 'She's nigh on death now but you have a fine calf in her place.'

Dodie sank his head on to Ealasaid's heaving flank and broke into a torrent of sobbing.

'I dinna want the calf! I want my Ealasaid! Ach my poor beastie, I've done for you so I have! You canny die, you canny!'

But Ealasaid had drawn her last shuddering breath and Dodie rocked on his knees, his calloused big fingers scrubbing his eyes.

'Come on, man,' Fergus said gruffly. 'Look at the wee calf. She's a bonny beast – and remember she's part of Ealasaid. It will be like having the old beast made new again.'

Slowly Dodie raised his tearstained face and a look of childlike wonder gradually diffused his sorrowful countenance.

'Aye,' he whispered, 'like Ealasaid reborn.' His voice grew eager. 'A new wee Ealasaid! I'll call her that! Mr McKenzie . . . it's yoursel' I've to thank. Without your help both would have died just.'

Fergus felt uncomfortable. 'Let's go now, man,' he said awkwardly. 'We'll take the calf down to Laigmhor till she's weaned. I'll get some of my men to come up and shift the old cow.'

Fergus hustled Dodie down the track, making him carry the new calf which he had already fallen in love with, whispering into its silky ears the way he had done to its mother. Fergus strode quickly in front. He was tired and hungry but there was something he had to do before he could rest or eat. Years of fretting, of living with his guilt, had finally culminated in an overwhelming desire to make his peace with Lachlan and simple, trusting Dodie had set the final seal in his mind.

School was allowed out early that afternoon because Kirsteen Fraser worried about the children living in farflung corners of the island and she didn't want them caught in the thunderstorm that was brewing. So it was that Niall and Shona were making their way home an hour earlier than usual.

'Come home with me for a wee while,' suggested Niall. 'Mother will maybe give us a scone in jam.'

But Shona was in a strange mood. Thunder never frightened, but excited her. She lifted her face skywards and Niall could see the tumbling grey clouds mirrored in her sparkling eyes. She laughed in abandonment showing a gap where one baby tooth had come out and been magically taken away in the night by a Fairy Moruach who had left a silver threepenny in its place.

'Och, it's lovely so it is!' she cried spreading her arms as if trying to capture the elusive force.

'I don't want to be shut up in a house,' she said breathlessly. 'Let's go somewhere. We've an hour to spare.'

'Where? To the caves at Sgor Creągs? I love watching the waves crashing into the caves and it's grand the way the froth skirls round the Creags!'

Shona shook her bright head. 'That would take too long. We'll go to the Kirkyard. It's creepy there in a storm. I love listening to the elms creaking and groaning. They talk to each other and the wee flurries sough through the bell tower and the bell rings – like a wee fairy bell.'

Niall snorted scornfully. 'There's no fairies.'

But the idea of the talking trees appealed to him and he took Shona's hand and they scampered through the trees to climb the steep brae to the Kirkyard. They opened the rustic wooden gate and made their way through the long grass. The tall elms bowed to them, their branches creaked and groaned, swayed and tossed, in the wind that was much stronger here atop the Hillock.

'Listen!' commanded Shona breathlessly. 'They're moaning like old Bodachs with the reaumys!'

She stood with her head thrown back looking at the tormented branches that laced overhead, shutting out any light there was to be had from the dark sky.

Niall looked about him and shivered. Some of the tombstones were very old and lay flat on the ground, the writing on them illegible, almost hidden by damp moss and twining ivy creepers. And Shona had been right about the bell, it was tinkling very softly in the bell tower.

'Old Joe told me a story about the bell,' said Shona in a hissed whisper. 'He said it's rung by a Moruach who got stranded and died on the shore and she rings the bell to let all the Moruachs and Caonteachs know what will happen to them if they stray too far from the water!'

Niall didn't dispute the story.

'It's skearie here, and these old trees are like ghosties moaning and wailing. Maybe they're the ghosts grown out of the bodies of all the dead folk, their spirits all mixing together and trying to speak!'

They stared at each other wondering if such a thing were possible, both of them feeling afraid but trying not to show it.

'I wonder what spirits are like,' whispered Shona.

'Todd the Shod says they give him a rare feeling,' grinned Niall deliberately misunderstanding.

'My mother's a spirit!' said Shona solemnly. 'She's here watching us.'

Niall shifted uneasily. 'Let's go home! There's still time for a scone in jam.'

But Shona was darting away to the newer part of the Kirkyard. 'I want to look at my mother's grave!' she called and Niall followed reluctantly.

They stood before Helen's grave with its white headstone. An old McKenzie vault lay in the older part of the Kirkyard but old Malcolm had been the last to be buried there.

Shona folded her hands behind her back and stared. She had been at the grave before with Mirabelle who occasionally brought a bunch of roses from the farmhouse garden. But it had been a year almost since her last visit because though she went to kirk on Sundays they always had to hurry home to get Sunday dinner laid. A year ago she hadn't been able to read but she could now, very slowly. Carefully she began to read out the words on the stone. Niall wasn't greatly interested and scrambled up the stone wall to sit astride and view the tossing Sound of Rhanna in the distance.

'Here lies Helen McDonald, beloved wife of Fergus McKenzie, Laigmhor. Born 14th June 1901, died 29th

January 1923. Wait for me beloved, on that distant shore, when my life has fled and the storms of life are o'er.'

Shona's eyes filled with tears. Wait for me beloved! How well her father had loved her mother. She wished she had known her, it would be lovely to have a mother. Niall was lucky. Phebie nagged him sometimes and he got an occasional skelping but more often she was loving, her round sweet face made beautiful with her love for her child.

Shona thought of Mirabelle. She was soft and round and her arms were loving. She scolded and skelped too but mostly she loved. Yes, Mirabelle was really like her mother though she was an old woman.

Something nagged at Shona's mind. It was to do with the writing on the stone. She read it again, slowly and laboriously while the wind wailed louder, shrieking and darting round the headstones. She halted suddenly. Something familiar nagged at the back of her memory. 29th January 1923. Why, that was her birthday! Why was her birthday on a stone that read death and not life! She had been born on that day and . . . She held her breath and for a second the storm paused. All afternoon, streaks of lightning and claps of thunder had played threateningly amongst the mountains. Now Glen Fallan was lit by a blinding glare and thunder reverberated in deafening roars directly above. Shona's scream was almost lost in the volley but Niall heard and came running, his face white.

'Shona!' He stared at her aghast. Her baby face was distorted with the agony of grief her discovery had brought her. Tears poured down her smooth round cheeks and her small slim body trembled with her sobbing. She couldn't speak, but just stood there, her eyes blinded by tears and her mouth twisted with shock. It was difficult to believe that a six-year-old girl could be capable of such emotions and Niall felt strangely frightened.

'Shona, what is it?' he asked softly, placing an arm round her shoulders.

'I know now why my father has never liked me – not really!' Her voice vibrated with intensity. 'It's because my mother died when I was born – like the sheep that died when its wee lamb came! He blames me for being born, that's why he can never love me! He'd rather I was dead and my mother alive. Och Niall.' She looked at him from swollen lids. 'I wish I never had been born!'

'Ach, don't say such daft things,' he comforted awkwardly. 'I'm glad you're born. So's Mirabelle and Mother and Father and lots more folk.'

'But Father isn't.' Her voice was dull and the life had gone from her. 'Every time he looks at me he'll be wishing I was dead and Mother here!'

The heavens opened then and they were soaked before they were halfway home. Shona ran to Laigmhor and Mirabelle into whose arms she tumbled with her heartbreak, and Niall, his fair curls plastered to his head, raced for Slochmhor. The kitchen was warm and no one was about so, while he dried his thick curls, he helped himself to a scone from a plate on the range.

At first he thought the house was empty. His mother wouldn't expect him for another half-hour and might be shopping at Portcull. Confidently he helped himself to another scone and munched contentedly, though he couldn't stop thinking of Shona. The clock ticked in the hall and the house was very quiet. Then he heard voices from his parents' bedroom. He went to the foot of the stairs to announce his arrival home but the rising note of bitterness in his mother's voice stayed him.

'Please, Lachy!' she cried. 'Don't let McKenzie run our lives any more. Let me have another bairn! Please!'

Lachlan was tired. All day long he had battled against the storm, from clachan to croft, tending his patients. Home was still the haven he so badly needed. He and Phebie had their rows like anyone else but he dearly loved the sight of her bonny face and her warm rounded body still moved him to passion. But now he kept a check on his desires and when they made love it was he who was the careful one when he reached climax and as a result their love-making lacked the spontaneity that was once plentiful.

Helen's death by childbirth and Fergus's accusations had affected him deeper than anyone realised. He loved Phebie dearly and wasn't going to lose her in the same way that Fergus had lost his wife. Phebie couldn't understand him. She longed to have another child but over and over he refused her. At first it hadn't mattered greatly and she had been confident that Lachlan would get over the matter. But time was passing, he had grown even more adamant, and lately their quarrels were heated and bitter.

Today was no exception. He had gone to lie down for an hour. He had wakened to find Phebie beside him, naked and desirable. Sleep went from him. She was tantalizing, touching him till he quivered, her silky body pressed against him, urging him to a frenzy and her hands did things to him till he cried out and reached for her roughly. But she kept eluding him till at the peak of his desire she whispered, 'Let yourself go today, Lachy! Don't hold back!'

But he had pushed her away and the flush of anger took the place of passion.

'You don't want me to love you!' he cried. 'You want to use me like a rutting stag! I'll not have it, Phebie! God, woman! Don't you know I do it for you . . . to keep you safe!'

That was when Niall heard Phebie's impassioned plea. He stopped, one foot on the stairs then turned and crept softly back to the kitchen. A few minutes later he saw Fergus McKenzie striding along purposefully. Niall held his breath. Fergus stopped and clicked open the side gate, pausing for a moment to look uncertainly at the house. At the same time Phebie came flying downstairs in a headlong flight away from Lachlan, the house, and her misery. She had dressed hurriedly and her hair and eyes were wild. She didn't even notice Niall but ran past him out of the door and came face to face with Fergus. He was taken aback at the sight of her. He was soaked, his clothes plastered to his body, rain running in rivulets from his hair and down over his face. In seconds she too was drenched but she appeared not to notice. The fierce storm that raged over Rhanna was nothing to the look in her eyes at sight of him. Her breath came quickly and her voice was high and unreal. 'Get away from here, Fergus

McKenzie!' she screamed above the peals of thunder. 'Get away and don't come back! I curse you for the selfish devil of a man you are!'

She ran from him and sped like a mad thing towards Glen Fallan. The next moment Lachlan shot out of the house. He stopped in his tracks at the sight of Fergus and his face turned white. For a long moment in storm-racked Glen Fallan the two men stared at each other then, with a look of contempt, Lachlan raced past to catch up with Phebie.

Fergus felt unreal. For years he had nursed his grievances, never stopping to think that they might affect the lives of others. He had felt himself to be the master of his own fate but had come at last to the stage when he wanted to bury the past. He had made the great decision and, having made it, nothing would appease him till he made amends. He had been sure of the forgiveness of easy-going Lachlan, and Phebie with her good nature presented no obstacle to the reconciliation.

He felt he had dreamed the scene but Lachlan, pleading and coaxing with Phebie while the rain poured in torrents round them was no dream, nor was Niall's face, white and frightened, at the window.

He stumbled away towards Laigmhor. There at least he was sure of a warm welcome. But another storm awaited him the moment he staggered thankfully into the warm kitchen. Shona jumped from the rocking chair. She had cried her heart out against Mirabelle's bosom. The old woman had petted and stroked and whispered endearing words, and her tears had dried leaving her heart heavy.

Afterwards she sat in the bath by the fire while Mirabelle bathed her. Mirabelle sighed and wished the unhappy little being would have a tantrum or utter words of anger but wrapped in her blue dressing-gown with her fiery hair tied back from her pale little face she was like a lifeless wax doll. But now the big wonderful man that she had loved devotedly was striding into the room and she felt at that moment she could never love him again. She faced him and her voice was strong and even.

'I know now why you don't love me, Father. It's because God took Mother and let me live. It was all on *her* gravestone!' Her voice rose and Mirabelle wrung her hands in dismay.

'If only you had told me, Father . . . about *her*! We could have loved her together but you wouldn't let me and I hate you for it – I hate you, Father!'

She fell to a storm of weeping and Fergus put his hand to his head and swayed dizzily. He had been without food since morning. The long struggle with Dodie's cow had left him exhausted, Phebie's words had shocked him but the worst nightmare of all was the sight of his little girl, an infant still but the words pouring from her baby mouth were those of someone whose emotions were developed beyond her years, who loved and hated with an intensity that matched his own. All the thwarted longings of her short life had given strength to her torrent of words. She had wondered at his rejection of her. Through the misty learning years of her infancy she had sensed the barriers between them; now she had discovered the reasons for them in a way that should never have been.

But he could give her no comfort – it was too late for that. He knew she would have rejected him and he also knew, with a choking sob rising in his throat, that it would be a long time before those slender little arms would entwine themselves round his neck.

Mirabelle looked at his chalky face and dazed eyes and felt alarmed. He's a man demented, she thought. Her kindly heart turned over and she cried, 'Fergus, come in and sup!' But he was turning into the fury of the storm once more. It seemed as if all the forces of nature had saved themselves for this day. The heart of the storm lay directly overhead . . . the wind tore at fences and trees and shrieked with an angry voice on the open moors.

Fergus bent into the wind, his mind churning like the sea. He was drenched to the skin but was aware of nothing but his tormented thoughts. He wandered without direction or sense of time but his subconscious guided him till finally he stood, a lonely figure battered by the elements, on the seething shore by the schoolhouse. The lowering sky had brought early darkness and a warm light shone from a downstairs window.

He stared at the light, trying to keep his eyes open in the sting of salt spray. The light signified warmth and he became aware of his numb extremities. He put his clenched fists to his frozen lips and murmured 'Helen'. But it wasn't Helen he saw in his mind. It was Kirsteen, warm, living, beautiful Kirsteen.

'Forgive me, Helen!' he cried into the wind and stumbled towards the schoolhouse door, the rain mingling with the salt tears that poured unheeded down his cheeks.

Kirsteen had bathed in her zinc tub before a roaring fire; now, in a faded pink dressing-gown, with her supper on a plate on her knee and a book in one hand, she was warm and comfortable. Rowan, her orange kitten, purred before the fire and the house was a cosy protective shell. Windows rattled, doors strained at their bolts, but the anger of the storm only served to heighten the peace and warmth of the room. Engrossed in her book it was some time before she became aware of the erratic tapping from the hallway. Vaguely she reminded herself it was time she got someone to prune the trees. They were always tapping the windows in a high wind. But the tapping became intensified and with a start she realised it was someone at the door. Annoyed at the intrusion she went to open it and drew an involuntary gasp of surprise. Fergus! The man she dreamed of had come to her at last but never had she imagined it would be like this. His face was grey and his black eyes sunken and full of a desperate despair. Rain fell in sheets around him and the bullying wind tore at his bedraggled clothes.

'Kirsteen.' His voice was soft with exhaustion. 'Help me! For God's sake help me!'

The plea was utterly heartrending and filled her with such compassion she wanted to take him into her arms, to love him with all the love she felt for him. But she stayed her wildly beating heart and drew him out of the storm into the warm shelter of her little home. She sat him before the fire and like a small boy he allowed her to dry his hair and help him struggle out of his wet clothes. It was like a dream; yet in all her wildest dreams she had never felt such tenderness for the vital young man who had come to her out of the storm and let her help and comfort him without protest. She dried him and wrapped him in a wool dressing-gown left behind by old Roddy. Leaving him by the fire she went to heat some broth which he took obediently and gratefully. His dark hair had dried and small tendrils curled round his ears. A feeling of such poignancy tore at her heart that she couldn't help reaching out and stroking his head. She had asked no questions since his arrival and he had uttered no words save those spoken with such pleading at the door.

He turned and looked straight into her eyes. Some of the pain had gone from his, replaced by a look of unbelievable longing.

'Kirsteen,' he whispered huskily and it seemed the most natural thing in the world that she should be in his arms, his hands gently stroking her hair, his fingers tracing the fine bones of her face. Her heart raced into her throat. She tilted her head and he kissed her eyes and nose. The warm smell of his drying hair filled her nostrils and the dear sweet nearness of him made her cry out.

'Kirsteen,' he said again and now his lips were hard against her own. The dressing-gown fell from her shoulders and the flames from the grate outlined her breasts and slim waist. He caught his breath and crushed her to him, his breath quick and harsh.

'Beautiful Kirsteen!' he cried pushing her to the floor. His pent-up emotions of many years were being released at last. She felt his gentleness turn into a passion that could only come from a man such as he. His mouth touched every part of her body till she trembled in ecstasy. She was as passionate as he, her feelings for him had smouldered for almost a year, now they kindled and caught fire till every fibre in her burned for him.

He was wild, almost rough in his eagerness but her frenzy matched his, their cries mingling with the shrieking moan of the wind that darted and howled outside.

Part Four

1933

Chapter Seven

They found the cave high on the Muir of Rhanna near the site of the old Abbey ruins. It was a hot glorious day in July. Bees droned lazily in the scrubs of heather. It was the school holidays and the days of every Hebridean child were filled with play. Groups of them were always to be found scrambling around the caves at Port Rum Point. At low tide it was possible to go into the caves to sit on rocky perches and watch the Sound breaking against the Sgor Creags. Wind and time had sculptured each crag to a sharp point to make pinnacles of treachery for the unwary boatsman. Rumour had it that long ago a stranger to Rhanna had been swept in his boat against the Sgor Creags one stormy night. His body had been harpooned on one of the Creags and because of the treacherous tides no one had been able to reach the body and it remained there till the gulls picked it clean and the skeleton was eventually washed away to sea.

It was one of the many legends that abounded on Rhanna. The old folk clung to the stories told by their ancestors and the children liked to believe all they heard. The story of the harpooned stranger was one of the most popular and Shona and Niall sat on the ledges to stare with morbid interest at the Sgor Creags, picturing the man's body slowly rotting away.

'It must have been terrible for the poor man,' Shona would comment, though her eyes shone.

'Ach, he'd be dead and never know,' Niall scoffed unfailingly.

'But he wouldn't be dead at first,' answered Shona trying to imagine such a plight.

It was also rumoured that the plentiful ledges high up in the caves had been used by smugglers to store their bounty. The caves filled at high tide but never quite reached the ledges so would have been perfect for the smugglers so familiar with the tides and the banks of slimy rock.

Shona and Niall, like many children before them, searched for signs of bounty but found nothing. Hopefully they also searched for parts of the legendary skeleton, one day unearthing an old bone which they excitedly took to Old Joe who was the leading authority on matters marine. He immediately identified it as a cow's 'knuckle' probably buried and forgotten by a dog.

As well as the excitement of the Creags there was swimming in Loch Tenee or in the calm little bay in which the harbour nestled. The latter was the best fun because the harbour was the heart of Portcull. Boats big and small plied in and out, and the fishermen let the children clamber aboard their boats to play among tarry ropes and lobster pots. Gulls screamed and old women leaned from rose-framed windows to chat with everyone who passed. Winter was the time for Ceilidhs but in summer, dances were held in hay-filled barns. The men got slowly but pleasantly inebriated while the young couples crept to haylofts to kiss and cuddle. Shona and Niall, with groups of other children, lingered at rickety doors and dared each other to rush in and grab handfuls of bannocks and fruit cake.

It was strange to see Wullie McKinnon, now a lanky youth of fifteen, march into a barn with a girl on his arm. His hair was neatly plastered, his shoes polished but he still sniffed continually and had long ago got used to his nickname of 'Dreep'. He had none of his sister Nancy's roguish good looks but like her he was extremely fond of amorous pursuits. It was a favourite game with the youngsters to climb into a hayloft before the start of a dance, to hide and await the appearance of the courting couples. 'Dreep' was the favourite. The watching children choked back their laughter while he panted and sniffed between kisses. He was awkward with his girls but usually managed to undo a blouse, and grab a breast to which he clung like a tenacious lobster till he was slapped on the face.

'Will *we* ever do things like that?' Shona wondered. 'It all seems a bit daft.'

Niall, tall and handsome at twelve years, scoffed at the idea but grew red in the face and changed the subject.

Shona was at the lanky stage, legs long and body shapeless though her plump cheeks were thinning, emphasising the cameo features of her infancy. She was inclined to untidiness and preferred her long hair to fly loose but Mirabelle made her tie it back with ribbons which she detested because of their femininity. She was a tomboy, perhaps through long association with Niall or perhaps in an unconscious effort to be like a boy in his eyes. There were times when he had gone off with boys to fish in the abundant rivers or to sneak into Burnbreddie to poach a grouse or pheasant just for the devil of it.

The first time he had deserted her she had sulked when next he sought her company. But Niall was not a boy to be trifled with and her mood had only served to drive him away for a much longer period and now she knew better than to have her girlishly subtle displays of disapproval, accepting him back from his manly sojourns as if they had never been apart.

But now he had changed again and they had spent that whole summer together, if anything closer than they had ever been before. Sometimes he put an arm round her and gave her an oddly affectionate hug which made her feel queer and protected, the look on his tanned boyish face near her own making the feeling of love she felt for her father steal into her heart, only with Niall there was something different and she didn't know why.

She loved her father with a love that was deep, her heated words of four years ago forgotten, but it was a love without the displays of affection she had shown so freely in early childhood. Now she felt even closer to him.

There were times when his strong arms reached for her, an indefinable longing in his dark eyes but something deep inside made her resist him, a pride, a stubbornness, she knew not what, but she recognised vaguely that it had all stemmed from the day she read her mother's headstone and discovered the secret that had shrouded her simple child's life for six years. She was happy but sometimes wondered what her life would have been like without Niall.

They had married each other when seven and nine respectively, a simple ceremony with Agnes as chief bridesmaid and Stuart Simpson as the minister. It had been a hasty affair, the 'marriage feast' that awaited them on a ledge of the cave which was serving as 'kirk', a much more attractive proposition.

Now they had found this other cave, stumbled into it really while playing amongst the Abbey ruins. The ruins dated back into the mists of time, nestling in a hollow and skirted by a rocky heather-covered hillock known as Dunuaigh which meant Hill of the Tomb. Because of the many ghostly legends attached to Dunuaigh the islanders usually gave it a wide berth but Niall and Shona found it an exciting place to play and defied the legends. They were children of whispering quiet places and anything with a legend to it enthralled rather than frightened. Niall had tripped and fallen on a tangle of gorse and bramble, then disappeared from view. Shona poised listening in the shadow of a crumbling wall, unable to pinpoint the direction of his calls. She went forward, tearing herself on the snagging bramble, then jumped when Niall's head suddenly appeared from a gorse bush.

'It's a cave!' he told her excitedly. 'All big and airy with recesses like beds.'

She crawled in beside him with difficulty. The cave's entrance was thick with overgrowth and the only reason that Niall had stumbled upon it was because a big slab of rock had fallen inwards. It was dry and very quiet without even the buzz of a fly to interrupt the silence. Niall pulled back a clump of gorse and secured it to a crack in the rock. Sunlight filtered into the cave which went backwards into the hillside for twenty feet. Several rough recesses had been hewn into the shelves of rock and two large stones in the middle of the floor resembled a rough fireplace.

'It's grand,' breathed Shona. 'So warm and dry . . . not like the smelly caves at Port Rum Point. But . . . you don't think it's a tomb of some sort? It *is* in Dunuaigh!'

'N-no, I think it's been a hidey-hole carved out by the monks *centuries* ago. Long ago the Norsemen came in great Viking ships and raided the islands. The ships were like dragons and the Norsemen plundered and stole things. I think the monks who lived here made this cave to hide their food. When the Norsemen came the monks likely came into the cave to hide – maybe for days, and they would sleep in these recesses till it was safe to come out again.' His eyes sparkled at the thought of the monks cowering in hiding while the mighty bands of Norsemen ravaged the island.

Shona drew in her breath. 'No one knows of it but us. It will be our wee house. We can come here to play, if it rains we have a shelter and if we want to hide from anybody we can come here.' Her enthusiasm grew. 'We can bring things to make it cosy. Mirabelle keeps a lot of old pans and dishes she's forgotten about. You can maybe bring things too. We can light a fire and cook things on it!'

Niall caught her mood. 'That would be grand. We'd be like explorers and Mother's always so busy with the baby she'd never notice if I took some bits and pieces.'

He referred to his little sister of four months who, with her constant baby demands, had caused quite an upheaval at Slochmhor. But it was a happy upheaval and Niall knew the atmosphere had changed since that long holiday last summer when he had gone with his parents to Stornoway. Lachlan, worn out after a bout of pleurisy, and Phebie, an unhappy shadow of her former self, felt they had to get away from Rhanna for a time. Leaving a locum to the tender mercies of Elspeth they went to Lachlan's brother in Stornoway.

Two months later they were back on Rhanna, the old boyish bounce returned to Lachlan, and Phebie sparkling in a way she hadn't done for a long time. In Stornoway, away from all the reminders of old quarrels, they had recaptured all the love and freedom of their early married life. Lachlan's hurt heart healed and Phebie forgot her grievances. Slowly they picked up the threads of their troubled marriage and twined them together again. Lachlan regained his confidence in his powers of healing, of delivering life and letting it go when nothing further could be done to preserve it.

Niall spent much of his time with his cousins, two boys near his own age, and Phebie and Lachlan walked hand in hand through summer days, discussing their lives in the frank manner of their youth. And the nights – Phebie never forgot the long golden nights with the scented air of summer drifting through the window. Those nights of love without fear were not to be forgotten and the result was little Fiona, pushing and bawling into the world after a short though violent labour, delivered by her own father who held her tiny form as if it were the most precious thing in the world. Phebie sang about the house again and Lachlan's manner was sure and firm.

Niall was fascinated by his tiny sister. He played with her and even changed her nappy when the need arose. He kissed and cuddled her, feeling proud that she was his little sister, but when she cried her loud lusty cry he was glad to let his mother cope.

Shona jumped into one of the recesses. 'Sit here till we eat our pieces, I'm hungry!'

She delved into the package Mirabelle had prepared that morning. Thick crusty bread with butter, apple pie, oatcakes and scones, nestled temptingly in their wrappings.

'Mirabelle's a great cook!' praised Niall, abandoning his own lunch to savour a piece of pie.

'I know and she's learning me. I can bake scones and make bread but it always turns out a wee bit wizened.' She sighed. 'Mirabelle's getting awful old – you know she was seventy-three the other day. I worry sometimes in case she dies because I love her so. I heard her telling Biddy she gets sick betimes and Biddy said it was like her heartburn and caused by old age. Biddy's old too, she's sixty-six and says she'll go on delivering babies till she dies. She's delivered nearly all the folk on this island except old ones like herself. She even helped give birth to my father.'

'How could she give birth? She's not your father's mother!' Niall's tone was scornful through a mouthful of scone.

'Och, you know what I mean. It must be funny to see babies you've delivered grow into people.'

'Babies are people too, only little ones!' snorted Niall in superior tones. His two years' seniority put him on his mettle with her and just lately he had felt an impatience because she prattled on so childishly while his thoughts and feelings were becoming more adult. Sometimes he felt protective and strongly affectionate towards her, at other times she annoyed him but he couldn't think of a life without her. Yet soon he must because his parents were sending him to a school on the mainland.

His love of animals had helped him to decide his career. He wanted to be a veterinary surgeon. He would be a doctor like his father but instead of helping humans he would help animals. Phebie had shared her home with many strange, wounded or orphaned animals through the years. One of these had been a seal pup, fortunately weaned but hurt and unable to search for food. Niall, with a dozen of his contemporaries, had carried the seal from Portvoynachan, four miles over rough moor, to dump it in Phebie's vegetable garden. It was a favourite trip for the Portcull boys, to hitch a lift aboard a fishing vessel from Portcull to Portvoynachan then to walk back to Portcull overland.

For two months Phebie tholed the seal slithering in the kitchen door whenever it could. She didn't even mind when the seal lay in pot-bellied splendour in the zinc tub out in the sun with Niall labouring back and forth from the burn to throw buckets of water over it. She even grew very fond of the young seal, indulgently christening it Salach because it smelled so strongly of fish. But when she found it snoring contentedly into Niall's back one night, with its silky head planted firmly on a pillow, she insisted it be returned immediately to the deep. Salach was thus returned to her natural habitat, fully healed but her mind imprinted with all the little homely comforts she had experienced in the land of humans. Niall had moped for a week till it was reported a young seal was haunting the harbour at Portcull and for a whole lovely summer he, with crowds of other youngsters, swam with Salach till the autumn came and she deserted Portcull to seek a life with her own kind.

Animals were Niall's vocation and his father had encouraged him to become an animal doctor; but he knew that his education would have to be furthered for such a specialised career so in autumn he was leaving Rhanna, his parents, and Shona who had been such a part of his growing years. The thought softened him and suddenly he put an arm round her. Fondly.

'You're a funny wee thing!'

'I'm not wee and I'm not funny!' she said hotly. 'And I'm going home because Uncle Alick's coming today. I promised Mirabelle I'd help her get tea ready. I like when Uncle Alick comes! He lifts me up and gives me hugs. I wonder why his wife never comes with him?'

'Because she doesn't like getting her feet covered in dung,' said Niall who had watched Mary on one of her rare visits picking her way daintily through a field.

'Manure!' corrected Shona primly.

'Dung!' spat Niall viciously. He was a bit wary of Alick. He hated the way he fawned over Shona and he didn't like the way Alick laughed. It wasn't real somehow. If anything he disliked Alick more than Fergus. At least Fergus was manly-looking and didn't prattle like an old woman. Alick was good-looking and women liked him but he was too smoothly handsome for rugged Niall.

'You're a vulgar boy sometimes.'

'I can be rude *all* the time if I want. Come on then, don't keep Uncle Alick waiting!'

They plodded through the heather and by the time they got to the hill track near Dodie's cottage they were tired and stopped to rest. Niall sprawled untidily in the grass and Shona sat hugging her knees.

'We'll get ticks,' said Niall uncaringly. 'You'll get them mostly in your bum!'

'Bottom,' she said evenly knowing he was egging her into a temper because he was still dwelling on Alick.

'Bum!' repeated Niall. 'Bum! bum! bum!' and feeling the laughter rising in his throat dispelling his mood, shouted daringly, '*arse*!'

'Arse!' echoed Shona and collapsed beside him on the grass where they both screamed in delight.

'He breath!' Dodie's doleful greeting made them sit up.

'He breeah!' they said together and Niall added, 'Are you looking for your cow, Dodie?'

'Aye and not findin' her. She'll be hidin' from me. I have her potash ready and I'm wantin' some milk for my breakfast!'

'We'll help you,' said Shona promptly and ran off with Niall in search of Ealasaid.

Dodie followed with his long loping gait. He had changed little over the years and no one knew quite what his age was, but the years he had spent on earth were the least of his interests. His first and foremost was Ealasaid whom he cursed constantly but loved with the same slavish devotion he had lavished on her mother. She was a cow with the wanderlust and all year round he tramped miles to feed her and milk her. He'd been unwilling to let her have a calf after what happened to her mother but Fergus had persuaded him that she was fit for such an event so he had succumbed, and Wee Ealasaid had arrived safely. But after a while Fergus had bought the calf from Dodie who couldn't cope with a wanderlust cow and a stubborn young bullock.

Dodie's second interest was his tiny garden out of which he coaxed amazing vegetables. He sold the surplus to make a few pence and altogether lived in a self-sufficient little world. Ealasaid was forever bringing her four-legged friends from the hill in an effort to trample down the fence that surrounded the little garden. Once they had succeeded, making a tasty meal before departing, leaving the patch a trampled mess of cabbage leaves and manure.

But Dodie wasn't easily dissuaded and now the garden was like a fortress into which he alone could penetrate through a massive gate made of a tangle of wood, wire, and flotsam, all bound together with heather. The fence was high with a disconcerting array of wire round the top over which not even the deer could jump.

'Only the sun gets in,' said Dodie happily.

Niall found Ealasaid in her shed behind the cottage happily munching a bundle of old hay.

'Ach the bugger!' cried Dodie. 'Me trampin' miles and her doublin' back on me! Ach well, I'll milk her now. If you go into the house I'll bring you a stick of rhubarb to chew when I'm finished.'

Niall and Shona were the only children that Dodie had ever honoured in this way. The island folk had seldom seen the inside of his cottage and few wanted to. Knowing his untidy ways they were sure his house must reek like himself.

The first time the children entered the dim interior they held their breaths. But the tiny room was amazingly neat. The two upright wooden chairs were rickety and an old dresser was almost in pieces, but treasures, reaped from shore and woods, decorated every available space. A lump of driftwood shaped like a seal was nailed to the wall above the fireplace, sea urchins scraped clean were strewn among the pine cones on the dresser. A pot of wild honeysuckle stood in the deep recess of the tiny window. True, the curtains were like cobwebs, ashes spilled from the grate but there was no 'Dodie' smell in the room. A string of onions hung from the ceiling and Shona decided they were the magic remedy for all unwanted odours.

'Sit you down now,' instructed Dodie coming back from Ealasaid. 'I'll make the wee polkys then I'll go and get the rhubarb.'

He was a most mannerly host. Nothing would do till the children took the two chairs leaving him drooping in the middle of the room so that his head would not touch the low ceiling. He went to fetch the rhubarb and the children sat obediently. They longed to wander round the room and look closely at the ornaments but were afraid they would break Dodie's trust and not be allowed back.

Two paper 'polkys' were filled with sugar and handed to the children with plump sticks of rhubarb.

'This is the best rhubarb I've ever tasted,' appreciated Shona, licking sugar from her lips.

Niall nodded in agreement. 'It is the best, Dodie. My mother has a good patch, so she has, all the best manure goes on it but never is it anything like this.'

'Not the best,' mumbled Dodie blushing with pleasure.

'I beg your pardon?' said Niall politely.

Dodie showed his stained teeth. 'Not the best manure!'

'Oh yes, the best,' stated Niall positively.

'Mine's the best,' argued Dodie.

'From Ealasaid,' said Shona, so taken up with the treat she hadn't wanted to stop and discuss the merits of manure.

'*Not* from Ealasaid,' grunted Dodie. There was a cryptic pause in which the youngsters waited patiently.

Dodie opened his mouth, hesitated, shut it again, and time ticked on. He seemed to be coming to some great decision and finally blurted out, 'If I tell you a secret promise you'll not utter it to a livin' soul.'

The children, their interest fully roused, agreed solemnly to keep the secret. Dodie's face was as animated as they had ever seen it.

'It's mine!' His head shook at the enormity of his confession and his carbuncle wobbled.

Niall looked puzzled. 'Your what?'

'*My* manure!'

'From Ealasaid,' said Shona again.

Dodie was growing frustrated at their lack of understanding and burst out, 'From *me*! I empty my po on the rhubarb patch every day!'

'Your *what*?' cried the children in horrified unison.

'*My chanty*!' babbled Dodie excitedly. 'The best I told you!'

Niall stared at his stick of rhubarb with new eyes and Shona looked at the remainder of hers with fascinated interest. She sniffed. It *smelled* like rhubarb, there was nothing unpleasant about its looks yet . . .

'The best?' urged Dodie with childlike enthusiasm.

'Did you wash it, Dodie?' asked Niall suspiciously.

'In the wee burn, always in the wee burn!'

'Och well,' grinned Shona and finished her rhubarb.

Niall giggled and ate his also and Dodie was delighted. He trundled to a pot on the fire and poked its contents with a bent fork. In the pot was a piece of venison. Every year the laird gave out venison and every year the islanders grumbled because the portions got smaller. 'Mean auld Bodach!' was the usual comment. 'He keeps the best for himself to feed the faces o' thon fancy folk from England!'

Dodie prodded his venison and commented mournfully, 'The joints I've seen at Burnbreddie. Great muckle lumps o' meat! Ach! It would make you sick so it would. And *he's* at it again! The things I'm seein' up there!'

Dodie had a knack of making cryptic comments which never failed to rouse the interest of his listeners.

'What things?' asked Niall.

Dodie shook his head slowly. 'Worse since my leddy lies up most of the time. I'm not sure what they cry her ailment.'

'Hypochondria!' proclaimed Niall, triumphantly repeating the word his father used when referring to Madam Balfour of Burnbreddie.

'A queer trouble just,' mourned Dodie. 'And *his* is no better.'

'What *is* his trouble, Dodie? persisted Niall.

Dodie blushed primly. 'I shouldny say.'

'We won't tell anyone,' coaxed Shona.

The old eccentric hesitated, not because his knowledge wasn't for children, but what he had to tell involved human relationships which were always such an embarrassment to him.

'I couldny help seein',' he said apologetically. 'I was workin' in the big hayloft and *they* came in . . . the laird and one of his fine lady guests with . . .' He cupped his hands in front of his chest. 'Big udders!'

Shona giggled explosively but Niall nudged her. 'And?' he encouraged curiously.

'They shut the door but I could see, plenty light in a hayshed. He was kissin' her and gruntin' like a pig and the next thing . . .'

'Yes?' urged Niall.

'He pulled out her udders – big they were – very big.' He paused and his vacant eyes were lit with an expression that could be described as humorous. 'I never knew a lady's udders could be like Ealasaid's!'

He stopped and a terrible screech escaped him and his big hands clutched his stomach. It took a couple of alarming minutes before the children realised he was not in pain but laughing, Dodie the doleful who had never been known to laugh, making a noise like a rusty hacksaw, his mouth stretched wide with enjoyment.

'Did he do anything else?' asked Shona.

Dodie nodded, his carbuncle wobbling wildly.

'Lots more! She was laughin' all the time but she stopped when he threw her on the hay and went at her like a ruttin' stag and she was bleatin' all the time like an old yowe. It was terrible just! Not natural at all, not like the beasts, no, oh no!'

Niall's eyes gleamed. When he was striding home down the winding hill track he turned to Shona. 'Let's get Agnes and Stuart and go up to Burnbreddie after tea! We'll get into that hayshed and wait for the laird. He just might bring a lady in there tonight.'

'But we promised Dodie we wouldn't tell anyone.'

'Agnes and Stuart aren't anyone, they won't tell. They kept all our other secrets – our marriage and everything,' he finished significantly. Shona hopped joyfully. Her hair had long ago escaped the ribbon and tumbled over her shoulders in silken strands. Her face and arms were a golden brown and Niall noticed these things that hadn't been important enough before for a second glance.

'Your hair's nice,' he said and touched it briefly.

She looked at him quickly wondering if he was teasing because sometimes he called her Caillich Ruadh which meant Red Witch. The name infuriated her and if he touched her hair it was only to pull it. But there was a new look in his brown eyes and for a moment they stopped and stared at each other. Then she pointed down to Laigmhor.

'Uncle Alick's here! I'll see you after tea!'

She was off, a rushing bundle of windblown hair and long legs. He watched her and kicked a stone vigorously.

'Bugger Uncle Alick!' he muttered and felt better. He raced home to help his mother lay the table, thinking about the adventure to come.

'Mother.'

Phebie looked at her sturdy son expectantly.

'I know that oldish folk like you and Father make love to make babies . . . that was why you had me and Fiona.'

Phebie hid a smile at being described 'oldish' at thirty-three but waited with suitable composure for the rest of the question.

'If you can do it and *really* old people can do it . . . well, you must like it a lot.'

Phebie looked slightly startled. She and Lachlan had always been frank with their son and knew that now he was at the stage of puberty his questions would become intricate but Phebie wasn't always prepared for the turn they would take.

'Y-yes I suppose so,' she faltered wishing Lachlan was home.

'Why is it then that big girls like Fiona Taylor and Annie McKinnon let boys kiss and cuddle them and enjoy it fine but if the boys put their hands on the girls' udd – breasts they get their faces slapped?'

Phebie searched for the right answer. 'Well – I suppose the girls do enjoy cuddling, it's only normal, but it's the girls who have the babies and no girl wants a baby out of wedlock.'

'Some do.'

'It can't be helped sometimes but it's best to wait for marriage.'

'It seems silly but I suppose you must be right,' said Niall and Phebie went thankfully to tend Fiona.

Shona flew to the farmyard and straight into Alick's arms. He lifted her high.

'My, but you've grown into a bonny big girl,' he laughed, holding her against the backcloth of sky till his arms ached. His handsome face was alight because he was truly fond of his niece and often regretted that she hadn't come to them as a baby. Mary hadn't given him children. She told him she was too delicate but she was strong enough to go gallivanting to the French Riviera. She was there now with a 'friend'. Alick didn't know if it was male or female and cared less. He had his own way of making his life bearable. He had a good job and Mary had been left a legacy by a great-aunt so they both had the means to indulge their whims. But he wanted a child and sometimes he thought the only reason he came back to Rhanna was to see Shona. He knew Fergus wasn't particular about his visits but they tolerated each other well enough.

He put Shona down.

'I've brought you a present.'

'Where? Och, where is it?'

'Hidden in your room. You'll have to search for it –

after tea. Mirabelle will spank me if I dare to hold up tea.'

'You're too big to be spanked!'

'Not by Mirabelle! She might even do it with my pants down.'

They roared in delight but Alick broke off suddenly, his gaze lingering on the slim young woman who had just come through the gate. Her short crisp hair gleamed gold in the sun and her breasts were firm under her thin summer dress.

She waved to Shona. 'I'm just handing in some things Mirabelle asked me to get at Portcull. I'll see you later.'

'Who was *that*?' asked Alick in admiration.

'Father's friend and *my* teacher,' said Shona proudly.

He whistled softly. 'I think I'm going to enjoy my holiday, Shona. Now, will you allow me the honour of taking my arm? We shall go in to tea in style.'

From the kitchen window Mirabelle saw the look Alick threw at Kirsteen. The old lady liked Alick. He was dashing and gay, bringing a lot of laughter into Laigmhor. He hugged her and made her laugh girlishly with his nonsense. But somehow she knew that this visit was going to be different. He had never met Kirsteen before because she usually went home to her parents in Oban for the summer. But this year she had decided to have a summer on Rhanna simply because she could hardly bear parting from Fergus. She was his 'bit mistress' in Rhanna language but she had borne the label well. At the beginning the gossips tore her to pieces but she had held her head high though she knew that if she hadn't loved Fergus so deeply she would have fled the island's malicious tongues and endless speculation.

How could anyone know of the heartache her love had brought? They couldn't know of the nights when her empty arms ached for him. These nights outweighed the ones he came to her in the school-house and they shared an intimacy that fulfilled her but couldn't compensate her aching heart. But they were the wonderful times when they shut out the world. Locked in his arms she was safe and wanted but the time always came for him to go back to his other world. In the four years of their relationship he had told her that she was beautiful, that he wanted and needed her but never once had he told her he loved her and she wondered if he ever would.

They had discussed Helen. She had persuaded him to talk of her and in time he poured out his heart till it really seemed he had brought the years of suppressed grief out of his heart forever. But Kirsteen asked herself if he clung to memories because they were safer than real life. You could think about them, laugh or cry then shut them away till something recalled them to mind again. She wasn't sure that Fergus really wanted to love again and sometimes she wondered how long she could go on with the affair. In her mind she left Rhanna many times but then he came to her and swept away all reason with his love-making. She was glad she had decided against going home to Oban for the holidays because that green and blue summer on the island was the most wonderful she had ever known. Fergus, once too busy to take time off, now left the running of the farm in Hamish's capable hands and spent every day with her. He cared nothing for the gossips and walked with his arm round her waist making her feel guarded against the covert looks that followed them. They walked for miles and picnicked in places as far away as Croy where tiny sheltered bays abounded. They swam in the warm waters from the Gulf Stream and made love on the hot white sands with only screaming gulls for company.

Once she cried against his broad chest and he was bewildered.

'What is it, my Kirsteen?' he whispered into her golden hair.

She looked away from him, far away over the blue-green waters of the Atlantic.

'I wish we could sail away over the sea, you – might forget then.'

He knew what she meant. 'I'll never forget, as long as I live, Kirsteen. It would be impossible to forget someone you were so happy with. Have you forgotten Donald?'

'No, but I wouldn't let his memories stand in the way of my happiness. He wouldn't want that.'

'Nor would Helen!' he cried, his black eyes clouding. 'She isn't standing in the way. She was a gay wee thing herself and liked others to be the same. Aren't you happy, Kirsteen?'

A look of incredible sadness came into her blue eyes and she turned away again but he cupped her chin in his hand and made her face him. 'My Kirsteen,' he said huskily. 'You're a daft wee thing sometimes. Don't be sad. When I say I can never forget Helen I mean it, but she is part of my past life. You are *now*. I'm not a fancy man with words but I could never picture my life without you now.'

He kissed away her tears and his strong arms held her close but she longed to cry out that she wanted to be his wife, to have him declare his love for her by marrying her, but instead she lay silently against him, content for the moment to be in the safe circle of his arms.

But Mirabelle did not mince words on the matter.

'When are you going to marry the lass?' she demanded regularly. 'The poor wee soul has waited well for you and had to thole a lot o' auld gossips into the bargain. How she's stood it I'll never know. She's a fine lass – too good for her name to be thrown about like a bit cow dung.'

'In my own time, Belle,' he told her unfailingly.

'Just like a man to think you can ay ca' the tune! A bonny lass like that could have any man o' her choosin'.'

Another time she told him, 'It's high time the bairn had a mother! Are you too selfish to see that?'

'She's done fine with you all these years!' he snapped.

'I'll not always be here!' she had said strangely.

'Are you ill?' he asked in some alarm.

'I'm old,' she said briefly and he couldn't argue with that.

Fergus couldn't really explain his reasons for hesitating. Kirsteen was sweet-natured and sensitive. He was happy when he was with her, she made him laugh. Her physical make-up was exquisite and his desire for her a constant torment when they were apart. She was an endearing, wonderful young woman and he knew he would never find another like her, but, he asked himself a thousand times, did he love her enough to let her take Helen's place in his home? Helen had loved him enough to tolerate his strange moody tempers but could Kirsteen? Did she love him deeply enough? Did he really love her or did she merely satisfy his physical appetites? He tortured himself with indecision. At times he cursed that storm-swept night when utter despair of mind and body had driven him to the refuge of her arms, yet common sense told him that fate would have found some other way of bringing them together in the end. She had haunted him since their first meeting in the wood and the night of the storm, when everything seemed against him, had merely provided him with the chance he had waited for. Sometimes the fear of losing her to someone else brought him out in a sweat. Mirabelle was right about Kirsteen. She was attractive and the openly admiring glances she drew from other men couldn't be denied.

The day Alick arrived his fears became stronger than ever. He came in to wash before tea and saw them together at the table, her golden head next to Alick's dark one. She was emptying her basket and Alick was making silly remarks that made her giggle. She turned when she heard Fergus and her face lit up but no one had time to speak because Shona came bursting into the kitchen holding an elegant and expensive doll. She didn't play much with dolls except in the long winter nights when her family were brought down to the kitchen to play at 'wee hoosies'. More often her doll's pram contained Tot who was very partial to being tucked up cosily with a frilly bonnet tied over her silky ears. But Tot had no time for such frivolities of late for she was the proud mother of five tiny pups. Their arrival had caused quite a sensation because they were purebred spaniels whose father could only be Hamish's gun dog. It was Tot's first litter. She had spurned every dog who had dared to attempt to court her but had obviously fallen for the charms of Whisky and was now too busy with her babies to share her time with such mundane things as dolls. But the dolls were neglected in summer anyway and sat droopily on the shelves in Shona's room, each one a reminder of every Christmas of her life, stitched patiently by Mirabelle so that a new doll would be hanging from the top of her stocking to greet her on Christmas morning. She loved her rag dolls but each one was really just a replica of the last so the extravagantly dressed 'town' doll took her breath away.

'I couldn't wait, Uncle Alick!' she cried happily. 'She's the most beautiful doll in the world!' She ran to hug Alick who lifted her to the dizzy heights of the ceiling.

Mirabelle, tired and hot at the stove, was hurt. She knew that the bought doll outrivalled all those she had ever made but love had gone into every stitch executed by the light of a paraffin lamp, causing her tired old eyes to smart with the strain. A lump came to her throat. She knew she was being childish but she couldn't help it. Lately her aching tiredness had caused her to be more than usually sensitive and the crushing pains in her chest made her come out in weak sweats. Lachlan had been blunt when she had asked him to tell her the truth and had told her she must ease up or he wouldn't answer for the consequences. But she had been as blunt as he.

'I'd rather go quickly, Lachlan my laddie. I've not been idle in my life and I'm not going to start now. You won't tell a soul, mo ghaoil?' she went on pleadingly. 'I'd not want anyone pampering me and looking at me like I was a frail wee chick just hatched.'

Lachlan looked at her ample figure and smiled, though his heart was heavy. Mirabelle's heart condition had shocked him deeply. She was the type of woman who gave everyone the impression she would go on forever; she was the tower of strength that people leaned on without thinking that she might possess the same human frailties as themselves. Her very appearance belied any hint of illness: she had been, and still was, a jolly rotund figure, ample of bosom and bottom. Her round face was cheery and her sympathy for others showed in the compassionate warmth of her grey eyes. Her skin was pink and white and she looked the picture of health except for a tiredness deep in her eyes.

Lachlan had been angry when he discovered she had felt ill for a long time and hadn't come to see him before.

'Ach, I was ay too busy,' she answered placidly. 'Besides I had too much to keep me occupied to have time to be ill. There's the bairn, a handful at times but a bonny bright wee thing. I love her with all my hert, Lachlan and . . .' She gave him a covert look. 'There's Fergus. If ever a lad was eaten up with loneliness it's him. If only he'd marry Kirsteen I'd die happy so I would. Shona would have a mother. I've done my best but I'm too auld to be much use. Ach, what will happen to my poor wee lass when I'm gone?' She gave a deep sigh. 'As for Fergus, he's my bairn too. I brought him up. Och, Lachlan! I wish you and he would make your peace. He's sorry for everything, I know. He tried to tell you a long time ago but it turned sour on him. I only know he's like a lost soul sometimes and my auld hert aches for him!'

Lachlan put his hands firmly over her bent fingers.

'Belle, Fergus nearly cost me my marriage. I think you can guess what I mean. That old windbag Elspeth must have overheard some tasty tit-bits and no doubt passed them on. But that's all in the past now. I'd shake hands with the man tomorrow but he won't give me the chance again. His pride has already been bruised and he won't risk it again and I'm damned if I'll go to him. But forget about Fergus for the moment! You must stop worrying that old head of yours! Time will tell all. You must rest more. I'll give you something to take for the pains and I'll come and see you from time to time.'

But she rose in alarm. 'Och no – no laddie! They'd find out then! I'll come and see *you*.' She winked. 'Who knows, the gossips might put us together and hint we've a wee thing goin' for us.' She giggled girlishly but he wasn't deceived by her jauntiness. He watched from the window and saw her heavy drooping figure go down the path, all attempt at gaiety gone now that she thought she was unobserved.

Lachlan sighed and tapped a pencil on his desk. He

had known great satisfaction in his life. He had plunged to the depths of despair and risen to pinnacles of glory and the joy of being able to save a fellow human was his euphoria. But when he had to tell people he knew and loved that their days on earth were numbered his heart plummeted to his boots. He had often been told that people who tended the sick became hardened to death but he had never found it so, he had simply learned to disguise his feelings in an effort to convey a strength he sometimes didn't feel to the people who relied so much upon his opinion.

'We'll sneak in at the back of the estate,' Niall instructed his three followers who were trudging through the heather at his rear. 'Near the old iron gate that's all overgrown. There's a wee bit we can get through – eh, Stuart?'

Stuart winked, the entrance being well known to most of the boys on their poaching expeditions.

Shona felt she should have been in on this secret long ago and she threw Niall a reproachful glance but he was looking ahead, his corn curls dancing in the scented wind blowing in from the sea.

'We could have climbed the stile and gone through the woods,' suggested Agnes who, hitherto a tomboy, was now becoming more careful of her appearance and didn't want her dress snagged. She was twelve, with black waving hair and brown eyes, and proud of her developing figure. She was beginning to giggle coyly at boys and Shona wasn't so keen on her company now that she was growing from a sensible child into a 'cackling yowe'.

Stuart was a tall lanky boy of thirteen with a keen sense of adventure. He was the best guddler in the school and could swim faster and further than most of his age. He was not in the least impressed by Agnes's efforts to gain his attention and at her suggestion he snorted: 'We'd get caught going over the stile so don't be daft. Do as *we* tell you or you'll never come with us again.'

They climbed to the top of a steep rise and could see for miles on either side. The sea sparkled in the distance, the deep blue contrasting breathtakingly with white sands and the green of hayfields. They were in Glenriach, behind them the steep crags of Glen Fallan misty blue against the heat hazed sky.

'It's bonny!' cried Shona spreading her arms and breathing clover and bracken, heather and thyme. But the boys were anxious to get into Burnbreddie and marched down to an ancient gate set in a tangle of fir and ferns. Niall pulled aside some branches to reveal a hole large enough for them to crawl through. Shona and Stuart did so quickly but Agnes grumbled when a branch pulled at her skirt and when another tore a gash in her frilly knickers she wailed aloud, 'I should never have come! Och, look at me! Mother will skelp me on the lugs! I think I'll go back. What way should I watch auld Burnbreddie kissin' and cuddlin' anyway?'

'Get going!' growled Niall, wishing he hadn't brought the vastly changed Agnes. He hoped Shona would never become all giggly and fuss about her clothes.

The boys led the way through a dense thicket then

skirted the cool waters of an amber river. To get to the courtyard and the haysheds they had to cross an open pasture and they were barely halfway over when they saw two riders: the laird was astride a gleaming chestnut mare and a glossy black pony carried the woman who fitted Dodie's description because her bosom was bursting out of her costume and her high giggle carried across the field.

Burnbreddie had visitors in all but the worst months of winter. Several island girls were employed by the laird and reported 'terrible goings on just' to the rest of the island. The honest people of Rhanna turned up their noses but listened avidly to the gossip. '*These* kind of folk make their own rules just,' was the general verdict. 'They're a gey mixed bag so they are indeed. A lot to answer for they have, not decent in the eyes o' God, oh no!' But the pious words belied the veiled curiosity over Burnbreddie affairs. Annie McKinnon was a reliable source of information. She was as fun-loving as her elder sister Nancy and though she could speak English perfectly, constantly annoyed the laird's wife by always conversing in Gaelic. One day she was busy with her duties when Mrs Balfour of Burnbreddie said tentatively, 'Annie?'

Annie turned, showing her white teeth mischievously. 'Mo Bantigherna?'

'Why is it you have never learned to speak English?'

'Och, Mo Bantigherna why does it ail you so?' grinned Annie. 'English is a foreign language to me, remember. Indeed I could ask you why 'tis yourself has never learned the Gaelic. It is a far more civilized language than your own, begging your pardon. Funny it is the way the English always expect others to know their tongue but are too put upon to learn another. If you'll be excusing me now, Mo Bantigherna . . . or would you prefer "my leddy" instead?'

She danced from the room and it took the laird's wife several astonished moments to realise that Annie had just spoken in the lovely lilting English the island folk used.

Stuart watched the riders from the cover of a bush. 'We might just go home or . . .' He brightened. 'We could guddle some trout while we're here.'

Niall was shading his eyes. 'They're not going, they're coming back. They'll go to the stables with the horses so we've time to race to the big hayshed.'

'How do you know they'll go there?' asked Agnes. 'And why the big hayshed? They might go to a wee one. There's a few up by the yard.'

'The big one has the only doors that shut properly, I was told by a reliable source. Come on!'

They scuttled along to the hayshed, arriving breathless and hot. It was a huge barn with sunlight slanting from the skylight to dance on dusty cobwebs that hung from the cross-beams. A mouse scurried and Agnes protested daintily.

'You played with them last year!' hissed Shona.

'Not this year,' returned Agnes primly.

They followed the boys into the hayloft which was warm and sweet smelling.

'This hay's awful jaggy,' complained Agnes who had been one of the happiest children on harvest hayrides.

'Och, you're a girny bugger!' scolded Shona.

'You *swore*!' said a shocked Agnes.

Niall grinned. 'You are a girnin' bugger! Shut up!'

Stuart lay on his back and watched the sunbeams. 'It would have been a grand night for guddlin',' he mourned.

Agnes wriggled up to him. 'Stuart,' she said in wheedling tones, 'do you like the way I do my hair?'

'It's not bad,' he said grudgingly.

'Do you notice girls at all? Their bodies and everything?' she asked gently, pushing out her growing bosom.

Stuart was now less interested in the roof. 'They're shaped nice,' he admitted placidly. 'But they're a bother mostly. My sister scunners me the way she giggles all the time. *You're* like her! She's older with bigger bosoms but you laugh the same.'

Agnes smiled secretively. '*My* bosoms will get bigger, Stuart. Will you like me then?'

Stuart wriggled uncomfortably and wished he was fishing. He yawned and folding his arms under head closed his eyes.

Fifteen minutes passed and they were all growing bored. Then a giggle came from below and two shadows darkened the doorway. It creaked shut and a bolt shot home, the bolt that the laird had had specially fitted on the inside doors. He liked to bring his ladies to the hayshed. There was something primitive about making love in the hay that appealed to him. He wasted no time in preliminary small talk.

'Come here, my bonny plump rose,' he grunted, pulling the lady to him. He had changed from his riding habit into a hairy tweed jacket, kilt, and lovat green hose. His legs were fat and very hairy and Agnes gave an explosive snort.

'Quiet!' hissed Stuart but the laird was making so many of his own he was oblivious to any other. Before long he was red and sweating. The children stared in amazement when, with a speed astounding in one so lumbering, he had exposed the lady's generous breasts.

Stuart gulped and Agnes whispered, 'I don't want mine to grow *just* so big! They'd be awful heavy.'

Stuart grinned. 'They'd make your back all hunch up and you'd be like an auld Cailleach. You might grow a big nose to match and you'd have a hump on your head because your nose would be such a weight.' He snorted into the hay in an ecstasy of silent laughter.

The laird was beginning to babble as his hands wandered. 'My kilt! Wore it specially – nothing underneath,' he groaned in Gaelic. The children understood but the English lady didn't. She was making sounds that fitted Dodie's description of 'an auld yowe bleatin'!' and soon discovered for herself the laird's urgent message. She threw back her head and giggled hysterically. Her mouth was large, painted liberally, and the children could plainly see her Adam's apple wobbling above her voluptuous breasts.

Dodie had likened the laird to a 'ruttin' stag' and he had never been more apt.

Niall blushed and wished he hadn't come. It was all very well listening to the description of something but the reality was embarrassing and somewhat crude.

There was no dignity about the old couple below and Niall, at a rather romantic and impressionable age, felt that love should have dignity. Even the young courting couples at the barnyard Ceilidhs had a certain respect in their attitudes towards each other. Niall felt he had cheapened himself and opened Shona's innocent mind to the wrong ideas about sex. His twelve-year-old mind groped for an idea of what love should really be like. It couldn't, just couldn't, be like that lustful scene below. He stole a glance at Shona and saw with surprise she was enjoying the whole thing.

'Look at his *bum*!' she hissed gleefully. 'It's pink and hairy and jumpin' the way the old boar does when he goes to the sow!'

Niall breathed a sigh of relief. She saw the scene with the eyes of the innocent. She had witnessed the mating of animals all her young life and to her the laird and his friend were two human animals doing the natural thing. Her ten-year-old mind lumped all living things together and nothing was more normal than the mating of two living creatures.

But Stuart and Agnes were different. They were older and more open to suggestive happenings. Stuart had forgotten about fishing and was fumbling playfully with Agnes, kissing her in an awkwardly eager boyish fashion and she was egging him on by twisting herself into all sorts of inviting poses. Niall watched them and wondered. Was Agnes an indication of all girls of her age, tormenting boys, teasing them, little witches who used their bodies like a commodity to entice, then to reject like the girls did at the dances?

Would Shona change so drastically? Would she flirt and tease and boldly flaunt her body? He knew her so well but he was going away and each time he came home he would see the changes in her such as he wouldn't if he stayed on Rhanna.

She was too engrossed to notice his stare, her twinkling blue eyes showing her obvious amusement. He was free to study the long sweep of her lashes. Mirabelle had tied back her auburn hair; it was swept up from her face but tumbled down her back in a cascade of thick rich waves. A dancing sunbeam lingered on the tresses and turned them the colour of autumn leaves. Her ears were like small pink shells. Niall noticed them for the first time. They were exquisitely shaped, so delicate in the sun they were almost transparent. She was thin to the point of being skinny but he knew that one day her whole shape would change. It had happened to all the bigger girls in school and it was bound to happen to Shona. Would she be like Agnes? Would she taunt the Rhanna boys with him away and not able to do a thing about it? For years he had calmed her stormy tempers, soothed her troubled heart and scolded if she sulked. They had spent their childhood together but when he was away she was bound to turn to others for company. Would it be another boy? He couldn't see the tomboy Shona playing dull games with other girls and the older she grew the more natural it would be for her to want a boy. Something churned in his heart but he was too young to recognize the bitter taste of jealousy.

He couldn't believe she would turn out like Agnes, he didn't want to believe it. He knew she had a strength in her, a pride and a sensitivity that went very deep and somehow he knew she wasn't going to be like other girls. She had confided so much to him but there had been times when the depth of her emotions shook him. She was usually so happy but sometimes he sensed a sadness in her that he was too inexperienced to reach. He knew the cause, of course, but who was he to turn the tide of time and make possible a more satisfying relationship between father and daughter. It was all too complicated for him. He had lost his dislike for Fergus McKenzie long ago – he admired his strength of character. It showed in every aspect of his bearing. He held his head high and ignored the gossips, his pride visible for all to see.

'Och, Niall, that was the best laugh ever!' Shona's voice startled him out of his reverie. She leaned over and whispered in his ear, 'Will yours be like that?'

'My what?' he said, puzzled.

'Like *his*! The laird's!'

'They've gone,' said Niall amazed.

'Och, you're silly *and* deaf, like Shelagh! They banged the door quite loud and you haven't answered me. Will you have a big rooster like his?'

Niall reddened. 'Will you have big bosoms like hers?' he countered.

'Ach, I don't think so, I'm too skinny. You're all red in the face, Niall. You never used to blush when you went behind a bush to pee. You never really bothered to hide, and I saw your rooster. It was a skittery wee thing – not like *his*! I hope you don't grow like that! You'd have to wear your kilt *all* the time because you wouldn't have room in your trousers!'

'*Shut up!*' he snapped and she fell back in the hay in a fit of laughter.

Stuart had become disenchanted with Agnes who knocked his hand away every time he became too personal.

'Let's go and guddle,' he grunted, pulling hay from his hair. 'If Robbie catches us we'll tell him we'll tell the laird we'll tell his wife he's a dirty auld man!'

Niall gladly accepted the garbled suggestion and all four trooped rather thankfully into a perfect summer evening.

Chapter Eight

A week later Mirabelle went up to her room to rest before tea. It was breathlessly hot. Not a leaf or heather bell moved and the sun shone faintly through a thick haze of heat. There was thunder in the air and Mirabelle felt tired and headachy. She sat on her rocking chair by the wide open window fanning her flushed face with a corner of her apron. Shona was in the garden. Mirabelle saw her pluck a red rose, sniff its glorious perfume absently before sitting down on the grass to hug her knees, her eyes gazing unseeingly ahead.

'Poor wee bairn,' sighed Mirabelle. 'She'll miss that laddie sorely when he's gone.'

Niall had told Shona because he couldn't bear to keep the secret any longer. He had told her in 'their' cave, now made homely with various items they had smuggled from their respective homes. At first Shona thought him to be teasing but the look in his brown eyes quelled her laughter.

'I want to be a vet,' he explained, his hand in her small grubby one. 'After school it will be a college like my father went to but there will be holidays, Shona. We'll still see each other.'

There was a long silence in which she sat like a stone, not even an eyelid flickering.

'I'll miss you like anything,' he hurried on, his sorrow at having to impart the news making him babble slightly. 'I'll miss lots of folk. My parents and wee Fiona. Tot too, she was so much with us. I'll miss Dodie and old Joe and even old Shelagh farting in kirk on the Sabbath. I'll be staying with a lot of other boys but it won't be like here on Rhanna. I'll miss our caves and the sea and the fishing boats and those lovely scones Mirabelle makes. I wish I could have known her better because it seems *awful* to miss her scones more than her. It'll be really terrible to wake up every morning and not look to the sea, because though it's a country place it's not near the water. There's a wee town not far away so I can send you a postcard sometimes. Would you like that, Shona?'

She was strangely, awesomely quiet. She saw the future stretching without Niall and the whole world was bleak. All along she had known that he would leave the island one day but one day was always in the future in her child's mind. Now that day was drawing nigh. A lot of Rhanna boys left school early to learn fishing and crofting, the two mainstays of the island. Some went away to the big cities like Glasgow and London, some to places like Canada and Australia, names that were other worlds to her, places on the big map in the classroom that she liked to hear about but they were foreign to her. Rhanna, the little green jewel in the Atlantic Ocean, was her birthplace and she loved it with every breath of her being. She would stay. Girls stayed on Rhanna – some went to take up nursing on the mainland but mostly they stayed. But she had known Niall would go. He hadn't been full of fancy ambitions for his future but had always clung to one, to be an animal doctor.

'I like them better than humans,' he once told her. 'They don't moan but suffer in silence mostly. They're nice to work with.'

Shona felt herself grow cold though the sun was streaming through the cave. She shivered suddenly and turned slowly to look at his boyish anxious face. His hand tightened over hers.

'I'll be back,' he said urgently, trying to dispel the dull look that had crept into her eyes. 'It'll be even better than when I'm here *all* the time because we'll have so much to tell each other. Och Shona, don't look so sad! 'Tis sad I am to leave. Think of the holidays! Every time I come home we'll run to this cave and talk till we're blue in the face. This cave will be our wee den! We'll always come here!'

He was so eager to please her he gripped her hand till it hurt, his tanned skin flushing with his need to make her understand how earnest he was. She put up a small brown hand and touched his golden hair briefly. 'We will, Niall,' she whispered in a small tight voice. She knew that if she gave way to her feelings she would explode. She would cry and shout and do all the things she tried never to do because they stamped her with the mark of her femininity and she wasn't going to give in now, not after all the years of reining her emotions. She drew her hand away and he was surprised and a little hurt that she hadn't shown more feeling. A lump came to his throat and he said defiantly, 'Mother and Father will miss me anyway.'

'Yes,' said Shona and turned away to hide a glimmer of tears. Angry at herself she stamped out of the cave.

'Are you in a bad mood?' he called.

'Yes,' she said again, keeping a wobble from her voice.

'Well you can just grow out of it!' Hurt made his tone snappy. 'You're a wee baby and I'm fed up trailing you about 'cos you're a girl! I'm *sick* of girls!'

He stamped after her. She stared at his tall sturdy figure. The wind whipped his hair and his cheeks were red. He stood astride a moss-grown rock, glaring at her, his brown legs apart and his arms folded. Her pent-up emotions came out in a flood of temper.

'Ach, away you go! You're a stupid daft boy and I wonder I've tholed you so long! I'm sick of you telling me what to do! You're glaikit, that's what you are, Niall McLachlan, and I'm that scunnered I'm glad you're going so I am! I hope . . . I hope a seagull shits on your head every time you travel on that boat – you deserve a whole flock of gulls shitting on your head for the rest of your days so you do!'

She scampered wildly over the heather. Her hair streamed like the tail of a wild pony and her blurring eyes saw not where she was going but she plunged on recklessly, the deep heart-rending sobs rising in her throat at last.

Niall was left to stare after her. Now he knew how desperately she had fought to conceal her tears from him. The wild burst of words, the tempestuous flight all proved it. His lips quivered slightly as her terrible wishes touched the humorous side of his nature but he sobered on a more serious reflection of the scene.

He realized it was the first time in years she had allowed her deeper feelings to come uppermost. She had tempers, yes; but nothing like the tremulous storm he had just witnessed. He cast his mind back, trying to remember that last time. It had been more terrible then because she had been very young and unable to restrain herself at all. When and where had it been? He searched his memory and it all came back: the Kirkyard, her mother's inscription, the deep terrible sorrow that her discovery had caused her.

Young boy that he was he felt sobered and very touched because she hadn't cried like that till today – and this time the tears were for him.

Two days had passed since then. He couldn't go to Laigmhor. He had never gone there and he couldn't very well start now. She wouldn't go to him because she was so ashamed of her outburst. Also there was the matter of her pride: it was difficult for her to apologize even when she knew she was wrong. So she mooned around and got under everyone's feet. Normally she was a good help to Mirabelle. She could do a lot of household chores and it had become her job to make the hens' pot. She also milked the cows sometimes and every morning she cranked the handle to start the generator that pumped water into the farm. But now she snapped at Mirabelle and not even Alick's cheerful chatter could dispel her gloom. A visit to Hamish's cottage lifted her spirits a little. Maggie was a cheery woman and stepped over dogs and cats to fetch creamy milk and biscuits for her little guest. Hamish showed her a baby rabbit he had rescued from one of the cats. It was in a little hutch especially kept for injured creatures and was happily munching lettuce leaves. Hamish made her laugh and she tripped home gaily but her mood returned when she saw Niall with a crowd of boys coming back from the harbour. It seemed he wasn't missing her at all, and she scowled. She didn't even have Tot for company and felt no one really cared for her.

Her father was surprisingly sympathetic. He knew what loneliness was like and could feel something of her sadness at having to part with the friend of her childhood. He saw how empty her life would be without the boy who had shared her innermost thoughts for so many years. She had made his mistake, that of attaching herself too devotedly to one human being. When that person went away the void that was left could only be filled by dreams and these were not things that made for a happy life. So he was gentle with her and for one lovely fleeting moment she allowed him to hold her close, his compassion overruling his fear of rebuff. He felt the warm smooth bloom of her cheeks against his and the sweet delicacy of her slim little body filled him with such overwhelming love that tears sprang to his eyes. She felt his dear rough face against hers. The smell of him was the night smell. His breath was fresh and his damp hair tickled her nose. He was stripped to trousers and vest and she could see where the brown weather-beaten skin on his neck merged with the paler skin of his chest. His arms were warm and very strong and she held her breath with the ecstasy of his nearness. But the feel of his arms was so unreal to her she began to feel uncomfortable and she wondered how she could break away. She wanted the lovely moment to last forever but moments never did. She knew he had hugged her on an overpowering impulse but it was over now and he too would be feeling uneasy. She broke away and immediately felt she had stepped back into a world of lonely uncertainty. His eyes were hurt and she knew she had done the wrong thing but she couldn't go back to him now. The beauty of the moment was over and they both knew it.

The next day she was irritable and snapped at her father during breakfast. He had spent a sleepless night wondering what to do about Kirsteen and snapped back. Alick ate his boiled egg and searched for something to say to ease the tense atmosphere.

'You two having love problems?' he said cheerily and immediately knew he had said the wrong thing. Shona got up and with great dignity marched from the room.

'Come back here and excuse yourself from table!' yelled Fergus, but she pretended not to hear.

'A good skelping she needs,' muttered Fergus and he too left the table. Mirabelle sighed. 'I wanted the bairn to help me this morning. I'm tired wi' her tantrums so I am. It's yourself to blame, Alick. Never could hold your tongue!'

He put his arms round her plump waist.

'Don't fret so, my lady. Alick will be a good boy and help with all the kitchen chores this morning. They take too much for granted, Belle. How have you put up with us all these years? Haven't you ever wanted a family of your own? You must have been a bonny lass in your day.'

She giggled and pulled a lock of his brown hair.

'Ach, away wi' you. You're a flatterer and a flirt into the bargain. You're such a different laddie from Fergus.'

'Aye, he was the big brother I worshipped and wanted to be like. But it didn't turn out that way, thanks to Mother. She strengthened my weakness by pampering me and setting Fergus up as my guardian. Oh aye, I've thought about it a lot, Belle.' His voice held an unusual note of bitterness. 'I should have fought my own battles but Mother wouldn't have it. Fergus was the strong one but just as much a pawn as myself. I think it was all wrong, Belle.'

'Ach, your poor mother did what she thought best for you both, but it's all in the past now, laddie.'

His smile was rueful. 'Aye, but it's our past that shapes our future, dear Belle. I was made to lean on Fergus even though he didn't want such a burden. All my boyhood days I needed that prop. Now, here I am, with a wife as flightly as myself. I'm just floating around like a cork in water. No bottle for me to fit into. I've lost my prop, Belle.'

'Ach, you're full of fancies, laddie,' she said lightly; but she wondered if anyone had ever credited him with the deep sensitivity he covered so well with frivolous words.

His mention about a family of her own had touched a chord deep in her heart. All day thoughts of the past came crowding in on her till she knew she had to be alone to think. Hers were very special memories but hers had been a very special family. She had a spare hour before tea so she folded her hands over her stomach and rocked herself by her window. A smile hovered at the corners of her mouth and a reminiscent dreaminess crept into her eyes. No one knew the secret she had kept in her heart for . . . how many years? She puckered her forehead. Fifty-four! It couldn't be but yes, it was, she was seventy-three now and had been barely nineteen when her husband and little son were taken from her in that terrible tragedy of 1879. She could see the face of her husband John so clearly. In her mind's eye she saw him smile, that jaunty gay smile of his, his boyish face alight with his love of life. And little Donald, just three months, beginning to smile his lovely toothless baby smile. She tried to remember his tiny face but couldn't. Panic seized her and she rose hurriedly to rummage in a drawer. The box was there beside all her bits and pieces. It was full of old photos, of her parents and sisters. The familiar crushing pain in her chest took her breath away and she sat down heavily, the box in her lap.

After a short rest she searched through the box, desperately eager to find that baby face that eluded her memory. There were several sepia photos of the child but she found her favourite, the one with John holding his tiny son. She looked gently at the young face of her husband and could see that he was bursting with pride, the sparkle of his eye and the upturned corners of his mouth gave him away but he had remained suitably composed till the photographer was finished. Now she could recall that day so clearly. When they got out of the studio he had burst out laughing, the sobriety of the occasion too much for his sense of fun.

She studied the face of her little son. His eyes were roundly agape at some object placed so that he would face the camera. He had kept sticking his fist in his mouth and John had to constantly take it out. It was a sweet innocent little face with big eyes looking into a future that was never to be.

Mirabelle sat back in her rocking chair and was transported back in time, far from Laigmhor and Rhanna. She remembered again that Christmas of 1879. It was a happy gay Christmas spent with her mother who dearly loved all her children and grandchildren. She was widowed, and Christmas was a time full of poignant memories for her, so Mirabelle had gone with John and little Donald to spend the festive season with her. She knew John would have preferred to stay in their own cosy little home for Donald's first Christmas but his kind heart was easily swayed and the journey had been worth the happiness it brought. Three days after Christmas they departed for home but at the station it was discovered they had left a case behind containing a lot of things essential to the baby's wellbeing. He was cutting a first tooth and wailing fretfully so it was decided that Mirabelle would go back for the case while John went on with the baby.

But there was no next train over the Tay that Sunday night or for many nights to come. The high girders on the wind-lashed bridge had collapsed and both engine and train had plummeted into the foaming waters beneath. Not a single survivor came out of the disaster and Mirabelle collapsed. For many months she lived like a shadow, unable to cope with reality, and her mother had nursed her through days of unending darkness. A year later her mother, too, was taken from her and she felt she had lost everything that made life worth living. Oh yes, she knew how dear proud Fergus had felt when he had lost Helen. The marrow had gone out of him, he had told her, and described exactly the way she had felt all those years ago. But at least he had the gift of his daughter, although unable to appreciate the fact. She had saved nothing from the wreckage of her young days.

Tears were coursing down her cheeks now but she wasn't aware of them. She was seeing the young Mirabelle, drifting, unable to settle into any kind of niche. She had lived with a married sister for a time but her natural sense of independence made her go out and find a job and she had become housekeeper to a demanding crotchety old lady who never seemed pleased with anything but who must have appreciated Mirabelle because she had left her several hundred pounds when she died. After that, each post was worse than the last and every ounce of her strength was drained by large demanding families or old demanding ladies and she had come to believe her life would contain nothing but meaningless service to others. Then came Laigmhor and the lovely healing peace of Rhanna. She had been thirty-seven then but had felt she was starting life afresh. She had become so used to keeping her private thoughts to herself she hadn't been able to change, not even on Rhanna. No one expected a housekeeper of many years' standing ever to have a life of her own. She was expected to immerse herself in the running of other people's lives and that had been easy enough at Laigmhor with two young children to love. But she had always felt herself to be part of the family, not just an outsider to be used as a convenience and she gave of herself every ounce of her loving heart. She had lost her own little son but the boys, then Shona, had fulfilled her motherly instincts. Two generations of children! She had been their mother really. When hurt or unhappy it was to her arms they tumbled. She thought of them as her own. She wiped away her tears and smiled, an inward happy smile of thankfulness for such a rich life.

Shona rocked listlessly on her heels. It was hot and she got up to seek some shade under the apple tree. She glanced at the house and saw Mirabelle at the window. She put up her hand to wave but there was no response and she guessed Mirabelle was asleep.

Miss Fraser was coming up the hot dusty road and she came through the gate and over to Shona. 'Hello,' she said warmly. 'Is your father about?'

She too had spent a sleepless night thinking about Fergus. She knew she couldn't go on in the present position much longer. Two nights ago she had lain in his arms but last night she was alone again and she was now convinced he only came to her to appease his physical appetites.

Shona nodded. 'He's in the big barn with Alick, stacking hay.'

'Thank you, Shona. I'll see you later.'

Shona watched her teacher walk away. She liked the way she held herself. She was quite tall and very graceful and there was that dignified tilt of the chin that had earned her the label of 'madam' by some narrow-minded locals. Shona liked the proud chin and the way the golden head was held high. She liked Miss Fraser altogether and wished she and her father would marry – that might put an end to some of the spiteful jibes she endured at school.

Kirsteen went into the barn. It was deliciously fragrant. Hens clucked lazily and poked for insects on the straw-littered floor. It was warm and quiet, and for a moment she thought it was empty.

'Fergus!' she called. There was a soft chuckle from behind a hay bale. She stepped inside and found Alick sitting beside a fat contented hen.

'Will I do instead?' grinned Alick. 'Fergus was called away to look at a cow who has hurt her foot. He and Hamish will be gone for ages. You know what they're like when they get talking about the beasts. I'm just resting from my labours. Brother is a hard taskmaster. He's making sure I earn my daily bread.'

'Oh . . .' she hesitated, 'well, I'll see him another time. Don't – don't mention I called will you?'

He looked at her standing poised for flight. She was wearing a very flimsy blue dress and her long legs were bare. He didn't answer but patted the hay at his side.

'Sit down and talk to me for a wee whiley. Och no, don't go! They're all in the doldrums here just now and I could be doing with a lovely lady to cheer me up!'

He was being very charming and she knew his eyes were taking in every bit of her body. She had always managed to avoid him on her visits to the farm because she knew he was a lady's man. Nevertheless she liked him and felt his cheery frivolities were just the tonic she needed to make her forget for a while all the problems her life held.

'Just for a wee while,' she acceded and sat, not in the spot indicated but on the other side of the hen. Before long she was laughing merrily. He had a way of making the most ordinary happenings sound funny. His dark eyes were sparkling. He knew his talent for making laughter had always been his greatest asset next to flattering women.

Kirsteen was enjoying herself so much it was a moment or two before she realised his flow of wit had stopped and he was looking at her with open desire.

'You're beautiful, Kirsteen,' he said in a low voice.

'No – Alick – no!' she cried and tried to scramble up. But it was too late. The fat hen ran squawking at Alick's lunge forward. He was quick, so quick that Kirsteen was pinned helplessly to the warm hay while he kissed her, small swift kisses on her face and neck.

'Let me go, Alick,' she panted. '*Please* let me go!'

'You're too good for him,' he mumbled. 'He doesn't deserve you. You're the kind of woman who could have any man.'

His mouth came down hard on hers and she fought for the breath to scream. His hands were caressing her body with such fierceness her flesh tingled with pain. Panic seized her. She couldn't breathe. The more she struggled the more he seemed to enjoy it.

'Will you give yourself or can I have the pleasure of taking you?' he whispered. 'Please let me, Kirsteen. I've dreamed of you every night since I saw you.

Touch me, dear sweet Kirsteen. I'm on fire for you!'

She screamed then, a half-sobbing sound that tore from her in a desperate succession of sound. The tall figure of Fergus darkened the doorway and he was tearing Alick from her while the cries were still choking from her throat.

Alick hardly knew what hit him. Fergus's sledge-hammer fists were raining down on him without pause. He put up his hands to defend his face but he was useless against the fury of his brother's onslaught. Kirsteen, wild-eyed and sobbing, could only watch while he was reduced to a bleeding mess.

'Stop, Fergus!' she cried. 'You'll kill him!'

Alick lay for several minutes. Blood streamed from his nose and frothy saliva mingled with the blood of a split lip. His face was a mass of bruises and one eye was already beginning to swell.

Fergus, his chest heaving, looked down at his brother with contempt. 'Get up,' he said softly, 'and walk out of here like a man. You'll get the next boat from Rhanna!'

Alick stumbled to his feet. He drew the back of his hand across his mouth and looked at the blood on it.

'A man!' He spat thickly. 'Oh yes, I'm that, despite the fact that you and Mother tried to turn me into a mouse! Not a man like you, Fergus, all fire and fury on the outside but soft like dung inside! People know what kind of man I am! Can you say the same, man? I show it when I feel afraid but you're too bloody proud even to be human!' He staggered outside and away over the breathless fields, swaying like a man drunk.

Kirsteen's eyes were full of tears. 'Och Fergus, you were too hard on him! He's not strong like you! He wasn't able to fight back!'

He looked at her, it was a strange look which she couldn't fathom. She couldn't know that he was seeing Helen again but this time as a lovely memory of the past. He would always see her because he knew he could never forget her. But the guilt he had felt, the uncertainty of being able to give his heart fully to another woman was gone and a burden lifted from him. He was certain now of his deep love for Kirsteen, the sight of her in his brother's arms had proved it and he felt light-headed with the knowledge. He held out his hands.

'Kirsteen, will you marry me? Will you share my life and make me a happy man? I love you, Kirsteen.'

The words were simple enough but they were the most beautiful she had ever heard. She ran to him and the whole world was at their feet in that magical eternal minute.

'Fergus, my dear Fergus,' she breathed. 'I've waited so long to hear you say that.'

He closed his eyes and held her close. Briefly he thought of his brother and felt both pity and gratitude. Pity because Alick was the unhappy, pleasure-seeking product of a pampered childhood, and gratitude because Alick had unwittingly brought him to a decision over which he had hesitated for so long. Later he would find Alick and make his peace with him, but not now when Kirsteen overwhelmed him with her dear sweet nearness.

*

Shona heard the rumpus coming from the hayshed. At first she paid no heed till she heard her father's angry voice followed by Alick's high-pitched tones, then she ran quickly and was in time to see Alick reeling over the fields. She stood by the big doors and heard the murmur of voices from within. Her father was asking Kirsteen to marry him and they were so wrapped up in each other they didn't notice her. She tiptoed quickly round a corner and leaned against the warm wood of the big shed. Hugging herself with joy she lifted her face to the sky. It was hot and hazy-looking with purple clouds piling on top of Sgurr nan Ruadh, the red mountain of the Fallan range. It was beautiful, everything was beautiful, Loch Tenee sparkling, the misty bronzed moors, the rough grass at her feet, even the midgie that landed on her hand, all were beautiful. But the midgie had a sting and had to be killed and her world of beauty was soon to turn to a devilish nightmare. But not now! Certainly not now when everything floated in such a happy haze. A bubble of joy rose into her throat and she knew she couldn't stand for long. She skipped away, over the cobbled yard and into the house to find Mirabelle. It was teatime, yet strangely there were no lovely savoury smells in the kitchen. It was empty except for Tot and her pups. She bent and stroked the bitch's silky ears. 'I'll tell you a secret, Tot,' she whispered. 'Father's going to marry Miss Fraser and we're all going to be happy. I'll have to find Mirabelle, she'll be pleased because she's getting too tired to be my mother and needs a wee help with things. After that I'll go and tell Niall, even though he's a boy. 'Tis he can keep secrets better than anyone I know.'

She looked into the parlour but Mirabelle wasn't there. She wasn't in the green taking in the washing that hung limply in the stillness nor was she searching the hen houses for eggs. Shona went back into the house. The grandmother clock ticked in the hall and the house had that strange empty feel when Mirabelle was out.

'Mirabelle!'

Her voice intruded into the peaceful house. Then she remembered – Mirabelle was in her room. She had been in her favourite rocking chair by the window and would be sound asleep forgetting all about tea.

'Lazy Cailleach,' chuckled Shona bounding up the stairs. Mirabelle's room was at the end of the landing. It was light and airy with its chintz curtains and gay patchwork cushions and covers. Shona knew it well. Mirabelle had often rocked her in the chair and crooned old Scottish lullabys. The room was full of knick-knacks but the reason she liked to go there was because it had a 'mother' air about it. Everything was homely and friendly, even the smell of the room. It had Mirabelle's smell of lavender and mothballs.

Shona giggled when she saw she had been right. Mirabelle was fast asleep, her chin sunk in her chest. She held something tightly and a box had fallen from her lap to scatter its contents on the floor.

Shona tiptoed forward. 'Mirabelle, wake up! I have something lovely to tell you. You're not going to be so weary now for Father and Miss Fraser are to be wed!' She shook the old lady gently by the shoulder. How fast asleep she was. Her head lolled strangely and there was something unusual about her face. It was all tinged with blue, nose, lips and cheeks, even her wrinkled eyelids, but her mouth was smiling and Shona sighed. 'Dreaming again! Och, wake up, Mirabelle till you hear my news!'

Mirabelle suddenly slid sideways against the arm of the chair. She looked like one of the limp rag dolls she stitched so often and the little girl's hand flew to her mouth. She backed away, frightened now of the stout old figure that had always spelled security.

'Mirabelle,' she whispered then turned and fled from the room, downstairs and into the kitchen. Sobbing she ran outside. A cool breeze had sprung from the sea and she shivered. Her head was spinning and the cold hand of fear gripped her heart with icy fingers. The farmyard was empty. Where *was* everyone? Normally Murdy or Mathew were about and Bob always came in for a cup of tea about now. She raced to the hayshed where she had last seen her father but he was gone. She was crying, a small whimpering sound that could have come from a lost puppy. Everything was blurred in tears, and fields and sky wobbled together. Then she spotted several figures on the road to Portcull. They were specks in the distance but she knew her father was there.

'Father! Father!' she screamed, knowing it was useless. The wind was strengthening and threw particles of dust into her brimming eyes. The masses of cloud over the mountains had changed to a muddy grey with wraiths of white mist sliding down over corries and scree. The sky was a slate-blue with curling smoky clouds creeping over the landscape.

She felt small, helpless and very lonely and ran forward to look for some familiar figure but she was all alone. The sweep of her glance took in the farmhouse and there was the open window with Mirabelle slumped in such a way that her white mutch was like a beacon in the dark window recess.

'No! No! No!' The scream tore from the child's throat in a series of anguished protests. She began to run swiftly like a terrified animal. She tripped half a dozen times but each time she got up and ran on, heedless that her arms and legs were grazed and bleeding. She had no notion of direction but her subconscious mind guided her tired legs to the haven of Slochmhor. She burst straight into Lachlan's surgery hour. Her auburn hair was windswept, her eyes wild like a young animal caught in a trap. Familiar faces swam in her vision. She opened her mouth but the wild hammering of her heart robbed her of breath to speak so she just stood there whimpering.

'Mercy!' exclaimed Kirsty McKinnon. 'The bairn hasny the wind to speak!'

Old Shelagh nodded knowingly and emitted a small belch. 'Ach the wind, a terrible thing just!'

Nancy Taylor, heavy and awkward in her eighth month of pregnancy, heaved herself up and put her arms round Shona's shaking shoulders. 'There, there, my wee chookie,' she soothed, 'come and sit down beside Archie and me and tell us what ails you!'

But the little girl shook her head violently. 'No – no. Get . . . doctor – I think Mirabelle's dead!'

There was a stunned silence.

'Ach no, she canny be.' Nancy spoke as if she was

convincing herself because she had a great affection for Mirabelle.

'God rest her soul,' said Kirsty piously and looked heavenward.

Elspeth's sharp nose hove into view in the dark passageway. The gathering clouds had brought early darkness and the small hall window gave little light. The people gathered for evening surgery looked like shadows and Shona's news had turned several faces pale.

'My, it's like a funeral to be sure!' barked Elspeth. 'And who's soul's needin' rested?'

'The bairn thinks Mirabelle's dead,' quavered Nancy. 'Could you fetch the doctor quickly?'

Elspeth turned pale. Mirabelle was her friend, the best she had because there were few who could stand her sharp tongue. Kindly Mirabelle could always be relied on for a sympathetic ear.

'Dead!' Horror made her tone sharper than ever. 'Are you sure, child? Did your faither send you for the doctor?'

Shona shook her head. She felt like screaming. All those questions and Mirabelle lying dead! Niall hovered in the dark hall. The commotion had brought him downstairs.

'Niall!' Shona's voice trembled with relief at seeing him. 'Please fetch your father! Mirabelle's dead!'

But Lachlan, ushering a patient from his room, heard. He reached immediately for his bag.

'You'll have to wait a while,' he told his patients. 'Niall, take Shona to your mother. I've no doubt the lass needs a bit comfort.'

But Shona broke from Nancy's arms. 'No, no, let me come! She might not be dead – she just looked it! Och, please let me see her! She's my Mirabelle!'

Lachlan rested his hand briefly on her head. 'All right, mo ghaoil. You're nearest her heart.'

He took her small hand firmly and hurried away.

'Ach, I'm goin' too,' said Elspeth whose features had softened with grief. 'Belle's my friend and if she's dyin' I have the right to say goodbye.' She peeled off her apron, threw it on a chair and grabbed her hat from the stand.

Nancy's eyes were brimming with tears. 'My, poor dear Belle! When I worked to McKenzie she was like an auld mither to me. Are you comin' up wi' me, Archie?'

In minutes the hallway was empty except for old Shelagh who hadn't the least idea what was happening. She shook her head and sucked noisily at her mint. The hall was warm and she folded her hands and dozed. Time meant nothing to her. She was quite content to wait in the doctor's house. It was a friendly house and Phebie would give her a cup of tea if the doctor was too long.

Mirabelle wasn't dead. Lachlan could see she had suffered a massive coronary and was deeply unconscious. Shona looked at the dear old face and her heart was heavy with love for the woman who had tended them all so devotedly. Now she was so helpless, unable even to move one finger, but she was alive! At least she was alive!

Lachlan had pulled the rocking chair over to the bed and was trying to lift the old woman.

'Fetch your father!' he panted. 'Quickly, lass, I canna manage myself.'

'He's not here, nobody's here! They all went away and I don't know why!'

There was a scuffle at the door and Archie fell into the room. A tight knot of Rhanna people were outside the bedroom all eager to help.

'I'll lift her wi' you, doctor,' offered Archie. Getting Mirabelle's ample proportions into bed was no easy matter but after much heaving the task was completed.

'Ach, my dear auld friend,' said Elspeth gruffly, 'can I help get her into a goonie, doctor?'

But he shook his head. 'She's almost gone. Her heart has been weary for long but she wouldn't rest.'

Elspeth stared. 'You mean she knew her heart was that bad and she never told a soul? Och, doctor, and her listenin' to all my troubles and never a murmur about her own!'

She sat on the bed and began to cry. No one had seen Elspeth cry before and they looked at each other uncomfortably. The realisation that she had such human emotions was quite a revelation and Kirsty patted her awkwardly on the back.

Mirabelle stirred and opened her eyes. She looked as if she had come back from a great distance. Everyone looked at her and Shona snuggled against the bosom that had always spelled security.

'What way is everyone here?' she whispered stiffly. 'Why are you here, Lachlan?'

Lachlan ushered everyone from the room. He knew that the old lady didn't have long. Her breath was coming in quick gasps making each word an effort.

'Weesht,' he soothed, taking her knotted hand in his. 'Don't talk, lass. It's come as I told you it would if you didn't rest.'

Shona didn't know what he meant but his voice was so gentle, his face so beautiful in its compassion that she could feel the deep pain he was feeling. She knew the laughing boyish Lachlan who was Niall's father. Now she was seeing the Doctor McLachlan whose love for his patients was so strong that the power of his love could reach out and comfort those in their last moments. Sometimes it was difficult for her to understand the world of grown-ups, the things they said were never easy to decipher, but at that moment, in the small dark room with Mirabelle dying, she understood one thing clearly. Niall's father could ease the fears of a mind that knew it was going to an unknown world. He had the gift of healing the body and an even more wonderful gift of bringing peace to a body he could no longer heal.

Shona could feel the peace in the room. Mirabelle's face was grey and old, but peace had replaced the weary look in her eyes. Lachlan held on to her hand, his brown eyes steady and reassuring as he spoke.

'There now, Belle, don't be frightened. You wanted it this way. No pampering an auld chookie – remember?'

She smiled. 'Aye, lad, a gey auld chookie.' She turned her head and looked deep into Shona's eyes. 'My ain wee bairn. Did I do right to bring you up and me too auld to see it through? I wish you could have had your own mother but it wasny to be.'

Shona felt the taste of salt from the tears pouring down her face. 'Och, Mirabelle you *are* my mother! The best in the world. Don't die, Mirabelle. Father's to wed Miss Fraser and we'll all look after you. I'll be a better help in the house and I won't get into tempers the way I do!'

A light came into Mirabelle's fading eyes.

'Fergus – to wed! Where is he? And Alick? My, these two laddies were a pair to rear. Alick was ay sae canty and Fergus – Fergus so proud but wi' a heart as big as a horse. Och, I'm glad he's to wed that bonny lass, but where is he? I'd like fine to see him before – before . . .'

Lachlan squeezed her hand. 'Don't worry, he'll be here in a whiley.'

She closed her eyes. 'If only you and he could let go of the past. He admires you, son, but he was ay too stubborn for his own good. Ach, the bothers we make in this life! It might be quite a wee change to get out o' it for a whiley.' She smiled but her eyes remained closed. 'Now, my wee lass.' She took the small hand in hers. 'I've a bit money put by and I've left it to you for when you wed. My lawyer will see to it for you.' She nodded smilingly. 'Oh aye, it sounds grand . . . auld Mirabelle wi' a lawyer, but even auld housekeepers can have their wee secrets. I never had need of money – not without John and wee Donald. It's a strange thought to think I'll see them in a whiley, John and my own bairn.'

Shona looked at Lachlan in puzzlement but he had Mirabelle's wrist between his fingers. She was breathing strangely. Shona could see the pulse beating under the thin skin of her neck but it was a funny beat, very jumpy and irregular.

Suddenly she gripped Lachlan's hand.

'Hold on to me, laddie. Shona, my wee chookie . . . coorie doon beside me – like you always did – when – your wee heart – was troubled . . .'

She drew a shuddering breath and the pulse in her neck stopped beating.

'Mirabelle!' screamed Shona. 'Please don't leave me!' She threw herself against the still figure in an abandonment of grief. There was the sound of sobbing outside the room and footsteps shuffling sadly away.

Lachlan lifted up the child. 'She's gone, Shona,' he said gently, 'we must cover her. Put her arms under the quilt.'

'She's holding something. It's like – like a piece of paper.'

Lachlan took the crumpled photograph from Mirabelle's clenched fist. He looked at a smiling young man and the tiny baby he held.

'Who are they?' whispered Shona.

'Who knows, except Mirabelle herself. People from long ago, no doubt, who meant a lot to her. Perhaps the John and Donald she spoke of a while back.'

Shona touched the white hair on the pillow. 'I'd like a wee bit,' she said softly, 'to keep in the locket she gave me for my birthday.' She began to cry again. 'Oh, I wish I had asked her to forgive me!'

'Whatever for, lass?'

'For sulking because Niall's going away. She must have been so tired and I've girned at her so. I was sulking today in the garden and saw her at her window. I should have been with her but I didn't even know she was ill. Och doctor, I loved her so!'

He sat down and gently pulled the forlorn little figure on to his knee.

'Weesht now, you mustn't blame yourself, she didn't want anyone to know she was ill. She loved you all and liked doing things for you. You were her life and she was happy. I know, she told me, you were like her own flesh and blood. Now, you are coming home with me. Phebie will see to you till your father comes home.'

Despite his gentle comfort she felt desolated. Mirabelle was dead and her father didn't know. His were the arms she needed more than she ever had done before. She felt cheated, deserted, and afraid. How could she live without Mirabelle? Who could she run to when she wanted to be the little girl she was and not the defensive dignified child her father thought her to be. How could she do without the homely routine created by Mirabelle? She had grumbled when told to do things that the old housekeeper had thought vital to her comfort but at the same time she had felt cherished and important. How often had she protested while Mirabelle brushed her hair till it shone? How many Gaelic lullabys had lulled her to sleep, how many fairy tales had been read to her while she sat in the inglenook hugging her knees? It must have been hundreds, perhaps thousands of times. Now these things would be no more. The homely 'mother' feel would be gone because no one, not even Miss Fraser, could fill the gap left by Mirabelle.

She sobbed quietly and allowed Lachlan to carry her

out of the room. She looked back but couldn't see for tears. 'Father,' she cried silently, 'Mirabelle's dead and you weren't here when we needed you!' She didn't know that only part of the nightmare was over or that her father needed help more in that moment than he had ever done in his life.

Lachlan carried her outside. The wind from the sea blew against them with deceptive calm and rain stung their eyes. She looked at Laigmhor through the mist of rain. It looked gaunt and empty against the grey sky. There were no flickers of lamplight to shine in the windows and they looked like empty dead eyes. She shivered. Mirabelle was in there. If she'd been alive the house would be warmly welcoming but she was dead and the house looked dead too and Shona knew it would be a long time before Laigmhor became alive again.

'We've left Tot in there,' she cried, making the house sound like an enemy.

'She'll be fine,' said Lachlan. 'I've got to go back with Biddy and I'll give Tot some warm milk and tuck her up for the night.'

She knew what he meant. Mirabelle had to be 'laid out' for her funeral. Biddy usually attended to such matters and was as used to dealing with the dead as with the living. But she and Mirabelle had been close friends and Shona thought how terrible it would be for Biddy to have to deal with such a matter.

Slochmhor was warm and friendly. Niall took Shona to the kitchen where Phebie made her drink hot milk and eat a biscuit. Little Fiona screamed delightedly at the cat who had recently adopted the house, and the belated surgery resumed. Shelagh wakened from a very satisfying nap and gave vent to her pent up 'winds'. 'Terrible just,' she consoled herself and rumbled into Lachlan's room leaving behind such a repelling odour that one or two people went home and the rest held their noses in disgust.

Chapter Nine

Fergus and Kirsteen were sitting in the hay making their plans for the future when Kirsteen looked up and saw the small knot of men coming towards the barn. They were very excited and shouted to each other in Gaelic.

'Come quickly, McKenzie!' panted Ranald McTavish. ''Tis your brother! Goin' to kill himself he is!'

'Aye, rantin' he was,' supplemented Todd the Shod. 'Says his life's not worth a bugger and he'd be better off wi' the de'il!'

'Says he'll prove he's man enough to kill himself!' said Canty Tam, named so because he was slightly simple and smiled at everything. He was smiling now despite the horror of his words.

Fergus's face had paled under his tan. 'What are you all rabblin' about?' he demanded, his fists bunching in a characteristic gesture.

Hamish placed a firm hand on his shoulder. 'Steady lad, 'tis true enough. Ranald was painting a boat when Alick came storming down saying he wanted to take a boat out . . .'

'It's true,' said Ranald who made his living hiring out small boats. 'Bad in a rage he was and I'm thinkin' it was odd because he's not like yoursel', Mr McKenzie – beggin' your pardon like. He pushed some money into my hand and I couldny believe my eyes, near on a pound he gave me. He was ay a kind-hearted chiel but a pound just . . .'

'For God's sake get to the point, man!' said Fergus grimly.

'Well, I gave him a boat – one of my very best and Canty Tam and myself helped him to push off. When he got out a wee bit he started to scream all the things we've been tellin' you. He was like a man demented, his eyes starin' out his head. It was a bit skearie, wasn't it, lads?'

Those that had witnessed the event murmured in agreement.

'It was to the Sgor Creags he said he was goin',' added Todd. 'Awful it was just. A man sair trauchled wi' life so he was!' Todd's eyes were round and the other men looked overawed.

Fergus stared. 'Did you say – the Sgor Creags?'

'Yes, terrible it was. He shouted he'd become like the chiel in the story my mother told me – the one who was caught on the Creags!'

'Aye.' Canty Tam nodded eagerly. 'He said the gulls would eat his flesh but his bones would stay there forever and we'd all have to remember him!' Canty Tam smiled in satisfaction at the thought.

'The tide, Ranald – what like was the tide?'

'Comin' in, sir – slow and peaceful like but – comin' in.'

Fergus strode away and the men followed, an assorted crowd but all curious, and eager to help. Hamish, kilt swinging and red beard jutting, walked beside Fergus.

'Don't worry, lad,' he said quietly, 'we'll get him safely aground.'

'Go home, Hamish,' ordered Fergus curtly but he was immediately sorry and put his hand on the arm of the man who had always befriended him. 'Don't worry about the McKenzies any longer. Maggie will have your tea ready and she'll wonder if you don't come home.'

'Ach, she's used to me bein' late but I'll ask young Mathew to run over and tell her I'll be a wee while.'

Mathew grumbled but went off over the hill. He was in a hurry to get the task over with and popped his head hastily through Maggie's door. Whisky rose quickly thinking his beloved master had come home but seeing it was just another human flopped back down, his nose in his paws.

Maggie raised her hand in greeting. 'Sit you down, laddie, and have a cuppy,' she invited. 'Hamish should be in soon and the kettle's on the boil.'

Mathew declined hurriedly. 'He'll be late home and thank you, Maggie, but I have no time to wait.'

He rushed off and Maggie took a pot of steaming broth from the fire. She looked at the table to make sure it was set properly and, content that all was ready for Hamish's return, made room between two cats and went for forty winks.

Mathew sped quickly over the fields to the village. He topped a rise and saw the unmistakable figure of Shona fleeing over Laigmhor fields below. He shouted and waved but she was beyond hearing range. He shrugged. She had Mirabelle and it might be better if she didn't know about Alick till his fate had been decided.

A skittish wind had turned the Sound into translucent green swells that broke in creamy foam on the boulder-strewn sands of Portcull. When Mathew arrived, the men were dragging a sturdy boat into the brown shallows. Fergus jumped aboard and many hands pushed him into deeper waters. Before the greedy sea took the boat out too far Hamish treaded water to his waist and jumped in beside Fergus.

'Get out, Hamish!' panted Fergus wildly.

'No.' Hamish's voice was calm but firm. His kilt plastered round his legs in wet folds and his fiery beard was bedraggled yet he still managed to retain the air of splendid dignity that was always his. 'You'll need help in yon sea,' he continued. 'It's rough out there by the Creags and if there's any swimming to be done better me than you. It was never one of your best assets.'

Fergus knew the truth of this. He feared the sea, its intensity and power. It could look calm and inviting but undercurrents were always a danger. He had swam a lot as a boy but never without fear. His head could be above the surface looking at the calm but underneath he could feel the water surging and swaying, restlessly roaming, tugging at the puny thing that was his body. In a way the sea reminded him of the unfathomed emotions of the human mind, the depths of which could be frighteningly strong yet appear so calm on the surface.

Alick knew that he feared the sea, but it was his unspoken triumph over the brother who was so good at everything else. During the days of their boyhood Alick had gloated quietly when Fergus floundered and had to be helped from some difficulty that was to Alick a simple matter of skill. Fergus now wondered if his brother was testing his boyhood fears. Was he throwing out a challenge that Fergus as his brother couldn't possibly ignore because if he did he would show the world there was something that could terrify him? Fergus was afraid. He felt it in every bone of his body. The sea was bucking at the boat and the Sound was growing rougher by the minute.

'Are you sure, Hamish?' he asked quietly.

'Will you try and stop me then?' grinned Hamish, looking with affection at the white-faced young man he had known since a baby. He saw Kirsteen on the shore. She stood to one side of the knot of islanders who had gathered like nosy gulls. He thought what a lovely lass she was with her slim body and fine sensitive face. Her eyes had shown her reluctance to let Fergus take the boat out but she had uttered no protest and now stood, quietly dignified, with her hands at her sides. Hamish wished that just one of the islanders would go up and offer her some crumb of comfort but the women were in clannish groups and the men too interested in the proceedings to bother with one unhappy young woman.

Fergus seemed to read his thoughts. As he pulled at the oars, he said in a quietly jubilant voice, 'We're to be wed, Hamish. I'll stop the gossiping old Cailleachs. She's a fine lass is Kirsteen and I've been a fool of a man not to have wed her sooner.'

Hamish smiled happily. 'That's what I've been waitin' to hear, lad. When is it to be?'

'Not soon enough, Hamish. It's strange, but I feel a

different man altogether, not like myself at all. I was so tightly bottled up this morning I felt I could burst, now I feel I could shout to the world how happy I am. I haven't felt like that in years and it's all because of Kirsteen.'

Hamish felt honoured by the confidence and touched by the eager happiness of a man usually so withdrawn. Hamish was a happy man himself. All his life he had been contented but it wasn't until he married Maggie he felt really fulfilled. Maggie had brought him an ever greater contentment. With her he had found the richness of companionship coupled with a steadfast love and he thanked God every day for having allowed their paths to cross.

'I'm happy for you, Fergus,' he said simply. 'You've been a lonely man these years.'

Fergus drew a deep breath. 'If only Alick . . .'

'Don't worry about him,' said Hamish who silently cursed Alick his childishness. 'He won't spoil things for you, son! We'll find him out there and a damt warmed arse he needs for doin' such a thing!'

They were well away from the shore now.

'Mind my boat, Mr McKenzie!' yelled Ranald anxiously. 'She's a good one so she is!'

Canty Tam smiled secretively at the green swelling waves on the Sound.

'The Green Caillichs will get them,' he said softly, but with devilish assurance. 'They're out there waitin', their auld hag faces smilin' because today they'll have a Rhanna man!'

'You're daft, man,' said old Bob but he turned his eyes quickly from the boat. Many of the islanders believed the legend of the Green Uisga Caillichs of Rhanna Sound. They were the spirits of witches of bygone days who had been cast from the island for various evil practices. Now their ghosts roamed the Sound and anyone venturing too far in a small boat were likely victims. The Caillichs took many forms but the most famous was a beautiful mermaid who turned into a green, one-eyed monster when the victim was lured far enough from the shore. Some claimed they had seen the mermaids sitting on the rocks near the treacherous Creags. The oldest man on Rhanna, ninety-seven-year-old Tam the Plough, claimed he had actually seen a mermaid turn into a green monster and had managed to escape. 'Just by the skin of my trousers' – because he had held a Celtic cross before him and shouted for St Michael to smite the hag. His simple faith had saved the day and earned him a reputation for bravery. No Ceilidh was complete unless Tam was there to repeat the tale which he lavishly embroidered with each telling. He and Bob had a friendly rivalry as to which was the best Seanachaidh but both were equally popular with their unending tales of water beasts, fairies, and witches. They spoke with reverence about St Michael who stemmed from the dim past of pagan rituals and who was the patron saint of all who were in danger at land or sea.

'St Michael will guard them,' muttered old Bob, but Canty Tam shook his head.

'Not, it won't be so. The Uisga hags are gaining strength. Look at them over yonder. I can hear their skirls of laughter from here. It's the kind of sea they like, all soft and swelling on the surface but below . . . boiling like a cauldron.'

Bob looked and saw the green swelling on the Sound and heard the thin threading moan of the wind rushing low over the water.

'You're daft, man,' he repeated but his voice was uneasy just the same.

Kirsteen stood nearby and listened. She knew all about the legends of Rhanna and she knew that the inhabitants held firm to their beliefs. Though they wouldn't always admit to it, they took precautions against those evil spirits that were said to abound in and around the island. Most of them wore Celtic crosses round their necks. Some of them were roughly carved from wood, but no matter how crude, they were a protection from a host of evils. Kirsteen had thought the ancient beliefs quite enchanting. She had been to several Ceilidhs in the homely crofts around Portcull. Curled warmly at blazing peat fires she had listened entranced as Gaelic songs filled the air or the plaintive notes of the fiddle brought the sigh of the sea and the rush of wind into the rooms. The highlight of the evening came when everyone settled to listen to the Seanachaidh, children and adults silently attentive while a lilting old voice told the tales that had passed through generations. Folklore, myths, and legends became frighteningly real in the warm, smoky rooms and, long after the stories were finished, the magic transmitted by the storyteller lingered on so that people scurried homewards clutching their crosses and children kept looking behind to make sure that no Caonteachs had deserted their water haunts in favour in haunting humans.

Since her affair with Fergus, Kirsteen had found her invitations to Ceilidhs growing less though she was still invited to partake of the odd Strupak. Suspecting that these gestures were merely a ruse to spier her into confiding her private affairs she had now started to refuse 'a crack and a cuppy' and by doing so incurred the islanders' hostility. Apparently nothing offended more than the refusal of a neighbourly gesture and she began to feel more and more outcast.

The charm of the islanders lay in their simple faith and barely concealed curiosity. Now that the curiosity was directed at her she was somewhat disenchanted and the islanders sensed her defensive attitude. Though she still received the customary exchanges she felt herself excluded from the vital centre of things though she knew a lot of it was her own fault. The folklore she had found so charming was crude and rather frightening when applied to everyday life and she shivered at Canty Tam's words of doom and moved away.

The boat was lost to sight now. Portcull lay in a bay, sheltered by rocky outcrops on the southern side, and by the steep cliffs that rose from Port Rum Point, a finger of land half a mile out to sea on the western side. It was on the other side of this finger that the Sgor Creags lay and the opening of the caverns known as Claigionn an Garadh which meant Caves of the Skulls.

Kirsteen made her way past the schoolhouse and began to climb the rough track to the high grassy base of the Point. She was aware that several islanders were dispersing to their cottages along the track and she quickened her pace to get away from their following eyes. A drizzling rain was beginning to fall and the mist was coming down quickly. She glanced inland and saw that the mountains were blotted out and thin curls of vapour floated in patches over the moors.

A group of sturdy mountain sheep were grazing contentedly on the short turf atop the cliffs but when she approached they bleated plaintively as if complaining about the weather. Kirsteen gazed at the greeny-grey waters far below and her heart leapt when she saw the boat heading round the Point. It looked tiny, the two men in it almost invisible. One of those men, a tiny dot barely discernible, was the man she loved more than her own life, the other a dear friend whom she knew had been a trusted member of the Laigmhor household for many years. Of Alick's boat there was no sign. She thought about him with pity and anger. She liked him and was sorry that his life was so shallow and empty but she was angry because he had ruined some of the most beautiful moments of her life. She cast her mind back to Fergus's marriage proposal, his words of love, the safe comfort of his arms, and his lips on hers, firmly sealing their love. Then those plans, so full of happiness. He had sworn his life to her and she had promised she would give him five sons, one of whom would surely carry on tilling Laigmhor soil. He had laughed then, a loud happy laugh, and swept her up in his arms as if she were swansdown.

It seemed impossible that a mere thirty minutes later she would be standing alone on top of a cliff with the gulls crying and the rain clinging to her eyelashes till she felt she was looking through a gossamer curtain. It was a fine rain but damp and cloying. Her dress was cold against her skin and she shivered again and wished she had stopped off at the schoolhouse for a cardigan. The mist was closing in fast and she could barely make out the sea below. A finger of icy terror curled round her heart. Abruptly she fell to her knees and put her wet hands to her face.

'Oh God,' she sobbed, 'keep them safe! And . . .' She stopped and looked far beyond the cliffs to the Sound of Rhanna. 'Please, St Michael,' she whispered, 'bring my Fergus back to me.'

Somehow just saying the words comforted her. She had dismissed all the tales she heard as folklore but she believed they had a grain of truth at their core and realised that below her so-called civilised veneer she was perhaps just as superstitious as the islanders themselves. She felt sick and dizzy and didn't hear the footsteps behind. Old Bob was there, his gnarled hands helping her to her feet, his voice rough but soothing.

'There now, lass, dinna greet so! My, you're cauld as ice. Here, take my jacket. Och yes now, I'm warm from the climb up!'

He tucked the hairy tweed round her cold body and put an awkward arm round her slim shoulders.

'Come away down now, you'll not do any good up here. The gods are wi' your man and as soon as the tide turns we'll all be out on that old finger down yonder, so dinna fear, lass. I came up to tell you we are all having a Strupak down at Todd's house. His wife says to tell you she'll keep you some hot broth. Come on now, there's a lass.'

Kirsteen leaned against him and cried. He was old and tough and it felt good to let herself be led by him. He murmured soothing words of comfort all the way to Todd's cottage where a small group of villagers had gathered. Without knowing how it happened she was sitting by a cosy fire with a mug of broth in her hands. Words of reassurance drifted to her ears and she looked up to see well-known faces whose concern for her showed in kindly glances. Somehow she knew she was in the bosom of the island once more and even more a part of it than she had ever been.

She listened to the men laying plans to man one of the bigger boats when the mist cleared a little and her heavy heart lightened with hope.

Alick wasn't out to sea ten minutes before he was regretting his hasty flight. It had been warm five minutes before but now a nasty wind knifed through his thin shirt. Boy of the seas of Rhanna many years ago, he was still master of the waves but years of soft living had weakened his fibres and he began to shake with a mixture of cold and the subsiding of an anger that had tensed his whole being. It had been a rare spurt of temper but extremely violent. In a welter of feelings he had stormed over the fields, hating Fergus for his strength. His face throbbed where his brother's iron fists had struck and the warm taste of blood filled his mouth. He spat out two teeth, dismayed to discover that one was from the front. His looks were his passport. His charming tongue and quick warm smile had won him endless nights of intimacy with endless women. He was a womaniser and knew it, yet there was never any fulfilment. Once he had won them over, his appetites satisfied, he soon tired of them and went on restlessly, hopelessly, plunging deeper into loneliness.

Kirsteen had been an exciting challenge. He had spent his nights at Laigmhor thinking about ways to win her over. She was even more of a challenge because she belonged to Fergus and because there was a dignity about her, a quiet, sweet burning of her inner strength that set her apart from all the women he had ever possessed. Today that slim body of hers had almost belonged to him. He wanted her more than any woman he had yet known and would have taken her against her will if there had been no other way. What a triumph then over Fergus, to have been inside the body of the girl that Fergus thought was his alone. The nearness of her had driven him crazy and all the time he was talking and laughing the heat inside him had risen to an unbearable pitch. Then the feel of her, the cool flesh under that thin dress, her breasts heaving with her struggles.

Then those awful pounding fists crashing into him, hurting every bone of his body. He was defenceless against the bullying power of his brother. He felt deflated and unmanly, humiliated beyond measure in the eyes of Kirsteen, the woman who moments before he had rendered helpless under his own lustful strength. What kind of man did he look now? She would pity him and wonder what he was made of. Only able to prove himself in the bedroom, a coward at all other times.

Well, he would show everyone what he was made of. He meant the words he hurled at the men on the shore. He wasn't afraid of the sea but Fergus was. They would go off and tell him and he could hardly refuse to come looking for his own brother. Let Fergus show them what he was made of . . . if he dared.

The boat rocked and Alick cried like a little boy. The tears mingled with the blood frothing from his nose. 'It hurts! It hurts!' he sobbed like the small boy who had ran to his mother with every little wound.

'Oh Mother! Fergus is a bugger for hitting me! I hate him so I do!'

He shipped his oars and buried his face in his hands. He had rounded Port Rum Point and was out of sight of Portcull. His little boat bobbed in the green swell coming in from the Sound and he sobbed, great heartrending sobs that were snatched greedily by the threading wind and tossed over the sea. For quite some time he cried out his heart and gradually felt better. Mirabelle was always saying, 'A good greet cures a host o' ails', and she was right. A man couldn't sit down and weep when he felt like it but he was alone now. Bobbing in his little boat out on the Sound he felt completely alone and very peaceful. The sea had always soothed him and he felt a regret that he hadn't stayed on Rhanna and become a fisherman. The water had peace and power; wind and tide decreed its moods and it was a force to be respected. But it could be kind to the unafraid. If a man could float and hold on to his courage the sea would carry him without the shell of a boat under him.

Alick stopped crying and looked about. The sea was strengthening. He had left the shelter of Portcull Harbour and was facing a glassy heaving swell at the tip of the Point. The tide was coming in quite fast but there was still a narrow strip of shore all round the high finger of land. He looked at the Sgor Creags standing out of the sea, stark and grey. The water seethed at their base and the glassy troughs of sea slid towards them to break in waves several feet high, washing the pinnacles in creamy spray. It was a wild sight. Alick was well aware of the presence of countless smaller rocks that surrounded Sgor Creags that were covered at high tide and a death trap to the unwary because they could trap a small boat and finally lure it against the Creags.

He stared up at the wind-battered cliffs that ran the length of the Point, getting steeper as they went inland. At their base they were barnacled and green, slimy with rotting seaweed, but above the tide line they rose dark and forbidding, hewn into fantastic patterns by wind and time.

The cold whipped through Alick's clothes and goose-pimples rose on his flesh. He was in a dilemma of his own making. The heat of his anger was burned out and he had no intention now of letting himself be battered to death on the Sgor Creags. But how could he go back with his tail between his legs? He would be the laughing stock of Rhanna. He couldn't stay out on the Sound too long either. He was hungry and cold and his whole face throbbed like a giant toothache.

For a time he rowed aimlessly, his dark head sunk on his chest, his shoulders hunched miserably. He was drifting nearer the Creags and he started when his keel crunched ominously against a hidden rock. He pulled away and came to a swift decision. He would hole up in one of the tunnels. He shuddered as he looked at the black holes in the cliff face but at least they would afford some protection from the elements. He knew the caves would fill with water but he would scramble to one of the tunnels higher up. He gave little or no thought to the men who would doubtlessly come looking for him. At the moment all his planning and motivation were for the comfort and preservation of Alick McKenzie, and time was running out because barely a foot of sand remained uncovered at the caves.

He pulled steadily and the keel grounded. Swiftly he jumped from the boat and, pulling it to one of the higher caves he knew never completely filled at high tide, tied it firmly to a rocky spur. He began clambering up the slippery rock but it was no easy matter: he slipped several times, tearing his clothes, cutting hands and knees on jagged holds. Eventually he slithered into a tunnel and lay panting. It was dark and smelled of rotting seaweed but at least it afforded shelter. He propped himself against the rough wall. He was trembling and sore all over and he sucked peevishly at his bloody hands. Edinburgh, with its clean streets and buildings, seemed a million miles away. He thought of a lot of things but most of all about his own plight. Something scuttled in the dark depths behind him and he stiffened when he heard the unmistakable high whistling of rats.

'Oh, God help me!' he sniffed. A thought came unbidden to his frightened mind. Those nights of the Ceilidhs of his youth and the old men with their stories of sea hags. What did they call them? Green water Caillichs? He looked down at the sea. It was green, a deep sea-green. He had laughed at the old men behind their backs and scoffed at the old legends but now – in this horrible dank tunnel with the waiting sea churning below – he could begin to believe anything. He would wait till dark then he would go back to Laigmhor, collect his clothes, and leave Rhanna in the morning. He was thankful that tomorrow was the day the ferry came: how awful if he'd had to wait a few days and everyone laughing behind his back.

The plan was simple and seemed quite feasible. Despite his state of discomfort a smile curved his cracked lips. He felt in his pocket, found his cigarettes, lit one, and leaned back against the damp wall to wait for the tide to turn.

Fergus and Hamish came round Port Rum Point and met the strong green swell from the Sound. They were surrounded by rolling mist and could just discern the looming cliffs.

'We'll use them to guide us,' said Hamish. 'But we can't go too far along or the damt Creags will tangle wi' us.' He laughed cheerily and Fergus, looking at his solid kilted figure, was glad of his reassuring company. It was eerie there in the mist with everything familiar blotted out. The slap of the waves against the boat seemed strangely loud but he knew it was because the thick blanket of har had deadened other sound.

'We'd better shout,' he said and proceeded to bawl Alick's name. Alick, dozing in his tunnel, heard the sound faintly. He recognized his brother's voice and for a reason unknown to himself his heart pounded with relief. He was feeling ill and miserable and didn't care now if he went back to Rhanna in disgrace. He had been a fool to behave the way he had and had deserved the beating he got. He crawled to the edge of the tunnel and cocked his head to fathom the direction of sound. There were two voices frantically calling his name and he cupped his hands to his mouth but only a croak came out. He swallowed hard and grimaced in pain. His throat was swollen and sore. He had slept with his mouth open because his swollen nose had made breathing difficult. Dried blood had gathered at the back of his throat and he swallowed again and again in an effort to relieve the dryness.

The voices were growing fainter. He cupped his hands once more and managed to shout, 'Here, I'm here!' but there was no answer. 'I'm here!' he cried again in despair. He sank to the floor and hugged his trembling body tightly. Fear made him feel sick and he vomited, retching agonizingly till he emptied his stomach.

Fergus had shipped the oars while he shouted. So eagerly did he listen for an answering cry that several vital minutes passed before Hamish noticed that the cliffs were no longer visible. Both men looked at each other in dread. Curls of mist drifted wraith-like over the water and the steady leaden rain soaked them to the skin. It was frightening not knowing which way to go. Too near the Sgor Creags and their boat would be smashed to driftwood, too far and they could drift into the open sea. Sweat broke on Fergus's brow and his eyes searched desperately for the cliffs but the mist had swallowed them up. The boat rocked alarmingly and his stomach churned in fear. It wasn't a particularly rough sea but there was a calm menace in the green swell that was far more forbidding than a superficial show of strength and Fergus knew that deep undercurrents were meeting and boiling.

Hamish wasn't afraid of the water, it was the mist that worried him. The sea was charitable enough as long as they could see where they were going but they couldn't and were in an extremely precarious position. He would have felt happier if they had been further out on the Sound away from the Creags and the numerous rocks surrounding them. The rain had drenched him. His red hair was plastered against his head and his kilt clung in miserable folds round his legs. He thought of Maggie and the warm meal she would have waiting. He thought of the warm happy feeling the sight of her always brought and just thinking about it brought a small measure of that feeling now. Life was so good; he loved his work but now he looked forward to the evenings, Maggie with her knitting, he with his pipe, Whisky and numerous cats draped over the furniture. They could be silent, so peacefully silent with Maggie's needles clicking, Whisky snoring, and the clock ticking sonorously. Or they could talk for hours about all sorts of things. Maggie wasn't just a woman who kept the house, she was extremely well versed in many subjects for she had travelled a good deal and could tell him about places he had never been to. He smiled when he thought about the intimate little habits they had adopted. Before bed they each had their own tasks, his to secure the hen runs and rabbit hutches, hers to wind clocks and settle the fire. Before he got back to the house she would hide from him then pounce from some dark recess and loudly cry, 'Keek a boo!' It was a kind of hide and seek they had played when first married and somehow the habit continued. It was 'their game'. They chuckled about it, wondering what the more sedate islanders would say if they knew. In kirk he only had to whisper 'Keek a boo' to make Maggie hide her laughter in a hanky.

He was still thinking of Maggie when an enormous silky swell hurled the boat on to a hidden spur of rock. For a moment he was aware of everything, the seething foam choking and blinding him as the boat tilted him into the sea, the wild crashing roar of water meeting rock, the white face of Fergus bobbing nearby, the cold ruthless water pulling relentlessly. He raised both arms and grabbed at the boat but even as he did so he knew he should never have pulled at the bow. It catapulted towards him. He heard the thud and knew it was deep inside his own head. He saw the blood foaming in the waves. Before the world and all his senses left him he heard Fergus screaming his name, over and over in nameless horror. His lips moved forming the name 'Maggie' before all that he had known and loved in life went blank and empty and the sea threw his body scornfully against the waiting Sgor Creags.

Fergus saw all that happened through a curtain of water. He heard a hysterical voice calling over and over for Hamish and hardly recognized it as his own. All the self-control that he had built round himself gave way and he began to scream in panic. He watched Hamish's helpless body being smashed over and over against the rocks till it was broken and bleeding. A giant wave lifted it and for a moment it was suspended before it was thrown high to wedge between two of the smaller pinnacles. Fergus looked at the once proud body, at the shining red hair, and the sightless staring eyes and he knew he was crying like a child. He thrashed wildly, trying to free himself from the horror of the Sgor Creags and their victim, but found that only one of his arms would work. The other hung in the water and now he felt the excruciating pain. His whole being had been so tortured at the sight of Hamish he had given no thought to himself. He tried again to lift his arm and cried aloud in agony. The sea was lifting him, taking him to the Creags, and he threshed wildly with his legs and one arm. He looked for the boat and saw that it had completely capsized and was being smashed to driftwood. With an awkward sideways scuttle he fought the tide and gradually took himself away from the rocks. His heart was pounding and he felt giddy. For a moment he stopped to rest and wondered why the water round him was tinged with pink. He looked up and noticed that the mist had cleared enough for the cliffs to be visible and thought bitterly that if it had lifted a few minutes before Hamish would still be alive.

He had managed to get well away from the Creags. They loomed like grey ghosts through the thinning mist. He shivered and his throat constricted when he thought of his friend dead because he had again wanted to help the McKenzies. His head was spinning alarmingly and he knew he could swim no further. Why had he come out here anyway? Alick! To find Alick! He tried to shout but couldn't. He blamed himself for everything. There had been no need for him to have beaten Alick the way he did. It was an unfair fight. Alick had never been good with his fists but it had been the sight of him with Kirsteen . . . Kirsteen, dear lovely Kirsteen, she was like Helen sometimes the way she laughed. Helen and Kirsteen, Shona and Helen, they all looked the same because their faces were blurring in his mind.

Mirabelle came to him suddenly – she darted into his mind and wouldn't leave it. She seemed very near and he held out his arm to cling to her motherly bosom. It was growing dim, and briefly he wondered if it was getting dark. His senses reeled; he was floating in the sky and looking up at wavering water and the sky he was floating in reminded him of a sunset because of the pink patches all round him.

Alick looked out of the tunnel and saw that the mist was clearing. He trembled with relief. It was horrible in the tunnel: rats scampered in the dark and insects crawled everywhere. He wondered where Hamish and Fergus were; it was a good half-hour since they had called. He hoped they hadn't gone out too far but knew that once the mist cleared they would be safe because a fishing boat would pick them up. Alick was worrying more about himself. The claustrophobic panic he had experienced in the dank misty tunnel had made him resolve to get out as soon as possible. It would be easy enough to scramble down the cliff for a few feet then jump into the water where he could swim to the cave where he had left the boat. The thought of the cold water didn't appeal to him but it was better than waiting in the rancid tunnel till the tide turned.

He stripped to his underpants and shivered. It wasn't cold but damp and cloying and he wasn't used to such discomfort. He peered out again and saw that the mist was clearing. At first it had hovered several feet above the water but a warm wind was dispersing it. He smiled to himself. No one would give him much sympathy when he got back, except perhaps Mirabelle. She would fuss discreetly and make him drink hot broth and a toddy or two. Yes, good old Mirabelle would salve the wounds of mind and body. He gathered his clothes into a bundle and tied them together to throw them into the water. He would have to change into the sodden garments because he couldn't very well prance through the village wearing nothing but underpants. He smirked. That would give the old gossips something to get their tongues round. He glanced at the dark object floating about a hundred yards from the caves and thought nothing of it. There was always flotsam coming in with the tide. But something oddly familiar about the object made him look again and he saw his brother's dark head sticking out of his brown working jacket.

'Fergus!' he cried and without hesitation dived straight into the water. He reached his brother with a few swift strokes. At first he thought the helpless figure was without life. The face was deathly pale and there was no sign of breathing, but a pulse beat faintly at the temple and Alick let out a sigh of thankfulness.

'Fergus!' he shouted again but there was no response and he realised his brother was deeply unconscious. He wondered what had kept him afloat then saw the piece of driftwood Fergus had clung to before his senses left him. It had wedged into his shirt causing a thick weal on his chest but at least it had saved his life – what was left of that life.

Alick worked swiftly. He pulled Fergus to him and removed the piece of wood, then he put him on his back, holding his chin above water. He had decided to swim to the cave where he would try and haul Fergus into the boat and get rid of some of the sea from his lungs. It was then that Alick saw something that made him feel faint with shock. His brother's left arm was a mangled bloody mess. Skin and flesh mingled together and the bone of the upper arm had splintered and projected several inches from torn flaps of skin. Alick looked away in horror. He retched but nothing would come from his empty belly. In that moment he felt a sorrow and a love for his brother that he hadn't experienced since those far-off days of hero-worship. He felt it was all his fault and he gathered Fergus to him and wept into his wet black hair.

'Forgive me, Fergie,' he whispered brokenly but he knew that his brother had a long battle for life ahead of him and the thought spurred him into action. He swam to the cave with his burden. The boat had risen with the tide till it almost touched the roof but he struggled gamely to get the helpless body aboard. It was an impossible task. Fergus was slim but muscular and heavier built than Alick, and after several exhausting minutes Alick gave up trying. He leaned against the boat wearily.

'It's up to God now, Fergus,' he panted, 'if He can give me the strength to keep us both afloat till help comes.'

He didn't know how long he floated. It could have been minutes or hours. Dazed with weariness he kept drifting into sleep only to jump into wakefulness at the feel of Fergus slipping from his grasp.

He had no idea of time, but in fact only thirty minutes had passed. Voices floated over the water.

'Here! Over here!' he croaked joyfully. He summoned his remaining strength and floundered out of the cave. The men saw him and two jumped into the water to help.

'Mind his arm,' warned Alick as his brother was taken from him and dragged into the boat. The men stared.

'Good God, what a bloody mess!' whispered old Joe. 'It's the doctor for him or he'll die if he's not gone already!'

Alick slithered into the boat. There was no willing hands to help him.

'What's become o' Hamish?' asked old Bob grimly.

Alick shook his head. 'Don't – know, Fergus was alone – no one else.'

'And where is my boat?' asked Ranald, but no one was listening.

The mist had cleared considerably and the sun was breaking through. It gleamed on the Sgor Creags and the men saw the small splash of colour that was Hamish's kilt. They looked harder and saw that the Sgor Creags had claimed one of the finest men of Rhanna. They hung their heads and in silence took the boat round Port Rum Point to Portcull.

Kirsteen was waiting with a knot of others. She saw Alick stagger from the boat. In different circumstances he would have been an object for laughter in his drooping sodden underpants but no one gave him a second glance. They were watching the helpless figure of Fergus being carried ashore. In a dream of horror she watched the men carrying him up the shingle and for several moments she remained in a trance-like state. Her hands had turned icy cold and she felt numb. She so desperately wanted to run to that beloved figure, to find out if he was still of this life, but she was paralysed with the enormity of fear that he had been taken from her. Then her feet took wings and she fled over the shore.

'He's in a bad way, lass,' said Bob before she could speak. He raised his voice. 'Will someone ride over for the doctor? Tell him to come quick!'

'To the schoolhouse!' cried Kirsteen.

Todd the Shod scurried off and the men carried Fergus gently away.

'Where's Hamish?' asked Mathew anxiously. 'I told Maggie he'd be late but I didny think this late. She'll be keepin' his supper warm. Is he comin' in another boat?'

'He'll never sup again,' said old Bob grimly.

Canty Tam smiled with satisfaction. 'I knew the Uisga hags would have a Rhanna man . . .' He glanced towards the group of men carrying Fergus. 'And maybe another before the night's over!'

Bob was old but his fists were iron hard and Canty Tam never quite knew how he landed with such force on the rough shingle because by the time his head stopped spinning old Bob had joined the rest of the men toiling towards the schoolhouse.

Chapter Ten

Fergus floated in a nightmare world of fever and pain. He knew not where he was. At times he felt himself bobbing in an inky black sea. The water roared in his ears and his bursting lungs fought for air. From afar he heard terrible groans that he knew came from himself yet they were part of another self over which he had no control. He was drenched in moisture and someone with gentle hands kept wiping his brow but how could they be so foolish as to think they could wipe away the sea that kept engulfing him. Hamish bobbed beside him but always just out of reach. It was awful the way Hamish stared at him, a blank stare from eyes of death, but how could anyone be dead who had been so vibrantly alive moments before? That sea near Hamish was spuming with red, bloody foaming sea, washing in and out of the battered gaping hole in Hamish's skull. That other self with so little control over its emotions let out a hellish scream and Fergus laughed and cried with pity.

Sometimes the black curtains that veiled his mind were pulled aside and he saw white muslin curtains blowing in the breeze and white wallpaper sprinkled with blue flowers.

Voices came to him and his senses struggled to place them in the faces that floated before him. A little girl with bright hair and blue eyes, a lovely little lass, but sad and lost looking.

And a young woman, with hair that gleamed like corn, and a delicate sensitive face. Her mouth was firm but soft and the very grace of her features made her beautiful. It wasn't Helen; no, she was of another life, one which he felt himself to be on the brink of. It was there, barely out of reach, stretching into the caverns of velvet infinity. It would be so nice, so peaceful, to let himself drift through those caverns, to reach Helen who floated like a dazzling star at the furthermost depths. He called her name and the sound of it reverberated back, back, into the black tunnels, vibrating till he felt he must scream. He was afraid now of those depths and he struggled; great weights pulled at him dragging him down, down, but he gritted his teeth and pulled against them. He tried to cry out but now no sound would come. He knew he was opening his mouth but his throat was paralysed with fear of the dark depths surrounding him. Over and over he tried to call out and the wet tears of weakness and frustration mingled with the salt sea dripping from his forehead.

Kirsteen watched his struggles and her heart lay like a stone in her breast. Once more she wiped away beads of sweat from his face with a hand that trembled. She was so tired but would let no one else nurse him till she knew he was going to get better.

The folk of Portcull were kind. Fresh bread, bannocks, and bowls of broth were brought every day. Kirsteen was touched by these gestures yet she was too tired and worried to listen to the solicitous condolences offered by all and sundry. No matter how Rhanna folk felt about each other personally, when sickness came to one of them it was a matter of duty to call in and offer sympathy and help. A steady stream came and went from the sick room. It was Kirsteen's own bedroom; she had moved into a smaller room and Shona slept with her, snuggled in close like a lost little kitten.

All day feet clumped up and down stairs.

'Terrible, terrible just!' Behag Beag said the same thing each day. 'Ach, the poor laddie! A dreadful thing to be sure.'

Kirsteen knew the postmistress disliked Fergus and each day she tried to tell her not to utter her hypocritical condolences but somehow she couldn't get the words out.

Shelagh wheezed in and did nothing but cry at sight of the deathly pale face on the pillow. 'Ach, my poor lad, he's like death warmed up and him not knowin' about poor Mirabelle and poor Hamish. It's terrible just! I don't think I'll ever complain aboot my winds again and all these good folk dead and dyin'.'

Her words weren't designed to cheer a flagging spirit and Kirsteen breathed sighs of relief when the old woman left.

Dodie was the most constant and surprisingly the most comforting of visitors.

'He breeah,' he unfailingly greeted, stooping low to allow his tall gaunt figure through the low door. Because of the camped ceilings he always stood in the middle of the room and from this vantage point offered all sorts of hopeful predictions about Fergus's future. He was gruff and shy but in his guileless way he gave Kirsteen hope. Each day he brought a small gift; perhaps a sea urchin dried and cleaned, an unusually shaped pebble, carefully chosen shells, or simply an early autumn leaf glowing with red and gold. 'To press into one o' these books you read, miss,' he explained shyly, anxious that so humble a gift would be acceptable to a fine lady.

Kirsteen was deeply touched by the gifts. Dodie's simple mind saw beauty in the treasures of nature. He looked at the sunset and saw its glorious colours where a man of keener mind might look and see nothing but the sun going down.

He clearly worshipped Fergus and stared at him for minutes at a time. Love looked out of the normally dreamy eyes. Each time he went away he left behind his peculiar odour but he also left a feeling of hope and Kirsteen was grateful for even a grain of that.

The forty-eight hours since Fergus had been carried to the schoolhouse were like a nightmare. Fergus, unconscious on the couch in her little sitting-room, and the blood, so much blood from that poor mangled arm; she sitting beside him; thoughts, reality, all mixing together while she bathed the deep gash on his forehead. Alick hovering, making demented half-statements, blaming himself, crying like a baby, looking to her for a comfort she could not give.

Lachlan had seemed a long time in coming but it was only because each tick of the clock was another moment lost in the fight to save Fergus.

Then Lachlan, white-faced from a day already filled with painful feelings. His examination was quick and he wasted no time making a decision.

'Get ready the kitchen table, Kirsteen. The arm will have to be amputated or poison will set in.'

Kirsteen felt faint but went to the kitchen. Water was already boiling on the fire. Kate McKinnon and Merry Mary had kept a big pot ready for the purpose of making tea. Bob and several of the men had stayed, suspecting their help was going to be needed. They were drinking mugs of tea and smoking their pipes with the slow deliberate enjoyment of their generation. Word had got round about Mirabelle and there was a lot for them to talk about.

Kirsteen hadn't known about Mirabelle and she leaned against the doorpost.

'No,' she whispered. 'Oh God no! Mirabelle – Hamish . . . the bairn, where is she?' Her voice rose. 'Poor little Shona, she'll be so lost already and she doesn't even know about her father yet! He's to lose his arm! I've to prepare the table, Lachlan is operating here!' Her voice broke with utter despair. Kate McKinnon put a heavy arm round her shoulders.

'There, lass, greet now for it will do you good. Don't worry about the bairn, she's wi' Phebie.' She led Kirsteen to a chair. 'Sit you down – we'll get ready the table. It's no' the first time an operation's been done o' the spot. Auld McLure had to tak' off a pluchie's foot that got mangled wi' a heuck. Right out in the middle o' a field it was. Poor Sandy, he died – pneumonia set in but it was himself to blame. He swung that damty heuck like it was a wee pocket-knife. And there's myself,' she puffed out her bosom proudly, 'all but brought our Wullie into the world without help. Nancy was there right enough but she was only a bairn and couldny do very much! Aye, there's many a thing has to be done in a hurry, lass!'

But Kirsteen was listening with only half an ear. She was watching the sturdy wooden table being scrubbed with soap and boiling water and she shuddered at the thought of Fergus lying on it, not knowing he was losing his arm. She dreaded to think of the time of his knowing. Another man might at first be shocked but would learn to accept what had happened, but would Fergus? Could he, with his stubborn, independent pride, be happy to live without every one of his faculties in perfect order? Would he in time thank God it had been his left arm or would he blame God for what had happened both to himself and Hamish?

She wondered if he knew about Hamish. He certainly didn't know about Mirabelle. She prayed for his recovery yet dreaded his awakening to a world from which he had lost so much. But he still had his little girl and he still had her. Would he weigh those things against his losses? Did he love them both enough? Tears coursed down her cheeks and she shivered though the fire had brought a flush to her face. Merry Mary handed her a cup of tea. It was laced with brandy and made her throat burn but the heat glowed through her and when the men came in carrying Fergus she was able to help lower him gently on to the table.

Biddy had arrived. She looked old and very tired and Kirsteen realised she had just come from Mirabelle's deathbed. Her eyes were red and Kirsteen shook herself from her stupor and went to the hall where Biddy was removing her coat. The two women looked at each other. Biddy's chin trembled and Kirsteen gathered her into her arms. Neither said a word but the unspoken bond of their heartache was enough. Biddy gave a watery sniff and blew her nose. 'I'm fine now, lass, just an old fool I am but she was – ach she was my good friend – none better – there's gey few o' them left I can tell you! But it's sair your ain hert must be, my poor lass.' She laid her hand on Kirsteen's arm and a smile lit her weary eyes. 'Come on now, into battle. We must patch together that young upstart in there.'

'Biddy!' Lachlan's voice was threaded with impatience and unease. It was a disquieting sensation to see powerful, self-willed Fergus McKenzie lying so helpless, so completely reliant on the help of others. Lachlan's profession made him only too aware of human frailties but he had learned to accept its demands. How to tell loving parents their child was doomed, how to impart the news of the passing of a loved one, how to speak of a wasting disease? Time had given him the answers but it did not lessen the pain or joy of each experience. He had learned much about people and, early in his career, found that the humblest of humans had their dignity.

Fergus had dignity – that was a good point in anyone – but he also had a fierce pride.

Lachlan looked at the waxen features of the man who had ignored him for ten years. God, was it really that long? Yes, it did seem a long time, yet, was it not just yesterday that Fergus had accused him of Helen's death? Fergus had killed everything with those accusations of long ago. For a long time he had wondered about his abilities. Could he have saved Helen? He had fought so hard for her life but the battle had been in vain. Doubts had crept into his mind like thick black poisonous threads. No one but Phebie had known about them but even her staunch love had weakened at his continuing refusal to let her have another child. In the end, love had won but it had been touch and go, just another example of how susceptible human beings were in the face of adversity, yet love itself was strength and its power couldn't be denied.

Love and hate. Which was the stronger emotion? Fergus had loved with an intensity that made love itself a frightening emotion. He had hated too. Lachlan still remembered the dour black hate in Fergus's voice but it had been a hate born of grief and Lachlan had known that Fergus would one day regret his bitter words. He had regretted them and tried to make amends but by then it was too late.

Lachlan felt the sweat break on his brow. Everyone was looking at him strangely. He was delaying too long, they knew it as he did. In that moment all his old doubts came back, but he knew now that ten years was too long for two men to hate each other. But he didn't hate Fergus, on the contrary he liked the man in a strange sort of way. In the old days Fergus had brought an excitement to him, not the thrill a woman brings, but the excitement of shared male pursuits. There had been an affinity between them, a feeling of respect for the other's mood, when they spoke it meant something, when they were silent it was a shared contentment.

Carbolic fumes and tobacco smoke filled the stuffy atmosphere and Lachlan's head reeled. He knew why he was delaying. Fergus had accused him once before of letting go of something he should have saved; when he woke, and found his arm gone, would he accuse Lachlan of removing something he could have saved? Lachlan knew he couldn't bear such an accusation again. From someone else yes, from Fergus no, because after all these years he wanted to know McKenzie again, he couldn't waive the chance of a reconciliation by removing that arm.

Biddy had sterilized the instruments and laid them on a small table by his side. Everyone was motionless, the silence only broken by old Bob wiping his nose on his sleeve. He was at the head of the table ready to hold Fergus still if he should move during the operation.

Kate McKinnon was presiding over pots of water, keeping them at boiling point. Kirsteen had come forward, ready to help if needed, though she looked so pale Biddy ordered her to sit down.

'No, Biddy,' she said with quiet determination, 'I must help.'

They all turned as Alick came through the door. He had gone back to Laigmhor to change from the baggy trousers loaned by Tam McKinnon. The memory of the quiet house, with Mirabelle dead in her room, was with him still and his face was gaunt and grey. He was exhausted but unable to rest.

'Is . . . it done?' he croaked painfully.

Lachlan shook his head. 'No . . . no I can't! It's a job for a hospital.'

A general murmur or horror filled the air and Biddy looked at him sharply. 'Havers, laddie! There's no way of gettin' him to a hospital in time!'

'I can't save that arm,' groaned Lachlan. 'Bone, flesh, nerves, they're all mangled together! It's not humanly possible!'

'We know that, lad!' cried Bob gruffly. 'Just tak' the bloody thing off! If you leave it it will just poison the rest o' him! McKenzie's not a god, man! He's flesh and blood like the rest o' us and can die the same!'

Sweat ran into Lachlan's eyes making them smart. His hands trembled. 'He'll never know how bad the arm was! He'll say I could have saved it! He'll blame me if I cut it off, damn him!'

It was a cry from the soul and Kirsteen knew what his thoughts were.

'Lachlan, listen to me,' she said quietly. He looked at her and she saw the naked doubts in his brown eyes. 'Bob's right – Fergus is no different from any of us. You're a fine doctor, everyone on Rhanna trusts you.' There was a murmur of assent. 'Take off the arm, he'll die if you don't. Fergus will thank you, not blame you. I love him, Lachlan! Och, please give him a chance to live! Take off the arm!'

Another murmur of agreement rippled gently but still Lachlan hesitated. Alick whispered to Kirsteen, then went to a cupboard and uncorked a bottle of whisky. He took it to Lachlan and held it to his lips.

'It will steady you, doctor,' he assured gently. 'Take

a good swig, we all know what it's like to have a bit of the shakes!'

Lachlan drank. The bottle was passed from man to man and Kate McKinnon took a generous mouthful.

'I'll have a sip,' said Biddy with dignity and gulped so much old Joe had to thump her on the back. The incident relaxed the tenseness of the atmosphere and Lachlan scrubbed his hands once more. 'Ready, Biddy!' he said evenly.

'Ready, lad,' she said and passed him the scalpel.

Kirsteen never knew how she managed to stay on her feet but every pair of hands was needed. Blood ran under the knife and she swabbed it away. In a sick dream she heard the saw rasping on bone. Her legs wobbled but she mopped the life blood of Fergus with one hand and wiped sweat from Lachlan's brow with the other. Biddy was busy with instruments and Bob, stolid and calm, held Fergus's dark head in his gnarled brown hands.

Fergus groaned but Bob cradled him as if he were a baby and spoke in his lilting voice though he knew Fergus couldn't hear a word.

The operation was finished by the dubious light of paraffin lamps and it was Alick who carried away the bucket containing the grisly remains of his brother's arm. He stumbled to the shore, barely able to see for the tears coursing down his face. It was a night of fresh salt wind and racing green waves. He waded into the sea and disturbed a flock of gulls resting on a sand bank. They rose and screamed at him. He swung the bucket, throwing the contents far into the water, the gulls wheeled and cried, then descended in a cloud of flapping wings and tearing beaks.

'Eat it, you filthy scavengers!' cried Alick, his voice choking with sobs. 'It's no use to him now! Eat it, damn the lot of you!'

Fergus was in bed when he got back, the thickly wrapped stump of his arm resting on pillows to stop the blood flow.

'He's needing blood badly,' said Lachlan. 'I must take samples from everyone to find his group. Will you go and ask Biddy to round up as many volunteers as she can, Alick? I've still a lot to do here.'

In the end it was Alick who was the donor. He watched his blood being drawn and felt strangely satisfied. The act was a salve for his conscience and he even managed to pull Biddy's leg, telling her she was the most glamorous vampire he had ever met.

Elspeth came in to relieve Kate McKinnon from tea-making and she reported that Shona was in bed and had cried herself to sleep.

Alick started up. 'That poor wee bairn! I'd nearly forgotten her and her heart bursting with grief. The devil take this hellish day! None of it will ever be the same again!' He took a few steps forward and collapsed in a dead faint.

Elspeth looked at him with contempt and her sharp nose went up in the air.

'A weakling if ever I saw one.' She inclined her head upwards. 'And the other, too proud for his own good. It's no wonder poor Mirabelle has gone to the grave. The McKenzies spell nothing but trouble. The Lord knows how the wee one will turn out! A wildcat like her father, I havny a doubt!'

Kirsteen went forward and deliberately slapped Elspeth on both cheeks. 'One for Alick and one for Fergus,' she said with a venom she hadn't known she possessed. 'Pity you only have one face, Elspeth, because I should have liked to have slapped you for Mirabelle who loved her family, and for Shona who's a lovely sweet child! Now please get out from under my roof! I'll make the tea.'

Elspeth held her red cheeks and backed away.

'You deserve Fergus McKenzie, you wee spitfire,' she spat. 'He might make an honest woman o' you yet!'

She flounced out and Lachlan put his hand over Kirsteen's.

'We'll have nothing but outrageous tempers and tight lips for a week now. Phebie will have a hell of a time and I'll be regaled with it all when I come in weary from my rounds.'

Kirsteen's chin trembled. 'Och, I'm sorry, Lachlan but I couldn't help myself.'

He grinned. 'Don't be sorry, she had it coming. Now, young lady, it's bed and rest for you. We'll dump Alick on the couch and let him sleep it off. He's just exhausted like the rest of us.'

The whole of Rhanna seemed to be gathered in the yard at Laigmhor for the double funeral. The two coffins lay side by side, set on chairs brought from the kitchen.

Hamish's body had been recovered the day after he had been smashed to death on the Sgor Creags. The men had found him washed up on the white sands of

Port Rum Point. He looked crumpled and small in death, so unlike the splendid figure that had graced Rhanna for nearly sixty years. His red beard was tangled with seaweed and his clothes were in tatters. The tide had tossed him uncaringly so that he lay face downwards, exposing the terrible gaping hole in his skull. Brain and tissue were gone, picked by sea birds, and the remaining shell had been cleaned out by the sea.

The men were sick at the sight. They were tough men, hardened by years of reaping the harvests of sea and land. They were used to grim sights and were not easily sickened but it was hard for them to look upon the pathetic sea-sodden man who had been beloved by all who knew him. One or two of his closer friends turned away quickly and young Matthew cried openly.

They wrapped him hastily and took him to shore. Maggie was there, old-looking, a black shawl thrown over her shoulders as she waited for the men to bring Hamish. They hadn't been sure of finding him. If the Sgor Creags held on to him no one would get near enough to bring in his body; if they released him the tides and cross currents of the Sound could take his body far away.

She gave a little cry when the shapeless bundle was lifted from the boat. She ran to it but the men wouldn't let her look. 'Remember him as last you seen him, Maggie,' said old Joe kindly. 'He was a fine proud big chiel and these must be your memories.'

She stood now at the front of the huge crowd that filled the cobbled yard. It was a warm blue day, bees droned, and the scent of roses from Mirabelle's garden hung heavy in the air.

Two minutes before, the crowd had been astonished at the arrival of Mr and Madam Balfour of Burnbreddie. The carriage turned into the yard and the islanders parted to make way. They looked suspiciously at Mrs Balfour. Was she simply being nosy? She had never come to an island funeral before. It wasn't unknown for the laird to make an appearance when the older inhabitants of Rhanna departed life. He had played with many of them in his boyhood and got quite sentimental over their respective deaths, but his wife attend an island funeral . . . never.

She stepped down from the carriage and her diminutive figure crossed the yard. The laird followed, splendid figure in lovat tweed jacket and swinging kilt. At his side walked Scott Balfour younger of Burnbreddie, not so spotty as in adolescence, but still weak of chin and pinched at the nose, his full, drooping mouth almost hidden by a large drooping moustache. His mother laid a posy of red roses on Mirabelle's coffin. For a long moment she stood looking down at the coffin lid. Wullie the carpenter had done a fine job. The wood of each coffin was as smooth as silk and a small metal plaque was affixed to each. Not all the islanders could afford such grand caskets – some were buried in no more than plywood boxes – but no matter the style the departed were always given a good send-off.

The laird's wife suddenly burst into tears and went quickly back to the carriage. She had genuinely liked Mirabelle. There had been a quality about her, a devotion to those she loved that went far beyond the call of duty. She also had dignity and a spirited defence for anything she thought unfair. She had given 'my leddy' the rough side of her tongue once or twice but that hadn't detracted from her character; in a way it enhanced it and all she stood for. Oh yes, she liked Mirabelle and she would miss – oh how she would miss the exquisite needlework that had enhanced Burnbreddie over the years. She would never get anyone else to do such lovely work. Madam Balfour of Burnbreddie sniffed into a lace handkerchief.

The laird stood, with his son, beside the coffins. The laird thought of Hamish. They'd had many a dram together, and sometimes a game of cards in the long winter evenings. Often they'd gone shooting on the moors and fished the rivers. He'd regaled Hamish with stories of his female conquests and the big man had laughed, his deep, full-chested laugh, that red hair and beard of his matching the fire of autumn's splendour. The laird did not know that Hamish laughed because the pictures presented in his mind were hilarious. The laird thought the laughter was sheer admiration for his wiles with women and he had puffed with pride. He hadn't seen so much of Hamish since his marriage to that Edinburgh woman. The laird glanced quickly at the unhappy widow and his watery eyes gleamed. He would have to see what he could do to take her mind off things.

Young Burnbreddie stared at the coffins with no feeling but resentment that his mother had coaxed him to come. He felt foolish and knew that many eyes were on him. One day he would be laird. He didn't fancy the idea much, but at least he could do a better job than the old idiot who was his father. He had caught the old boy too many times fooling around, his hands up the skirts of those giggling middle-aged frumps who were never away from Burnbreddie.

He knew Hamish of course, but Mirabelle – she was that old woman who, according to his mother, had licked the boots of McKenzies most of her life. Mirabelle . . . a thought came to mind . . . a sunny day on Rhanna, himself a small boy tripping and falling into bramble thorns his screams bringing a nice motherly-looking woman from a nearby farm. She had taken him in, bathed his wounds, then plied him with freshly baked scones and strawberry jam. He had gone back several times and played with Fergus and Alick, who was about his age. But he had been sent to boarding school and had learned social refinements that had taken away his natural ability to make friends from all walks of life. School taught him to speak in a rather nasal way, certain things just weren't done, but it was considered smart to laugh at nothing and to browbeat those weaker than oneself.

A pang went through young Balfour's heart. He looked again at Mirabelle's coffin. The sun was hot and the scent of roses strong. The impulse that took him to the rose garden was entirely unpremeditated. He took a penknife from his pocket and cut a single pure white rose which he took back to place on the old housekeeper's coffin. 'Goodbye, Mirabelle,' he said softly and went quickly back to the carriage.

A few of the men were drowning their sorrows. One of them held up the bottle and shouted, 'Will you drink to our departed friends, laddie?' It was a jeer more than an invitation because few liked the 'college cissy' who would one day be laird.

Young Balfour hesitated, then he turned into the crowd and took a hearty swig from the bottle. His back was slapped by several crofters. 'Guid on you, lad,' said one. 'Share our bottle and our spit. You're no' so proud after all.'

A smile touched Scott's lips. 'I'd sup whisky from a chanty,' he commented cheekily and the crofters smiled dourly, recognizing a wit to match their own.

It was time for the coffins to be taken to the Kirkyard. The pony and cart were brought into the yard. Maggie watched dry-eyed. She hadn't cried yet, her grief was too deep for tears. Whisky was whimpering at her feet, a small puppy-like sound of utter misery.

Shona watched Mirabelle's coffin laid next to that of Hamish and she clutched Phebie's hand tightly. She had lived at Slochmhor for the past three days, though she slept at the schoolhouse. Occasionally she was allowed to see her father but the sight of him made her want to cry. She could hardly believe he had lost one of those lovely strong brown arms. She wanted to hold his dark head in her own arms, to touch him and tell him she loved him but he didn't know her, he didn't know anyone and tossed in his own world of dark fantasies. It was awful to hear him cry out. She wanted to comfort him yet she herself so badly needed comfort. At night there was Kirsteen's warm arms and soothing words but during the day Kirsteen was so busy nursing her father and had little time for much else. Slochmhor became a haven with its smells of baking and medicines, baby powder and wet washing. She played with little Fiona but for some reason couldn't talk to Niall. He comforted her in his awkward boyish way and she wanted to feel safe in his arms but he wasn't mature enough and she was too young to put her feelings into words. She mourned for Mirabelle yet didn't really believe she was dead. Tomorrow or the next day she would go back to Laigmhor and the familiar smells of baking and lavender would greet her.

She felt the same about Hamish. It was all a bad dream. He was still in his homely cottage with Maggie fussing and the animals weaving in and out of his legs. Soon things would be back to normal and Mirabelle and Hamish would be back where they belonged. Her father would get well – he had to get well. Nothing could take away the tower of physical strength that was her father. So she set up the pathetic barriers of self-deception.

The cart trundled on to the road with the line of mourners, stretching behind like a curving caterpillar. Hamish had relatives from as far as England, but Mirabelle had no blood relations to weep for her. Her sisters were long dead, nieces and nephews scattered afar. Nevertheless there was many a wet eye as she was laid to rest.

Elspeth stood apart and tears cascaded down her thin cheeks. She felt she had lost her last friend. Mirabelle had been the only one who had been kind enough to give her comfort or advice. Now she was gone and she felt very alone. She didn't even have the stimulation of an argument with Hector to sharpen her life. He had died the year before. The manner of his death had surprised everyone and dumbfounded Elspeth. He had gone to bed one night, very intoxicated, and was found dead the next morning choked by his own vomit. Elspeth couldn't believe that, after all the years of wishing a dreadful fate on him, he should die so suddenly and uneventfully in his own bed.

In a strange way she missed him. Life had held a certain uncertainty when he was alive. She had something to anticipate even if it were only a verbal battle during which they poured out venomous words and malicious jibes. He taunted her for not being woman enough to bear children and she goaded him to fury by pointing out that their childless marriage was caused by his impotency through drink. 'Your very seeds are burnt dry, you drunken pig!' she would rage and in a blind anger he would throw her on the bed and forcibly take possession of her angular body. Secretly she had loved those times, the feel of him ripping into her rousing her in a way that none of his ordinary attempts at love-making had ever done. The brute force of him inside her, his animal cries of satisfaction, thrilled her every fibre and she had pressed her hands to her mouth to stop from crying out in pleasure. Guilt at such heathen feelings took her hastily to kirk on the Sabbath where she prayed half-heartedly for a deliverance from her barbaric desires.

Without Hector she was lost, without Mirabelle she was alone, and she cried sorely as the minister's sombre words boomed into the hush of the Kirkyard. Biddy bustled over. 'Here,' she hissed, passing Elspeth a small hip flask. 'Take a droppy, it will do you good.'

Elspeth quickly composed herself and looked disdainfully down her nose. 'I don't drink – thankin' you just the same!'

Biddy straightened her hat. 'Och well, if you feel like that . . .'

Elspeth looked at the old nurse's moist sad eyes. 'Och well, a wee drop then . . . to bid Mirabelle a guid journey.'

Biddy guided Elspeth round the bole of a large tree. 'To Mirabelle,' she whispered hoarsely.

'And Hamish,' said Elspeth taking a large gulp without a sign of distaste.

'You've tippled before?' said Biddy, whose eyes were rather dazed.

'Betimes,' agreed Elspeth and gulped greedily.

Far below, a little girl with sun-bright hair walked to the schoolhouse clinging to Alick's hand.

'Father might be awake,' she said, trying not to sound too eager because she knew that Hamish's death and her father's illness were all somehow linked to Uncle Alick.

'He might,' said Alick too brightly. He lifted his face to the breeze from the sea and prayed to God for strength. He thought briefly of Mary and his life in Edinburgh but it was unreal. Rhanna, the dear green island of his boyhood was, for the moment, his reality and he would not leave it till he had made peace with his brother.

Fergus wakened peacefully. He saw the shaft of sunlight dancing on the blue counterpane and wondered what time it was. It must be afternoon because the sun didn't come round to his bedroom till then. But what was he doing in bed in the afternoon? And it wasn't his bed or his room. There was a huge bowl of roses on the window ledge and the breeze from the open window wafted their scent to him. There was another smell, a smell of medication, the way Shona smelled when Mirabelle dressed the many wounds of childhood. Fergus hated the smell, it made him feel sick it was so strong. His mouth was dry and he felt himself floating strangely. He sat up quickly and his head swam. The room wavered and he blinked to clear his vision. It was a glorious day. The fields were green and a bee buzzed frenziedly in the bowl of roses: a summer sound. He had always liked to hear the bees droning and he smiled with pleasure. He could see the Kirk Brae from the window and a long procession winding slowly to the Kirkyard. It was very bright and he raised his hand to shield his eyes but something was wrong! His hand wouldn't come up: he looked and saw the bandaged stump at his left shoulder. For a long moment he stared, frowning in puzzlement, then the shrouds unfolded from his mind and he remembered. It all came back slowly but the weight of each memory pushed him back on the pillows where he lay staring unseeingly at the ceiling, his thoughts turned inward, raking up each hellish memory that had been the nightmare fantasies of his unconscious brain. The search for Alick, the mist that had caused the boat to drift on to those terrible Sgor Creags that had killed Hamish. But no! It wasn't the Creags, it wasn't the Creags, it was the boat! Hamish had grabbed the boat and the bow had smashed his head to pulp. Fergus felt his heart twisting in pain. The memories were growing clearer by the second. He remembered knowing that something had happened to his arm but he hadn't felt anything, just the blood flowing round him in that awful sea of death. And Alick! They hadn't found Alick! Was he dead too? He looked again at the window. The funeral procession, could it be his brother? But how could it be? They wouldn't bury him so quickly. Everything had happened so short a time ago. He gave a short cry of terror and sat up to look at the procession again. He saw the cart turning and twisting up the brae and on it were two coffins. Alick and Hamish! His heart pumped wildly and he dragged himself from his bed to stare from the window but his legs wouldn't hold him and he fell in a crumpled heap on to the window seat.

Kirsteen rushed into the room. 'Fergus! My darling, come back to bed!'

She gathered him to her and led him back to bed and she sat beside him and smoothed his dark hair. His forehead was hot and he was coughing, a harsh dry cough. She looked at the pallor of his cheeks and his black eyes staring at her intensely. She took his hand gently.

'How are you feeling, my Fergus?'

He ignored her question. 'Kirsteen, you're ill,' he cried with concern. 'You're so – so white and there's black circles under your eyes.'

'Don't worry about me, Fergus. I'm just a wee bit tired.'

He closed his eyes and his breath was laboured. 'Everything . . . so strange,' he whispered. 'I'm in your bed . . . that's right, isn't it, Kirsteen? We've loved in this bed, haven't we?'

'Yes, Fergus,' she answered huskily.

'My arm . . . it's gone . . . I knew it – out there in the sea – I knew I'd never use it again.'

She breathed a sigh of relief. The moments of truth were coming but the one she had dreaded most wasn't so bad as she had expected. He was struggling to ask more questions, feebly astonished that he had been unconscious so long.

'That's why – the funerals . . . I knew about Hamish! God, will I ever forget the sight of him . . . but the other – Kirsteen . . . ?'

Footsteps came quietly upstairs and Alick entered the room with Shona. Fergus struggled up, his eyes burning into Alick's.

'Alick . . . y-you're not dead?'

Alick's chin trembled. He wanted to cry, he wanted to run to his brother and beg his forgiveness. Instead he said, 'No, Fergus, 'tis me still here – though I deserve to die for all the ill I've caused.'

Fergus shook his head. 'Havers, man! Everyone here knows I'm at fault, I shouldny have been so hard on you. I wanted to . . . say I'm sorry before but I'm saying it now . . . maybe too late for a lot of folk.'

Alick opened his mouth but could think of nothing to say. A breeze blew the muslin curtains, tossing the scents and sounds of summer into the room. The words of a well-known hymn were born faintly.

Fergus licked his dry lips. '*Abide With Me* – 'tis my favourite.'

Suddenly he noticed his daughter standing quietly by the window. He held out his hand. 'Shona, my wee lass, her hair all bonny with a blue ribbon.'

She ran to him and buried her face in his neck. He took some of her hair and fondled the silken strands. Suddenly he remembered something. 'The other coffin – was it old McTavish? I know he's been ill.'

'Oh Father,' Shona began to sob. 'It's Mirabelle! She's dead, Father! She died three days ago, she was ill and didn't tell anyone!'

'Oh dear God, no!' He turned his head on the pillows but too late to hide the glimmer of tears. Kirsteen went to him quickly. 'It was very quick, Fergus. She wanted it that way.'

He didn't answer but went on stroking his daughter's silken hair.

Alick shuffled uneasily. 'Don't worry about the farm, Fergus. I'll see to everything till you're well.'

Fergus remained silent. He was staring at the window but he wasn't seeing cotton wool puffs in a blue sky. His thoughts were bleak and he saw no glimpse of blue in the black of the sky. He felt drained. All his old power of mind and body were gone. Mirabelle floated into his mind but he pushed her quickly away. Hamish, tall and laughing, strode past the eyes of his mind but he blotted him out. He didn't want to think. His arm throbbed and pains shot through his chest. He turned to look at Kirsteen and the love in her eyes made him shut his own tightly. He didn't want to see that shining selfless love because he knew he couldn't marry her now. How could he ask a lovely girl like Kirsteen to tie herself to a one-armed cripple? His thoughts were wandering: he was going up and down; one minute it was light, the next dark.

'Lachlan – want to see him,' he mumbled. 'Must see Lachlan.'

But Kirsteen had already sent Alick to fetch Lachlan. She knew that Fergus's racing pulse and burning fever weren't normal.

Lachlan pronounced the diagnosis that Kirsteen had dreaded.

'Pneumonia! I was afraid of it, but luckily only one lung is affected! Even then it'll be a fight, his body hasn't got over the shock of losing that arm.'

Fergus slowly came out of the stupor into which he had sunk. 'Lachlan,' he rasped hoarsely. 'I'm – sorry . . . friends again?'

He lifted his hand from the coverlet and Lachlan took it almost roughly. 'Friends!' he said, swallowing the lump that had risen in his throat.

That night Shona slept at Slochmhor. She tossed and turned but sleep refused to come. The barriers she had erected in her mind were falling fast. She could no longer deceive herself into believing that Mirabelle and Hamish were going to come back. Her father would never be the same again. His arm was gone for good and he was ill, so ill that Kirsteen had made up a bed in his room to be near him all night. Biddy had been with him all evening and all visitors had been turned away. Not even Dodie, with his unquestioning faithful love for Fergus, had been allowed into the sickroom. Shona remembered the quick childlike glimmer of tears in his eyes when he heard that Fergus was worse.

He had stood in the schoolhouse kitchen, awkward and gangling, his huge wellingtons making scuffling sounds on the linoleum. To many he would have appeared a comic figure with his wobbling carbuncle and strange, inward, dreaming eyes. To Kirsteen and Shona he was a figure of tragedy. The tears had spilled and sobs choked him for a moment. Then he fumbled in his ragged pocket and laid something on the table.

'He'll get better,' he whispered huskily, convincing himself. 'This will make him better, och yes, it will just!'

It was as if he were trying to summon all the powers of healing to hasten Fergus's recovery. 'He'll get better,' he repeated and stumbled out of the kitchen to make his way back over the hills to his lonely little cottage.

Shona picked up the horseshoe he had laid on the table. It was an old one but it had been polished over and over till it shone. She could picture the old eccentric spending hours of love and devotion on the horseshoe. His initial was scratched on it, sprawling and untidy, but another mark of his faith.

Kirsteen took the horseshoe gently. 'We'll hang it beside your father's bed, it *will* help him to get better.'

Shona turned her face into the pillow and the hot tears spilled over. She heard Fiona crying and Phebie coming up to her. It was a nice house, homely and comfortable. She was in the little guest room and the sheets smelled of lavender. Lavender! Mirabelle!

Mirabelle and lavender! Laigmhor and Mirabelle! Laigmhor and her father! All the years of their life together. Lovely moments like today when he had caressed her hair and called her his bonny lass. His neck had been so hot and she could hear his heart thumping loudly in her ear. She loved his heart, it was a strong wilful heart but it could be so loving, so dearly loving.

In the still darkness of the little room she thought she could hear his heart beating-beat-beating, then she realised the beat came from within herself. She had never paid much attention to hearts before, they were just another part of the body to be taken for granted, now she knew when they stopped everything that had been a person stopped too. What if her father's stopped! He would be gone forever, all that lovely big man person would go away from her life! She couldn't take any more of her thoughts. Terror made her sob loudly and she could do nothing to stop herself.

The door opened softly and Niall padded in, holding aloft a flickering candle that threw leaping shadows all over the room. 'I heard you,' he whispered. 'My bed's right next to yours through the wall.'

'Is it?' She felt oddly comforted.

'Yes, we can tap out wee messages to each other.'

She felt the bed sagging as he sat on it. The tears were still catching her throat. He laid the candle on her dresser and his hand caught hers.

'I know how you feel,' he whispered sympathetically.

'Do you? Do you really and truly, Niall?'

'Yes – well, about Mirabelle anyway.'

'Do you know how I feel about my father? Is your heart all funny with wee shivers all through you?'

'N-no, but I'm trying to think what I'd feel if my own father was very ill.'

'It's terrible, Niall, so terrible you wish you were dead yourself.'

'Don't say that,' he scolded. 'Your father will get better, my father will make him, he's a good doctor. He's going to be friends with your father after this, I heard him telling my mother so. Grown-ups are awful daft, they wait till they're dying before they start speaking and then it's too late 'cos they might not live to speak to each other.'

She sucked in her breath and immediately he knew he had said the wrong thing. She was crying again, great sobs that shook the bed. Frightened, he tried to make his unthinking words sound reassuring, but it was no use. In despair he lay down beside her and stroked her warm brow in a shy attempt to soothe her. 'Och weesht now,' he whispered, 'we'll say our prayers and God might help your father. Don't greet so.'

His curls tickled her nose and she felt better.

'Stay beside me, Niall.'

'Very well then, give me a bit blanket and the coorie in. I hope you don't snore.'

She giggled, suddenly warm and secure in the embrace of his thin arms. 'Kirsteen said I talked a wee bit.'

'I don't think I'll hear you,' he mumbled into her hair and in minutes they were both sound asleep.

At the schoolhouse, Fergus was delirious and Kirsteen sat at his bedside bathing his forehead. Oh, how tired she was; every bone in her body ached for rest. Her eyelids were like lead weights and several times she almost dropped off. Lachlan had said he would come back after he'd snatched a few hours' rest. He'd wanted to let someone else sit with Fergus but she wouldn't hear of it.

It was a warm night. The window was ajar and soft moorland scents wafted in, a mixture of peat, bell heather and thyme. A dog barked from a distant farm and a sea bird 'cra-aked' close by. Kirsteen lowered her head on to the counterpane and slept.

She woke with a start and looked at the clock – 1.30 – she had been asleep for an hour. Fergus was moaning, repeating something over and over.

'Can't marry you, Kirsteen – not now – not now, Kirsteen. It's a better man deserves you. One arm – only one arm – can't marry you, Kirsteen . . .'

Her heart was like a cold heavy stone. She had been stupid enough to think he had taken the loss of his arm lightly, how wrong she was. He was too proud, his pride was like a disease, there was no fighting it, no curing it, she was a fool to think he'd come out of the accident unscathed in his mind. She covered her eyes with her clenched fists. She couldn't cry, all her weeping had been for Fergus and his battle for life. For herself she could only feel the exquisite agony of a mourning soul. She had lost Fergus as surely as if he had died. Her love for him was a growth, swelling in her heart till she felt it must burst, yet she must relinquish him if she were to keep her sanity. She would nurse his dear beloved body back to health then she would leave Rhanna while she could still go with some dignity. The decision left her drained. Lachlan found her sitting by the bed, her golden head resting on Fergus's hand, her blue eyes empty, gazing at nothing. She didn't even stir at the opening of the door.

'Kirsteen, are you all right?' asked Lachlan sharply.

'Yes, Lachlan, I'm fine.'

Her voice was hollow. Fergus stirred, coughed feebly, and once more began his fevered ramblings.

Lachlan took Kirsteen's hand. 'He doesn't know what he's saying, the man's delirious!'

She withdrew her hand gently. 'But he knows what he means, Lachy, the thoughts are there.' She shook her head and he saw that she had turned very pale.

'Are you ill, Kirsteen? You're tired, I know – exhausted, God knows – but is there something else troubling you?'

'No, Lachlan – nothing . . .' But she gripped his arm looking deep into his eyes. 'You're such a good man, Lachlan, you understand things – maybe . . .'

'Yes, Kirsteen?'

But she shook her head again. 'Don't worry.' She inclined her head towards the bed. 'Whatever way it goes – and God knows I pray he gets better – I'll be leaving Rhanna. I couldn't stay here now.'

'But your job! Dammit girl, you can't just give it all up!'

She smiled wearily. 'I'll write to the Education Authorities pleading illness. Don't worry, they'll send another teacher!'

'I'm not thinking about your job!' He was angry now. 'I'm thinking of you . . . and him, you can't leave him now, not when he needs you most!'

'Oh dear heaven, don't you think I need him! I need him so much I don't know how I'll live without him but I can't take any more, Lachlan. You've heard the gossips. I thought that was all going to be finished with but it seems not and I'd rather go before he tells me to! At least I owe myself some self-respect!'

His brown eyes were sad. 'There's nothing I can say?'

She shook her head vehemently but couldn't stop the brimming tears. 'Nothing, but thank you for caring enough to want to help. Now I must go and make us both some tea.'

For four days Fergus hovered on the brink that separates life from death. At times he was quite rational and recognized everyone who came and went. Alick was constantly at his bedside and the brothers rediscovered the kindred spirit of their youth. When Kirsteen was resting it was Alick who spooned broth into his brother's mouth. Fergus was inclined to refuse the nourishment but Alick was firm in a way he had never been before. It wasn't because Fergus was too physically weak to protest, for even in his fight for life he wasn't to be taken advantage of. The assertion that Alick had lacked all his life was at last coming to the fore. The last week had brought out a strength in him he hadn't known he possessed, but it was a strength of mind, a power born of a realisation that the thing his life lacked was the opportunity to make decisions for himself. During his brother's illness he had been responsible for the farm. There was no Hamish to turn to and he'd had to make many decisions. The men came to him and asked him things he knew little about, but his quick brain had helped him work out the best methods for coping.

Such a lot of tragedy had happened that summer on Rhanna yet he felt happy. Oh, he would go back to Edinburgh but Mary might not get so much of her own way in future. He wanted children and she was going to provide them. Perhaps a firm hand was what she needed. He had also decided to pull himself out of the rut of his easy job and look for something where he would have a say in decisions of importance.

His new mood must have showed. Fergus saw something in his brother that hadn't been there before. 'You're doing grand,' he would assure Fergus when his breathing was at its most difficult and he hadn't the strength to clear his lungs. Alick made him sit up and his back was pummelled till he cried aloud in pain but there was no mercy till he coughed up the thick red sputum.

Shona flitted from house to house like a pale little ghost, feeling she didn't belong anywhere. Phebie was gay and warmhearted but her life was a busy one. Alick was occupied with the farm. Kirsteen was loving and sweet as always but Shona sensed a withdrawal of the spontaneous affection she had displayed so readily in the past. Shona wondered why and shed lonely tears. She so badly needed to love and be loved. It was a time of great adjustment in her life and she needed to turn to someone. She couldn't know that Kirsteen, knowing she must soon leave all that she loved, was unconsciously steeling herself for the parting. She loved Shona whose every glance was her father's. His blood flowed in her veins, his defiance and pride were hers, and Kirsteen wanted to hold on to any spark that reminded her of the man she loved. Instead, she turned away and fought to hide her feelings from Fergus's child. Shona was hurt, but the pride that had been born in her wouldn't let her show it.

She went every day to the schoolhouse. She bathed her father's head and held the cup to his lips when he was thirsty. He smiled at her, a funny wistful smile and held her hand tightly. Often he fell asleep holding her hand and she liked to sit there just looking at him. He had always been so active and elusive she hadn't often had the chance to study him closely. How beautifully sensitive his mouth was; his jaw was strong with a tiny dimple in the middle of his chin; the tip of her pinky fitted in perfectly. It was strange to watch the pulse beating in his neck, it made her afraid, yet it fascinated her. Often she counted it beating to a hundred and more. It was a funny sad feeling to see him lying in bed. She hadn't often seen him in bed till this awful illness. His lashes were long and dark, curling a little at their tips. His hair was so black; she had always loved the way it clung round his head in crisp waving curls. Sweat plastered tiny baby curls at his ears. It was during one of her 'private looking times' that she noticed one or two small white hairs in his sideburns, they were very wiry and stood out from the black. The sight of them made her want to cry. She had always thought of her father as a big boy but those little white hairs belonged to a man not a boy. Each day after the discovery she studied his black curls and was thankful she could find no more of the wiry white ones. Eventually she grew to love the tiny white hairs; they were part of him and she loved all of him. She even knew how many there were, seven at the right side and three funny jaggy ones on the left. She hugged herself because they were her secret. Probably not even Kirsteen knew *exactly* how many of the little white hairs he had.

She could never look at him as long as she would have liked because either Biddy or Lachlan hustled her away. She didn't have Niall to talk to. He had gone to an aunt in Dumfries for a few days, to be fitted for his school uniform. He had grumbled about going.

'I canna stand the way Aunt Elly fusses,' he confided. 'She hops about like an old chookie and makes me eat salads all the time. I don't think she's *heard* of mealy herring or chapped turnip and Uncle George does awful things like picking his teeth at the table.'

Nevertheless his eyes gleamed. He liked the shops in Dumfries. His father had given him a whole pound to spend and he liked Aunt Elly's two boys who were very worldly without being superior.

Shona longed to see Niall's sturdy boyish figure. She wondered what it would be like when he was away all the time. There were only three weeks left but she pushed the thought far away and took Tot over the moors to the cave. Together they snuggled on a mattress of moss and heather. She was as lonely as Tot whose babies had been taken from her. Each afternoon they slept together on the bed, snug in the cave.

*

The days dragged on, each one feeling like a year to Kirsteen who spent most of her waking hours by Fergus's side. When he was asleep she just sat looking at him, engraving a picture in her mind that she might carry it with her forever. One day Biddy caught her staring trance-like at the strong handsome face.

'Aye, he's a bonny man, my lassie,' said Biddy with assurance. 'But time he had a woman to look to him.'

Kirsteen looked at the old nurse. 'What was he like, Biddy . . . when he was a wee boy?'

'A fine laddie but a strange one. Always quiet – not in a shy way but a quiet kind of strength – funny in a wee laddie but then his mother put too much upon his young shoulders. It wasn't right to make him feel he should never give in. But it was her way. She loved her bairns but ended up making one too reliant and the other . . . ach, poor Fergus – to him it's a sin to show weakness. It's hard to shake off the habit of years but I see a change in him, he's learnin' we're all weak in one way or another.'

Kirsteen looked over her shoulder at Fergus and a wry smile twisted her mouth.

'His pride is his weakness, Biddy.'

Biddy frowned in puzzlement. 'He's proud I'll grant you, too damty so for his own good, but what way is it a weakness, mo ghaoil?'

'Because he is not its master, it rules his head and his heart. His pride is the master . . . and oh God! how I wish he'd get the better of it! It has touched too many lives with its greedy need for power. A little pride is a good thing, Biddy, we all need it, but too much is a curse!'

Biddy looked mildly astonished. She didn't understand Kirsteen's logic but sensed that the words were a cry from the heart. 'There, my lassie,' she soothed kindly. 'You have a queer way of putting things but I think I understand a wee bit. Now, let's get his bed changed, you'd think a herd o' cows had trampled it for weeks!'

Kirsteen had already informed the Education Authorities she was leaving her post for health reasons and had asked that a replacement teacher be sent for the start of the autumn term. It was short notice but she didn't care, she was beyond caring about her responsibilities, she only knew she had to leave Rhanna. Every moment spent near Fergus weakened her resolution to leave him. Every sense in her was dulled except those that reeled with the engulfing love she felt for him. All else was unimportant and she knew she had to get away so that she could get a truer perspective of her feelings.

She tried not to think of a life without him, she only knew she wasn't going to wait for the moment when he must tell her he couldn't marry her. She couldn't bear that, she couldn't bear to go on as before, so she had to break away while there was still time.

The day dawned when Lachlan examined Fergus and pronounced him well.

'You've a heart like an ox or you'd never have come through. We'll fish the Fallan yet! It's been a while since I had a nice fresh trout for supper.'

Fergus glowered at the stump of his arm. 'Fish? With this? Don't haver, man!'

'The Fergus I once knew would let nothing stop him. Is it letting a little thing like losing an arm stand in the way then?'

Fergus struggled up. 'Dammit!' he exploded. 'It's fine for you to stand there and . . .' The rueful twinkle in the doctor's brown eyes compelled him to smile. 'Aye,' he said slowly, 'we will fish the Fallan and a damt red face you'll have when we weigh in our catch!'

With returning health came a growing awareness of all that had passed since the scented summer evening of his marriage proposal. He had lost so much, yet, when he thought of Alick and Shona, he felt he had gained a lot too. He felt closer to them than he had ever been. Alick was no longer a boy, the days of crisis had turned him into a man; Shona was a loving little girl again, throwing her arms around him with a zeal that sent him flying backwards on the pillows. His journeys near the deep valleys of death and his eventual escape from them made him vividly aware of the dear things of life. It was so good to feel those child's arms, the sweet, near, earthly touch making him respond with equal warmth.

In the lonely hours he journeyed back in time, reliving the years with Mirabelle. She had always been in his life and her going left a gap that he had only begun to appreciate. He still expected her ample motherly figure to come bustling through the door, scolding or fussing in the way they had all taken for granted, and tragically had never realised how much it meant till her motherly arms were no more. He couldn't bear yet to think of Hamish. The loyalty of the big Highlander was too near, too poignant to remember. Instead he forced his mind into the present and Kirsteen. In his darkest hours she had always been there. Even when his strength had reached its lowest ebb and his mind sank into one timeless abyss after another he had been aware of her presence, the power of her love reaching down, down into those dark depths, willing him to struggle out of them and upwards to meet her love with his. Because of her he had wanted to make that awful endless struggle to live and because of her he had won.

Propped up on pillows he watched her. He noticed that she was very pale with dark smudges under her eyes. His heart turned over with love. Her nights of nursing him had drained her, yet she uttered no word of complaint. She was quietly jubilant that he was getting better, yet he sensed a change in her. It was indefinable, but he knew that in some way she was different. He was suddenly afraid. He couldn't bear it if she loved him less than before the accident. He looked down at the useless stump of his arm. Was that it? Did his appearance repel her to some extent? But not Kirsteen! They had loved too deeply, he knew her better than that. Yet he needed reassuring, he had to know.

'Kirsteen.' He reached out for her, his voice husky. 'My dear little Kirsteen . . . do you still love me? I watch you and thank God for you! Are you still just a wee bit glad we met that day in the woods by Loch Tenee?'

She was taken unawares. She had steeled herself for such a moment but when it came she wasn't ready. She looked at him, at his hand reaching out for her, the naked doubts of her love for him in his burning dark eyes.

A sob caught in her throat and she was beside him, holding his head against her breasts. She ran her fingers through his thick hair and kissed the nape of his neck.

'I wish – oh how I wish we could have that day again,' she whispered brokenly. 'I loved you the moment I saw you. I wish we could have a thousand moments like that again, my Fergus!'

He wiped her tears away with a gentle finger. 'We'll have a million moments like that, Kirsteen.' He kissed her tenderly on the lips.

Three days later Kirsteen watched Rhanna fade into the blue of the sky. It was a hot day and there was no horizon. Sky and sea were one and the green island with its blue mountains was ethereal in the distance.

A group of sheep huddled on the boat, their plaintive cries rivalling the lost threading mews of the circling gulls. To Kirsteen the whole scene had a dreamlike quality. She felt she must soon waken to see Fergus smiling at her. She hadn't said goodbye to anyone, not even Phebie or Lachlan, because she knew they were hurt at her going and would try to talk her into staying.

The cross currents in the Sound swayed the boat, making her feel sick and giddy. Deep in her womb something quivered and stirred and she knew that she was leaving Rhanna with a child growing in her, its tiny foetal heart already pumping the blood of Fergus McKenzie through its living tissues.

Part Five

Spring 1934

Chapter Eleven

It had been a winter of severe winds tempered by mild damp spells. A short, cold snap in February brought the deer down from the hills and it was quite usual to see them sharing a potash from the same pail as an unruffled cow.

Dodie kept a special little supply of hay for the deer. Strewn a few yards from his cottage it attracted a number of the gentle-eyed, gracious creatures which he loved to watch.

Dodie was very contented with his lot these days. He had acquired several hens who supplied him with his breakfast eggs; as well as Ealasaid, he had a ewe in lamb. Fergus had given him the sheep in return for the horseshoe which he said had helped him to get well.

When March came the ewe gave birth to twin lambs and all three were housed cosily with Ealasaid because Dodie couldn't bear the idea of the baby sheep weathering the high winds. The ewe and her family trotted after him like devoted dogs and he shouted at them or waved his arms but to no avail. Inwardly his heart brimmed over with love for his animals and he strode over hill and moor in his flapping raincoat and flopping wellingtons with the sheep plodding faithfully behind.

He was helping with the lambing at Laigmhor and three figures in the field watched his coming.

'Dodie had a little lamb . . .' chanted Shona, giggling.

Mathew shook his head. 'Ach, he'll never sell the damty things. He'll make pets o' them and keep them forever! It's wondering I am you gave him the yowe, McKenzie.'

Fergus looked at the stooping tattered figure whose mouth was forming the familiar 'He breeah!'

'He has more in him than meets the eye,' said Fergus quietly. 'Dodie is smelly, dirty, and eccentric, but his heart's as big as his head! When he came to see me . . . the time of the accident, he left behind his stink but he also left behind his faith and I needed all I could get then. He's a cratur nearer to God than any of those kirk-going hypocrites who talk behind each other's backs. Aye, Dodie's a good man.'

Mathew said nothing. It was hard-going, working side by side with Fergus. Mathew was grieve now and honoured, yet awed, that he had been given such a responsible position. He was eager to please, yet in his own reserved way tried to appear nonchalant before Fergus. He was also embarrassed at having to give orders to men twice his age yet they had been pleased that he had been given the job. He was the likeliest choice. The other men had their specific skills whereas he knew a little about everything. It was what he didn't know that frightened him. He was marrying in the summer, the little cottage that had been Hamish's awaiting him and his bride. Fergus had given Maggie the option of staying on but she was unable to bear Rhanna without Hamish and had moved back to Edinburgh to live with a sister.

The prospects of the job excited Mathew. He liked and respected Fergus but he wished a thousand times that he had some of Hamish's strength of character and maturity.

'Bide your time, lad,' advised Bob. 'McKenzie didny pick you for your looks! Just ca' canny and don't put these muckle great feet o' yours in the shit afore it sets. McKenzie canny eat you, damn it! He's a thrawn bugger and respects a body wi' a bit gumption but see you don't tell him his business. Mind you . . .' Bob stroked his grizzled chin reflectively. 'He's no' so girny since his accident. I'd say he's learnt a bit about patience.'

Mathew took Bob's advice. He didn't indulge in superfluous chatter; he respected Fergus's supremacy yet, if he felt he was right and Fergus wrong, he clung to his opinions and was surprised to find that the older man acceded quite agreeably.

Shona ran to meet Dodie at the gate. He handed her a little bunch of snowdrops he had found growing in a sunless corner of his garden. It was March, late for snowdrops, so they were therefore all the more precious.

'Thank you, Dodie,' she breathed and held the frail white drops against her cheek. Snowdrops made her think of her mother because two months before, on her eleventh birthday, she had gone with Phebie to the Kirkyard and on her mother's grave had placed a huge bunch of snowdrops. Phebie had helped her to understand so much about her mother that she had missed because all the jealously guarded memories had been hoarded from her. Shona thought the story of her mother and father was a lovely one and she cried in bed when she thought about it; but for her it was really just a story – when she looked at her father she saw him not with her mother but with Kirsteen whom he had been going to marry but didn't. She wondered why. She had thought about it over and over and could find no answer. She didn't know why Kirsteen had left so suddenly and her father didn't seem to know either. No one seemed to know, not even Phebie who had been Kirsteen's close friend, but Shona suspected that all the evasive answers she received were the usual grown-up solutions for things they didn't want to discuss.

She would have found out from Mirabelle. Mirabelle had been evasive in her own fashion but in her guileless way she would let little things slip. She had solved many a mystery through the old lady's unguarded remarks.

Thinking of Mirabelle still brought a lump to her throat. A lot of the cosiness had gone from her life. Laigmhor had lost a lot of its homeliness since Mirabelle's going but the old housekeeper had taught her well. She was now adept at baking and could prepare reasonable meals. Kate McKinnon, all her family married except William, came in three times a week to clean the house and wash clothes. With her earthy tongue she was a colourful intrusion into the drowsing quiet of the farmhouse. Sloshing clothes about in a big tub, with soap suds piling over on to the floor, she regaled Shona with accounts of her family's latest exploits.

Shona knew that Nancy liked the physical aspect of marriage, everyone on Rhanna knew, but Kate had the privilege of knowing more than most.

'Aye, in heat is our Nancy,' she informed Shona as she lustily swished clothes on the scrubbing board. 'She tells me she makes poor Archie so tired of a night he can't get up in the morn to milk the cows. His father's sick o' it I tell you . . . mind you, he was a bit of a lad himself in his younger days! Aye, fine I know it too! We came home from a Ceilidh one night and he got me into a shed. Before you could blink, there they were! All hangin' out! Balls on him like a prize bull! His hand was up my skirt in no time and I had to slap his face for him. 'Tis a pity we have to pretend not to like the things we like but a lass had to hold on to her self-respect in those days.'

Despite Kate McKinnon the winter had been quiet. Niall's going caused a huge gap in Shona's life. She had plenty of friends. She played with them and Ceilidhed in their houses but there was no real intimacy, none of the real talks or lovely easy silences she had known with Niall. Always there was the feeling she was suspended in a world of expectancy, waiting for the holidays that brought Niall. When he was home she dropped into place again, and Rhanna, the lovely green island of wheeling gulls, windblown heather, ice-cold burns, and fragrant peat fires, was the same dear place of her yesteryears.

Christmas had been the loveliest she remembered at Laigmhor. For a week the weather was like spring with warm winds blowing in from the sea. It had been a Christmas of Ceilidhs, each one going into the small hours of morning. Tables groaned with turkey and mince pies, mealy black puddings, and potted herring. The fiddlers played and the Seanachaidhs told their well-worn tales. It was Shona's first experience of such traditional revelry, for her father had lately become less reserved than she ever remembered. Whether it was due to the influence of the McLachlans she never knew but he had changed.

While Ceilidhing, he sat quietly in a corner, but his feet tapped to the gay tunes of the fiddle. Sometimes he caught her eye and winked and a happy glow warmed her heart yet, though he appeared happier, sometimes there was such a look of sadness in his eyes that her breath caught and she wished there was some way she could dispel the look.

But that week of Christmas was no time to be sad. It was enough that for the first time in many years her father was mixing more with the folk of Rhanna and they admiring and respecting him for it. Many had thought that after his accident he would become even more of a recluse but he had gritted his teeth and faced the world, doing things with his one arm that astounded the observer.

Shona had completely accepted his disablement. It was no surprise to her that he could hoist her up in his one arm and carry her home from Ceilidhs. In the safe circle of that strong right arm she felt herself being jogged home through a world of night breezes and twinkling stars then being helped into pyjamas and tucked into bed, the last thing remembered the warm, fleeting touch of his lips on her cheek.

The Hogmanay Ceilidh at Laigmhor was the

loveliest of all. The whole of Rhanna seemed to be packed into a parlour that normally knew only the ticking of clocks; now it rocked with merriment. Biddy, praying that no Hogmanay babies would decide to arrive, got slowly and deliciously inebriated on the rather uncomfortable perch of the coal box.

'The wee buggers will keep till the morn,' she told a large glass of whisky and lapsed into a garbled Gaelic lullaby.

Elspeth had swallowed her indignation at the way Fergus had treated her in the past and condescended to help in the kitchen. She had smuggled a bottle under her apron and took frequent sips in the privacy of the pantry. Within half an hour she was humming untunefully while she buttered hot scones. Each utensil she used brought quick tears to her eyes.

'Ach, they were used by you once, Belle,' she sighed, gazing dazedly at a bread knife. 'It's honoured I am to be in your kitchen.'

Lachlan and Phebie came crowding in. Niall immediately armed himself with a handful of scones and deftly escaped Elspeth's scathing tongue. That night he tasted his first glass of wine and got up quite unbidden to sing one of the loveliest Hebridean boat songs. The lilting tune filled the air and everyone hummed quietly, swaying dreamily on the crest of each note.

Shona watched Niall. The room was lit only by one lamp and his tall kilted figure was outlined in firelight that made his fair hair gleam. It was then she noticed the change in him. His face was still soft but hovered on the brink of young manhood. His skin was smoothly tanned as always but on his upper lip was the faintest shadow, a mere breath of downy hair. His voice was different too, still sweetly falsetto, but occasionally an unaccustomed gruffness crept into the child's tones. She clasped her knees and swayed with the others but she thought about the changes in Niall. Barely five months had elapsed since he had left Rhanna but already she was seeing things in him she might never have noticed if he hadn't gone away. She wondered if she had changed and looked furtively down at her long legs and skinny arms. No, she decided quickly, she was still the same, perhaps a bit taller, thinner too. How awful! She was so shapeless and lanky. She wondered if she would ever get fatter. Mirabelle would have fussed and given her cod liver oil. Mirabelle! How she would have loved this night; a banquet would have groaned on the kitchen table. She would have grumbled a bit and been very hot with her mutch slightly askew and her long white apron floury from a day spent baking.

Shona dashed away a tear. This was no night to be sad, not with Todd holding the floor with his melodian and Shelagh 'hooching' loudly, her skirts held aloft to allow her black-clad legs better freedom. Her 'winds' forgotten for the moment, she gave a delightfully wrong interpretation of an eightsome reel, till finally she collapsed on top of an unwary Bob who was unfortunate enough to be lighting his pipe at the moment of impact. The pipe broke, Bob cursed, and Shelagh staggered to a seat leaving behind a loud 'Trumpet Voluntary' as an encore.

'Dirty auld bugger!' fumed Bob but Shelagh, sweetly oblivious, was sipping rum by the fire.

It was some time before Dodie was discovered waiting at the gate. Fergus had gone outside for a breath of air and saw the familiar, stooping figure, embarrassed, wiping his nose on his sleeve, and muttering profuse apologies because he hadn't known 'Laigmhor was Ceilidhing'.

Fergus had to hide a smile. The Laigmhor Ceilidh had been the talk of Portcull for days, everyone knew about it. 'Go away in, man,' he invited gruffly. 'It's daft you are hanging about here! They're having a good time in there.'

Dodie protested feebly. He had never been known to Ceilidh, a Strupak yes, a Ceilidh never.

'Come on, I'll go in with you,' offered Fergus. Dodie showed his teeth in a nervous grimace but allowed Fergus to push him gently in the direction of the door. Fergus got the impression that Dodie looked different somehow but for a moment he couldn't think why. Then he realised. Dodie had left off his greasy cap to reveal a head covered with fine dark hair. It had been combed into a middle parting, but though tamed by water, still sprouted upwards in jagged clumps. It was like a field of new grass and Fergus could not help staring; everybody stared when Dodie tripped on the rug and catapulted into the room. There was a sudden silence and Dodie patted his head self-consciously while his face grew bright red. Instinct had made the folk near the door move away, thus leaving Dodie all alone in a little clearing. But there was no need. Dodie had made history appearing at a Ceilidh hatless; he had broken all records by also having a bath. Carbolic fumes wafted from him and were even more powerful than his usual peculiar odour.

A loud bellow from the window broke the silence. Lachlan pulled back the curtains to reveal Ealasaid blowing steam against the glass.

Bob roared with laughter. 'The damty cow has followed you, Dodie! She wants to Ceilidh too!'

Everyone joined in the laughter and Tam McKinnon slapped Dodie's back. 'You'll be havin' a dram, Dodie! A large one. This is an occasion we must celebrate!'

Dodie grinned with relief and raised the glass. 'He breeah!' he said dismally and downed the drink in one gulp.

Shona smiled whenever she thought of that night. Dodie had become completely intoxicated and had been carried home by four equally merry crofters. Ealasaid had trotted behind the unsteady revellers, her bellows breaking uncaringly into the velvet blackness of the wee sma' hours.

The rest of the winter passed uneventfully except for the weather. Gales churned the Sound of Rhanna into fury and strong gusts forced the lobster boats to stay in harbour. Trees were uplifted by the roots and one had fallen over the schoolhouse, badly damaging the roof. The children were given an unexpected holiday while Mr Murdoch, the balding new teacher, tried to hustle the placid Rhanna builders into unaccustomed speed.

The winds screamed round Laigmhor making the inside feel all the cosier. Shona liked the evenings when it was just herself and her father. She read or knitted while Tot snored and Fergus smoked his pipe, his slippered feet up on the range. The clocks ticked and the firelight flickered and at bedtime she made hot milky cocoa. Sometimes the McLachlans left ten-month-old Fiona with Elspeth, and came over to spend an evening with Fergus. They brought a warm, happy feeling with them and when Shona went up to bed Phebie tucked her in and read to her. Afterwards she liked to listen to the murmur of voices from downstairs and it was so good to hear her father's deep laugh ring out.

It was good to fall asleep listening to the wind and the sound of laughter.

Now it was spring, with daffodils poking green buds to the sky, and the lambs arriving in ever-increasing numbers. She watched Dodie and Mathew go off to the lambing fields, then she ran into the kitchen to put her snowdrops in water.

Lachlan was coming along the road on the bicycle he used for his local calls and Fergus went to the gate to have a chat. He took out his pipe.

'Like to see my new trick?' he said, with his rueful grin. He'd had trouble lighting the pipe with only one hand. Now he placed the pipe in his mouth, held the box of matches under the oxter of his stump, and, with his right hand struck the match against the firmly held box.

'How's that?' he asked after the triumphant demonstration.

Lachlan smiled. 'You're nearly there, man, just as good as new.'

Fergus frowned suddenly. 'Do you think I'm as good as any man?'

'Better than some.'

'Then why . . . dammit why did she leave me, Lachlan? I've overcome most things. Did she think I'd be less of a man than I was? Why did she go away?'

Lachlan sighed. Fergus had confided in him over Kirsteen and he had been asked the same question several times. There were times when the trust Fergus placed on him felt like too big a burden, yet he was honoured that Fergus had trusted him with his innermost thoughts. 'You know why, man,' he answered firmly. 'She had some dignity left and she went before it was all taken from her.'

'But we were to wed! I told her that before the accident!'

Lachlan nodded and asked gently, 'Would you have wed her after the accident? Would that damt pride of yours let you?'

'In time yes . . . oh God yes, Lachy! I've been lonely too long!'

'But she didn't know that, she was at the end of her patience. She knew you weren't going to marry her and she had no guarantee you would do so.'

'Dammit, man I was raving! She believed things I said when I wasny my own master! She could have waited!'

'For what? You were rantin', man – aye, I'll grant you that! But these were the wanderings of what was in your mind. Admit it, Fergus! When you knew I'd amputated your arm you had already decided not to marry Kirsteen.'

Stark misery looked out of Fergus's black eyes. 'Aye

– you're right. But that was then. Now I'd marry her a thousand times over!'

'Then go to her – tell her! Don't let that proud heart of yours rule you any longer!'

'But she left me! And I've written! A dozen times . . . aye, and more, yet never a word back.'

Lachlan placed his hand firmly on the other man's shoulder. 'Go to her Fergus. For once in your life think more of her happiness than your own. She left Rhanna with a broken heart. You could heal it – and your own.'

'I'll think about it,' said Fergus gruffly, embarrassed that he had bared so much of his thoughts to another human. He returned to everyday talk with characteristic brusqueness. 'Have you a busy morning ahead?'

'No more than usual. I've to lance a boil, change a few dressings, Shelagh insists she needs an enema . . .'

He waved cheerily and pedalled away. Fergus walked slowly to the fields, his head bent, his thoughts going back to the time he realised that Kirsteen was no longer on Rhanna. He'd sunk into an abyss of lonely despair. Over and over he asked the same question. Why had she left him? They'd loved together – oh God, how they had loved. She'd given herself to him completely. He'd done things with her he hadn't even done with Helen, things that only a man of experience and maturity could know of. The exquisite beauty he'd known in her love for him couldn't be denied and he'd loved her with a depth he didn't think possible after Helen.

He had admired her sweetness of character and her quietly happy personality; there was so much about her he had loved and he had thought that she returned that love, that life would be an impossibility for her without him just as it was such an impossibility for him to exist without her. The realization that she had shown she could live without him had hurt him deeply.

After the misery and aching longing, came anger. How dare she leave him? He could well live without her, there were other things in his life! She could go to hell for all he cared. He went through a spell of being angry at everything. The curious, guarded looks of his neighbours goaded him to fury. They were waiting – waiting to see what course his life would take, now that he had a disability to contend with, now that Kirsteen had fled from him, leaving him to look a fool in the eyes of everyone. His temper had acted as a good barb for his pride; it was temper that first took him among the people he had known all his life, inwardly he fumed but outwardly he showed the world he wasn't a maimed object of pity.

Maintaining a deliberate calm he threw himself into the work of the farm. The men watched him, hearts in mouths, while he attempted impossibly difficult tasks, but he conquered each one and the men nodded their heads and told each other, 'Nothing will beat McKenzie!'

It was defiance that took him to the first Ceilidh but a joy in renewed acquaintances that took him to the rest.

Anger wore off and gradually the old feeling of hurt took over. He thought about Kirsteen continually; sometimes he could spend a whole evening staring into the fire, reliving some experience they had shared in the past. He grieved for her and his grief was all the keener because it was for a beloved person who was still of the earth. Often he would stop and wonder, What is Kirsteen doing at this precise moment? Was she thinking of him? Did she think of him with the deep ache he felt for her? Was she well? Was she – happy? But how could she be? Was not every one of her waking and dreaming hours tortured by memories in the same way that his were?

He wrote letters and tore them up again. Why should he write? She left him! But there came a day when he could no longer bear the burden of his thoughts. He poured out his heart and sealed and posted the letter before he could change his mind.

For three weeks he waited and hoped. The sight of Erchy whistling cheerily along made his heart lurch. It became an obsession to look out for Erchy's stubby; weatherbeaten figure. Mail came, but not a word from Kirsteen. In desperation he wrote one letter after the other but to no avail. There was nothing, not even a polite note to tell him not to hope any more. He'd written the first letter in January, now it was March and he felt empty. Was there really so much in his life? He had recaptured the love of his little daughter and in return he treasured her for the precious gift she was. There were Lachlan and Phebie, warm and trustworthy, so much more than mere friends. The rift between them was healed, and he valued them perhaps even more than if they had never known those years of misunderstanding.

Alick! Yes, there was Alick too, so close to him since

his accident and turning into a real man at last. He and Mary had paid a short visit just recently and everyone was astonished at the change in Mary. She was helpful and kind and so amusing with her dry sense of humour that everyone held her with a new regard. She was even persuaded to don wellington boots and explore the farm. Murdy's son, Hugh, was mucking the byre at the time, and the aroma of disturbed dung was somewhat overpowering, but she had held her breath and doggedly plodded into the milking shed.

She no longer spoke to Alick with contempt. Instead they wandered off for walks and laughed a lot. Inevitably they argued but Alick no longer gave her her own way and Mary looked at him with a new respect. He had left his office job and had found a less comfortable post in an Edinburgh store. He was assistant supervisor, his pay was less but the job was so much more rewarding.

Yes, Alick was a brother worth having, no other child was as endearing as Shona, no friends finer than the McLachlans; yet, despite them all, he was empty, feeling the hunger pains for a love which had no fulfilment.

He thought about Lachlan's words. 'Go to her, go to her, man!'

He'd reached the lambing field. Bob was whistling orders to Kerrie and the sounds of new life filled the air. New lambs wobbled on unsteady legs, tails bobbing frantically as they darted under their mother's belly for sustenance.

Dodie was skinning a dead lamb and putting its fleece round an orphan in the hope that a bereaved ewe would accept it as her own. Tears were coursing down Dodie's face because the task was distasteful to him but if such ruses helped orphans to a new mother then the job was worthwhile.

It was a mild, fresh day, and the scent of new heather blew down from the mountains. Fergus lifted his dark handsome face. He had always loved the rugged changing hills on Rhanna. They were like himself. Sometimes stormy and moody, at others peacefully calm. Today they were clear, slate blue scree showing through the bronze of last year's heather on the deep corries of the higher masses, new grass and bracken furring the lower slopes.

Fergus took a deep breath and made up his mind. At Easter he would go to Oban. If Kirsteen was teaching again she would be on holiday then. Shona would have Niall for company. Mathew was a good efficient lad, well able to run the farm for a spell. There was nothing, nothing at all to stop him going to Oban, to see Kirsteen again, to talk to her, be near her. His breath caught and suddenly he was like a small boy, wishing the hours away till the Easter holidays.

Fergus felt very strange leaving Rhanna. It had been a long time since he'd left the island. There had been cattle sales in Oban but that had been some years ago; he had been inclined to leave such things to Hamish who had enjoyed the buzz of the sales and who had needed little help when it came to choosing good dairy cattle.

The day was cold with a fresh wind blowing from the east. Fergus shivered slightly with a mixture of cold and nerves. A tight knot of apprehension coiled deep in his belly and he wanted to shout to the boat's captain to turn round, to head back for Rhanna and security; instead he picked up his small suitcase and went below to the saloon.

The picture of Shona and Niall waving him off from the harbour was still with him. Shona's chin had trembled slightly but Niall had placed a firm arm round her shoulders and she was soon smiling. He had watched them till they were tiny specks against the white blur of Portcull. Alick and Mary were staying at Laigmhor for Easter, and Kate McKinnon was coming in to help with the meals. Alick had been aglow at the thought of helping Mathew to run the farm and Fergus had felt strangely superfluous.

He was awkward and uncomfortable in his suit and he was also very conscious of the loosely pinned left sleeve. In his working clothes it didn't matter but in the suit he felt conspicuous and very aware of his disability. He lit his pipe awkwardly in a little corner and settled down to the long journey. Only Lachlan and Phebie knew where he was going, everyone else thought it was a holiday, a break after all his sad experiences.

He thought of Kirsteen. The idea of seeing her again made his heart beat strangely. A quiet elation gripped him but it was tempered with doubts and the terrible fear she would reject him. He didn't want to think beyond that, he couldn't think of a life that held no hope of reconciliation with the woman he loved.

Oban seemed big and busy after Rhanna. How different the busy harbour was from Portcull. Men shouted and groups of noisy children helped the crew with the ropes, hoping their labours might earn a penny or two.

The town had changed little since Fergus had last visited, there were more shops but the happy bustling atmosphere was still the same. He booked into a small hotel. It was homely and its unpretentious character suited Fergus. After a wash he felt better and, it being teatime, he went rather nervously into the dining-room. It was almost empty. The season was quiet because of the cold weather and the hotel was peaceful and uncluttered. Nevertheless he was careful not to dunk bread in his soup. Mirabelle had snorted disapprovingly at the habit but in his own kitchen he hadn't cared; now he was in unfamiliar ground and felt hot and uncomfortable. Though there were only two other people in the room he was aware of every move he made. The stump of his arm grew in proportion till he felt it filled the room and when his pudding came he pushed it away untouched and rose hastily.

He strode into the cold air and took a deep breath. He looked down at the piece of paper that carried Kirsteen's address and his hand trembled. A passing fisherman gave him directions and he climbed to the top of a steep hill with legs that felt like jelly. He looked at the house. It was clean and whitewashed with tiny attic windows. It was perched on top of a hillocky garden filled with crocuses and budding daffodils. A light shone in a downstairs window. It looked warm and inviting yet he felt a stranger, an intruder into a scene that held no invitation to him. It was an oddly sad experience. On Rhanna he had been so sure of Kirsteen's welcome – he had expected it – now he felt he had no right to expect anything.

He looked again at the house she had grown up in. How often her light, eager step must have trod that path – this road. He pictured her toiling up the hill, the long climb behind her, her face flushed and her breath coming quickly. He wished she were coming up the hill now, it would make his task so much easier. The light of welcome would surely come into her eyes. They would look at each other, not speaking for a moment, then they would laugh, take hands, and he would know that she loved him still.

For several minutes he waited, his eyes straining downhill. The lights of the town twinkled, a boat tooted, and a crowd of young men laughed in the street far below. His ears listened for the sound of those well-known footsteps uphill but he knew he was waiting in vain.

Again he looked at the house. The wind whistled up from the sea and, pulling his collar closer, he went slowly towards the little green gate set in the wall. For a long moment he hesitated at the door then he knocked demandingly before his courage left him. Seconds of eternity passed then quick, light steps could be heard within.

His heart pounded into his throat. Kirsteen! At last, Kirsteen!

But it wasn't Kirsteen who answered the door, though for a moment the dim glow of a paraffin lamp gave the illusion that the woman who stood there was the one he had come to find. The likeness was so marked he nearly cried out but in time he saw a woman much older than Kirsteen and her hair was brown instead of fair.

'Yes?' The voice was softly Highland but it held a note of impatience.

'Can I . . . is Kirsteen here?'

She held the lamp higher and stared at him. 'And who might you be?'

'Fergus – Fergus McKenzie. I knew Kirsteen on Rhanna and I was in Oban for a few days . . . and – I thought I'd look her up . . .'

The hissing sound of her indrawn breath made him falter like a small boy.

'So,' she breathed, 'you've come at last, McKenzie! Just a wee bit late, I'm thinkin'.'

'You – know of me then?'

'Know of you! My poor lass nigh broke her hert – aye – and her health too because of you!'

'But I wrote – my letters – she never answered!'

She inclined her head backwards. 'I never thought I'd be askin' you over my doorstep but you'd best come inside, for it's cold standin' there.'

The house was warm, with a cosy lived-in atmosphere, but Fergus was barely inside when he sensed that the homeliness was an echo of the past. The shabby furniture had known a lot of use, the polished floors and squares of carpet were well trampled and on the piano top the faces that smiled from photographs were of happy years the house had known. The firelight danced over the shadowy figures. There was Kirsteen, a tiny girl on her father's knee; Kirsteen, her arm thrown round the shoulder of a friend, happy tomboys with bare feet sinking in the sand; and

Kirsteen, lovely in young womanhood, her eyes solemn but a smile curving the corners of her mouth. And pride of place, Kirsteen on her graduation, the sombre gown and cap serving only to heighten the sweet youth of the girl who wore them.

Fergus felt an indescribable sadness creep over him for he knew, as surely as if he had been told, that photographs and memories were the only things of Kirsteen left in the house. There was no feel of her tangible presence and he wished that he had never made the journey to Oban.

'Sit down, McKenzie! Let me see the man that tore all our lives apart. I'd like to look at you properly!'

Mrs Fraser's tone was imperative and Fergus felt angry at being addressed in such a derogatory fashion. She was a match for him, he had sensed the ruthless strength of her instantly, and he resented her for it.

But he sat down on the edge of a chair. 'Where's Kirsteen?' he asked flatly.

'You may well ask.' Her tone was so bitter that he looked up quickly. 'Gone she is, my own daughter. She wouldn't bide wi' me and all I wanted was to take care of her, even after all the shame she brought on us! It's no wonder her poor father died! A broken hert it was. Och, he doted on that girl so he did!'

'Her father . . . dead?'

'Aye, just six months ago. She wouldn't do as we asked! We wanted her to go away and have the bairn adopted when it came! But no! She got heavier and the whole of Oban seeing it – and her – like a hussy she was! Holding her head high, saying she was *proud* to be with child!'

Fergus turned white and stood up to face her. 'Did you say . . . Kirsteen is having a child?'

'*Had* a child, McKenzie! Your child, two months ago! A wee mite of a thing he was and her so ill she nearly died. But she came through, she and the wee laddie! Och, a bonny wee thing – dark, like you, McKenzie. We can only beseech the Lord he doesn't grow up to have your selfish streak in him!'

Fergus sat down heavily. He stared at Kirsteen's mother. 'Oh, God no,' he breathed, 'why didn't she tell me? I loved her! I wanted to marry her. I didn't know about the baby. I swear I didn't know!'

'Hmph! And the pair o' you livin' in sin! *She* said you didn't know but how could we believe her after all the lies she told us about her nice, clean-livin' life on Rhanna! We brought up that girl to tell the truth and she was a good God-fearin' child till you warped her, McKenzie. *Proud* of her pregnancy she was! She wanted the child to remind her of you! When I think of her poor father! Och, he was a good man, and he'd already forgiven her when he died. It was too much for him . . . the shame, the disgrace of it all! He sacrificed so much for that girl and that was how she repaid us.'

'Where is she?' Fergus's voice was tight.

'God knows, I wish I did but I wouldn't tell you! She walked out taking that poor wee mite with her!'

Fergus gritted his teeth and stood up again. 'WHERE IS SHE?'

Her hands clenched together till the knuckles showed white.

'I tell you I don't know and it's the truth. She said

she was going to one of the big towns to find work. I begged her to stay but madam was too proud. Didn't want to be beholden to her own mother. Despite all, I was willing to keep her in my house. I knew all the neighbours were whisperin' behind my back but she was my lass and I stuck by her and that was my thanks. Gone three weeks now and not a stroke of a pen. I could be dead for all she cares!'

In a flash Fergus saw it all. The long weary months of pregnancy, Kirsteen, that lovely head of hers held as high as it had been on Rhanna; her father's death; the recriminations, the hints that it had been all her fault. Her mother's continued air of martyrdom; the birth of the child. Kirsteen's lonely soul tortured in a world where it must have seemed everyone had turned against her. He could almost feel her ceaseless torment till finally she had fled from all that was familiar in her life to an uncertain existence in some noisy, frightening city.

He put his hand to his forehead in an agony of remorse. But something nagged at him, his letters! He had poured out the love in his heart, his pen had written things that he hadn't felt himself capable of expressing. Surely Kirsteen must have known that he had mourned for her.

He looked directly into Mrs Fraser's eyes. 'Did she not get my letters? I asked her over and over to come back to Rhanna to be my wife.'

Mrs Fraser could not hold his look. She fidgeted but when she spoke, her voice was coldly defiant. 'The first came when she was in hospital too ill to be bothered with anything. The others came when she was home but I made sure she never got them! I didn't want her to go to you! Not after you treating her like a hussy! I wanted her to stay here – with me – her and the wee one, but she went – just like a stranger she walked away from her own mother . . .'

His hand dug deep into her shoulder and she cowered under the strength of his blazing fury. 'She never got my letters! You call yourself her mother yet you wanted to rob her of any chance of happiness! I love her! Do you hear me, woman? Now, because of you she's in some God-forsaken place and we might never find her!'

She struggled to free herself. 'Let me be,' she demanded furiously. 'Yes! I'm at fault, McKenzie, and I'm sick with the knowing of it, but who put her with child then said he couldn't wed her! You, McKenzie, live with that on your conscience if you will!'

All at once he was deflated. 'We're all to blame,' he said softly, 'but you're right, I am most of all. I want now to find Kirsteen and I want you to tell me of anyone who might know where she is.'

Her own fit of indignation had subsided and he got a glimpse of a lonely woman.

'Do you not think I've asked? Her friends, everyone she knew – aye, and they were many for she was a popular lass, but not a soul knows of her whereabouts after me burying my pride to ask. Fancy, her own mother not knowing, eh? Aye, the tongues have been wagging here for sure!'

'If you hear, will you let me know?' he asked abruptly.

She smiled coldly. 'If I hear.'

'And the letters, can I have them back? If I find her I'd like to show her those letters.'

'I'll not be having them any more.'

'You destroyed them?'

She didn't answer but was already at the door to usher him out.

'I'll be bidding you goodnight then, Mrs Fraser.'

'Aye, goodnight.' Her voice was so distant he got the impression that she had already dismissed him from her thoughts. He took a last look round the room. Kirsteen smiled at him from the piano. A photograph . . . if he could even have a photograph.

But she had read his mind. 'I'm sorry but I have none to spare.'

The door closed behind him. A cold wind whipped round his legs and he felt that what had passed had been a dream. He had imagined it all and in a minute he would knock on Kirsteen's door and she would answer it. But already he was in the busy part of the town, that little house in the dark hilly street far behind him. His mind was numb. All that he could think of was that, somewhere unknown to him, Kirsteen struggled to keep herself and their little son. Their son! He caught his breath and was only then aware that he was crying, there in the street, where people could see him. The salt breeze whipped him and his legs carried him aimlessly. Light streamed on to the pavement in front of him. He looked up and through a glimmer of tears saw a public house. He didn't remember opening the door but suddenly he was surrounded by talk and laughter, warm smoke, and the fumes of beer and whisky.

Two hours later he staggered once more into the cold night air. He was drunk, so drunk that he had to lean against a wall for several minutes. Shadows passed and the disapproving ghost glances of strangers made him laugh, a slurred lunatic laugh, induced by the disposal of nearly a full bottle of whisky. Fergus was used to a good dram. He had always been able to hold his drink but now he careered along the streets in the weaving motion of the drunk. He fumbled and found a cigarette. Standing still to light it was an even greater problem than walking. Over and over the wind blew out the matches.

'Bastard!' he shouted stupidly. 'Daft bloody bastard!'

He staggered on, gulping in smoke and coughing, the inside of his head feeling as if it were stuffed with cotton wool.

'Kirsteen!' he shouted into the wind. A light rain began to fall but he was unaware of it. Tears of self-pity poured down his face; his nose was running and tears and mucus mingled together. He bounced against a wall and hung there, his shoulders hunched and his eyes staring wildly.

'I've a son!' he told several passersby. They gave him a wide berth and he bawled out his lunatic laugh, over and over, till his ears rang. He was so drunk he felt neither grief nor pain. His cigarette burned into his fingers and he giggled; he unpinned his sleeve and let it flap in the wind from the sea, and all the time his numbed thoughts for Kirsteen and the son he hadn't known existed were expressed in the hopeless tears that kept trickling from eyes that were swollen and red.

He lurched and mumbled through the quietening streets. He began to feel sick and the lights in the streets were wobbling alarmingly. He was sweating and shivering and had to urinate. Drunk though he was, he looked round desperately for a toilet. There was none. Deep in the recesses of his mind his human dignity struggled to assert itself. He tried to make for a doorway but had no time. A young couple were courting in a dark little wynd. They were kissing and giggling and the girl was making little noises of protest. They saw Fergus at the exact moment he saw them. He felt the hot liquid coming from his bladder and he was horrified even in his stupor. Quickly he undid his buttons and the stream flowed from him, weaving down through the cobbles in little steaming rivulets.

The girl stared and giggled. The boy grabbed her hand and tore her away. 'Dirty drunken pig!' he hissed at Fergus. 'You should be locked up, so you should!'

Even then Fergus was unable to stop. He stood where he was till his bladder emptied itself then he leaned against a wall and was sick. Afterwards he felt better but still dizzy and drunk. He stood in the rain till his head cleared, then he made his way back to his hotel, thankful that it was quiet and he was able to creep up to his room unseen.

He fell on to the bed, dimly aware that he smelt of alcohol and vomit. His sleep was deep but unsatisfying and he woke early, shuddering when he saw the state of his clothes. He coughed and knew that sleeping in wet clothes had brought on a bout of bronchitis. Lachlan had warned him to guard against damp because his pneumonia had left him with a weak lung.

He lay back and looked at the ceiling. His head ached and he felt fevered but over-riding all were the hopeless thoughts that crowded into his mind. Dimly he remembered his drunken wanderings of the previous night and bitter shame made him cry out. He felt he had sunk to the very depths of degradation by allowing himself to get into such a condition. He was Fergus McKenzie, strong of mind and body; he wasn't some poor helpless animal who cared nothing for dignity. He was a man, a *man*!

He put his hand over his eyes and tried to will his aching body to move from the bed. He craved for a drink of water but his body wouldn't obey his mind and he fell back exhausted on the pillows and sank again into the abyss of sleep.

From a long way off a voice called him. He forced his eyes to open and the plump, good-natured face of his landlady wavered above him.

'Are you ill, Mr McKenzie?'

'A drink . . . just want a drink . . . water . . . that's all.'

She touched his brow. 'Why, it's fevered you are, sir, and you're coughing real bad, heard you on the stairs I did! It's the doctor I'm fetching. Now, now, lie back, I'll get Maisie to bring you a nice cup of tea and a bit toast. But first we'll get you into pyjamas . . . in your case are they?'

He struggled to sit up. 'Mrs Travers, I'll be managing these myself!'

'Ach – a thrawn one I see! You can put them on

while I phone the doctor. You're in a terrible mess so you are! I didn't think a gentleman like yourself would get into such a state.'

'Nor did I, Mrs Travers,' he said ruefully. 'Just a wee thing I had to sort out for myself.'

'Aye.' She folded her hands over her stomach and looked at him. She was a cheery little woman with pink skin and greying hair. Her experience of human nature had made her a good judge of character and she could tell that the crumpled big Gael was no habitual drunk. 'Aye,' she repeated softly, 'you'll sort it out in this bed for that's where you'll be bidin' for the next few days I'm thinkin'.'

She was right. Dr Mason was slow and lumbering but he discovered Fergus's weak lung immediately.

'Bed,' he said briefly, folding his stethoscope and stuffing it into a large pocket. 'For at least four days. I'll give you some pills to clear the inflammation and a bottle to ease your tubes.'

Mrs Travers had come into the room to hear the verdict. 'I'll see he takes them, doctor . . . and don't worry, the laddie will get the best of attention here.'

The doctor winked at Fergus. 'A real tartar but a heart of gold for all that. You stopped at the right hotel, lad – Maggie Travers is the best unqualified nurse in Oban.'

Fergus was strangely content to stay in bed in the bright cheerful room; it was a little haven; he felt shut off from the world and for the moment he didn't want the world so he was as happy as it was possible to be. He knew he was living in a fool's paradise but he didn't want to think of the future. One half of him wanted to go back to Rhanna but the other half rebelled against it. For the past seven months he had fully believed that the day would come when he must meet Kirsteen again, it had been there, always at the back of his mind, that lovely romantic illusion of their reunion. Now it had all been taken away and he was numb. He didn't want to think of a life without Kirsteen, he didn't want to face the thought of the empty years ahead, so for the moment, he pushed Rhanna, with its familiar things and people, far into the recesses of his mind. It was enough just to lie and listen to the outside world, the sounds of the waterfront, people laughing and shouting, just as long as he didn't have to take his place in that demanding world outside his room he was content.

Mrs Travers coddled him and reminded him so much of Mirabelle he put his hand out once and squeezed hers gently.

'You're good to me so you are. Why are you so?'

'Och, because I always wanted a laddie like you, and because that old bone-shrinker's right – I enjoy nursin'. My poor old Murdy only has to sniff and he's in bed cuddlin' a hot bag . . . besides . . .' She patted his hand. 'I liked you, son. You have a troubled hert and though I might not mend it at least I can try and keep it cheery.'

Murdoch Travers blustered in to see Fergus. He brought beer and a pack of cards and amiably helped Fergus to forget himself. He spoke about shinty and fishing, sunsets and boats, showing a breezy enthusiasm for everyday topics till even mundane things like having a bath sounded like a crazy adventure.

Maisie Travers dimpled into the room with washing bowls and food trays. She was the Traverses' only child and at the age of twenty-five giggled coyly like a schoolgirl and blushed prettily. She flirted with Fergus, bending low over his bed so that he got an unparalleled view of her smooth firm breasts.

One day he ran his fingertips over the smooth skin of her face and the feel of it brought back memories of what it was like to love a woman.

'You're a nice girl, Maisie,' he said softly. 'Why have you never married?'

'I've never met the right man,' she answered. Her green eyes looking into his and her lips parted showing small white teeth. On an impulse he drew down her dark head and kissed her briefly on the mouth.

'You will, Maisie,' he said gently. 'You're a bonny lass.'

He was well enough now to go into that world which had seemed so hostile to him. He stepped into a world of spring. Daffodils were bursting everywhere and the birds were singing. He looked around. This was Oban, Kirsteen's home town, he had to know the places she had known. He walked to the school where she had been a teacher; like a small boy he peered through the railings and pictured her there, blowing her whistle, calling the children to order.

He went to the hospital where she had given birth to his son and tortured himself with mental pictures of her writhing in pain, the way Helen had writhed giving birth to Shona. He trod again up the hill to the cottage with its gay blooming garden and its air of waiting for people of the past to step into the present to bring it back to life. A curtain fluttered at a window and he knew he was being observed. In a way he felt sorry for Mrs Fraser. She was like him, lonely and waiting and knowing it was hopeless.

He was grey and tired when he got back to the hotel. Mrs Travers tutted disapprovingly and made him go back to bed.

'First day out your sick bed and you tramp the streets for hours. Are you demented, laddie?'

He pulled the sheets round him. 'Aye, you could say that.'

'I know fine. It's a lass, isn't it?'

'You know too much!' he said grimly.

She folded her hands over her stomach in characteristic fashion. 'No, laddie, not enough! You puzzle me, you puzzle us all.'

'You've been talking! I should have guessed.'

'Discussing more like. A fine young man like yourself shouldn't be alone! You are alone, aren't you? Why else would you be here breaking your hert?'

He sighed and put his hand over his eyes. 'I was married . . . a grand lass she was! We were happy, very happy, then came the bairn, my daughter Shona, and Helen died having her. I was a bitter man for a long time – dammit I even resented my own child! But the years healed and a time came when I met another lass, fine she was, too good for me but we were to be married, then . . .' He indicated his empty sleeve. 'This happened. I thought she wouldn't want me and she knew it, she'd waited too long already! So she went away and it's nigh on eight months since I last saw her.'

She nodded. 'So you came looking for her?'

'Aye, I'd written but her mother kept back the letters, now Kirsteen's gone and no one knows where, she never even told her mother. What chance have I of finding her . . . she could be anywhere in the world!'

Mrs Travers sat down slowly on the edge of the bed. 'Kirsteen . . . you wouldn't be talking of Kirsteen Fraser, would you?'

He looked at her wildly. 'You know her? You know Kirsteen?'

'Of course I do,' she said softly. 'Oban's quite a big place but we all know the other and Kirsteen being a schoolteacher was well known – aye, and well loved too. Poor child, her mother wanted her to be a saint and her father just fell in with everything Maudie Fraser wanted. He was a kindly wee man but henpecked if you know what I mean. He loved his daughter and was proud of her – they both were – maybe too proud. When she came home from that island where she went to teach she came home with child and they nearly died of the shame! Oh . . .'

She stared at him and he nodded. 'Aye, Mrs Travers, my son – and I swear I knew nothing about him till that first night I set foot in Oban. Mrs Fraser would barely let me over the door but she told me enough to make me wish I'd never been born.'

'Your son, Mr McKenzie?' She studied him. 'Aye, right enough, that dark hair, and the dimple, just plunk in the middle o' his wee chin. A bonny wee mite he was. Kirsteen brought him round here often before she went.'

'Kirsteen's been here?'

'Aye, she was never a stranger in this abode. Near demented she was with her mother accusin' her o' bein' a hussy and a shame to the family. Blamed she was for her father dyin' and he with a weak hert for years. The lass was so good to her parents too, she kept them in bread and butter ever since she graduated. Her father wasn't strong enough to work, you see, and it was Mrs Fraser going out on wee jobs that saw her girl through college. But Kirsteen paid them back in full . . . oh aye, she did! She even sent money from Rhanna. Mrs Fraser was always going on about her good lassie.' She nodded sadly. 'That was why she took it so bad – the bairn, I mean. She gave the girl no peace. Oh, she offered to give them a home but can you picture it? The accusations and the tears? She could turn them on like a tap could Maudie Fraser. Yes, Kirsteen came round here often, Mr McKenzie, I saw her getting near to breaking, then I heard she couldn't take any more and she just went away one day and never came back.'

He grabbed her arm eagerly. 'Do you know where, Mrs Travers? Oh please God that you do!'

'Ach laddie, I wish I did but somehow I'm thinkin' we'll not be seein' Kirsteen again.'

He lay back on the pillows and her kind heart turned over when she saw the long dark lashes glistening with tears. 'There, laddie,' she said huskily. 'I know fine you love that lass and she will be loving you too. Ach, it's a funny old world so it is, but God will let you meet again.'

He opened his eyes and looked at her pleadingly. 'If you hear anything . . . any little thing that will help me find Kirsteen . . . will you let me know?'

She pulled a hanky from her apron and blew her nose loudly. 'You can count on me, son. I'd like nothing better than to bring the pair o' you together again.'

He looked at her seriously. 'I'm glad I met you, Mrs Travers, I don't take to a lot of folk and they don't take kindly to my dour tongue. Last year I lost two of the finest friends I had in the world and I've felt a gap at their going. You're a nice body and Murdy's a fine man, I'd like fine if you'd befriend a man like myself – maybe come to Rhanna for a holiday now and then. Laigmhor's a big place and there's only myself and Shona.'

Her face beamed with pleasure. 'Och, I'd like nothing better. We're quiet here out of season. I've never been to the Hebrides and Rhanna sounds a lovely island.'

Fergus looked out of the window at the grey clouds scudding across the sky. It was a windy, salt fresh day, the kind of day Shona loved. All at once he felt homesick.

'Rhanna is lovely,' he said quietly.

'And Maisie too?' Mrs Travers was saying.

He came back from his thoughts and smiled.

'Yes, Maisie too, though Rhanna might be a bit quiet for such a spirited lass.'

'Och, Mr McKenzie, Maisie's a shy girl, she's country

bred . . . and she's very fond of yourself too and I'm sure would love to stay at that bonny farm you talk about.'

But he wasn't listening, his mind was wandering over the sea to Rhanna, and he knew he was ready to go back. There was nothing now to keep him in Oban.

Part Six

Summer 1939

Chapter Twelve

Shona raced to the top of the hillock behind Laigmhor and shaded her eyes to look towards Portcull. She had heard the ferry tooting its funny little horn while it was still in the Sound of Rhanna.

It was a morning of pearly mist and though it was nearly the end of June the dew lay heavy in the fields. There was the promise of another long hot day and she was breathless when she reached the top of the rise. Her breasts rose and fell quickly and when she saw the ferry tying up in the harbour she fell to her knees on the wet grass and a soft little chuckle of pleasure escaped her slightly parted lips.

'Niall.'

She spoke the name gently, savouring the sound of it. The smell of peat smoke drifted lazily from Portcull and she breathed in the scent of it ecstatically. Everything was going to be wonderful that day. Niall was home. They had the long summer days ahead. He could forget about his studies at the veterinary college in Glasgow. Together they would roam Rhanna and while away the lazy hours of all the lovely lazy days. They always had so much to talk about yet just being quietly together was a queer intimate kind of happiness.

Tot came labouring up the hill. She was eleven now,

rheumaticky and slow, but still willing to leave her basket to follow her mistress.

Shona swept her up and kissed her silky ears. 'You're a lazy Cailleach,' she said lovingly, 'and I'm going to carry you the way I did when you were a silly wee pup. It seems a long time ago, I was just five and Hamish gave you to me for a birthday present.'

She stood with the old dog clasped to her and that day of her fifth birthday came back with blinding clarity. She remembered all the moments she thought were forgotten. Her father giving her the purse she still treasured; Mirabelle and the patiently knitted black stockings she had hated; Hamish with the wriggling bundle inside his coat. That had been the day she'd fought with Niall in the post office and Mirabelle had smacked her for her rudeness. She remembered it all as if it had only just happened but Mirabelle and Hamish were dead, her father was still as lonely as he had been on her fifth birthday. Tot was old and no longer romped.

Shona felt a little catch of sadness in her throat. For a long moment she stood, a slender graceful figure silhouetted against the sky, then her deep blue eyes looked again to the harbour and bubbling joy took the place of poignant memories.

She hoisted Tot against her shoulder and ran over the field path, taking the short cut to Portcull.

She saw him first and for a second she said nothing but stood among the trees watching. Every few months away from Rhanna brought changes in him. She had noted each different aspect of his growing years with surprise but with an acceptance that it must be so. Yet, though there were the inevitable changes, he had still remained boyishly handsome, his voice was gruff and a fine fair stubble grew on his tanned face if he forgot to shave, but the boy had been more predominant than the man.

Now she gave a little gasp of surprise at sight of him. She hadn't seen him since Christmas because he hadn't managed home at Easter. He had broadened and his chest was deep, his bare arms muscular and strong, and he was even taller than her father. But more than anything she noticed the fair little moustache. It changed his whole appearance and made the boy a man.

She shrank back among the trees, afraid that because he looked so different his whole character and personality would be different also. Then she heard the gay jaunty whistle and saw the corn curls bobbing in time to the tune.

A leaf tickled her nose and she sneezed. He looked up and she went flying out to him, a jumble of petticoats, sunburnished hair, and breathless giggles. He threw out his arms and she ran into them and he hugged her so tightly Tot wheezed in protest.

'Shona,' he breathed against her warm silken hair. He tore her away from him. 'Let me look at you – you skinny wee thing.'

'Och, Niall I'm not.' She laughed protestingly, wishing he hadn't pushed her out of his arms so quickly.

He saw the beauty of her slender, sixteen-year-old figure, and his heart beat swiftly. She was wearing a flimsy white dress and he could see the top of her breasts, the skin there was white and looked like satin and her neck was long and graceful. His eyes travelled to her face and he could see the tiny fair hairs on her smooth, peach-bloom cheeks. She was standing against the breaking sun and gossamer strands of hair gleamed like copper.

'You . . . look nice,' he said casually. 'You've filled out a wee bit since Christmas.'

'Is *that* all you can say?' she cried angrily. 'I don't like that silly wee bit hair on your face! You don't look like you at all!'

He threw back his head and roared with laughter. 'Well, *you* haven't changed! Still a damt wee spitfire! Caillich Ruadh!'

'I hate you, Niall McLachlan! Gordon McNab from Portvoynachan thinks I'm beautiful!'

Niall glowered at her. 'And who's he then?'

'Just – a man! I've Ceilidhed with him and I danced with him at Neil Munro's wedding. Four nights it went on – it was grand. I was drinking port and got quite merry and he kissed me twice.'

Niall grabbed her arm. 'You've never mentioned him before! Did he only kiss you?'

'I'm not telling! Anyway, it's none of your business. *You* never kiss me – well only like a brother – not that I'd be wanting it any other way,' she added hastily.

'I'm not letting you go till you tell me about Gordon McNab!'

His fingers were digging into her bare arm and she winced but he wouldn't give in.

'What about all the girls at the college?' she countered. 'Don't tell me you haven't kissed some of them!'

'And what if I have?'

Her nostrils flared. '*Oh*, so you have a fine carry on in Glasgow have you?'

'That I have, and a girl called Isabel is my special favourite. She lets me cuddle her a lot . . . nice wee arse she has too.'

Her cheeks were scarlet and tears of rage danced in her eyes. 'Och, you're a dirty bugger, Niall McLachlan – always did swear like a heathen!'

'You're swearing!'

'Who's Isabel?'

'Who's Gordon McNab?'

She looked at him and a twinkle shone through the tears. 'A lonely old man of sixty who's just come to Rhanna and does odd jobs at the farms.'

'And Isabel is the college cat who sleeps on my bed and has kittens twice a year.'

They burst out laughing and he threw his arm round her and hugged her close.

'Silly wee thing,' he said affectionately.

Dodie came loping behind them. 'He breeah!' he greeted mournfully. 'I have just come from Shelagh's house! She is asking for the doctor.'

'I'll tell him, Dodie,' said Niall.

Dodie paused to study Niall. 'My, but it's growing you are just. I thought you might have failed a bit in Glasgow. I hear tell it's a dirty smelly place with thon motor cars killing people all the time.'

Niall laughed. 'It's not like that really, Dodie. It is noisy and a bit smelly but it's interesting and I appreciate Rhanna all the more for being away.'

Dodie rubbed his grizzled chin thoughtfully but his

eyes were far away. 'Aye, there is that! I'll be goin' now, I'm needin' my dinner. Shelagh gave me a nice bit salt pork she couldny eat herself. Roarin' like a bull so bad in pain she is . . . terrible just so it is. He breeah!'

He galloped away over the hill track. The years had made little changes in him except that the stubble on his chin had changed from a dirty brown to a dirty grey.

Shona stopped at her gate and Niall squeezed her shoulder.

'The cave after dinner,' he whispered. 'I have something for you.'

The colour tinged her face. 'It's not my birthday.'

'It's a special thing, something I hope . . . och well you'll see for yourself. I'll be a bitty late for I have something to tell my folks.'

He strode off and she fancied his jauntiness was somewhat forced but she dismissed the idea as a mere whim of her imagination and flew up the path to burst into the kitchen.

Fergus turned from the sink where he was washing. 'Niall's home then?'

'Yes, did you see him?'

'No, but you're all pink and there's a sprite in your eye.'

'Father.' She smiled and reached up to kiss his sideburns. They were almost white, though the rest of his hair was still jet black. The touches of white only served to enhance his strong handsome features but it was one of Shona's favourite jokes to tease him about it. It was one of their 'alone together' intimacies, and he would laugh and retaliate by calling her his

'Sibhreach'. She had been thin and elfin-looking for years and the endearment had infuriated her at times. Now her mirror told her she was no longer an awkward bundle of arms and legs and she could laugh at the idea of being likened to a fairy spectre.

'I'll get dinner, Father,' she told him, putting an apron over her dress, and bustling about with a gay tune on her lips.

Fergus sat at the table and watched her. 'You're so happy when Niall's home,' he observed.

She set soup on the table and pulled in her chair. 'I'm happy all the time, Father – with you here – we're so warm and peaceful together. But – with Niall I feel a big bubble – just here,' she placed her hand over her heart, 'and I feel it growing to a million bubbles all bursting in funny little excited pops! Does that sound daft, Father, or have you ever felt like that?'

He stopped with his spoon in mid-air. 'Aye, I've felt like that, Shona, but it all seems so long ago I've almost forgotten what it feels like.'

She studied him and wanted to reach out and transfer some of her happiness to him.

'It'll happen again, Father, you'll meet her again. I know you loved her so much.'

For a moment he was startled and angry. He had guessed that his daughter knew far more about his thoughts than she ever revealed. She was quick and sensitive and a strange telepathy ran between them. He appreciated her deep intelligent mind, she knew how to be diplomatic, but at times she was too aware of his innermost mind and he resented it. A quick retort rose to his lips but her incredible deep blue gaze held his with unwavering love. 'I hope you'll never be hurt too much,' he found himself saying. 'A little hurt must be expected, we all know we can't go through life with our head in the clouds, but too much hurt can tear a heart to pieces and somehow the bits never fit into the right places again.'

It was the most he had ever divulged about himself. She felt honoured but tried not to show that the moment was so laden with intimacy.

'Och Father, be quiet and sup your soup,' she scolded. 'I've all those greedy hens to feed yet and I want to collect some eggs to take later to Shelagh. Poor old Cailleach, an egg is about the only thing she enjoys now.'

Soon she would be alone with Niall in the cave. The cave! Her eyes gleamed. It was their haven and as soon as she was free she ran over the heather with winged feet. The sun was shining in a blue sky and the world was a wonderful place.

The cave was cool and dark and she pulled bracken and heather back from the entrance so that sunlight found its way inside and dappled on the floor of mossy earth. She had come the day before to add new touches. The bed of stone was soft with sheepskins and cushions; the stone ledges were full of knick-knacks and some of Mirabelle's rag dolls sat next to cups and plates. Two old wickerwork chairs were positioned on either side of the fireplace on which stood a spirit stove and a paraffin lamp. It was like a real little home, each item lovingly gathered bearing a memory. She thought back to the day when the chairs had been smuggled from a shed at Laigmhor. She was twelve, Niall fourteen. They hadn't wanted the risk of anyone seeing them so had arranged to meet at dawn on a June morning. Five o'clock saw them struggling over the moors, each with a chair humped over their head. They had arrived exhausted at the cave and after fortifying themselves with liquorice sticks and chocolate fell asleep together on the sheepskins.

Shona fell on to the bed in a fit of laughter at the memory. A shadow darkened the doorway and Niall stood looking at her. He had changed into a kilt and old sweater, his favourite Rhanna clothes.

'Niall!' she said, the breathless laughter still in her voice.

'I thought I was hearing a demented spook of the Abbey laughing his lunatic dying laugh!' he chuckled, sitting down beside her. He looked round appreciatively. 'It's nice, mo ghaoil,' he said quietly. 'A real wee hoosie, is it not?'

'And would his lordship like a Strupak?' She giggled, placing an old kettle on the stove.

'And tea too? It's setting up house we should be.'

Her eyes were suddenly serious. 'And what could be nicer in the whole world than that? You and me in this cave and no one knowing where we were.'

'Ach, you'd tire of me and start throwing cups,' he laughed, but his tone was strange. She was kneeling, lighting the stove, and suddenly he bent and taking her face in his hands looked directly into her eyes. 'You're beautiful,' he said simply.

She felt hotly embarrassed and so acutely aware of his manly nearness that she rose quickly. 'I suppose you say that to all the girls.'

'Only the ones I like,' he teased.

She took down the cups and, keeping her face deliberately turned from him, asked, 'Niall, be serious and tell me – have you made love to a girl – really I mean?'

He clasped his hands round his knees and studied a patch of sun on the floor. 'We've known each other a long time, Shona, and we've always been honest. I'm a man now and I'm as human as the next lad. Yes, I did make love to a girl once but . . .'

She turned to face him and her eyes sparkled with unshed tears. 'Niall!' she cried.

'Let me finish, you wee spitfire. I did make love but I couldn't see it through because – because I kept thinking of you – dammit, I just couldn't do it!'

She turned once more into the shadows to hide her look of relief.

'Are you such a saint yourself?' he questioned roughly. 'I've been away a lot and – and I know for a fact there's a lot of lads daft on you! What about that then? Are you so prim as you make out?'

She met his blustering questions with a steady gaze. 'No, Niall, I'm not prim, I never was and you know it. I have been out with a few of the lads – I admit to it for you'll hear it anyway. Ti Johnston kissed me once and do you know what? I nearly spewed so I did. His mouth was wet and he smelled of potted herring!'

They looked at each other and laughed till the cave echoed.

'Och, Shona!' Niall wiped his eyes. 'You're a terrible girl but I'm glad Ti wasn't nice to kiss for you might have enjoyed it.' He grew suddenly serious. 'I've something to tell you, something you might not like, so promise you'll hear me out and not go running off in a temper.'

She glanced at him quickly, knowing now she hadn't been mistaken when she sensed the restraint in him. 'I half promise,' she said, forcing a smile. 'I can't help myself sometimes so it's no use making a real promise.'

He watched a spider making a web between some ornaments. 'I'm only going to be on Rhanna for a week then I'm going off to training camp. I volunteered for the Army and passed my medical and everything. There's a war coming, Shona and I don't feel right just sitting back and doing nothing. I want to fight for my country. I'm a man – and – and anyway, I'm going.'

There was a stunned silence. Shona couldn't believe her ears. The war and all it meant seemed very unreal to her. Rhanna was like another world. The islanders listened avidly to the progress and destruction of war but it was like an adventure story. Most of the men on the island couldn't possibly be spared because their existence, and that of their families, depended too much on the harvests of land and sea. A few of the young boys had spoken tentatively about joining up but families too often depended on young hands for the heavier crofting tasks and, as yet, it was all just a topic of conversation to most people.

Shona could feel nothing but an incredulity.

'Och, Niall, stop pretending! Your parents won't let you go. They've given you all those chances of a better education. You can't let them down.'

He took her hand gently. 'Shona, my parents know already. Och – of course they wereny pleased – not at first! I've just had an awful row with them! Father can understand but Mother is near demented.' He smiled indulgently. 'She has me dead already and me not even begun my training. She was begging Father to stop me but he's a sensible man my father. He's not pleased but he can see I must do what I feel is right. I'm young, Shona, I can go back to my studies later. Try to understand, mo ghaoil.'

Shona was barely listening. She was thinking how senseless it all was. She had read about the bloody massacre of the First World War. Between the wars there had just been enough time for boy babies to grow up and go marching into another bloodbath. They could all go if they wanted; if they had to prove they were men. Let them fight for medals that were often granted to them after they were dead – but not Niall, she was already proud of him, she knew the stuff he was made of, he didn't have to prove it.

She tore her hand away and raced outside to lean against the sunbathed rocks. It was very hot but she felt cold and trembled. She could do nothing to stop the tears coursing down her cheeks. The sunshine was blotted out and Niall appeared through a watery veil. 'Shona – my dear little Shona,' he breathed, 'do you cry with anger or with sorrow that I am going?'

She turned her face away but he took her pointed chin and gently made her face him. His head was very near; she saw the golden threads caught by the sun; his eyes were close and held her own with such a powerful intensity she couldn't turn away again. His skin was flushed and small beads of perspiration stood out on his forehead. He put out his hand and touched her hair and in a dream she felt his own hair running through her fingers. She hadn't even been aware of reaching out to him. Somewhere close at hand a bee buzzed but it was a sound outside of the world into which she had stepped with Niall. She heard her heart beating very fast then, in a rush of beauty and wonder, she was in his arms and he was kissing her. They had kissed before; short little pecks of affection, but now she was drowning in a tide of excitement. His lips were warm and firm and for a brief moment she could feel his tongue touching hers. But it was all so quick and changing. Their mouths were mobile instruments of pleasure. She heard a little cry at the back of his throat and felt his breath quickening. She sensed rather than felt his hands on her breasts, his touch was like a feather, yet it sent electric impulses deep down inside and awakened chords of desire she hadn't known existed. The feeling reached down even further till she was throbbing with a heat that had nothing to do with the sun. She too cried out and it was then he pushed her away almost roughly. She was still in the trance and he put her head on his shoulder and stroked her long burnished hair. 'Shona – I love you,' he said savagely. 'I've known now for a long time and – and there have been times in the last year when I didn't dare touch you or come too close in case – in case . . .'

She traced the curve of his ear and whispered, 'I've loved you since you were a wee boy and I was always so afraid you would meet someone each time you left

Rhanna. I love you, my Niall, and now you are going away.'

He didn't answer for a few moments but kept stroking her hair. The nearness of her, her sweet female scent, made him burn with desire. She had grown so beautiful; each time he came back to the island he saw some change in her. She wasn't very tall, her head came barely to his shoulder, she was fragile looking but so beautifully proportioned and so very feminine that, in the past, it had been difficult for him to be near her without wanting to take her in his arms. Now she was, and her lips, and that fleeting moment of touching the firm roundness of her breasts, had driven him so crazy with the need for her that he couldn't trust himself to keep her in his embrace.

He pushed her gently away and held her at arm's length.

'My little tomboy, when did you grow up to be so bonny? I've known you most of my life yet in a way I'm just getting to know you properly. You're new somehow, not like the old Shona at all!'

'That's how I feel about you,' she breathed. 'I feel we've played and talked all these years but we were just marking time – waiting for the moment when we would throw our old selves away and – and put on our grown-up selves. Does that sound daft?'

He smiled. 'It sounds like the old Shona, but I'll settle for a mixture of the old and the new. Now, would you close your eyes for a wee minute?'

She squeezed her eyes shut and felt him placing something round her neck. It was a gold locket, beautiful in its simplicity and when she opened it a tiny heart-shaped picture of Niall gazed out at her.

'Put one of yourself, next to it,' he said, 'and we'll be together even when I'm away.'

Tears of sadness and happiness made her voice funny. 'Niall – it's beautiful – I think I'll treasure it for the rest of my life.'

A return of boyish embarrassment made him redden slightly but again he clasped her hand in his.

'It's – it's a kind of engagement present really. I didn't want to get a ring in case you wouldn't accept it but – it's as good as a ring . . . isn't it, Shona?'

He looked at her anxiously and she leaned forward and kissed him tenderly. 'Better,' she murmured, 'much much better! You can't put photos into a ring.'

He pulled her close and whispered. 'You know it means I want to marry you . . . after the war.'

'I hate that man Hitler.' Shona's voice was vehement. 'With his silly wee moustache and cow's lick! Oh, I wish I wasn't a girl! I'd go to the war myself, so I would!'

'I'm glad you're a girl,' he cried with such passion that she held her breath. 'So very very glad! Sometimes you were a wee pest but that was a long time ago. I'm glad you're Shona McKenzie and I'm glad you belong to me.'

For the rest of the afternoon they walked hand in hand in the sunshine, not speaking much because the wonder of their love was too overpowering to be expressed verbally. Their eyes spoke volumes, they laughed at little things and squeezed hands, hearts pounding with the awareness of each other's nearness. Everything was doubly beautiful, a droning bee, the sea shimmering in the distance, the smell of earth from which sprouted the tough, swaying moorland grasses. Time flew on wings and Shona gasped when she looked at her watch. 'It's almost teatime, I'll have to run! Father will be in and not even the table laid!'

Niall clung to her hand at the gate. 'After tea?'

She nodded breathlessly. 'Yes, I promised Shelagh some eggs but later we could go down to the harbour. It's lovely there in the gloaming.'

Kate McKinnon had left scones and bannocks to keep warm on the range. Fergus had washed and was laying the table.

'Och, Father, I'm sorry!' gasped Shona.

He chucked her on the chin. 'When are you ever late, lass? I'm early. Mathew's a good lad, we got those bottom fields cut today. If the summer's a good one we'll have two crops this year. It's needing it we are. Last winter there was little feed for the beasts.'

She was dreamy and withdrawn all through tea. He watched her and knew that something big had happened in her life. He was afraid of change yet knew he couldn't hold it back. He had watched his daughter changing from a gawky child into a beautiful young woman. It was to him she had turned when, at the age of thirteen, her bodily changes had manifested themselves. Phebie had told her what to expect so she wasn't afraid but nevertheless needed reassuring. He remembered her pale child's face that day and thinking she was still too much of a little girl for such womanly things to be happening to her. She had looked too young with her long hair tumbling over her shoulders and her big blue eyes looking up at him as she sat in the inglenook hugging the hot bag he had given her to ease the cramp.

She hadn't been embarrassed, speaking to him with a natural ease about her changing body. Her simple trust in him had swept away any reserves he might have had and in the years that followed they discussed life and its facts with a freedom that made him proud of her faith in him. But he had known that one day she would have her secrets from him.

In the years since Kirsteen's going from his life he had desperately needed comfort and he had found it in the child he had once rejected. She, lonely without Mirabelle, and lost without Niall, sought to fill the needs of her warm and loving spirit and turned to the father she loved so unashamedly. All the love she had yearned for in her infancy was now hers a thousandfold; there was a kindred intimacy, so richly fulfilling, it was enough for her to be near him without the need for words. Her greatest wish was that one day he would find the happiness he had waited so many years to find. Even she had never been very successful at drawing him out but she loved him enough to let time work for them both. But that was when her own heart was happy and carefree. Now she struggled with a welter of powerful emotions, her mind whirled with thoughts of Niall and the implications of their love for each other.

Absently she fingered the locket at her neck and Fergus leaned over the table curiously.

'That's new,' he remarked. 'A present?'

'In a way, an engagement present from Niall, instead of a ring. Oh Father . . .' She sucked in her breath and her eyes swam with tears. 'Niall wants to marry me – after the war! We love each other! I suppose we've known for a long time but today it all just came out! I think it was when he said he was joining the Army. I'm happy . . . yet at the same time my heart is all funny and achey! I'm so much in love I could burst, yet I'm so frightened I could cry and cry! *You* know how I feel, don't you, Father?' The tears poured over and she ran to him.

'There now, my lassie,' he soothed, stroking her hair gently. 'Yes, I know how you feel – so well I know – only with you and Niall there's so much youth and hope. I'm losing my hope – and my youth!'

She tore herself away. 'No, no,' she cried fiercely. 'You're not getting old! You're so big and strong and I've always thought you were like a big boy! Even when I was a tiny wee girl you were just such a boy. You're not even forty yet!'

He laughed. 'Thirty-nine, mo ghaoil, but I've heard tell life begins at forty, so maybe there's hope for me yet. But you are just beginning and have all the strength of your convictions I once had. I'm glad about you and Niall. He's a fine lad and he'll come marching out of the war with his head held high. I'm not surprised he joined the Army, he's got Lachlan's spirit.'

She buried her face into the warm hairy flesh at the top of his neck. It was good just to feel his strength and listen to his soft lilting voice and by the time she had put eggs and cake into a basket and was walking to Shelagh's cottage she was feeling much better.

A gay whistle made her turn and Niall came up to

her. They said nothing but their finger entwined in an unconscious gesture of affection.

Shelagh wheezed and grumbled at them but they knew she was glad to see them. She was eighty-three. Her hair was snowy white and her skin unblemished and smoothly pink though in the last six months she had failed rapidly, her once pear-shaped bulk thin and frail. She was dying of cancer. Lachlan had discovered it long ago and had wanted her to go to a mainland hospital for treatment but she was adamant that her pains were merely caused by her 'winds' and no force on earth would make her leave Rhanna.

'I won't be having a strange doctor prodding at my belly,' she scolded Lachlan. 'And I won't be lying in some foreign mortuary like a lump o' frozen meat and maybe gettin' cut up like a yowe on a slab and me never there to do anything about it. No, no, laddie, it's the Kirkyard for me beside the friends I've known all my days.'

Niall seated himself on a raffia stool beside the old lady's chair.

'And how's my lass these days? Still driving all the men crazy, are we?'

'Ach, dinna be daft,' she answered with asperity. 'The only way I ever drove anybody daft was wi' my farts! Mind you . . .' Her old blue eyes twinkled. 'There was a time when I had the lads at my skirts but the dirty buggers were all after the one thing!' She chuckled wickedly. 'I watched you two holdin' hands outside. Is it in love you are?'

'Yes, Shelagh,' said Shona simply.

'Ach well, keep a grip o' your dock, mo ghaoil. This one looks a real buck.'

'You know then, Shelagh?' grinned Niall cheekily.

Shelagh was enjoying herself enormously. 'Aye, we all have our moments, and of course there's the things I was after seein' when I worked to the gentry. I could write a book but it would never be published for it would indeed shock the Sunday people!' She giggled.

'I brought you some eggs and a cake, Shelagh.' Shona wanted to divert the conversation. It was strange. She had always enjoyed the earthy humour of the islanders but now she didn't want to hear it in front of Niall. She felt embarrassed and a little angry that he obviously had no such reserve. His corn curls were almost touching Shelagh's snowy locks as they laughed heartily together. The old lady's high-pitched cackle filled the little cottage. A late sunbeam streamed through the open door and shone on the two heads, turning one to gold, and the other to silver. The anger left Shona and in its place came sadness. Shelagh had so little time, yet she showed no sign of fear and could still laugh merrily though she suffered constant pain. Shona's anger was turned against herself for grudging the old woman a little pleasure. 'I hope you like the cake, you daft Cailleach,' she smiled. 'I made it myself with a wee spot rum to warm you up.'

Shelagh smiled coyly. 'Oh did you now? And what would I be wantin' wi' rum in a cake? It's a good measure in a glass I'm needin' but I'll eat a wee bit o' your cake though it will likely give me a bad dose o' the winds.'

A spasm of pain twisted her mouth and Shona saw that she was very weary.

'We'll be going, Shelagh,' she said gently. 'Let you get on with that awful shocking book you're going to write.'

Shelagh gripped her hand. 'I doubt if I've enough time to write a letter, my wee lass. Away you go now, it must be good to be young and to know that death is far away. I'm glad the pair o' you have discovered each other. All those years . . . I've watched you both growin' . . . never one without the other . . . it's right you should fall in love. And thank you for the eggs, they're grand so they are. I miss a fresh egg since I had to give up my own hens.'

Old Joe came in, his cheeks as smooth and round as ever, and his sea green eyes twinkling but not quite so brightly when he looked at Shelagh.

'How's the whining old bugger?' he greeted his cousin with brusque affection. 'Still weathering the storm, is it?'

'She'll see the snows of many a winter yet,' said Niall too brightly.

Shelagh nodded her head calmly. 'The autumn will see me out. I'll go wi' the leaves o' summer.'

Niall bent and kissed her on the cheek.

'You young bull,' she cackled but she was thrilled.

'You're fond of old Shelagh,' observed Shona when they were strolling down to the harbour. 'It was nice – the way you kissed her.'

'I know she won't be here when next I come back to Rhanna,' he said quietly and when she glanced at him she saw the glaze of unshed tears in his brown eyes. She knew his heart cried for the dear, familiar people they had once thought immortal.

It was peaceful at the harbour. The smell of tar hung in the air and the gulls mewed placidly as they rummaged in the seaweed for small marine creatures. The sky was pure blue with a touch of gold on the horizon and darkness would never fall completely on such a June evening. Hand in hand they ran over the wooden planks of the pier and stopped to look breathlessly at the unbelievably brilliant royal blue of the Sound of Rhanna.

'Such a night,' whispered Shona. 'It's perfect.'

He drew her close and kissed her full on the lips. 'I'll never forget this day and I'll always remember how you look now – with your hair on fire against the set of the sun, and a smudge of peat soot on your nose. Hold still till I wipe it off.'

He took out a rather grubby handkerchief, wet it in a salty puddle, then scrubbed her nose till she giggled, 'Och Niall, they'll be peeking behind their curtains and thinking we're daft. You know what they're like.'

'I want them to know about us. The world can watch me kissing you and washing your face with water from the sea. I want to shout to everyone that I love you. I don't care what anyone thinks!'

He grabbed her hand again and they ran to the end of the pier. A number of fishing boats were bobbing gently, shadowed waves slapping against their hulls. A dog barked from one; an old fisherman, pipe hanging from his mouth, worked with lobster pots on another, but several craft were deserted.

'C'mon,' said Niall and they clambered aboard the

nearest to snuggle among tarpaulin and ropes. They lay in each other's arms and the sea rocked them.

'I love boats,' said Shona. 'They're lovely, smelly, exciting things.' She propped herself on an elbow. 'It's lovely to see Portcull in the gloaming. The men will be eating supper and the children maybe having a scrub in the zinc tub before bed. Look at the reek from the chimneys – spiralling into the sky without a breath to blow it away.'

He propped himself up to look at the picture she described but her nearness disturbed any attempt at concentration. He slid his arm round her waist to pull her closer. For a moment she was dimly aware of the cloudless sky above before his head blotted everything out and she was once again oblivious to all but his lips doing things with hers that made her feel she was drowning in a world of ecstasy. She knew she was responding to him with the desires of a full grown woman. That morning she had still been a child; tonight she was a woman and she knew her life would never be the same again. She would think of Niall but her thoughts would hold all these lovely intimate secrets that were happening now. For a moment she was afraid of the strength of his passion. Fleetingly she tried to remember what he had been like on his last visit home but strangely she was unable to visualize the boyish, mischievous Niall of yesteryears; not now, when he was groaning deep in his throat and she could feel the hardness of his young body pressed to her own. He was murmuring her name over and over and his brown eyes held a look she had never seen before. She ran her fingers through his hair, feeling the warm dampness at the nape of his neck. Again his hands caressed her breasts and she closed her eyes, wanting the night of warm desire and clinging bodies to last forever, but a screaming gull, and voices on the shore called her to reality. 'Niall,' she whispered urgently, 'stop now please.'

He fell back on the deck his breath coming quickly. After a while he caught her hand and kissed it. 'I'm sorry, mo ghaoil. You make me forget everything when I'm near you. It's as well you stopped me.'

She kissed his warm forehead. 'I heard people but – I think I would have stopped anyway. We – we don't know each other well enough yet.'

He saw that she was serious but he couldn't suppress a yell of mirth. 'You dear funny wee thing!' He leaned on an elbow. 'Look, the water's lovely. Let's go for a paddle, I need something to cool me down.'

They were carefree again, divesting themselves of shoes and stockings to splash in the clear brown shallows. A few Portcull children watched longingly till, unable to resist, they too were dancing in the water, risking a scolding from parents for coming home with damp hems and wet knickers.

Morag Ruadh came along, combing the beach for driftwood. 'A fine night,' she observed, looking disapprovingly at Shona's skirt tucked into her knickers, 'but 'tis chilled you'll get with the sea splashin' up your backsides.'

'Och, it's lovely, Morag,' laughed Niall. 'It's up with your skirt, off with your shoes, and in you should be yourself!'

'Havers,' sniffed Morag, 'it's stiff feets I would be

getting and not able to get a note of sense out of the harmonium on the Sabbath, forbye the fact that I would not be able to spin my cloth and there's some of us must work for a living.' She glanced proudly at her long nimble fingers. 'Without me our house would go to ruin. I tell you. My mother has hands like cow's feets and my father just spends his days damping the peat with his spit. But the day will come . . .' She was already drifting away . . . 'when I'll be after marrying and where will we all be then?'

Shona giggled. 'Poor Morag Ruadh, she's waited for a man for years and thinks that the world will fall to pieces if she ever gets wed. I know for a fact Totie Little has waited years to get a chance to play the organ and poor old Mr and Mrs McDonald love it when Morag's out the house so that they can get a rest from her tongue.'

Niall grinned. 'It's her red hair that makes her tongue go – just like yours. All you Caillich Ruadhs have bad tempers!'

She bent to pick up a shoe to throw at him but he was already halfway up the beach, leaving a trail of footprints in the sand. She ran after him and they walked hand in hand through Portcull carrying their shoes. They took the path through the fields and the delicious fragrance of new-cut grass filled their nostrils. At the top of the field they stood for a moment, looking down at the roofs and chimneys of Laigmhor.

'Father will be making cocoa,' she said softly. 'I'd better put on my shoes and stockings or he will wonder what I've been doing.'

She squatted down on the grass and Niall sat beside

her. He caught her hand and kissed her briefly. 'We won't give him any reason to worry,' he said seriously. 'We won't give ourselves the opportunity for being alone very often. I love you too much to want to do anything to harm you so I think it would be a good idea to take Fiona with us. I promised her a picnic and a day in one of Ranald's boats. She's a wee pest I know but she'll keep me in order. Do you mind?'

'No, I don't mind, Niall, it would be for the best and I don't think Fiona's a nuisance at all. She asks a lot of questions but so did I at seven.'

He grinned. 'You still do, and daft ones at that, but I can thole them now – because I love you.'

She held his hand briefly, then she was flying downhill, her hair a mane of red in the setting sun.

Fergus had the milk ready for the bedtime cocoa. He studied her flushed face as she buttered scones at the table.

'You're late in,' he said lightly, trying not to sound as if he were interfering with her life.

She giggled. 'Do you know what I've been doing, Father? Paddling with Niall down at the harbour! It was lovely – the water so cool!'

'Paddling?' He laughed. 'And not a finer night for it. I wouldn't mind myself but could you imagine what Portcull would have to say about that?'

She gave Tot milk, then sat opposite Fergus to sip her cocoa.

He looked again at her face, which was partially curtained by her long hair and knew that the time had come for her heart to hold its secrets. 'Take care,' he said softly, 'now that you're a woman.'

She looked up quickly but knew instantly what he meant. 'Yes, Father, I'll try.' She shrugged her shoulders, looking at him pleadingly. 'There's so much that's new – feelings I never knew existed. I know I still look the same – but – inside I've changed. I think I grew up today, it's a wee bit frightening.'

His strong, dark face relaxed a little. 'You're still such a little lass really. Mirabelle would have you in black stockings and blue ribbons.'

'Do you remember these things, Father?'

'You'd be surprised at what I remember. I see everything, though you might not always think it. I'm not old and feeble yet, you know.'

She looked at his slim, powerful body, and burst out laughing. 'Och Father! Do you think I see you as a withered old Bodach? You're so good-looking I'd marry you myself if I could. Oh – if only Kirsteen could come back – we could all be happy.'

He stopped laughing and the shadows of his loneliness veiled his dark eyes.

'You know too much,' he said angrily. 'I can't remember discussing my private life with you!'

'Father, don't shout so,' she chided angrily. 'Perhaps if you did talk to me of such things it would help. I'm old enough to understand now.'

'I never could talk about myself,' he growled, his voice tightly controlled, 'and I don't know what makes you think you'll have a privilege no one else ever had.'

She got up and touched his shoulder lightly. 'It might be because I'm your daughter,' she murmured and bent to kiss his bowed head before she turned and went upstairs to bed.

*

The week flew past. Shona and Niall were seldom alone and never even managed a return visit to the cave. Niall's original idea to take Fiona on an occasional outing turned sour on him because Phebie took a bout of summer 'flu and had to take to bed. Elspeth was kept so busy managing the house and the surgery she had no time for anything else.

Niall was assigned the task of shopping and each morning left the house with Elspeth's shrill orders ringing in his ears. He refused to carry a shopping basket. The first morning they set out Fiona skipped at his side, swinging the basket high in the air, and imploring him to give her some pennies for sweets.

'Oh shut up, you wee nuisance!' he rapped. He was in one of his rare tempers. Elspeth had nagged him since breakfast which he'd had to get for himself because he'd lain longer than normal and arose after everyone else had breakfasted.

Tears sprang into Fiona's eyes at her adored big brother's sharp words. She was a tiny sprite of a child with straight brown hair cut in a heavy fringe and button bright eyes alive with mischief. She was the opposite of her brother, both in looks and temperament. He had always been easy-going but she was stubborn and had tantrums that were the despair of Mr Murdoch at school and a puzzle to her good-natured, placid parents. But despite her moods she could be angelic and loving when she wanted and Niall could always get the best from her with his easy calm manner and quiet affection.

Now they were both out of spirits and trudged

sullenly along the road. A twite uttered a note of alarm from its nest in the heather and a group of scaup crooned contentedly on the calm green waters of Loch Tenee. A frog hopped unhurriedly into the moss at the road's edge and overhead, soaring in the wide blue of the sky, a skylark trilled notes of pure merriment. Normally, one of these things would have brought Niall at least from his mood, but not this morning, and the very fact that Fiona ignored the frog showed that her stubborn little heart was badly hurt.

They trudged into the post office in disgruntled silence and while Niall purchased groceries Fiona made a face at Behag behind his back. Behag sucked in her thin lips and banged a packet of tea viciously on the counter. 'Cheeky wee upstart,' she sniffed. 'Got your mither's sense o' humour, I see.'

Niall looked up quickly. 'What's that about my mother?'

Behag sniffed disdainfully. 'I was just sayin', your mither has a funny wee way o' sayin' things – sarcastic if you know what I mean – and the wee lass has the same quirk, only she's not so open natured – oh no, makes faces at folk only she's to hide behind her brither's back to do so.'

Niall's jaw tightened as he paid for the messages. When he was lifting his change he looked steadily at Behag and said, 'My mother was never one to make sarcastic remarks but it might be there's a wee quirk in your own nature that brings out the worst in people. Good day to you, Mistress Behag.'

He left the postmistress with her mouth agape and pulled Fiona outside. Without a word he lifted her frilled petticoats and smacked her hard on the bottom. For a moment nothing happened, then she dropped the bag of sugar she had been carrying and simply bawled with hurt pride.

The sugar had burst all over the road and Niall's face was red with temper and embarrassment.

Shona had come out of Merry Mary's at that moment and she ran over to survey the scene with amazement. Suddenly she burst out laughing and had to steady herself against the wall of Morag Ruadh's cottage. Her peals of mirth made several people turn and smile but Niall's face was a study of indignation. He glowered at her. With the sun in her hair, laughter creasing her face, and a pale green dress setting off her glowing tan, she was the picture of summer freshness but he was angry that she was enjoying his obvious plight.

'Girls!' he snapped. 'Nothing but pests!'

'Niall,' she gasped, 'it's just so funny – you slapping poor wee Fiona – funny strange I mean – history repeating itself in a way! Don't you remember? That time we met in the post office? You called me a baby and I said you were glaikit and we bawled at each other till your mother pulled you away and Mirabelle took me outside and skelped me on my *bare* bottom! I was so mortified I couldn't even cry!'

Fiona wiped her tears and giggled at the idea of lovely, graceful Shona being spanked for being naughty. Niall relaxed and chuckled, his eyes dreamy as he travelled back over the years. 'Yes, I do remember that day now,' he said, 'but I never knew Mirabelle gave it to you.'

'Right here – outside the post office – she was so

ashamed because I'd thrown a tantrum in front of your mother and nosy old Behag in there.'

Niall handed Shona the basket and put his arm round her, then he put out his other hand and grasped that of his small sister. 'Do you know what, bairns?' he grinned. 'I'm going to treat you to a bar of chocolate and we'll get down to the harbour to eat it. The old bitch Elspeth can wait for her messages! It was through her Fiona and I were grumpin' at each other in the first place.'

After that, the morning trip to Portcull became a treat instead of the drudge Niall thought it would be. With Shona everything was different. Whenever she could she went to Slochmhor and helped Elspeth with the chores, and prepared pretty trays for Phebie. As a result Elspeth was less put upon and her tongue lost its edge.

In the little spare time left, Shona and Niall took Fiona for picnics and in the process taught her to swim. They also spent lazy hours fishing offshore in one of Ranald's boats. Fiona was a lively interested child, always engrossed in whatever she was doing. Niall and Shona could steal the odd kiss and hold hands occasionally.

'Go ahead,' Fiona told them once. 'I know big boys and girls enjoy these things. Kiss all you want – I'd rather kiss a cat myself.'

Shona had smiled. 'I used to feel like that too, Fiona.'

The little girl screwed up her face. 'I'll *never* change. I don't like boys at all. They're dirty and cheeky and try to lift your dress so they can see your knickers, *and* they do awful things like picking their noses behind their reading books!'

The day before Niall's departure Shona went over to Slochmhor to prepare lunch for Phebie who was up but still feeling shaky. She was a young thirty-nine, plump and pink-skinned.

'My doctor is allowing me to Ceilidh tonight,' she smiled as she sprinkled salt over cold lamb, 'so I was wondering if you and your father would come over. We could have a nice crack.' She placed her hand over Shona's. 'It's sore your heart is that Niall's going.'

It was more a statement than a question. Shona nodded. Her heart was brimful of suppressed emotions. It had been a week of restraint both for her and for Niall. There had been so much they had wanted to say but no opportunity except for brief assurances of their love for each other. She couldn't trust herself to say too much to Phebie because she knew she might break down so she merely nodded at Phebie's words.

Phebie sighed. 'Och my lass, I wish he wasn't going. I know the war's not right begun yet and if we're lucky it might not get off the ground at all but I can't help fretting for my laddie.'

Shona bit her lip. 'Please don't talk about it,' she whispered.

Phebie saw the blue eyes brimming and she put out her arms and Shona went into them and cried quietly.

'There, there,' soothed Phebie, 'have a good greet. Niall's going from us and we would all like to grab him and hold on but Lachlan and I have talked it over. It won't be easy for any of us but he has to do this thing, Shona. He'd grow discontent and sour if we held him back. But yet our hearts will be heavy. It's the ones who are left behind who should be given the medals right enough.' She held Shona at arm's length and chuckled suddenly. 'Why do women always cry for men? Do they cry for us I wonder?'

Shona gave a watery sniff. 'In a different way I suppose.' She put her hands over her breasts. 'They cry more in here – in their hearts. Father's been doing it for years and it hurts him so. First it was for my mother, now it's for Kirsteen. I watch him and I want to take away the ache but there's nothing I can do.'

Phebie looked into the girl's incredible eyes. 'You've been doing something all your life,' she said softly. 'You've loved him and without you he'd be a sorry man today.'

'Do you really think so, Phebie?'

'I know so, mo ghaoil, and Fergus knows it too. If Kirsteen Fraser came back tomorrow she could turn round and thank you for holding together the body and soul of her man.'

'I wish she would come back to Rhanna. I'd love to see Father really happy. D'you know, Phebie, I don't believe I ever really have – not really.

Phebie looked thoughtful. 'No, I don't suppose you have. It must be terrible – to be so deeply unhappy. Thank God he and Lachy made up their differences or he could have been even worse.'

Shona nodded. 'I know, thank God for that at least.'

Phebie's little crack snowballed into a gay Ceilidh that went on till the small hours of morning.

'Och, Mother, you shouldn't have bothered,' said

Niall, looking at the laden table in the kitchen.

Phebie placed her hand briefly on his fair head and said softly, 'It's not every day my son gets himself engaged, so be quiet and put those pancakes down. Engaged or no' I'll skelp your lugs for stealing. Your eyes were ay bigger than your belly!'

The house was filling. Todd the Shod came in bearing his bagpipes and old Bob was settling down to play the fiddle. Todd's daughter, Mairi, now Mrs William McKinnon, came into the kitchen to see if her help was needed.

'Ach, it's all ready you are, Mrs McLachlan,' she said with her simple but radiant smile. 'I've brought some wee buns so I'll just leave them on the range. They're nice warmed a bitty. If you'll be excusin' me I'll just go and see will William dance with me. My mither's mindin' wee Andrew so I can have a good time.'

Faithful, doting Mairi spent a restless night looking for Wullie while the pipes skirled and the fiddles haunted the soul. Toasts were drunk to the newly engaged couple till everyone was crapulous and merry. Doors and windows were flung wide to let smoke and whisky fumes escape.

Niall and Shona held hands and tapped their feet to the pipes and each wished they were alone with the other.

Lachlan danced with Phebie and kissed her warm brow gently. 'Are you happy, my bonnie, plump peach?' he whispered.

She looked at her son with his bright hair and eager young face. 'Yes, happy that our son is going to marry Helen's bairn. It's strange the way of things, eh Lachy?'

He knew what she meant and his brown eyes were thoughtful. 'Aye, strange, if I'd saved Helen and lost the bairn or lost them both . . .'

She put her fingers over his mouth. 'Hush, no more of that, things are as they were meant. I wish Kirsteen had never left Fergus though – look at him – Shona's right – I doubt if we've ever seen him really happy for years.'

Fergus was sitting in a corner getting quietly drunk. His thoughts were crowding him that night and he couldn't sort one from another. He wanted his daughter's happiness yet he knew that her marriage to Niall would mean more emptiness for him. It would be a while yet but it was there, looming on his bleak horizon.

He looked at the revellers and noticed that nearly everyone had a companion of some sort. Even empty-headed Mairi, dithering about in her search for Wullie, had someone to look forward to. When Shona went he would have no one, what then would he do with his life?

Fiona Taylor, flushed and breathless from a gay highland fling, threw herself down on the seat near him. She was the child Lachlan had saved on the night of the awful storm of Helen's death. She was now in her early twenties, dark and vivacious with a firm bosom and a neat waist. Fergus looked at her and felt an open desire for her warm, young body. It had been so long since he'd held a woman close to his heart. He had lived with thoughts and hopes too long now and he was hungry for love. Kirsteen had taken all that was left in his heart; she had robbed him so that he knew he could never love another woman mentally. But the physical need in him for the contact of a female body couldn't be denied. He worked hard on the farm so that most nights he fell into bed exhausted but there were those other nights when sleep wouldn't come and he throbbed with heat.

These were the nights he conjured up the memories of Kirsteen till she beckoned in the dim mists of his mind. Sometimes it was difficult to get a clear image of her lovely face but he could imagine loving each part of her body that his memory could provoke till he could almost feel her beside him in the warm bed. His mind could make his body love, but when it was over there was no real, living body to snuggle into with contentment, only the big double bed with himself, humiliated and unhappy beyond measure.

He could smell Fiona's perfume and the smile she threw him raised a response in him. He leaned forward to ask her to dance but she was already jumping to her feet. 'Och, that Jimmy,' she laughed, her eyes sending messages to the young man who was beckoning her from the other side of the room 'he won't sit still for a minute – loves dancing he does and just because we are to be married at Christmas he thinks he owns me.'

She was off, her petticoats whirling and a wild skirl breaking from her. Fergus put his head in his hand, letting his veneer fall away for a moment of longing. A light touch on his shoulder made him look up. 'Would you dance with an auld wife like me?' asked Phebie quietly.

'I prefer to dance with the bonniest lass in the

room,' he answered lightly and whirled her away.

While the Ceilidh was still at its height Niall and Shona stole away unnoticed into the summer night. Biddy was ensconced in Fiona's swing, her hip flask clasped to her bosom while she rocked herself gently back and forth to the lilt of a Gaelic boat song she was humming untunefully. She didn't notice the two shadows stealing past. Shona stifled a giggle and Niall took her hand and they ran beyond the halo of light from the house.

It was a soft velvet night of country scents. The sea sighed in the distance and a dog barked from a distant croft. They walked to the small wood at the top of the field above Slochmhor, stopping to listen to the laughter that drifted from the open windows. Laigmhor was a dark shadow and Portcull a blur of whitewashed cottages against the subdued shimmer of the Sound of Rhanna.

Niall pulled Shona close. 'It's been a grand night, mo ghaoil. But it's glad I am to have you to myself for a wee while.'

She turned to him with a sudden movement and buried her face into his neck. 'Och Niall, I love you so much. I've got so much I want to say yet I don't know where to start.'

'That's how I feel,' he whispered into her hair. 'I've wanted to be alone with you all week; now all the words have gone I wanted to say. Now, tomorrow, I must leave you and I am wishing tonight would last forever. Promise me you'll write. I'll be lost for a time and looking for your letters.'

'Niall, of course I'll write,' she chided gently. 'But

will you answer I wonder? You never wrote much before.'

'This is different,' he assured her. 'Before we were just bairns playing ourselves – now one day you'll be my wife.' His voice was full of awe at the overwhelming implications of his words. He held her hand tightly. 'I'll miss you,' he said huskily. 'Will you think at all of me?'

'Maybe sometimes,' she answered as lightly as her heavy heart would allow.

He smiled in the darkness. 'It's a skelped bum you're needing, my girl.' He reached for her but she eluded him and like children they played hide and seek in the rustling wood. When he caught her he kissed her over and over and whispered, 'No more kissing Ti Johnston or flirting with Gordon McNab or I'll spank you when I get home!'

'And when will that be, my canty lad?' She tried to keep her voice steady but in the darkness tears were on her cheeks.

'I'll not be knowing for a while but I'll be home whenever I can.'

'I'll try and be here. Who knows where I might wander? I might even join the ATS and be away when you get back.'

'Don't dare!' he said fiercely. 'You're mine and a man has a right to claim what's his! When I come back to Rhanna I want my Shona here to welcome me . . . Now, turn round till I pee.'

She giggled loudly at the sudden change of mood. 'Och, you're rude, so you are, Niall McLachlan. It's so unromantic to say such things.'

'I can't help it, I'm burstin' with all that beer big Tam McKinnon kept giving me. I think he makes it himself for I'm sure I've smelt it coming from that wee wash-house near the cowshed. He must drink gallons of the stuff too for every time I've been with Tam he's always burstin' to pee and when he does it's like the wee waterfall up by Brodie's burn – never-ending. I remember one time –' he chuckled at the recollection – 'Tam was burstin' and a crowd o' lassies coming along. He couldn't wait so he popped the milk can he was carrying inside his breeks, did up his buttons, and was peeing merrily into the can as the girls were passing. It made quite a noise and between that and the bulge in his trousers the lassies' eyes were goggling. He looked like a prize bull with breeks on!'

Shona shrieked with mirth and she and Niall returned to the Ceilidh in a light-hearted mood.

Next morning she overslept and was kept so busy there was no time to see Niall off from the harbour. In a way she was glad because she knew she would have cried at the parting.

She was in one of the top fields, driving two straying cows, when she saw him on the road far below. He looked up and waved, shouting something she couldn't hear, then he was off, his beloved, familiar figure a dark little blob on the road to Portcull. She stood silhouetted against the sky. She knew he turned again and again because she could see the tiny stick that was his arm raised in farewell. She sank into the lush grass, the cows forgotten. She watched the boat leaving the harbour and kept on watching till it was just a speck in the misty distance.

'Ca' canny, my Niall,' she whispered and a cold little wind dried the tears on her cheeks.

That summer Alick and Mary came with their four-year-old twin sons. The farmhouse rang with wild yells and screams of joy. Shona was an adored cousin and she took the boys for picnics to the sheltered little bays at Nigg. She taught them to ride Thistle, the tiny Shetland pony she had long outgrown, and they clattered along with her to feed the hens or help with the milking.

She was laughing and gay, yet Fergus looked at her and could feel her loneliness.

The twins departed and Laigmhor reverted to its drowsing norm. Erchy the postman paid more than his usual number of visits and he lumbered slowly through a Strupak while Shona fingered Niall's letters nestling in her apron pockets and wished she was alone.

'Love letters, is it?' twinkled Erchy unfailingly. 'That young buck must have it bad, I'm thinkin'. His poor mither only gets half of what you do.'

Niall's letters were colourful and his descriptions of life in the training camp so full of wit that Shona often laughed aloud, but there was also a yearning for her in every line he wrote and she hugged each little intimacy to her heart.

The summer days grew shorter and autumn came with a sharp tang. The rowans winked fiery eyes and woodsmoke hung in the misty air. The bronze of beeches and the twinkling golds of silver birches turned Rhanna into a patchwork quilt of colour.

Bracken rustled on the mountains and towards the end of September the deer rut came and the strange, plaintive roar of the stags echoed in the glens.

Biddy was seldom away from old Shelagh's cottage and one morning the old lady said to her, 'See that I have my teeths in when you lay me out, mo ghaoil. The damt things were never much good to me when I was alive but they'll help me to look better when all my friends come to see me in my box. And . . .' She laid a frail hand on Biddy's arm. 'Will you be saying a wee prayer for me in the Gaelic when they put me into the Kirkyard? I know God has all the tongues but thon minister is not even speaking English right and I'd like fine for God to know I'm coming so that all my friends up yonder will know to greet me.'

Biddy brushed away a tear and said gruffly, 'Ach of course I will, you old blether, but it's a bit early to be talking of such things.'

But Shelagh, a small wizened figure in a bed full of patchwork quilts, shook her head. 'You should know better than to try and fool me. I've lived too long to be taken in by kind words. Just say that wee prayer for me, Biddy, and don't worry. If I have any trouble getting into Heaven I'll just blow my way through the gates, my winds will see to that.'

Three days later, on a morning of gentle sun and mellow amber tints, she passed peacefully away. Everyone who had loved the kenspeckle old sprite who had spent her entire eighty-three years on the Hebridean island, toiled up the leaf-strewn path to the old kirk.

Old Joe watched his cousin laid to rest. 'Gone with

the winds right enough,' he chuckled but there was a mist of tears in his green eyes and he blew his nose loudly on a spotted red handkerchief.

Dodie, resplendent in a black coat and grey soft hat no one had seen before, wept quietly into his big tobacco-stained hands. 'He breeah!' he said in a funny choked voice. He was conscious of the strange hat on his head but proud that he had managed to dress decently to see his old friend off. He had 'borrowed' the clothes from Burnbreddie many years before and was pleased of the chance to wear them, even if it was for such an unhappy occasion.

He looked at Biddy, who was standing by the open grave saying a beautiful Gaelic prayer that brought the tears to the eyes of all the Gaels present, and his broken teeth showed for a moment. It was nice to see her wearing the gift he had given her a number of years ago. She too was wearing her very best in honour of old Shelagh.

Chapter Thirteen

Shona rubbed at a pair of thick woolly socks with an energy that had nothing to do with enthusiasm. Mrs McKinnon had been unable to come to Laigmhor because of a bout of sciatica and Shona had had to contend with all the chores both in and out the farmhouse for nearly a fortnight. She had been so busy she had deliberately ignored the pile of washing, but when Fergus came down to breakfast that morning, with no socks to wear under his wellingtons, she was so ashamed she set about the tasteless task after lunch was over. Soapsuds spilled out of the tub to the floor and Tot, who had skated the length of the kitchen twice, was now taking refuge under the table.

The kitchen was warm and the door was thrown wide to let in the few stray breezes from the Indian summer day outside. Sunlight streamed over the flagstones and Shona sighed, raising her head for a moment to look at the russet gold shoulder of Sgurr na Gill outlined against the deep blue sky. She longed to be outside to feel the sun on her skin. The outdoor sounds were enticing, a Hebridean song-thrush 'tchuck-tchucked' from the apple tree, cows lowed gently from the fields, and the hens clucked peacefully and every so often wandered into the kitchen, combs waggling and beady eyes bright. Shona rushed at them with a besom and they flew clumsily outside, shrieking indignantly amidst feathers and droppings.

'Silly fools!' Shona spoke vehemently to the empty kitchen, and the ticking of the grandmother clock from the hall, and Tot's snorting, only served to heighten the silence.

She sighed again and rubbed her nose with a soapy hand before going back to the sink. Clothes slopped once more and she looked absently at the calendar. October was halfway through and it was three and a half months since Niall had left Rhanna. She had been parted from him for longer spells but it was different now; now that their love was no longer the secret of the other, the months apart were like years.

Her hair fell over her face and she was so engrossed in her thoughts that she didn't notice the shadow that loomed on the sunlit flagstones.

'Is this the wee hoosie where the washwife lives?' Niall's voice was full of suppressed joy. She looked up, her expression one of startled disbelief. His strong young figure filled the doorway, a handsome stranger in his Army uniform. With a few quick strides he crossed the room and lifted her high; then the warm firm mouth she had dreamed of was on her own and she gasped for breath.

'You smell and taste of soap,' he grinned, holding her away to look at her. She wiped her hands on her apron and backed away from him, trying to take in the fact that the suntanned young man in the neat uniform, his hair severely cropped under his cap, was really the same person who had left her months before.

'Hey!' he laughed, 'it's me – Niall! Remember – the glaikit wee laddie you played with!'

'You look so different, it's difficult to believe you're Niall McLachlan!'

'I'm just the same, it's the uniform that's different – aye, and the Indian crop! C'mon! Are you not pleased I'm here?'

She went into his arms then. 'I've missed you so,' she whispered into his ear, 'and I imagined when you came home I would be beautiful and perfect and instead you've caught me with my peenie on.'

'You *are* beautiful and I've longed for this moment so much I wouldn't care if you'd nothing on.'

They burst out laughing then she grew serious. 'How long, Niall?'

'Seven days but I'll miss two of them because of travelling so it leaves only five. I'm being posted to France.' She turned pale and went quickly back to the sink but he was at her back, turning her face gently towards his. 'We must make the most of the time, mo gaolach, so it's off with your peenie and out with me. I've been home and sent my folks crazy with delight at sight of my bonny face. Mother has made me a big parcel of sandwiches so we can go off for the whole afternoon.'

'I can't,' she wailed. 'I look like a spey wife and I'm in such a guddle with the washing! Father hasn't a single pair of socks to wear!'

He slapped her gently on the bottom. 'Give me your apron and you get along and clean yourself up.'

She left him wrapping the apron round his uniform and she could hear him singing while she washed and tidied herself in her room. She surveyed herself in the mirror and sparkling eyes and rosy cheeks looked back at her. She put on a blue dress and brushed her hair till it shone. For a moment she stood still and thought, 'Five days, five precious days with Niall. I'll hold on to every minute and turn them into hours.' She put down her brush and flew downstairs, chuckling when she looked outside and saw Niall hanging out the washing, his singing somewhat distorted by the rows of pegs sticking from his mouth. She didn't dare inspect the newly washed clothes too closely. They were hanging in comically unusual positions but looked clean enough in the searching rays of the sun.

Niall came back to the kitchen and threw his apron on to a chair. 'All set?' he said, crooking his arm in a dashing manner.

She nodded breathlessly, 'I've left a note for Father in case he comes in and wonders where I am. I just said you were home.'

They went outside. 'Where will we go?' she wondered though she knew what he would say.

'Where else but our own wee hideaway?'

It was a day borrowed from summer and Niall took off his jacket and threw it over his shoulder. He put his arm round Shona and they walked with their heads together, their feet light and swift on the dry moor grasses.

They hadn't been to the cave since June and it was full of cobwebs. Shona dusted them away and made tea on the spirit stove while Niall washed the cups in the nearby burn. It was too warm to stay in the cave so they spread a rug outside and sat on it to drink tea and eat chicken sandwiches. The ruins of the Abbey made a perfect sun trap. Through the crumbling walls held together in places by an overgrowth of tree roots and fern, they could see the moor stretched for miles, a sheet of golden ochre merging with the blue-green mists of thc sea.

Shona looked far into the distance and felt frightened, knowing that Niall was soon going to a place where the serenity of Rhanna would be very far away. She shivered and snuggled against him.

'Hey, why all the shivers?' he asked gently. 'The sun's warm enough for July.'

'I'm afraid, Niall. You are too – I can feel it. It's happened – I've tried not to think about it but now the time has come – you're going off to fight and you might get hurt.'

'I am a wee bit scarey, Shona,' he admitted. 'I think most of the lads are, but we're not going out there with the idea we're going to get hurt. We're going to fight and probably not even right away. I'll maybe get a chance to come home if things aren't too bad.'

She pulled herself away from him angrily. 'When are you going to give me peace of mind? When will you stop leaving me? I can't deny it any longer, Niall! I've always hated you leaving but I didn't want to behave like a silly wee girl so I pretended not to care every time you went. It's different now! I love you! And you're supposed to love me but how can you when you worry me so with all your stupid ideas about adventure? War's not an adventure. You might get killed, Niall and have you thought – you'll have to kill other people if you want to stay alive!'

She burst into a torrent of tears. Niall's face had turned white with anger. 'I know it's not an adventure, Shona,' he said harshly. 'I've lain nights in the billet sweating when I think about it. I don't want to kill anyone but you're right – if I don't, they'll kill me, even though they might not want it either. It's the whole conception of war that's rotten and evil but if I don't fight, and thousands like me, there would be no freedom for anyone! Everything would be swallowed up by all the greedy little Hitlers of the world! Do you want that to happen, Shona? Would you like to see Scotland taken over by the Nazis?'

She had never seen him so angry. She hadn't realised his convictions were so strong and she wanted to run to him and hold him but her stubborn nature wouldn't allow it. The sun was still shining, but the beauty of the day was ruined for both of them. She began to gather up her things while he watched miserably.

'Will I see you tomorrow?' he asked.

She flounced about, her chin set in the determined lines he knew so well.

'I really don't know,' she answered, coldly polite. 'I have so much to do with Mrs McKinnon not well. You'll be about no doubt and know where to find me if you need me!'

She hardly dared look at him because she knew if she did she would melt. From experience she knew how he was looking. From the side of her eye she saw him sitting dejectedly, his hands hanging over his drawn-up knees. What she couldn't see, but could guess, were deep brown eyes, dark with growing misery, and tanned skin flushed with fading anger. A lump came to her throat but she forced herself to walk away, her head high and her step nonchalant. He didn't come after her and her face was pale with hurt when she arrived home. Tot wheezed to greet her but it was still too early for anyone else to be about.

She held the old dog close and went to the cobbled yard then through the little gate to the drying green. Niall's washing, a gay jumble on the line, made her cry out with remorse and shame. She wanted to run back over the moor to tell him how sorry she was but instead put potatoes and turnip to cook on the range and laid the table with a precision calculated to pass time quickly.

Fergus came in smelling of dung and he stripped to the waist and ran water into the sink. 'I hear Niall's home,' he called through a lather of soap. 'Well, you can go off and enjoy yourselves while he's here. Mrs McKinnon sent a message that she'll be here in the morning.'

He reached for a towel and wiped the water from his eyes, expecting to see his daughter's radiant face. Instead she was at the stove, her back to him while she furiously mashed turnip and potatoes.

'Clapshot tonight, is it?' he asked, wary of her mood.

'With salt beef,' she snapped.

'I'll mask the tea then.' He poured boiling water into the teapot and set it on the range. He sat down, still wearing only his trousers, and drew his plate towards him. 'I hear tell Dodie's ram's been going at the yowes up on the hill,' he said conversationally. 'The crofters from Nigg will be moaning about it though they know fine none of their rams can compare with Dodie's. He should be charging a fee, so he should.'

'He should have sold that ram,' said Shona sullenly. 'And you should never have given him that old yowe in the first place. One of her lambs just had to be a ram and one of these day's there's going to be a fine stramash over the whole thing – that's if the old ram doesn't drop dead first from all its matings!'

'There's already been a stramash, I think. The sun's gone out of your eyes, my lass.'

She lifted her head, an angry retort on her lips, but the look of caring in his black eyes made her instead jump to her feet and go to him. His body was warm and still damp from his wash, and she bent over to put her arms round his neck.

'Oh Father, I'm a bad-tempered bitch and deserve a skelping! Niall's going off to France and all I could do was shout at him that he thought it was all just an adventure. I'm afraid for him and when I'm frightened I get crabbit.'

He smiled strangely. 'An inheritance from me! It's a devil of a thing to control and even worse if there's a bit of thrawn pride alongside it. You're the one who should apologize but I know how hard that can be.'

'You understand so much, Father.'

'I've been through it all, that's why. When I was your age I could never bring myself to admit being wrong. Now I see all the time I wasted with my pride and it's too late to be sorry. Don't make my mistakes, Shona, or you'll live to regret it. How long has Niall got?'

'Five days – and one of them nearly gone.'

'Precious hours,' he said briefly and turned back to his meal.

That evening she wanted to run over to Slochmhor but she didn't. Her father was going up the hill to old Bob's biggin for a night of chess and when he had gone she curled herself on the inglenook and gazed into the leaping flames in the hearth. Minutes passed, then a tap at the door made her leap up, her heart racing. Niall had come to her! But it was Nancy on her way to Portcull to visit her mother.

'I'm just dropping in for a crack,' she dimpled, her merry dark eyes full of life. 'Archie brought me over in the trap and now he's away to Ranald's for a dram and a game o' cards. Och – but you and that bonny Niall will make a fine pair. If you just let me put Jeemie down and give me a cup o' tea I'll give you a few hints for your weddin' night.'

Shona listened to the busy tongue and felt that Nancy's vivacity could be somewhat overpowering at times.

Half an hour later she left in a whirl of laughter and Shona sat down thankfully, feeling tired and unhappy. At nine o'clock she took her cocoa, her hot water bottle and Tot up to bed and lay gazing at the small damp patch on her ceiling. She had loved the patch from childhood because it was shaped the way she imagined Jesus's head would be. The slates of the roof had been fixed and her ceiling repapered but still the little patch came through till the paper was stained in the gentle profile that always brought her a certain measure of comfort. She turned and snuggled into Tot who groaned in ecstasy. It was the time the old dog loved best; the dregs of cocoa from the saucer, the cosy bed, and the warm loving arms of her mistress hugging her close.

Shona pictured Niall sitting in the homely parlour at Slochmhor. Fiona would be in bed and he would be talking with his parents in that intimate close way they had with each other.

A tear slid on to Tot's ear and Shona whispered, 'Oh dear God, let Niall know it's because I love him I'm angry he's going away and – and I'm so frightened.'

Tot snored and Shona heard her father come in. It was comforting to hear him moving about. The light from his lamp illuminated the crack under her door. She knew he had stopped and she could picture him, a tall lone figure surrounded by the darkness of the house, listening for a sign from her that all was well. He wouldn't say anything for fear she was asleep, and he would go to his empty room, with its masculine traces of untidiness, without the comforting sound of a human voice bidding him a good night.

'Goodnight, Father,' she said gently.

His soft lilting voice floated back. 'Goodnight, Ni-Cridhe.'

'Ni-Cridhe'. My dear lassie! The unaccustomed endearment made her heart swell with love for him and feeling oddly comforted she buried her face into Tot's silky ears and slept.

The next morning was one of calm mists and damp dewy grass. Mrs McKinnon came and talked incessantly while she made bread and prepared vegetables. It was good to hear her earthy tongue and Shona laughed despite her restless mood.

'Are you not going out?' asked Mrs McKinnon, looking from the window to fields and moors now bathed in mellow sunshine. 'I hear tell Niall's home for a wee while before going off to fight. You should be making the most of your time together. When I was your age the blood was leapin' in my veins – rearin' to be off I was.' She chuckled. 'Aye, and look where it got me – a man that could still teach a young buck a thing or two about ruttin' and a gift for breakin' everything he touches. Still, I'm happy with my Tam, no brains he has but he's done not bad without them. Yon Niall's got brains – and a fine handsome laddie into the bargain. He'll go far, will young McLachlan.'

'If he stays alive,' said Shona, unable to keep the bitterness from her voice.

'Och havers! You mustny think so! Bide a wee – he'll have the Germans runnin' like gowks and thon wee man Hitler will be frothin' like a bull without its balls, mark my words. Now, away ben and get me some dripping from the larder.'

The morning passed quickly, thanks to Mrs McKinnon, but when she departed after lunch and the house was quiet again Shona still had not thought of a way to make amends with Niall. She didn't want to go to his house because that would make her appear too anxious. He hadn't come to her so she knew he was still hurt and angry and was making it clear that the first move must come from her. But it was so hard to apologize when stubborn pride seethed within. Unable to bear the house any longer she threw a cardigan over her shoulders and went outside.

It was another day stolen from summer and the heat

from the sun made her shed the cardigan quickly. Tot had opted to come out too and the golden dog and her slim, golden-skinned mistress walked together over the shaggy amber moors. Without conscious intention Shona was breasting the Hillock of Dunuaigh and looking down at the ruins of the Abbey nestling in the hollow. There was still a good half mile to go and Tot, pink tongue lolling, was tired and lagging behind. Shona picked her up and went on down the hill. The ruins of the Abbey loomed against the blue sky and she paused for breath, hoisting the sleeping old dog higher against her shoulder. Through one of the crumbling windows of the Chapel she suddenly saw Niall. He was sitting in the same place she had left him the day before and she might have thought he had spent the night there but for the fact he had changed from his uniform into his old kilt and jersey. Her heart pounded and she felt faint with her love for him. How dearly familiar he looked in his Rhanna clothes. He was disconsolate and sullen-looking and idly threw pebbles into the foaming little burn that wound its way from the mountains.

Tot had wakened and was struggling to get down. The lovely scent of rabbit was in the air and she still enjoyed a mild chase. She whimpered with excitement and stood for a moment, torn between going to greet Niall or going to sniff out rabbit.

Niall looked up, a pebble poised in his fingers. He stood up and, though he was more than a hundred yards from her, Shona sensed the tension in him. He began to run towards her and her own feet took wings, his name a soft breath on her lips. For a moment it seemed eternity divided them, then she was throwing herself into his outstretched arms, her mouth meeting his in a kiss she knew would hold in her heart forever.

'Don't ever walk away from me again,' he gasped, holding her face and covering it with kisses.

'I'm sorry, my Niall. I didn't mean half of the things I said – please forgive me.'

They walked to the cave, arms entwined. Shona fell on to the sheepskin rugs, her legs weary from the long walk. Niall sat beside her and stroked her hair. 'I couldn't sleep last night,' he whispered, 'and all because of you, you wee wittrock.'

'Love me, Niall,' she breathed her blue eyes serious and her lips, warm and inviting, parted to show her even white teeth.

'I do love you.'

'Love me with your body, Niall. I thought about it last night. Father was out and all I could think about was you. I love you so much I want to give you all of me – my heart and my soul – and – and my body. Please, Niall, give me something to remember when you're gone. I want to be able to think of us belonging to each other. Our memories are the only things we're going to have for a long time.'

He had turned away from her and didn't speak for a few moments. Outside Tot barked and a light wind rustled the ferns. 'I want you, Shona,' he said at last. 'God knows I've wanted you for a long time now. You're beautiful – so beautiful that I can hardly bear to be alone with you without wanting you. I've watched you growing lovelier each time I came back, but because I love you I can't do anything that might hurt you. When we're wed your body will belong to me but, till then . . .' He spread his hands helplessly, unable to express himself further.

'We are wed,' she laughed softly. 'We've been wed for years. Don't you remember our marriage in the cave at the Point?'

'Och, Shona, it's teasing you are. Get up from there and we'll go for a walk . . . or something.'

But she lay where she was, strangely inert, and tears fell helplessly on to the sheepskin. 'I'm afraid, Niall, I'm frightened you'll be killed and I won't ever know what the completion of our love would have been like. I won't be able to remember because you won't give me now what would be my memories later.'

He looked at her intently. 'You really mean it, mo ghaoil?'

'You know I do. It's not the sort of thing to speak of lightly.'

She was exquisite, with her burnished hair spread over the white sheepskin and he felt his heart beating up into his throat. 'We'd better go outside,' he mumbled before his resolution left him. 'I won't be tempted to do something we might both regret later. Please Shona – don't look at me like that – those eyes of yours all soft and with a look I've never seen . . .'

His words were lost because she had reached up a slender arm and pulled his head down to her breasts. He heard the throb of her heart and felt the softness of her. His body wouldn't obey his mind. He was beside her, their mouths meeting and parting over and over, their bodies pressed together till he could think of nothing but her. Briefly her hands touched his hardness and for a moment he was embarrassed because he was still in possession of his sensibilities and he thought she might be shocked that the playmate of her childhood could have changed to a virile young man, capable of doing all the things they had once thought so foolish. But her touch had been no accident, and she caressed him again till he felt himself to be on fire and the hard swelling of his passion became a thing apart, something that seemed to move and press without any conscious direction from him. His pelvic muscles seemed to be made of fluid, so easily did they allow him to move up and down, and her body was a supple thing of wonder, moving with his in such perfect unison they might have been of the same flesh. But not yet; he wanted to keep the ultimate moment at bay, to enjoy her lips and the feel of her breasts for as long as he could. The cave was warm and quiet, an intimate little world into which no one could intrude. Slowly he undressed her till she lay naked on the sheepskin. For a moment her blue eyes looked at him, an awareness in them of everything that was happening. 'Shona,' he whispered, 'are you sure?'

But she closed her eyes without answering and he looked at the sweep of her long lashes and the pulse beating in her slender neck. His eyes slowly travelled to her body, seeing how white was the skin of her torso compared to her arms and legs. He reached out and his hands cupped her small high breasts, then he bent and kissed her hard pink nipples, over and over again till she was making soft little moaning sounds.

She put out her hands and again caressed those intimate parts of him till there was no turning back. Trembling, he undressed. For a moment she opened her eyes to look at him. Her gaze travelled over his penis. She looked at it wonderingly and touched it again, like a little girl who had unlocked a secret door and discovered adulthood. Their childhood was far behind them now – those long days of innocence, of exploration of the things of nature, now turned in on themselves and the joy of finding such ecstasy in each other.

But the real ecstasy was still to come. Niall quivered at her touch and could wait no longer. He gathered her to him in a frenzy of excitement and went into her with the drive of an animal. She hadn't expected the pain and bit her lip to stop from crying out. He had forgotten everything but the intense pleasure he was getting from her body. His brown eyes were glazed and each thrust he made inside her brought a strange low moan from his throat. She endured the pain, it was the ultimate proof of her love for him, and she stroked his neck and shoulders till he finally let out a cry that echoed through the cave. Still he kept moving, releasing every bit of fire that burned in him till finally he fell against her exhausted.

'Shona, my lovely Shona,' he whispered and tears glistened in his eyes while he kissed her with such tenderness that she cried soundlessly. They were still joined together but he made no attempt to withdraw, falling asleep with his young, boyish face so close to hers she was able to study every little detail. His skin was smooth, the little fuzz of his moustache a shade deeper than his fair head. She put up her hand and touched his firm, sensitive mouth and he awoke with a start, withdrawing from her almost guiltily. 'Shona, I'm sorry.' He was full of remorse. 'I shouldn't have done it – oh God – after all the times I kept from touching you!'

'Please don't be sorry, Niall. I wanted you to love me, I'm not sorry and . . .' she giggled unexpectedly. 'Shelagh was right, you are a young bull. Now I know something else about you I didn't before.' She leaned on her elbow and touched him. 'Look at it now, it's a wizened wee Bodach, yet before it was so – big. Does it go like that often?'

'Sometimes,' he said evasively.

'When you think about girls?'

'When I think about you – and if you don't stop poking at it you'll make it happen again.' He reached for his clothes and noticed a stain on the sheepskin. 'Shona, I've hurt you, you're bleeding!' he cried in alarm.

'Only a little,' she confessed. 'But don't worry, my Niall. I loved the pleasure I could give you. The bleeding only means I'm no longer the virgin I was.'

He fell on his knees and cradled her head. 'I'm sorry I hurt you so. I should have been gentle but you drove me crazy. It was wonderful but it can't have been very good for you.'

'It will be – the next time.'

'The next time?'

'We only have five days together, Niall, and I want to belong to you every minute you're here.'

'Let me bathe you,' he requested, still ashamed that

he had hurt her. 'I'll get some water from the burn while you dress.'

He made tea and while it was masking he cleansed her with warmed water. She had protested but his argument stilled her.

'Please let me, I drew the virgin blood from you and it is my right to clean it away.'

'Are you not shocked?' she asked when it was finished.

'No, I love every bit of you and besides, I know what girls are like. I've bathed Fiona manys the time; you're much the same, though bigger with fluffy red hairs. It's funny, I often wondered if they'd be red.'

She gasped. 'You've thought of me in that way then?'

'Of course – a long time ago in fact. I used to try and see but you always had knickers on.'

'NIALL MCLACHLAN!' She threw a cushion at him and he lay back on the bed and roared with laughter.

It was growing dark and the air was damp and frosty when they arrived at her gate. He took her hand. 'I loved you so much this morning I didn't think it was possible to love you more – now I know I was wrong.'

'Do you, Niall – really? I wanted to prove to you how much I care. I don't want you to think I'm just a cheap . . .'

He put a finger over her lips. 'Hush, don't dare think the thing. Now I must go. Will you be over tonight? My mother will be expecting you – and your father if he's not busy.'

'I'll come even if he doesn't.'

She was halfway up the track when she stopped,

wondering suddenly how she would face her father. He had an uncanny knack of reading her mind and always knew what her mood was even if she tried to conceal it. Tonight she felt jubilant and very womanly. She didn't feel ashamed or guilty. Her father had warned her indirectly about the trappings of emotion and she had promised him to be careful. Today she had thrown caution to the wind and she was afraid now that he would guess at her indiscretions.

But the warm kitchen was quiet and empty. She lit a lamp and saw a note propped against her place at the table. Her father had been asked over to Burnbreddie to dine and discuss farming business with Scott Balfour, laird of Burnbreddie for two years now since his father had died.

The new laird of Burnbreddie had made slow progress with the wary Rhanna crofters. They didn't trust a 'college cissy' to handle their affairs but gradually they realised they were getting a fairer deal from him than they'd ever had from the whisky-loving womaniser who had been his father. He was generous with the harvests of his land and distributed game and venison equally to all and even those who had criticised him with the sharpest tongues had to grudgingly admit he had some gumption after all.

His wife was no society girl either but a sensible young countrywoman of Scottish landed stock, and she endeared herself to the islanders by taking an active and genuine interest in their lives. Little boys of two and four livened the former gloom of the big mansion house wherein old Madam Balfour, under the firm hand of her daughter-in-law, simpered and ailed less, complained still, but less vehemently, and even enjoyed her two little grandsons.

Shona took her dinner on a tray by the fire. Tot lolled on one side of her and two cats sat grimly to attention on the other. Three pairs of eyes watched her emptying plate intently and Tot's mouth watered profusely. Normally, such blatant bad manners would have earned a rebuke, but Shona was barely conscious of her surroundings and sat for a long time gazing dreamily into the fire. Eventually Tot's snuffling and wheezing brought her to her senses. Shona patted the silky ears and went to the larder and soon the cats were lapping milk and Tot eating her fish and oatmeal.

Shona went outside to shut the hen-houses and check the cowsheds. Her breath clouded in the air and she looked up to see a million stars. Mirabelle had taught her the various constellations and she stared at the panorama of the heavens, her arms folded over her breasts in delight.

'Oh great God up there,' she breathed, 'I thank you for this lovely day with Niall and for all the things I have that are so good. Mirabelle – if you're listening don't think bad of me. What I did today was for love, I don't feel it was wrong though I know you won't think it was right. Tell Hamish and my mother I send my love – and old Shelagh too.'

She always prayed in the fashion of her childhood, simple words that gave her great satisfaction and, since the old housekeeper's death, she had passed messages through her to others who had gone from her life.

She went indoors and damped the fire. She had

already laid the table for breakfast and the big kettle was filled for bedtime cocoa and hot bags. She stepped once more into the frosty night air and met Dodie hovering at the gate.

'He breeah!' he moaned unhappily.

'He breeah! Is something not right, Dodie?'

'I'm lookin' for my damty ram so I am. He's having a fine time with the yowes on the hill and I hear tell the lads from the sheiling of Nigg are girnin' about it. It's just talk with them for Dan Russell was blawin' last spring about his fine lambs and knowin' fine my Murn was the father.'

Shona had to hide a smile. After his experience with Ealasaid's offspring he had decided that the females of the domestic animal kingdom were easier to manage and had hopefully bestowed feminine names on the lambs at birth. When the mistake became apparent the names had stayed because the young ram would only answer to Murn.

'We ought to call him,' suggested Shona. 'Was he seen hereabouts recently?'

'Not long since.'

After a few minutes of calling Shona paused for breath. 'You know, Dodie, you ought to sell Murn. He's just causing trouble and with Ealasaid to look after you have enough of a handful. I've seen you tramping miles with her potash.'

'Ach, she's worth it – and I'm not selling Murn. He would miss me too much.'

'Och, c'mon now, Dodie, it's not right that a fine ram like Murn should be mixing with all those common yowes on the hill. Murn should have hand-picked yowes and you'll never manage that letting him roam freely.'

Shona could be very devious when she liked and Dodie stroked his grizzled chin thoughtfully. 'I never thought on it that way just. Murn is a fine ram, I'd like to see him get goin' with good yowes. That lot on the hill are a scruffy lot.'

'Well, just you have a good think about it. I'm having to go now.'

'Is your father at home? I'd like fine to ask his advice about Murn.'

'He's out tonight, Dodie.'

'Ach, what a pity just.'

She expected him to lope away but he trailed behind her and it was obvious he was in the mood for company. She paused at Niall's gate. 'Are you coming in to Strupak?' she asked kindly.

'Ach, the doctor will be busy.'

'I'm sure he'll be delighted,' she said uncertainly.

'Ach well, maybe for a wee while. I'd like fine to ask somebody about Murn. I'll hold the gate while you go through.'

Phebie was less than delighted to see Dodie. She had scrubbed the house till it smelled of soap and disinfectant and she knew that a few minutes of Dodie in any enclosed space would allow his odour to linger for hours but she concealed her feelings admirably and ushered both callers into the parlour.

Lachlan was dozing by the fire. Dodie immediately settled himself in the opposite chair and very soon the heat from the hearth was coaxing all the trapped smells from his boots.

Niall came pounding downstairs and burst into the room, his eyes meeting Shona's in a brief moment of unspoken love.

'Hello, Dodie,' he acknowledged cheerily, holding his breath as the smell hit him. 'It's yourself then?'

'Just for a whiley. I'd like fine to ask the doctor here what he thinks I should do about Murn.'

'I saw him chasing some of Croynachan's sheep,' volunteered Niall. 'Just round about teatime.'

'Aye well, that's the trouble, chasing too many damty yowes and myself gettin' into trouble because of it. Wee Shona here thinks Murn's just wastin' himself on thon scruff on the hill. She thinks I should sell him and see he gets a chance with some better yowes.'

Lachlan's eyes twinkled but when he spoke he sounded so seriously concerned about Murn's welfare that Dodie listened intently.

'Shona's right, Dodie. I've watched that ram and thought what a fine beast he is. I know old Jock from Nigg is looking for a good ram.'

'Is he that now?'

'Aye, I heard him telling Johnston just the other day.'

'Well now, that would be fine. Murn would be happy with Jock for he's a kindly wee man and loves his beasts the way I love mine. But I wouldn't know what price to be askin'. Murn might be a fine ram but he's been usin' himself up you might say. Not that he'll run dry on Jock – oh no, never that, but it's a wee rest he's needin'.'

Phebie, coming in with a laden tray, could hardly keep a straight face and Fiona, a sparkling nymph in a white nightgown, came in for a scone and looked sympathetic at Dodie's words. 'Ach poor Murn,' she consoled. 'I think he plays too much with the sheep. I saw him jumpin' on a scraggy old yowe yesterday and her wool must have tickled his belly for his eyes were rollin'.'

It was the cue everyone needed to release their laughter. Phebie lifted her little daughter high and kissed her. 'On up to bed, ye wee wittrock. Remember to say your prayers.'

Shona helped Phebie to hand round the Strupak but when she made to put milk in Dodie's tea he stayed her with a big hand. 'Not in my tea, lass, over my bread in a saucer.'

'But Dodie, there's jam on the bread.'

'Aye, lovely just. I like a bit jammy bread with milk over it. Merry Mary makes me jam from my own rhubarb and quite often she gives me bits of her new baked bread. I spread on the jam and pour over Ealasaid's best cream and have it for my dinner. It's a fine meal, you all should try it.'

He scooped the soggy bread from the saucer and smacked his lips to catch the dribbles on his chin. 'Lovely,' he approved. 'You make fine bread, Mistress McLachlan. I'm thinkin' now you'll be tryin' my recipe on the family.'

'Aye maybe,' said Phebie while Shona smiled as mention of Dodie's rhubarb brought a memory of two suntanned children listening round-eyed while the secret of the thick, juicy sticks was divulged.

Dodie was sublimely happy eating his Strupak and chatting in his native Gaelic. Most of the islanders, except the very old, had a good English vocabulary and the youngsters could speak both languages equally well but Dodie, with his speech difficulties, was sadly lost trying to pronounce the 'foreign' words. Rumour had it that an English visitor, lost in the hills, had come upon Dodie and had asked the way back to Portcull. Dodie, arms waving and carbuncle wobbling, had tried to give directions but the Englishman was unable to understand. Eventually Dodie had summoned Ealasaid and tied a rope round her hairy neck. The stunned visitor was bidden to climb aboard and, with a proud Dodie coaxing and pulling, Ealasaid lumbered into Portcull to safely deliver her ashen-faced passenger.

He dusted the crumbs from his knees and got up reluctantly.

'I'll have to be going now.' He patted one of his voluminous pockets. 'I have a neep here for Murn and I'd like fine to see he gets it for supper.'

Phebie sighed. 'Och Dodie, no wonder there's a smell,' she scolded. 'The neep's near roasted with the heat from the fire! I've been trying to fathom the reek.'

'Ach well, that's what it was,' said Dodie who was sublimely unaware of his own strange scent no matter how many innuendoes were cast at him.

'I'm going over to Nigg in the morning,' said Lachlan kindly. 'If you want to see Jock about the ram I'll pick you up around ten. I'd like fine to see you get a fair price for Jock's gey canny with the shillings.'

'Och, it's kind you are.' Dodie's broken teeth showed for a moment. 'I'll be off now, bidding you thanks for the Strupak. He breeah.'

He backed to the door and Phebie held her breath as his ungainly figure narrowly missed tables and other obstacles. Lachlan went to the door and watched till the untidy flapping figure was lost in the dark though the moaning cry of 'Murn! Murn!' could be heard for a long time in the calm frosty air.

When Lachlan got back to the parlour he chuckled to see everyone fanning the air with newspapers.

'I'm sorry about bringing him,' grinned Shona, 'but he was so forlorn out there I couldn't leave him. Poor Dodie, he must get lonely sometimes.'

She was on the sofa beside Niall and he squeezed her hand. 'Will you think of me, a poor lonely soul, out there in muddy, smelly trenches with bullets whingin' round me?'

It was meant to be a light-hearted comment but everyone in the room tensed.

'We'll think of you, lad,' said Lachlan quietly. 'Every day we'll spare our thoughts for you.'

Shona's eyes glinted in the firelight. 'Will it really – be like that?'

Niall made his answer sound uncaring. 'I canny really imagine what it will be like. It might be a bit like going into a dark room and not knowing if there's ghosties there or not.'

Shona shivered despite the warm room. 'I can't imagine you in a strange country,' she whispered.

'Ach, I'm used to being away from home.'

Phebie was clearing the tea things but she stopped to look at her son and when she spoke her voice was sharp. 'Are you used to fighting? And what about killing. You that never hurt a living cratur no matter how wee. What about a man, Niall? How will it be killing a man?'

She didn't wait for an answer but rushed from the room, her face crimson.

Lachlan sighed and studied his slippered feet intently. 'Take no heed of your mother, Niall,' he said gently. 'She's having a hard time trying to cope with her feelings. She canny believe you're going off to war. We're all feeling a bit strained at the moment.'

Shona got up silently and went to the kitchen to help Phebie.

Lachlan tapped his pipe on the grate. 'How's she taking it?'

Niall played with his thumbs. 'Bad at first. She ran from me yesterday when we spoke of it.'

'I thought you were out of temper last night but you're sweethearts again I see.'

Niall flushed and his bowed head glinted in the firelight.

Lachlan looked at his son and felt such a rush of love that he wanted to cradle the young head in his lap. Ah, it seemed but yesterday that a merry little boy laughed and played at his feet. Was it not a short time ago that the harvest carts trundled homewards in the gloaming and his sleeping son lay heavy in his arms? How could he ever forget the family outings with Niall, the only child in their lives then, leaving a trail of tiny footprints on silver sand? Those had been the days of picnics in sheltered coves, the thundering foam of the Atlantic spuming high in the air while Niall, a suntanned sprite, embraced the world with his outstretched arms, screaming with joy as the frothing spray bathed his sunkissed body.

How golden had been those far-off days and how easy it had been to laugh. Lachlan didn't feel like laughing now, knowing that each interlude with his son would become a precious memory later – later when all he might have would be memories.

Niall stirred restlessly and Lachlan sensed his impatience.

'I'll see Dodie gets a good price for his ram tomorrow,' said Lachlan trying to take the strain from his son by keeping matters on an everyday level.

Niall looked into his father's brown eyes and felt the love and understanding reaching out to him.

'I'd like fine to come over to Nigg with you. I want to see Tammy and one or two others. Could Shona come too, do you think?'

'Well, it's only a wee trap but Shona's just a wee lass so I think we'll manage, but don't blame me if you're all squeezed up against Dodie.'

Niall put his hand on his father's shoulder and his usually laughing eyes were serious. 'I know there's a lot you'd like to say, Father, but thanks for not saying it. I always knew I chose a sensible father.'

Lachlan's fixed smile did not betray his inner emotions. 'And I always knew I picked a lad with a lot of gumption. Now see me over those tuffers before the fire goes down and I get a warmed lug from your mother.'

It was a mild misty day when Niall left Rhanna. He felt himself doing things as in a dream yet he was so aware of individual sensations he felt he could reach out and put each one in his pocket. Shona's head nestled on his shoulder as they walked away from Slochmhor. The smell of her was of roses and shining hair, mingling with all the scents of Rhanna the breeze brought to him. The healthy smell of dung and hay came from Laigmhor. A herd of cows, scratching hairy necks on the fence, blew clouds of steam and chlorophyll into the air. Smoke, fragrant with peat, floated lazily from chimneys and over-riding all was the faint, ever-present tang of salt sea.

The memory of saying goodbye to his father was keen on his mind. It hadn't been a spectacular farewell, just a few murmured words, and a pair of strong hands gripping him on the shoulder. He was glad his father had turned away quickly because he felt the hot tears blurring his eyes, his throat constricting as he watched the tall, familiar figure striding away, clutching the black bag that marked him as a healer of men. How often he had watched that beloved man going off on his rounds. When he was a little boy he'd sometimes gone with his father, thinking it a treat to visit croft and farm, biggin and cottage, where constant Strupaks were offered and dogs and cats would submit to being his very own 'pretend' patients, obediently sitting with patient resignation while he prodded the old stethoscope his father had given him into furry bellies and examined tongues. In the dogs' cases that had never been difficult as a pink tongue was usually lolling anyway, but cats were never quite so forthcoming and he often ended with a scratch or two which the real doctor had to see to.

He had waited that morning for the final wave from the striding figure and when it didn't come he had felt like the little boy of long ago, cheated out of something he felt was his right. Then he saw his father's hand go up to his eyes and he knew, with a poignant tearing of his senses, that his father wept too.

The time for leaving came quickly. Shona came breathlessly from Laigmhor and his mother, wiping floury hands on her apron, kissed him briefly and promised she would come to the harbour to see him off. She was aloof and too bright and he was grateful to her for giving him the obvious opportunity to spend those precious last minutes with Shona.

She was very quiet on the walk to Portcull and he wondered if she was in the same wakeful dream as himself. Tot trotted beside them and her squatting on every patch of grass that appealed to her brought a sense of normality to the morning.

The gulls were whooping and screaming in the harbour. He could see them in the distance, looking like torn fragments of paper blowing in the sky.

He kissed the delicate shell of Shona's ear and felt that even if he were to die in the war his last days on Rhanna had brought a fulfilment to his short life that could never be surpassed. He had loved Shona with his body and his soul. She had given herself to him with such unquestioning love that he had cried in the act of joining with her and she too had wept so that their tears mingled as their bodies became one.

Suddenly she twisted her head to look up at him, her incredible eyes dark with emotion.

'Oh Niall' she murmured, 'I feel so unhappy – yet

in the last week my life has been so full I think I could live for ever and never know such happiness again.'

He put both arms round her and held her close. 'You even steal my thoughts, Caillich Ruadh. Is it not enough you already have my heart? Five days ago I came home my heart afire with love for you, now I leave, knowing that what burned before was only a candle to what I feel now. Oh God, I love you, mo gaolach! These days together will be my crutch when I'm low in spirits and I ask you to spare your thoughts for me whenever you can.'

'It's going to be a long winter, Niall, there will be time to think and wonder – what you are doing, when you'll be home.'

'I might get a bit of leave if things are quiet.'

'Not enough to allow you to travel to Rhanna. It would be fine if you could walk over the sea because those daft ferries of ours only come twice a week *if* the weather's good.' She fingered the gold locket at her neck. 'I have something for you. Niall – nothing as grand as this locket but it's a wee keepsake to remind you of home. I made it when I was nine and think well of it, Niall McLachlan, for each letter was sewn in tears and blood. I hate sewing but Mirabelle made me unpick it and do it over and over till it was as perfect as I could get it.'

It was a sampler of rough linen, beautifully embroidered in different coloured silks. Tears shone in his brown eyes as he whispered the words of a Hebridean poem: 'From the lone sheiling of the misty island, mountains divide us and the waste of seas; But our hearts are true and our hearts are Highland, and we in dreams – behold the Hebrides.' He gathered her to him again. 'I'll treasure it, mo gaolach, but I won't need reminding of home. I can assure you of that.'

The harbour was strangely quiet. Usually, when the boat was due there was a subdued excitement in the knots of people waiting about. Today there was hardly a soul to be seen. A few cows, waiting to be shipped to the mainland, lowed dismally in a nearby pen, but otherwise Portcull was deserted.

The boat appeared like a ghost ship on the horizon.

'I thought Mother would have come,' said Niall looking towards Glen Fallan. He felt strangely deflated. He was leaving the island of his birth to fight for its people and not one familiar figure was there to wish him luck. His thoughts were self-righteous and with them came an unaccustomed pang of self-pity.

Shona squeezed his hand. 'Your mother will come, Niall. She'll leave it to the last because she won't want time to cry.'

The boat came closer and they watched in silence, suddenly finding nothing to say to each other while the boat loomed, filling the span of their vision. Ropes were thrown, men shouted and the ever-present gulls glided in the warm air from the ship's funnels.

The boat was unloaded. Chickens clucked in subdued tones from several crates and a young bull swung gently in the cradle of the sling attached to the derrick. Old Joe sauntered from nowhere and lit his pipe, keeping a nonchalant eye on the sling. His appearance was like some kind of trigger. All at once the harbour swarmed with all the warm-hearted, familiar faces that Niall had known all his life. They gathered round him showering him with gifts.

Morag Ruadh pressed a small parcel into his hand. 'A wee bit tablet, just the way you like it. Mither moaned at me for using up the sugar and Father just missed the pan I was making the tablet in with his spit.'

Niall wasn't sure if she meant the tablet had been made with a recipe using some of old McDonald's spit but he took the package gratefully and kissed Morag Ruadh on the cheek. She looked astonished for a moment then she smiled slowly, a rueful gentle smile that softened her ruddy, weatherbeaten features.

Ranald beamed into the scene, pushing a bundle of rather tattered magazines into Niall's hands, and Todd the Shod gave him a tiny horseshoe. 'Just for luck,' he said in his apologetic fashion, though the keepsake had been cast with exquisite attention to detail.

Canty Tam smiled in his vacant fashion, murmuring something about no horseshoe on earth being a match against the evils of 'furrin parts' but his mother, a widow woman of mighty girth, prodded him sharply in the stomach, leaving him without further breath for his prophecies of doom.

Merry Mary, who had simply shut up shop for a few minutes, handed Niall a parcel, her usually radiant smile somewhat forced on this occasion. 'Just a wee bit sweets,' she whispered sadly. 'Not so good for the teeth but fine for the nerves – the wee kind in your belly that can make you feel sick.'

Righ nan Dul came limping along from his cottage perched close to the lighthouse at Port Rum Point. He had inherited the name from his father who had manned the lighthouse before him. It meant governor of the elements and Righ thoroughly deserved his title. His limp he owed to a fall on the twisting stairs inside the lighthouse but, despite it, he still kept his lonely night vigil, year after year. His weatherbeaten face creased into a grin at the sight of Niall and he shouted, 'I'll keep my torch burnin' for you, laddie, and may the Lord guide you home safe.'

'Thank you, Righ,' said Niall, feeling a lump rising in his throat as Righ's horny hand took his in a firm grasp.

Old Bob had stolen away from the fields to see Niall off. He was extremely fond of the doctor's son but his words were gruff as he hastily slipped a small heavy package into Niall's pocket. 'For fear you get drouthy, lad,' he mumbled and seized Niall's hand in his large calloused one. Niall couldn't speak. He knew if he did he would make a fool of himself. His dreamworld was growing in proportion yet still he felt and saw everything with an intense clarity.

Dodie galloped into the crowd. 'He breeah!' he sighed dismally, 'I thought I would miss the boat for I couldn't find Murn and old Jock comin' for him early. He's away now so he is and I just hurried down to give you this wee present.'

He was embarrassed and unsure of himself. Tears had sprung to his odd, pale eyes and Niall wasn't sure if they were for him or the going of his beloved Murn, but when he looked down at the exquisitely polished conch shell, with a shaky 'N' laboriously scratched on its surface, he knew that eccentric old Dodie wept for him.

'It's a bonny present, Dodie,' he said brightly.

'Ach well, you were a fine brave laddie,' came the reply and Niall knew that he was already as good as dead in Dodie's simple mind.

'Niall, Niall!' Fiona's small figure hurled itself at him. 'Old Murdoch let me away to say goodbye!'

He swung her into his arms. 'We said it this morning, you wee wittrock.'

She giggled, her dark eyes snapping with mischief. 'Old Murdoch doesny know that for I said you were in bed when I left for school.'

He nuzzled her warm neck and put out his free arm to his mother.

'I'm late,' she apologized, her concealed emotions putting a sharp edge to her voice. 'Mathew tore his knee on barbed wire and I had to bind it for him.'

Shona stood to the side. She felt shut off from Niall's world but she knew she was being foolish. She wondered if love was always such a strong influence on a person's normally sensible reasonings. Portcull was alive with people all claiming Niall's attention. A short time ago it had just been the two of them and selfishly she wanted it to stay like that, to have all his thoughts directed at her. She wanted to be the last person in his vision of Rhanna, instead it seemed the whole of Portcull would predominate over his final impressions.

She folded her arms behind her back and let the sounds wash over her. The cry of the gulls seared into her brain, the babble of voices made her want to scream.

A terrified bellow came from above and she looked

up to see a shaggy cream-coloured cow rigid with fright on the sling. It was perfectly safe in the strong canvas sling and the men winching her aboard were experts but the poor cow could know none of these things. Her eyes rolled and the rigid limbs thrashed the air. Shona felt sorry for the frightened animal. It was terrified of the unknown and, like herself, didn't know what the future held.

At the moment her own future looked bleak and she felt sick and empty. But a warm arm came round her neck to hug her close and Niall whispered, 'Don't desert a sinking ship! All these folk seeing me off as if I were some sort of hero and now all I want is you, mo gaolach.'

She was secure again but in minutes he was gone from her, striding up the gangplank to the deck to become again a dear, familiar, but unattainable figure.

Phebie gripped her arm. 'Hold on, mo ghaoil,' she urged. 'I know well how you feel but don't let go now.'

A sob rose in Shona's throat but she choked it back, looking up to smile and wave at Niall.

Fergus burst into the scene, tall and wonderfully calm. He slipped his arm round his daughter and drew her close. 'Thought you might like a shoulder,' he murmured. 'They come in handy betimes.'

She leaned against him and he felt hard and strong. The boat was casting off. Niall leaned on the rail shouting something she couldn't hear for the bellowing cows and the ship's loud, mournful horn. The crowd cheered and Niall raised his hand, a handsome slim figure in his Army uniform. For a moment

Shona swayed against her father. Her times of loving Niall were already folded into the caverns of her mind, the memories that would sustain her in the long days ahead. Already quarter of a mile of swirling green water was between her and the young man she loved. He was just a dark speck, indistinguishable from the other little specks that merged around him.

She was inclined to linger but her father pulled her away.

'I'm going back to make a Strupak,' said Phebie lightly. 'Anyone care to join me?'

'Just what we all need I'm thinking,' said Fergus leading his daughter firmly in the direction of Glen Fallan.

Barely a week later Shona was restless and unsettled. She had looked forward to the annual visit of the Travers family but a letter came from Oban containing the news that Murdy had fallen and broken a leg so their holiday would have to be cancelled.

'Maisie would have come alone,' wrote Mrs Travers, 'but she is going steady with a nice boy and doesn't want to leave him alone.'

'Frightened he would get away,' said Fergus with a grin.

Shona tossed her mane of bright hair impatiently. 'Och Father, you've never been very kind to poor Maisie.'

'Ach, it's just my way and if you must know the truth I was always frightened she would get me in a dark corner.'

Shona giggled absently and fingered the letter. 'I like

old Murdy, and Mrs Travers is such a cheery wee body. I could fair have been doing with them for a whiley. Alick and Mary won't be till Christmas and that's a long time away.'

Fergus tapped out his pipe on the edge of the grate. He looked at his daughter's brooding young face. 'Why don't you go to the Traverses'? The break will do you good, stop you thinking too much.'

She turned to him in surprise. 'But I'd have to leave you and you'd never manage on your own. Who would get your meals and darn your socks and feed the hens and – and . . .'

'I don't put a hole in my sock every few minutes,' he smiled, 'and I'm not a baby to be coddled by a daughter who's fast becoming a Cailleach before her time.'

The tears, never far away lately, sprang to her eyes. 'Och Father! How could you?'

'Because it's true. I know you love Rhanna but I think the time's ripe for you to get away. We all need fresh stamping ground at some time in our lives. Your time has come.'

She hesitated, her elbows on the table, the letter clutched in her hand. She knew her father was right. The things that had charmed her from babyhood now seemed to have no meaning. Her lonely walks could only take her to the places she and Niall had haunted. The white beaches and long stretches of moor now seemed bare and lonely and she returned from her lone wanderings disconsolate and uneasy. She tossed in bed unable to sleep and as a result she felt weary and disinterested. She reached across the scrubbed table top and caught her father's hand.

'Will – you write and ask, Father?'

'Get my pen and paper and I'll do it now. If we hurry we'll catch the boat before she leaves. Erchy says she had to bide in harbour for a minor repair but she'll be leaving soon.'

Mrs Travers's reply came the following week. She wrote saying she would love to have Shona, they were all looking forward to it, especially Murdy who was wearying and needing a 'cheery wee soul like Shona to cheer him up'.

'I don't feel very cheery.' Shona stared from the window at the blue-green Sound of Rhanna in the distance. It was a windy fresh day, the sort she had always loved. Behag Beag, her black coat flapping, was making her determined way to Lachlan's in time for morning surgery and Bob, his pipe hanging precariously from his lower lip, had hold of a ram by the horns and was dragging it to a small field of noisy sheep. The scene looked so familiar and dear that she suddenly felt she must sit down and write to let Mrs Travers know she couldn't manage after all.

Fergus was reading over the letter. 'They're expecting you by the next boat – the mail boat to Oban . . .' He paused as a memory came back to him. 'So you'd better iron your petticoats, mo ghaoil.'

'I wonder if Kirsteen ever goes back to Oban.' She said it absently, still staring from the window, but he looked at her quickly.

'Why do you say that?'

'You went there to find her, didn't you? I was only eleven, I think, but I remember you coming back. You had changed in a funny kind of way. You were so gay but your eyes – all empty and sad. I think I loved you more then than I ever did. It was after that I became your wife – yes, in a way, Father. I've looked after you and worried about you the way a wife would. Now I feel like you must have then – lonely and terribly empty.'

He put his arm round her. 'You'd better start packing. I know women take long over such things.'

'I think I'll only stay for a week, Father, so I won't need much. Now, you'd better get over and help Bob with that ram. I've never seen one so unwilling before.'

Her week dragged into a month and Fergus had never been so keenly aware of his own loneliness. The nights were long. Clocks ticked, Tot and the cats snored peacefully while he gazed into the fire and thought his lonely thoughts. He made work for himself, gathering in peat till the shed was piled high, scrubbing the milking shed till the cows looked uneasy at such cleanliness, and redecorated Shona's room for her return. Before bedtime each night he took to going to the byre to smoke his pipe in the company of the cows. They were such peaceful animals with their calm, long-lashed eyes, and they transferred some of their serenity to him. The cobbled byre was a place of warm breath, rich smells, and solid hairy backs to lean on and St Kilda, who had lorded the byre for years, would bellow at him till he was obliged to put a few strands of hay into the racks.

Letters came from France and he readdressed them to Oban knowing how eagerly his daughter waited them.

She returned to Rhanna three weeks before

Christmas and he was quietly pleased to see the change in her. Her eyes sparkled with life, her cheeks were pink, her slim body had filled out slightly. She flung herself on him and he felt his heart bursting with the joy of having her back.

'Oh Father, I've missed you so but I've enjoyed myself with the Traverses. I've got all my Christmas presents – the shops in Oban are bonny. Murdy's a terrible man, he taught me all the card games there are, so you and the McLachlans had best be careful if I'm playing with you.' She paused to look at the fields and the blue-grey shoulder of Sgurr na Gill. 'Och, isn't Rhanna beautiful?' She turned back to him, her blue eyes quizzical. 'It's strange, Father – I had to get away from Rhanna and I love you for making me go but I *knew* when I was ready to come back. I was pining for you and for my island. I suppose Phebie's told you Niall's well? He doesn't really describe what it's like out there but he never did explain things – even when he was away at school.'

She danced into the kitchen and Tot grunted delightedly to meet her. 'Oh, it's lovely to be back.' She was ecstatic. 'Dear old Tot and everything just the same. I hope it's always like this!'

'Things change,' he said lightly.

'Not Laigmhor, not you, Father. Now, I must unpack and hide my presents! I don't want you poking about . . . oh, Mrs Travers gave you this, she said she was going to send it but I was coming home so she gave it to me.'

She tossed a package on to the rocking chair and raced upstairs.

Fergus heard her exclaiming over her room as he picked up the parcel. It was wrapped in brown paper and tied tightly with string and he put it on the mantelshelf to open later.

He served out dinner and Shona felt like a queen being made to sit down while he ladled steaming soup.

'Just today,' he smiled ruefully. 'Tomorrow it's back to normal. I've a pile of socks to be darned and all my shirts need buttons.'

'I knew you needed me, Father,' she said triumphantly.

She was exhausted that evening and went to bed early. He sat for a time beside the fire, drinking his cocoa and sucking his unlit pipe. He reached to the mantelshelf for a taper and his hand brushed the parcel. Suddenly he felt quite excited about it and opened it quickly. He recognized the contents at once and his heart lurched into his throat. They were his letters to Kirsteen, each one opened but still in their envelopes. It had been so long since he'd written them yet it seemed only yesterday he'd painstakingly scrawled each loving word. But why were they sent to haunt him after all this time? There was a note from Mrs Travers and he read it, his hand trembling:

'Dear Fergus,

I should have written before but with Shona here the time has flown by so quickly. Mrs Fraser died two weeks ago and I went to clear out her bits and pieces for, though she was a selfish wee body in many ways, she grew to trust me over the years and would let no one else do things for her.

As you know I tidied for her now and then so it was natural enough for me to clear the things out. She has a sister somewhere and one or two nephews and the lawyer tried to trace them without success.

I found some letters from Kirsteen to her mother. She had been writing after all but Maggie Fraser never once hinted this to me and myself her good friend the besom. However I'm not one to speak ill of the dead. It was obvious Kirsteen had been sending money to her mother but there was no address on the letters and never a hint where she was staying so it was easy to see she never wanted her mother to know of her whereabouts.

The old lady has eaten her heart out these years since Kirsteen left. I used to see a tear in her eye on the few occasions she spoke of her lass. I know she was sorry for driving her away but she was a stubborn old lady and would never admit to being wrong. There's a hint she's left her house to some charity. She hadn't much else but her house and her memories. The lawyer will likely put something into the leading papers in an attempt to let Kirsteen know that her mother has passed on and if I hear anything I'll let you know.

The letters are your property, I think, and I feel it's your right to get them back. I didn't look at them, well, maybe just a wee keek and they were that lovely I had a quiet wee greet to myself.

Murdy and Maisie send their regards. I think the

break here has done Shona some good. She's a bonny bright lass and we'll all miss her. Take good care of yourself, my lad.

Your friend
Maggie Travers.'

Fergus picked up the sheaf of letters and crushed them to his breast. 'Kirsteen, Kirsteen,' he murmured brokenly, 'it seems everyone has read my letters but you.' He cradled his head in his hand, the firelight giving the dark curls on his brow the sheen of a raven's wing.

He remained where he was for some time, a strong motionless figure in his thick tweeds and Fair Isle pullover, lovingly knitted by Shona. The room was dark behind him and a faint wind rattled the window. A daring mouse nibbled crumbs by the dresser and Snap's ginger fur bristled but he was too lazily comfortable on the hearth to bother further.

The fire's glow found every hollow in Fergus's handsome face and iridescent colours broke on a tear poised on his lower lashes. His knuckles tightened on the letters and the sudden movement of his arm, drawn back to hurl them into the fire, made Snap sit upright, nostrils aflare with fright.

The bundle landed on a piece of unlit turf and remained unharmed but for the wraiths of smoke already blackening the edges. Fergus watched, his chest heaving. A flame curled greedily and with a small strangled cry he snatched the bundle back from the fire. Something that was beyond his understanding made him want to keep this reminder of the past. The letters were a link with Kirsteen, the girl who lived somewhere in the world and who cared for the son he had never seen. If he ever found them, the letters were proof of a heart that had never stopped mourning for a love he couldn't let go of.

Part Seven

Christmas 1939

Chapter Fourteen

The smell of snow was in Shona's room when she woke three days before Christmas. She was aware of it, even as she was aware of the feeling of nausea that was becoming a familiar sensation of her first waking hour. She lay snugly under the patchwork quilt she had started with Mirabelle's help when she was nine years old. She loved the quilt, it was a dear familiar thing in her life because each triangle and square was a memory. There were several patches from Mirabelle's thick tweedy coats and from old jackets of her father's. Many bits were from her own childhood clothes and two very precious patches had been begged from Niall to mend a torn square. He'd been fifteen when he'd given her the fragment of tartan from one of his discarded kilts. She ran her fingers over the rough homespun and thought about him. He wouldn't manage home for Christmas or New Year. He had leave but not enough to allow for all the travelling time necessary to get to Rhanna. She searched under her pillow and found his letter from the week before. One passage tormented her with its unconscious pathos:

'The thought of you is the one thing that keeps me going out here, mo gaolach. It's a cold place, a different cold from Rhanna, and it curls inside till it reaches every bone. I make myself remember each moment we shared then I get warm again. It's not that I find it hard to think of you but a man gets gey tired playing at soldiers and weariness does odd things to the memory.

'It will be strange not being home this Christmas. I've always had Christmas on Rhanna with my ain folk but I'll imagine you all, the peat fires, the plum puddings, and Bob playing his fiddle. Give your father my regards. Funny, I used to be a wee bit skearie of him, now I'm glad that one day I'll be his son-in-law.

'I look at the sampler you gave me often and, in my thoughts, I can see those misty islands.

'I love you, mo gaolach . . .'

She folded the letter and slid it back under the pillow, her arm frozen though it had only been exposed a few minutes. She covered herself again, reluctant to leave the warm bed. She heard her father in the kitchen and felt guilty. He was always up and about by six and in again for breakfast at half-past eight. Usually she had the fire going and his breakfast ready. Lately she'd felt too sick to move from her bed and the cold searching light of a winter dawn was something she hadn't seen for almost a week now. She'd felt the same nausea when she'd been staying with the Traverses but it had passed quickly and hadn't detracted from her enjoyment of the holiday. Oban seemed far away now and her visit belonged to another time.

Cups clattered in the kitchen and with quick decision she got out of bed, making Tot groan at the intrusion into her slumbers.

Shona was aware of the heavy dull soreness of her breasts as she swiftly pulled on clothes. She'd been aware of the feeling for some time but her mind was always so active with other things that she hadn't bothered very much about it, she always got it before a period only this time the heaviness was more acute. She pulled on a cardigan and her eyes fell on the calendar above her bed. She stared at it, her eyes growing big, while her hand went slowly to her mouth. She hadn't stopped to think before, to count the weeks, or to analyse the reason for the lack of menstruation. She sat back heavily on the bed and her hands went automatically to her stomach. She was going to have a child, Niall's child, it was growing inside her now and she hadn't been aware of it! The surprise of the discovery made her feel faint. She tried to think, to count the weeks of her pregnancy, but she couldn't. Pregnancy applied to people like Nancy and Mairi, to animals like sheep and cows, dogs and cats, not to beings like herself, in love but unmarried, and barely seventeen. Her time of loving Niall had been a time of joy, of innocent wonder of the untamed passion they had shared. It was their secret, a thing of beauty to be held in the heart and unlocked from the mind in the dark hours when others slept. She was shocked by her discovery but she wasn't afraid, there was going to be time enough for all those emotions later. The only real emotion she felt at that moment, other than surprise, was a growing certainty that she'd known all along that this was the thing that had motivated her to give herself so freely to Niall. She was afraid he wouldn't return to her and she'd wanted him to leave a part of himself, his seed was growing inside her, into a baby that would be like him.

In a daze she got up and splashed her face with cold water from the basin but the freezing water did nothing to rouse her from her trance. Her father shouted from below, 'Are you up yet, lass? The porridge is bubbling!'

'I'm coming, Father!' she cried and went downstairs with Tot at her heels. Warming flames leapt in the grate and the porridge made soft plopping sounds in the pan. Fergus was pouring water into the teapot but he turned to look at her.

'It will snow before the morn's out,' he forecast. 'I'll have to go out with Bob and Jock and put out neeps for the hill sheep and you'll have to look for Thistle again – he got out from the field, the rascal. Most of the beasts will need extra hay so it will be all hands to the plough.' He looked at her keenly. 'You look wabbit, Shona. Are you sleeping bad of late?'

She forced a laugh. 'Och no, Father, it's just lazy I am and afeard of the cold outside the bedclothes. I'm sorry you had to get breakfast and you out so early. It won't happen again.'

But he wasn't deceived. He ate his porridge thoughtfully and noticed she only toyed with hers. He'd noticed the change in her after her return from Oban. She was different in a subtle way. Her lovely elfin face was still rosy and her summer tan hadn't faded completely but there was a pinched look at her nostrils and her morning lethargy was very noticeable. She'd hardly missed a morning since Mirabelle's passing, therefore her behaviour was all the more noticeable.

There was something about her that stirred chords

somewhere in the recesses of his mind but he couldn't think what it was. He was used to Helen's fragile loveliness looking out from her face so it wasn't that which tormented him. He knew she missed Niall more than she would admit and he decided it was his absence so near Christmas that was causing her such distress. He remained silent till she was clearing the breakfast things then he said casually, 'I'll have an hour or two to spare this afternoon. Mathew has a few wee firs growing near his cottage and I thought we could cut one down and decorate it for Christmas. Alick and the bairns will be here next week and it would be nice to have a tree for them.'

Shona's eyes sparkled. 'That would be grand, Father. I'd like that fine, so will Alistair and Andrew. Oh, it will be nice to see them again. Mary's so different now. Do you know, she made better scones than me last year.'

The first flakes of snow began to fall while she was looking for Thistle. Somehow, the thing that she had discovered about herself that morning was so unreal that she pushed it to the back of her mind. Later she would think about it, later she would worry about telling her father, but not now, not with the calm cold air stinging her cheeks and the Sound of Rhanna glinting dull silver in the distance; not when snowflakes fell like silent fairies and were draping fields and dead bracken in white.

She found Thistle sharing a meal of sliced turnip with the shaggy sheep of the hill. He was unwilling to go with her because he was a creature of the wilds himself but she tied a rope round his neck and led him back to the pony shed where fresh oats soon settled him down.

By early afternoon the snow was two inches deep and Shona put on her wellingtons to cross the cobbled yard with her father so that they could check the outbuildings before setting off. The snow was powdery and crunched under their feet and she looked at her tall handsome father looming above her and felt a quick upsurge of happiness. He strode briskly, his pipe in his hand and the axe under the stump of his left arm.

Rhanna was like a Christmas card with the croft and byre huddled under a white blanket. Snow clung to bare trees and turned everyday objects into things of beauty. The crags of Glen Fallan blurred against the leaden sky and the tiny huddled houses of Portcull sent smoky banners into the snowflakes. It wasn't often snow came to Rhanna, it was therefore a novelty to the young but a hazard to the more mature who knew of the danger it could bring to livestock.

Shona lifted her face appreciatively. 'Oh, isn't it lovely, Father?'

'It's nice stuff to look at I'll grant you.'

'And to play in. I used to have such grand snow fights with Niall.'

Fergus had half-expected the snowball but hadn't bargained for such an exact aim at his neck. The snow melted and some slithered down the woollen neck of his jersey. Very deliberately he laid down his axe and pocketed his pipe. Shona yelled and looked for cover but there was none. His aim was even better than hers and the absence of an arm was no deterrent to him in the battle that ensued. Shona's cheeks glowed and even while she darted about she knew she was sharing with her father a precious moment. He loved her and trusted her and now she carried a secret, the disclosure of which could only be a matter of time. When he found out . . . She dared not think further and the tears of laughter in her eyes mingled with the tears of sorrow.

Lachlan joined them on the way. 'Tina's near her time,' he informed them, referring to Mathew's wife. 'Are you walking my way?'

'The very place,' said Fergus. 'We're cutting down a tree for Christmas. Mathew has some nice firs, some that Hamish planted a few years back. He never thought they would survive that wind that whistles up from the sea but they have, though they're a wee bit twisted.'

Lachlan looked at Shona. 'The fishing boat brought in some extra mail at dinner time. Erchy's just brought a letter from Niall so no doubt there will be one for you too. It's a shame he can't be home for Christmas but Phebie sent him a food parcel. She's certain he's starving to death out there. There's enough shortbread and tablet to go round the regiment.'

Shona drew in her breath and wanted to run home to Niall's letter but she marched steadily beside the men. 'I've sent a parcel too, not a foodie one, I knew Phebie would do that. I knitted him gloves and a scarf that just got longer and longer without my realising. Poor Niall, he'll be sharing it too with the regiment, I'm thinking!'

They scrunched up to Mathew's cottage. Three-year-old Donald drifted to meet them, a purring cat draped round his neck. The little boy followed Fergus and watched solemnly while the tree was being cut.

Shona went straight to the kitchen to make a Strupak while Lachlan examined his patient. Shona felt at home in the cottage. It was little changed from Hamish's day. Dogs and cats were heaped by the fire; the sofa was covered in hairs, and Tina always half-heartedly apologized to visitors, but she was a pleasant, easygoing, young woman who spent her life dressed in a smock and slippers. She muddled through each cluttered day and she and Mathew were extremely happy.

Fergus came in with the tree and Donald, still with the cat round his neck, went to sit on the rug to gaze dreamily into the fire and pick his nose. His mother, oblivious to his bad manners, sat on a chair beside him, her body arched forward so that she wouldn't squash a large ginger cat who had lost an ear in some nocturnal battle.

Shona plucked a hair from her tea and studied Tina quietly. Was it possible that one day she would look like that, her stomach an enormous protuberance and her breasts hanging heavy with milk? Tina looked like St Kilda, the old cow who lorded the byre, somehow always escaping the fate of most cows past their best; a trip to the slaughterhouse on the mainland. St Kilda's udder swayed with the slightest movement and almost touched the ground.

Tina bent to re-turf the fire and Shona could see right inside her loose garments. Her breasts flopped heavily, and there was darkness where the belly swelled relentlessly. There was no grace or dignity, from the shamelessly splayed legs to the hair scraped back with kirbies. Shona shuddered. She couldn't get like that – she was too slim, her breasts were high and tight. Tina was normally a pretty girl but inclined to plumpness and there was simply no comparison. Nevertheless she was aware of Tina's every move, noting the awkward walking gait, with the belly thrown out and the feet spread to withstand the weight.

'When is the bairn due?' she heard herself asking.

'Och, it will come at any time now.' Tina patted her stomach affectionately. 'It's a wee bit skearie I am with Mathew out all day. I'm thinkin' the snow will last a while and me here all by myself. It's a quiet wee corner and sometimes it's only Erchy I'm seein' in the daytime. My sister from Croy said she would come and bide with me for a whiley but I hear tell she has a bad cold and in bed. I dareny think how auld Biddy will get up in time to deliver me. I was so quick with Donald! Just came out like a wee skinned rabbit he did after only four hours' labour. 'Tis afraid I am just.'

Lachlan patted her arm reassuringly. 'Don't worry, lass. When has Biddy ever let anyone down?'

'Och, I know she's a good sowel but she's a mite too auld to be gallopin' about in this weather!'

'I'll come.' Shona's impulsive offer surprised her own ears. 'I'll manage to sit with you in the afternoons till your time's past.'

'Ach, it's kind you are, Shona, mo ghaoil.' Tina beamed with gratitude and Fergus smiled quietly at his daughter's sudden look of apprehension.

They stood up to go and Tina ushered them to the door with Donald toddling at her back, wiping his sticky fingers on her apron.

'No skinned rabbits at Christmas,' ordered Lachlan jokingly. 'It's turkey for me that day and a dram, with my feet up at the fire.'

Snow was still falling heavily and it was good to get back to Laigmhor and the cosy kitchen. They seldom used the parlour now but after tea Fergus went through and lit the fire. Coal was piled on and the flames licked it greedily. The air of gloom, always present in a room that hadn't been fired for some time, dispersed quickly. He recalled the days when the parlour had been one of the most used rooms in the house and he remembered vividly the family Sundays with he and Alick sitting stiffly to attention while their father read from the enormous family bible. He had spent some of his happiest days in the parlour when Helen had been alive. The warm fragrant kitchen was Mirabelle's domain in those days but the parlour had been his and Helen's kingdom. In it they had made their most important decisions and, huddled cosily on the big settle, they had sometimes made love there.

He looked round at the dark walls where phantoms made by the fire cavorted and darted. The dresser held the best china and two large soulful-looking plaster dogs guarded the hearth. The mantelshelf was covered with photographs and from the top of an old wind organ that he and Alick had pumped to death as boys, the sepia-tinted features of his parents regarded him solemnly.

It was a room with a feel of the past and Fergus

shuddered. Shona called on him to help her with the tree, already potted in an old tub.

'I think I'll do up the parlour,' he told her. 'It has an odd feel about it now. It would be nice to brighten it up with some paint. It feels as if it's waiting for something to happen.'

She dusted her hands on her apron and looked at the dark walls. She seldom came into the parlour except to dust but now she took stock of it and knew what he meant. It was a 'dead' room, full of reminders of people long departed life.

'Yes, Father,' she said slowly, 'it's fusty and needs doing. Mirabelle used to say "Make the old thing new and meet again an old acquaintance".'

He didn't reply but heaved the tree up to the window and she decorated it while he sat on the settle and watched her. The decorations were mere paper chains and fir cones, baubles of silver paper and cotton wool, but they nestled against the dark green of the needles and looked lovely.

Shona stayed on in the room long after her father had gone up to bed. 'Don't be too late,' he warned before going upstairs. 'You know you can't get up come morn.'

She lay down on the settle, staring at the tree and wondering for the first time what Niall's reaction would be to a baby. Till now he was the one whose opinion she had feared the least but now her thoughts were crowding in on her and she was afraid. Niall might be horrified at the idea. He would come home from war, expecting the slim girl he'd left behind and instead he'd find a lumbering monster. Even though it was his baby he might not want it. They'd barely courted each other and suddenly he would be confronted with the enormous responsibility of fatherhood. Then there were his parents, how would they take it? How would her father react to a daughter who shamed him so? She felt she couldn't bear any of it and she felt sick and utterly lonely.

A star was twinkling in the window behind the tree. She was so dejected she was ready to grasp at any straw and she saw the star as a symbol, a sign that Niall would love her no matter what happened. She sat up and wiped away a tear with a slim delicate hand then rose and went to the window, rubbing away the steam to see a moon-bathed snowscape. The sky was ablaze with stars and the moon spun a pathway of silver on the sea. A movement at the wire fence surrounding the garden caught her eye and she laughed softly. The deer had come down from the hills and were eating some old kale stalks, past their best and higher than the fence. For a long time she watched the graceful creatures then she went to the kitchen, put on her shawl and her boots, and went out to the hayshed and scooped out forkfuls to spread behind the outhouses. The deer had magically disappeared but she knew they would be back. It was bitterly cold. She huddled into her shawl and looked at the sky and particularly at the brilliant star she had noticed before.

'Twinkle, twinkle little star . . .' she chanted childishly and scooped a handful of snow to throw in the air. It was strange to be out there on the sleeping island. Lights from fishing boats were visible though they were well out at sea and the world was hushed and very peaceful. Small sounds were to be heard, a rustling from the byre and a snort from the pony shed, but otherwise all was silent. Tot waddled into the path of light from the kitchen and sniffed the air. She shook a paw, disgusted by the snow, then squatted hastily before turning back to the warmth. At the door she stopped to look at her mistress, undoubtedly puzzled by the quirks of human nature.

'In a wee minute, Tot,' called Shona softly and reluctantly abandoned the world of white peace. The clock in the parlour was at half-past eleven and guiltily she remembered the promise she had made her father to be in bed early. She took the lamp and went upstairs. The halo of light revealed Fergus outside his door.

'Where have you been?' he demanded rather sharply. 'You should have been in bed long ago.'

'Yes, Father, I . . .' Impulsively she wanted to throw herself at him and unburden her heart. How interwoven the pattern of their lives had become when he was unable to sleep because she had broken their usual routine. His face was dark and angry and she could only say, 'I'm sorry, Father, the tree was so bonny and the deer were down from the hill. I gave them some hay.'

'Aye well, you won't get up in the morn.' His voice was softer now.

'I will, I promise you won't come in to a cold kitchen again.'

'It's not that, lass, it's . . . never mind now. Goodnight.'

'Goodnight, Father.'

*

Tina was pacing the floor when Shona arrived on the afternoon of Christmas Eve. Donald was playing with lumps of peat from the turf box, mixing small bits with saliva and spreading it carefully on a black and white collie who looked dejected but resigned to such happenings. Two hens squawked in the kitchen, cocking beady eyes at a black kitten who was stalking them under cover of dirty pans on the floor.

Shona grabbed a besom and chased the hens outside and Tina sighed gratefully. 'The buggers came in when I was fetching water and I was putting them out when the pains started bad.'

'Pains?' faltered Shona. 'You haven't started, Tina? Did you tell Mathew when he was in at dinner?'

'Och well, they weren't bad enough then. It's hard to tell because you get a lot o' funny wee pains in the last month. I didn't want to worry poor Mathew, he was going to thraw some turkeys this afternoon and he never did have a stomach for such things.'

Shona held her breath and wondered at girls like Tina. She was a grotesque figure with her belly lumped before her in menacing splendour. Her pleasant pink features were twisted in pain and all she could think of was Mathew. She was the most unromantic sight on earth yet she loved with utter self-denial.

'Are you sure . . . now?' asked Shona, hopeful of a negative reply.

'Aye, sure as daith! My waters came you see, near as much as came out o' Brodie's burn in a week . . . but och . . . I shouldny say such things to a wee lass like you.'

'I'm nearly seventeen,' asserted Shona faintly, 'and I'd better go for Lachlan and send a message to Biddy.'

'Ach, the puir auld Cailleach will never manage. She near died when Donald was coming. She was so wabbit from the walk I'd to give her brandy and me the patient!'

Shona darted to the door but Tina let out such a cry that she turned back and helped her to lie down on the sofa. Donald turned, and with an angelic smile, rubbed his lovely muddy mixture into the sole of his mother's slipper.

Tina grabbed Shona's arm and her usually calm brown eyes were gently worried. 'My – pans – the dishes – could you wash them, mo ghaoil? I know I'm not very tidy but the doctor will need hot water and he can't have it mixed with clapshot can he?'

'I'll do them later, Tina! I'd better go! Lachlan might be out on rounds and it will take Biddy a while to get down from the Glen. If I see Father, I'll ask him to fetch her in the trap – if he can get it through.'

Tina let out a cry and gritted her teeth. She was unable to speak for a moment, then her face relaxed and resumed its usual beatific expression. She lay amongst patchwork cushions covered with cat's hairs and suddenly looked so radiant it was difficult to believe she was in childbirth.

'It'll be a girl, I know it will be a girl! A bonny wee lass that I can cuddle and dress in fine frocks.'

Shona smiled with affection at the bulk on the sofa. 'I'm going now, Tina. I'll run if I can.'

'Och, mo ghaoil, wait a minute. Och I wish my sister was here – you can be more at home with your own.

I meant to have everything ready but I never seemed to have the time. Shona, would you get me a pair o' knickers? The others got all wet with . . . well you'll find them in the top drawer in the bedroom – the pink ones with the wee bits o' lace at the legs.'

Shona was exasperated. 'Tina! The doctor will just make you take them off again!'

'Och, I know, but a lass has to be respectable.'

Shona fetched the desired garment and left Tina pulling them on with Donald, an interested spectator, admiring the bits of lace.

Lachlan was out. The pony and trap were gone and with it seemingly the whole family. Shona rapped the door till her knuckles were sore but no Phebie or Fiona appeared to greet her. She looked round desperately. Sometimes her father was about but today the fields were deserted and she knew he had gone to the high ground with Bob and Mathew to bring the sheep to lower ground in case there was more snow. Her eyes searched in all directions for a sign of life. The children were on Christmas holidays and those who lived in the Glen were often to be seen making the journey to and from Portcull but today the road was empty. Panic gripped her. She had to get a message to Biddy. If she went herself it meant leaving Tina on her own for at least an hour, probably more because of the snow.

Something black and ragged flapped in the distance. She recognized Dodie coming from the hill track, obviously bent for the village. She almost screamed his name but for a moment he appeared not to hear, then she realised he'd slipped on the hill and couldn't stop for a time but his arm was raised and she heard his familiar, 'He breeah!' with something akin to hysterical laughter. He loped up, dusting snow from his coat, his stained teeth showing his pleasure at being hailed.

'He breeah!' she greeted him swiftly. 'Could you take a message to Biddy for me, Dodie?'

His face fell and his peculiar mourning eyes brimmed with tears. It was obvious he was disappointed and she suspected he'd been hoping to partake of a cosy Strupak at Slochmhor.

'It's a fair walk,' he pointed out sadly, 'and Merry Mary was keeping my baccy.'

'Father will give you some later and . . .' She gripped his arm impulsively. 'Come over tomorrow for a bite of Christmas dinner. I'm cooking it myself though Kate McKinnon made me the dumpling but – hurry now to Biddy and tell her Tina's baby is coming.'

His face lit with joy. Christmas dinner for Dodie was hardly different from any other day. People were kind and gave him tit-bits but other than that his festivities were sparse. He flapped away with his giant lolloping gait.

She scrunched back through the snow to the cottage. A squadron of hens raced helter-skelter to meet her and she realised they probably hadn't yet been fed.

'Where's the hens' pot, Tina?' she called.

'On the bunker,' answered Tina through clenched teeth.

Shona spent the next half-hour washing up and boiling pans of water. She was glad to be doing something because the moans coming from the sofa frightened her more than she could have believed. She piled peat on the fire and removed a skelf from Donald's finger.

'Muvver's greetin',' he observed in his childish lilting voice. 'Muvver's belly sore.' He drew his hand across his eyes and screwed his nose with the back of a dirty hand. The threatening tears spilled over to be scrubbed away on Dot the collie's floppy ears.

'Weesht,' soothed Shona. 'We'll get mother cooried in bed. Doctor will be here soon because there's going to be a new baby. Biddy will be here too.'

'Biddy,' beamed Donald who loved the green-cloaked, kenspeckle figure. A visit from her meant a boiling to suck and spectacles to play with and the most amazing teeth that simply lifted from her mouth in two whole pieces.

Tina didn't want to go to bed. 'A nice cup o' tea first, mo ghaoil. I've such a drouth on me.' She got up and began to pace again, her hands gripping her back, her legs splayed wider than ever.

Shona got the tea and wished someone would come. She looked from the window and saw a blanket of whirling snowflakes.

'Is anyone coming at all yet?' asked Tina who had collapsed again on the sofa, her face very pale and her eyes showing her pain.

Shona shook her head wordlessly.

'God, make them hurry,' prayed Tina aloud. 'The pains are coming so fast now, I don't think it will be long. 'Tis hell so it is, lass, just hell!'

She let out a sharp cry and both Donald and Shona stared wide-eyed.

'Muvver's dyin',' yelled Donald and his nose frothed profusely.

Shona ran to the door and looked out along the path. Nothing moved in the swirling snowstorm, only the trees stood like sentinels on the fringe of the fields. Another cry came from within and she hurried inside. Tina was writhing and the sweat stood on her brow. Shona felt sick and giddy but she took Tina's hand. 'They won't be long, Tina. It's just the snow's so heavy and walking will be difficult. I'll put on my boots and go up the track for a wee bit. I can give Biddy an arm though Lachlan will most likely be there . . . pray God!' she ended in a fervent whisper.

But Tina kept hold of her hand. 'Stay wi' me, Shona. Och please! The bairn's coming, I can feel it! It's been making me push for the last two pains. Could – could you have a wee look? Just a quick peep. Biddy could tell me the colour o' Donald's hair at this stage.'

Shona's heart was racing and she pushed copper strands from her eyes. 'I'll – I'll get a bowl of water first! I think I'll bathe your brow.'

Her hands trembled as she lifted a heavy black pot from the fire. The fact that she had to step over cats and dogs strewn uncaringly on the rug, made her task all the more difficult, but she held the steaming bowl aloft and went to Tina.

Donald sat solemnly amidst the animals, his thumb in his mouth, watching the bulk of belly, all that he could see of his mother, heaving on the sofa.

'You'll need some sheets and cotton wool,' whispered Tina, her eyes dark and pleading. 'It's all in a wee bag under the bed. The – baby's shawl is in there too.'

Shona's eyes were very blue in her white face. 'Tina – I – I – can't. I've brought forth a lamb before and helped my father pull the calves from the cows but never – never a *baby*!'

'It's the same thing,' urged Tina. 'Easier than a calf. I'll do most of it but you've got to help a wee bit. I'll tell you what to do. Och – mo ghaoil – one day you'll have a bairn of your own and you'll need all the help you can get.'

Shona looked down at the young woman and said gently, 'Tina, tell me what to do for I'm shaking like a newborn lamb.'

'Have – a wee look and tell me how much you can see o' the bairn's head.'

Donald sucked his thumb and rocked himself, looking calmly up the dark tunnel of his mother's legs ending in a pit of blackness where, from his position, nothing was visible. But Shona saw a crown of fine hair and the sight made her draw in her breath and feel unaccountably thrilled.

'Your baby's got fair hair, Tina.'

'Never! Och, it'll be a girl, I know – I wish I could see the other end.'

Shona tucked the sheets over the sofa then bathed Tina's face and gave her sips of cold water. She was panting and pushing and gripping Shona's arm till it was red and bruised.

Half an hour passed. Shona went to the door again

but the snow was heavier and she could see nothing. Mathew will be home soon, she thought. Father won't keep him in weather like this.

The cottage was unbearably warm and she wished she hadn't piled the fire so high.

'Shona!' Tina's cry pierced the air. 'The bairn's coming now!'

She was pushing, her face red and her lips clamped in a straight line. Her legs were spread, one braced against the back of the sofa, the other waving in mid-air. She grabbed the limb and held on to it, uncaringly displaying the huge pale dome of her belly with its untidy sprinkling of pubic hair. Donald looked up from the absorbing pleasure of licking butter from a scone.

Shona had no time to be afraid. She stared breathlessly at the gleaming circle of the baby's head. Tina's whole being was absorbed in getting the child out from her body. Her face was upturned, her eyes were closed, and elbows dug into the couch to further the terrible, supreme effort a woman has to make in childbirth.

The small circle grew bigger. Tina gave a mighty push, her voice catching in her throat in a half sob. Suddenly the small head was expelled and with it a rush of amniotic fluid. Instinctively Shona supported the warm slithery little head. She was still apprehensive but now a sense of wonder held her and she wanted to help the small thread of life all she could.

Tina lay back exhausted and the baby's head hung helplessly. Tina gathered her remaining strength and strained for a moment. The baby shot out in a rush of fluid to lie still and lifeless in the pool that had buffered it for the last nine months. The waxy white coils of the umbilical lifeline were yet attached to the placenta inside Tina and Shona stared helplessly at the awesome sight.

'The – the baby's a funny blue colour,' she whispered.

'So was Donald, it's natural, hold it up by the feet and smack its wee bum.'

But there was no need. The tiny form jerked and gasped, its mouth opened, and it cried loudly and clearly.

Donald toddled over and pointed. 'Doll's crying!' he reported happily and clapped his hands. Tina lifted her head to look and the tears of joy sprang to her eyes. 'It's a wee lass, och, wrap it in the shawl away from the mess. Everything else will keep for a whiley.'

Ironically, everyone arrived at once. Biddy, supported by Mathew, slithered in, her coat hem soaked and her spectacles askew. As always she was slightly indignant about everything. Dodie's rude awakening of her cosy afternoon nap had given her 'bellyache' and he'd been no help at all on the treacherous Glen road. She was soaked and frozen and needing a 'cuppy' but as always the sight of the newborn softened her kindly old face and brought forth as much excitement as the new mothers felt themselves. She stared at Tina's new baby and threw up her hands. 'Mercy! It's come! And the deliverer wee Shona McKenzie none other! Mathew, get the whisky. We'll all be needin' a dram, I'm thinkin'!'

She went to cut the birth cord and deliver Tina of the placenta. When Lachlan arrived he found a clean mother and baby and a slightly inebriated old midwife, minus teeth and spectacles, reclining beside two cats in the armchair. Donald peered from behind spectacles and grinned at him with a mouth grossly misshapen by its burden of extra teeth.

Mathew, overjoyed by his tiny daughter's arrival, was in danger of collapsing on Biddy's knee as he refilled her glass from the almost empty whisky bottle. 'It's a wee lass,' he greeted Lachlan, 'a bonny wee lass. I couldny have given Tina a nicer Christmas present if I'd tried – eh?' He grinned in a gluttony of self-satisfaction and knocked Biddy's hat off for the third time.

Lachlan had to smile. It was usual for new fathers to take most of the credit for their offspring till sleepless nights and cold meals, served late by a disgruntled wife, brought them quickly to their senses. Mathew was wallowing in his hour of glory and Tina, only slightly weary looking, was letting him have his way. She was quietly radiant and it wasn't easy to believe she had just endured an afternoon of agonising labour. Her daughter slept warmly and peacefully by her side and she stared at the tiny red face in wonder.

Lachlan went over to admire the newborn infant. 'A bonny wee lassie right enough and she arrived on the eve of Christmas. She'll be a blessed bairn.'

'Doctor, you have just given me her name, I'll call her Eve.' Tina's satisfaction was complete. 'It's a bonny name for a bonny wee lass.'

'And thank Biddy for getting here in time to deliver her,' said Lachlan. 'It's a treacherous road over the

Glen today and myself out with the family would never have got here in time.'

'Och but doctor, it was not Biddy either! Wee Shona McKenzie brought my bairn forth and the Lord be thanked for her. I don't know what I would have done without her. She fetched and carried and saw to Donald.'

Biddy staggered upright holding her glass aloft. 'Praise be to the Lord for Tina's safe delivery and thanks be to our Shona.'

Lachlan turned his dark head to look at Shona and saw that she was fast asleep on a small hard rocking chair. She looked very young with her smooth flushed skin and long tresses of silken hair hanging over her shoulders. Biddy's words brought back the long ago night at Laigmhor with the storm freezing his marrow and the terrible tragic aftermath of the weary struggle with the dark angel of death. The results of that night had been many but the most loving and lasting had been Shona. She and his son loved and because of them the lives of all of them were inextricably bound together. He knew she was missing Niall badly. Despite her vivacity and spirited nature there had always been an aura of contentment about her; now he sensed a restlessness and looking closer he thought there was a weariness in the youthful shadows of her face. She stirred and uttered a small cry but smiled when she realised where she was.

Lachlan took her hand. 'Doing me out of a job, I hear. It's proud I am of you, lassie, and thinking you deserve a cuppy. If our new father would care to stop patting himself on the back he might make us all one.

After all – though he did most of the work according to what I'm told – there were other parties who just *might* have helped a wee bitty.'

Mathew reddened and hastened to put on the kettle and Biddy, toothless and barely able to see, nodded with satisfaction. 'Just what we all need. The daft bugger might have given the bairn birth himself the way he's carryin' on. Ach well, I suppose it's only natural.' She fixed her dim eyes on Shona who was yawning and stretching. 'It'll be the same wi' you my wee lass when your time comes. Young Niall will take all the credit – it's the way o' things.'

For a moment Shona's arms remained in mid-air. She wondered wildly if the cunning old midwife could possibly have guessed her secret. But Biddy was toasting her feet and had apparently forgotten her surroundings. Her smile was very toothless and alcohol appeared to have taken her mind faraway.

Shona held her breath because she wanted to cry. She was beginning to misconstrue innocent remarks and knew she would go on doing so till the truth was out. She glanced at Lachlan and wondered sadly if she ought to unburden herself to him. He was always so fair about everything and wouldn't be likely to fly into a rage like her father. But telling Lachlan would be the easy way out and something in her make-up had always prevented her taking the easier course. She was proud and stubborn but above all else she was true to herself and that had always meant being true to those she loved most. No matter how nasty or unpleasant, her father was the person to know first. She fingered Niall's letter in her pocket. If only he were coming home that would solve a lot but his leaves were not long enough and the war was getting more serious which meant young men like Niall were desperately needed in the fight.

She sipped her tea and felt very scared because she alone carried the burden of her knowledge. The man she loved could do nothing to help her. She wasn't even going to tell him about the baby, not until it became more real to herself. At the moment it was all like a dream. She looked at Tina crooning over her baby but the sight did nothing to cheer her. Her baby wasn't real like Tina's and she couldn't imagine herself going through the ordeal she had witnessed that day.

Childlike, she turned her mind away from herself and thought about Christmas. The snow made it all very real and created just the right atmosphere for presents, turkey, and plum pudding, Christmas trees and carols. Alick and Mary were coming with the twins: the thought of their cheery, lively presence at Laigmhor made her smile.

She jumped up. She had a lot to do and she had to get home. Biddy groaned and began pulling on her boots. Everyone was making a move to go and she wasn't letting Lachlan away so easily when he might offer to take her home in the trap. She didn't relish the thought of plodding up the Glen in the snow. She sighed and wondered how long she could go on. She was seventy-three and beginning to feel it but she would be lost without her patients and her babies. She was greying and old-looking, with her grizzled thin hair escaping her hat and her cheeks wrinkled and sunken, but there was still a dignity about her bearing.

She gently prised her belongings from Donald and went through to the kitchen to rinse her teeth.

'Let's go, mo ghaoil,' she said to Shona, grinning resplendently. She took the girl's arm and wanted for a moment to hold her close and tell her not to worry. She wasn't going to find the months ahead easy and the old woman prayed that Niall would come out of the war alive so that Shona's child would have his name.

Her throat felt tight with sorrow for all the torrential emotions that girls like Shona must bear alone. She had given herself away so easily, the reddening of the face and the long silence at Biddy's words. Oh, they had been innocent enough until they were uttered, but the reaction to them had caused the seemingly unobservant old midwife to note all the usual signs, the thickening of a normally diminutive waist, the pinched face, the tired pallor, all so plain to an expert looking for them.

Biddy sighed again and hoped that Helen McKenzie's daughter would give birth easier than her mother had done all those years ago.

Part Eight

1940

Chapter Fifteen

The swelling sounds of spring filled the air, the most compelling being those of the newborn lambs. Shona, coming from Portcull with a laden basket, paused to catch her breath and gaze at the lambing fields. She saw her father with some of the men, dark specks in the distance, with two smaller dots that were sheepdogs frisking busily.

Biddy was coming down the hill-track from Nigg, her green cape lifting in the gentle breeze from the sea. She was panting and slightly askew as usual. A smile lit her face when she saw the girl leaning by the dyke.

'It's yourself, lass? My, I'm damty tired so I am. Been sitting with Mamie McKinnon for three hours so I have and then the pains go – just like a puff o' wind. It happens sometimes. How is it with you, my wee one?'

Her scrutiny appeared careless yet she took in everything.

'I'm fine, Biddy,' answered Shona pulling herself up quickly. Her clothes were loose-fitting and she was neat to be in her sixth month of pregnancy but nevertheless she knew she couldn't hide her condition much longer.

'Aye,' Biddy gazed into the distance, 'fine you look too, mo ghaoil – for a lass so far gone with child.' She heard the surprised intake of breath but stayed the stammered protestations with a gentle touch of her hand. 'Weesht, lassie,' she whispered kindly, 'I'm an auld hand at the game – remember? I was tendin' pregnant lasses afore you were born and I know the signs fine. I've known for a long time about you and I'm thinkin' it's high time you told your father. You haven't yet, eh?'

Shona shook her head miserably.

'Aye well, the time has come, mo ghaoil. You canny hide it any more. It's a wonder Lachlan hasny spotted it.'

'I – I haven't been over for a time.'

'Aye, he mentioned that you were keepin' away these days. I knew why of course. He's a doctor and a good one. Mind you, he wouldny be lookin' for such a thing and you're such a mite of a lass still. We're all inclined to think o' you as a bairn yet. Some are wed at your age, I know, but you have the look o' a wee lassie just out o' school . . .'

She was expecting the tears and her arms were ready. She hugged the sobbing girl to her scrawny bosom and uttered words of comfort, 'Weesht, my bonny one. Tell your father, you'll feel the better o' it. He's near at hand to give you comfort whilst Niall, the poor laddie, is too far away to help at all. He'd be pleased I'm sure if he knew someone here was helpin' you.'

'But he doesn't know either,' wailed Shona. 'I meant to tell him in every letter but somehow I'm afraid it will take away all the lovely things we shared!'

Biddy nodded significantly. 'And wasn't the making

o' the bairn a thing you both had a share in? Och, pull yourself together this meenit, girl! You must be near out your mind keepin' such a thing to yoursel' so long. Niall wouldny be pleased. Surely he's more o' a man than you're givin' him credit for. It's time for the truth, my lassie. Mirabelle taught you well, don't let her down any more than you have already!'

Shona made her way home, oddly comforted by the old midwife's blunt words. She made up her mind to tell her father that night.

But there was no need. He was kept late in the lambing field and when he arrived home she was asleep in the inglenook. He tiptoed to retrieve his dinner from the oven and sat to eat it quietly. He looked at his daughter and wondered at the little naps she seemed to find so necessary now. It was so unlike the vivacious, almost untamed vitality he was so used to, that he was beginning to wonder about her health and the very thought of anything wrong made him pause, the fork halfway to his mouth. He studied her intently, knowing there was something different yet unable to place it. Living with someone, seeing them every day, it was difficult to pinpoint changes, yet he knew there was change in her. She was lying awkwardly, her head pillowed on her arm in a familiar childlike pose. Her dress had caught under her and was pulled into the contours of her body. The thing he had imagined to be so subtle now glared at him and he drew in his breath sharply, his meal forgotten. He tried to tell himself it wasn't true, the distortion of the slim child's figure had something to do with the way she was lying, but how could anything lumped into such an obvious place be a figment of his imagination? It all fitted, the sickness, the fatigue, the gradual change from flimsy garments to the loose smocks and dresses he'd thought to be a mere girlish whim.

He got up and went to look down at her. He could feel the muscle in his face working the way it always did when traumatic feelings seethed in him. He knew of course whose child it was but at the moment he had no thoughts for the young man at war in France. His fury was all for his daughter, the child he had come to trust and love with an intensity that he was afraid of at times. She was all he had, he knew his life revolved round her too much but he couldn't help himself. They needed each other, each a buffer for the other's loneliness.

The strength of his presence reached into her sleeping brain. She stirred and her eyes opened, a smile of pleasure lighting them. 'Father!' She struggled up. 'I left your dinner in the oven. Did you get it?'

The black fury in his face deepened and when he spoke his voice was hoarse with the depth of his hurt. 'Tell me, girl, tell me about the thing that has turned you from a bairn into a clumsy tired Cailleach! You're with child, aren't you? Dammit, I should have guessed but I thought you had more sense! You're having Niall McLachlan's child after all my warnings and all your ill-kept promises! You're no better than a tramp!'

The whiplash of his words made her cringe back against the cushions, afraid of the temper that was boiling over in such frothing fury. She had seen his rages before but never one so furious as now. Her heart pounded and the room spun round.

'Say it damn you,' he roared. 'Let me hear from your own lips you've lain with McLachlan and now carry his child!'

She felt faint and strangely breathless. 'I tried to tell you, Father, I wanted to but I was afraid! I was going to tell you tonight – Biddy knows and thought you should too! But you were late and I fell asleep . . .'

'So – the word is already getting round! Biddy knows – before your own father! Soon the whole of Rhanna will know that McKenzie's daughter's a slut!'

'I'm not ashamed, Father,' she sobbed. 'I love Niall and because of that I am proud to be carrying his child! It might be the only part of him I'll have left in the end. I am *not* ashamed, Father!'

His hand came down and crashed into her face with such force that she fell back against the cushions. Tot whimpered and struggled up to lick her mistress's bleeding lip.

The door slammed and the house was quiet but unnaturally so. Shona's tears were soundless though she wanted to scream and run to someone for comfort. She thought of Niall but even he was unreal in her mind. He was her life yet he could not help her. Somewhere he too fought a lonely battle in some stinking trench in faraway France. Seas and mountains divided them when they needed each other most. She couldn't know if there was any comfort in his life but she had people she could turn to, those who were the flesh of her beloved Niall. She rose from the couch and ran from Laigmhor to the warm beckoning glow of Slochmhor nestling in its shelter of Scotch pines.

Fergus walked as he had walked on that other night of tortured mind and spirit, blindly without thought of direction.

The infant Shona had pointed the screaming finger of accusation at him then, her child's mind infuriated because of the tight band of secrecy he had woven round the truth of her existence. Now he was the accuser and his hurt wouldn't let his seething mind see anything, other than the fact that the child he had come to worship had deceived him by her very silence.

The cool night wind lashed over him and he was aware of the sound of the sea. He walked on, stumbling over rocks on the shore, his head bent in misery. He came then to the place he had sought once before. From the lonely washed shore he looked towards the schoolhouse, its windows aglow from the soft lights within. It was the same place it had been on that other night, a dark mass of stone and chimneys outlined faintly against the endless moors. But within moved little Mr Murdoch and his family. There was no Kirsteen beckoning him wordlessly with the beauty of her body and soul. He could run to no one for the comfort he so desperately needed.

He sat on a barnacle-encrusted rock and cradled his dark head in his hand. The sound of the sea and the soft sigh of the wind gave peace to the night and gradually his reeling senses cleared. He began to collect each of his thoughts and sort them out.

An hour passed. The beautiful peace of the Rhanna night seeped into him and he raised his head to look at the soft glow of silver on the water. He reached for a pebble and threw it into the water and as it sank it seemed to carry all his furious feelings to the bottom of the sea.

Now his heart cried for the little girl who had wreaked so many emotions in him throughout her life. She had always been there, wanting only his love and gradually he had given her all the love that should have been hers in her infant years, yet, despite his love she had been afraid to tell him about herself because she feared he would love her less.

He hurried now, back to Laigmhor, his heart full of remorse, seeing in his mind's eye a pale little wraith without Niall, carrying on her duties at the farm, tending to his every need and all the time a child growing within the confines of that delicate body.

But the farm was quiet, with only the animals sleeping by the kitchen range. He ran upstairs to her room but it too was empty. He guessed though where she was, the people she was with, the folk who had been her comfort and stay from her early years.

It was Phebie who answered the door and she looked wordlessly at his wild dishevelled figure.

'Where is she?' he demanded urgently, looking past her into the dimly lit hall.

'Upstairs – in Niall's room! Lachy gave her a sedative, she was worn out but couldn't rest. I've never seen a lass so lost of heart.'

Phebie's voice was softly accusing but Fergus was only aware of his need to see his daughter. He pushed past and went upstairs to Niall's room. It was a real boy's room with all its boyish collections of model planes, pictures of animals, and fishing tackle propped in a corner. In the bed, with its gay patchwork quilt, was Shona, half asleep, her face warmly flushed, and her copper hair cascading over the pillow.

At sight of him she started up quickly, the sleep going from her eyes leaving them big and frightened. He stood for a moment looking down at her; noting the lovely elfin little face, eyelids puffy from heart-broken weeping, he saw the bruised cut lip caused by the brutal strength of his own hand and his heart twisted in a rush of remorse and terrible shame.

'Shona.' The whisper of her name was barely audible. He bent and took her to his heart, crushing her to him in a moment that gathered the years together and brought forth all the love he felt for her. Her silken hair was smooth against his lips and the warm heat of her body surged through his hand and at last the flesh of his flesh was openly acclaimed for its worth.

She lay against him and sobbed quietly, giving herself up to the exquisite moment. After a time he pushed her gently away and taking her hand looked deep into her eyes 'It – it's difficult for me, Shona – you know that. I never could show my feelings much.'

'I know, Father,' she said softly.

'This – thing that has happened – we'll see it through together. I'll take care of you till Niall comes home then we'll get the pair of you to the altar as it should be. Bugger the auld Cailleachs and their wagging tongues!'

'Aye, bugger them, Father,' she said softly. 'They will

talk and though I'm not shamed at having Niall's baby I'm sorry for the disgrace I'll bring on you.'

He was silent for a time and his dark eyes were faraway. His hand gripped hers tighter. 'My lass, I've never spoken to you much – of things. I loved your mother. God knows I loved her too much and when she died I didn't want to love another. I was afraid of love and I didn't even want to own you, my own bairn. But no man can be an island forever. I met Kirsteen, you were just a wee lass then. I loved her –' he lifted his face to the ceiling – 'I loved her in the way a man loves a woman but I couldn't bring myself to wed her. She was all any man could want, more, God knows, but I didn't want to commit myself – not after your mother. Then, something happened that made me ask Kirsteen to wed me but then . . .' He paused and she held his hand tightly, her love reaching out to him in the agony of his revelations. 'There was the accident. Kirsteen knew I was too proud to ask her again to be my wife – so she left Rhanna – carrying my child!'

Shona gasped aloud, her mind racing with the implications of his words.

'It's true, Shona,' he said softly. 'Somewhere I have a son I've never seen and . . .'

'I have a half brother,' she finished in dazed tones.

'Aye, it's true you have. The words you spoke tonight of being proud to carry your lad's bairn were spoken nigh on six years ago by Kirsteen herself. I found it all out that time I went to Oban. I was looking for Kirsteen but she had gone and me not knowing where to this day.'

'You'll find her again one day, Father.'

'Aye, maybe.' He touched the cut on her mouth gently. 'I'm sorry, mo ghaoil, I've hurt you but I couldn't believe the truth of my eyes. I'm a fine one to judge but at the time I saw black with rage. I had thought better of Niall yet I'm no better myself.'

She looked at him, a strange mixture of pride and pleading in her eyes. 'I wanted him to love me, Father, I asked him. I was afraid of the war, I had to know what love with him was like in case – in case . . .'

'Weesht now, he'll come back. It'll take more than a war to put down that young de'il.'

She lay back on the pillows, blue smudges of weariness under her eyes. 'Now I can tell him about the baby,' she whispered.

'He doesn't know?' His words held disbelief.

'No, somehow I couldn't tell him without you knowing first and I was afraid to tell you so I couldn't tell anyone.'

Something tightened in his throat at her confession and his voice was sad when he spoke. 'You've borne your burden alone, my lass, and I know what that feels like. Aye, you're a McKenzie right enough.'

Her eyes were closing despite herself. 'You'll let me bide in Niall's room tonight, Father? I'm so tired.'

Lachlan appeared at the door. the eyes of the two men met. 'Let her rest now,' said Lachlan quietly.

Fergus stood up. 'Aye,' was his brief answer before he went quickly from the room.

In the hallway Lachlan gripped his arm. 'My son's a young bull and deserves to be whipped for this. I'm sorry, McKenzie.'

Fergus drew a deep breath and looked straight into the deep compassionate eyes of Lachlan. 'I'm not – not now that the first shock is over. Those two were created for each other and the coming of a bairn is but a bit sooner than any of us expected.'

Lachlan's eyes crinkled with relief. 'Good God! Are you not a man of surprises? You're mellowing, Fergus, and it's as well. Will you come down now and have a dram to celebrate the fact that soon we'll both be grandparents?'

Fergus stared. 'I hadny thought of that! I'm not yet forty!'

'And I have just a year over you and poor Phebie only thirty-nine like yourself. It's a nasty shock for us all.'

Phebie appeared in the hall below. 'Are you not coming down? You'll waken Fiona with your blethering!'

'Coming, Grandma!' answered Lachlan and both men gave a bellow of mirth.

Fergus had been right about the gossips. Shona's condition provided ample fuel for the wagging tongues who openly declared their piety by regular church-going but who kept stout keys for the many skeletons rotting in the cupboards of their past. The more sensible islanders gossiped eagerly in the beginning but soon grew tired of the subject, even solicitously asking after Shona's health when she appeared in the shops at Portcull.

Behag Beag remained tight-lipped and distant whenever Shona's ungainly little figure appeared on her premises.

'Serves McKenzie right,' Behag told her cronies. 'His nose might come out of the air now his lass is known to have such lusts of the flesh.'

'You're a jealous auld Cailleach,' grinned Erchy. 'It's for want of a man up your own skirts you're such a greetin' baggage.'

Erchy had always enraged Behag by his teasing remarks which were too much near the truth for comfort and she flounced to kirk on Sundays to stare at the stained glass window and pray for the salvation of Erchy and sinners like him.

Tina gave Shona endless cups of tea and lots of advice and Mairi delighted in detailed accounts of each of her confinements always ending up with, 'Ach, poor Wullie was always afeard I wouldny come through and promised never to touch me again. But he's a man! He's a man so he is and likes fine his wee bit play.'

Nancy came more to the farm than ever with her four sticky children trailing at her heels. She beamed at Shona's hard lump of a belly and became motherly and comforting, all the while listing gory details 'Ach, but never mind, you'll be fine. Biddy might be an auld Cailleach but she'll see you come through. My, she must have seen more bums in her lifetime than she's had cups o' tea.'

Shona listened and waited and grew increasingly impatient with her clumsy stomach which was tight and neat to be harbouring an eight-month foetus but which nevertheless made her feel ugly and untidy.

The war was worsening and she fretted for news of Niall. His last letter had been angry that she hadn't told him about the baby sooner. 'It is the child of our love, mo gaolach, and it was my right to know about it. I dream of you and our times of love and I long to be back on dear clean Rhanna. The stink of war is growing worse by the minute. I smell of it, the mud and the filth and the first thing I'll do on Rhanna is sit naked in Brodie's burn and let the sweet cold water from the mountains wash the war out of me. I love you, mo gaolach, and I'm worried and unhappy that I can't be with you when you need me most.'

It was the beginning of June and the warm winds of the Gulf Stream fanned gently the sweet new heather on the moor. Cows and sheep grazed contentedly in the lush pastures and the island had the browsing lazy feel that summer brings to green places.

Shona felt hot and uncomfortable and spent a lot of time by the open window of the parlour, now fresh with new paint and white muslin curtains. Fergus had acquired a wireless set, powered by accumulators which had to be recharged occasionally by the generator on the young laird's estate. The islanders were dourly impressed by the strange piece of machinery that could make enough power for such a modern wonder as electricity to come on at the turn of a switch.

Todd the Shod already owned a small generator which proved its worth in the smiddy and he had felt himself to be a man of some importance since its acquisition. But he guarded it jealously and continually bemoaned the cost of its running, considering it unprofitable to use it for anything other than the blacksmith business. The arrival of the young laird's generator, and the fuss of its unloading on to the harbour, was a day to be remembered in Portcull. The huge piece of machinery swayed precariously on the end of the cattle pulley and Todd watched from his doorway and wished mildly that the whole contraption would go crashing on to the cobbled pier.

But stout ropes and many hands loaded it safely on to a strong cart and two wheezing Clydesdales trundled the burden away on the steep twisting road to Burnbreddie.

Few on the island owned wireless sets but those who did took their accumulators to the laird who proved most obliging and didn't charge a penny for the use of the ever-running generator.

'Noisy damty thing!' spat Todd, his self-esteem much lowered in his own eyes.

News of the war wasn't good but to most of the island it didn't mean much. There was the excitement of watching extra vessels sailing up the Sound and British reconnaissance planes roaring overhead but, other than that, the threat of war didn't touch the peace of Rhanna.

But Shona hung on every report that crackled from the wireless in the parlour. Niall had been very hopeful of a leave that would give him enough time to come home but now now, not when the Germans had invaded Holland, Belgium and France and were pushing the British Army on to the beaches at Dunkirk. The sombre voices of the newscaster intoned the bloody massacre the Germans were leaving on their trail and Shona shuddered and wondered about her dear Niall. He had only hinted at the horrors of war and it was difficult for her to think of him in any setting other than that of the island.

She forced her mind away from her imaginings of what the war must be like and looked towards the green fields where she had so often walked with him. Her memories carried her back to the times she had run nimbly over the fields and into the trees to await him coming off the boat. She sat by the open window, her face cupped in her hands, and dreamed of the past, till the familiar strong movements in her belly brought her to reality and she sighed with the knowledge that she could barely walk let alone run.

Her fears of becoming like Tina had been allayed. Her breasts were still firm and high and her loose garments gave no sign of the round little dome beneath.

'Are you *sure* there's a bairn in there?' laughed Lachlan, but his careless merriment was only for the benefit of her spirits. He was keeping a sharp eye on the small child-like form who carried his grandchild. He had examined her and found her perfectly healthy; nonetheless he was watchful and Phebie was aware and tense, spending more time at Laigmhor than before.

Fergus was snappy and irritable. Lachlan and Phebie knew that it was because his daughter's time was drawing near and he was recalling, with a painful reawakening of buried memories, that other time when the birth of a child had brought tragedy. Then he had lost a wife who meant his world, he had gained a baby whose tiny helpless life had meant nothing but which was now everything he couldn't bear to lose.

Shona sensed the mounting tension building round her. Coupled with her inner anxiety about Niall, she became withdrawn and no more did the rooms of Laigmhor echo with her singing and laughter. The one thing she feared no more was the actual birth of her child. During the earlier months she had come out in sweats of terror remembering Tina and the awful pain of her labour. Now she was strangely peaceful and thought no more of the pain her baby would bring in its struggle into the world. Instead she tried to imagine what it would be like and formed the picture of a tiny boy with Niall's corn curls and deep brown eyes. She knitted tiny garments and cleared a drawer to keep them in, hardly able to believe they were for a real baby and not one of Mirabelle's dolls that still smiled at her from the shelves in her room.

One hot night she undressed and stood naked before the wardrobe mirror. She was a small girl with tumbling copper hair and eyes big and tired in a pale face. Looking at her head and shoulders she still looked like the restless tomboy that Mirabelle had scolded to be still while a ribbon was tied to keep her shining mop of hair in order. But her eyes travelled her rounded breasts and the swelling that began just beneath them. Briefly she touched her breasts then her belly for a long breathless moment. She tried to remember what it was like to be flat but couldn't. The hard tight little mountain seemed to have been part of her for a long time now; she couldn't visualize herself without it yet how she longed to be rid of it.

A picture of Mirabelle smiled at her from the dresser. 'Oh Mirabelle,' she whispered and the tears spilled over. 'I wish you were here just for a wee whiley. I miss you, so I do. You would have grat at me in the beginning but then you'd have mothered and loved me and I could have talked to you. Father's worried in case I'll die like my mother, I can feel it. Lachlan and Phebie know about that time too and they think they're being kind not mentioning it at all. Niall's away so I've no one – not a soul to talk to – not *really* talk.'

She hugged the photo to her breast and fell on the bed to weep sadly but silently so that her father wouldn't hear.

He lay in the darkness of his room and tried to still the restless agonies of his mind. He was afraid for his daughter but, by very reason of his manhood, felt inadequate. He wanted to comfort and reassure her and tried his best to do so, knowing all the time it was the understanding of a woman she needed. He was grateful to Phebie but she couldn't spend all her time with his daughter and in the still emptiness of his room he listened to his own heart beating and wished that Kirsteen could fill his arms and his life once more.

June grew hotter and the island merged with the sea in a haze of heat. Shona sought the coolness beneath the spreading boughs of the gnarled apple tree but mostly she liked to sit in the cool parlour by the window.

One morning she stared towards the hazy blue sea and imagined Niall was coming home over the water from France. She watched the mail boat gliding through the smoky horizon towards the harbour and wasn't aware that her nails were digging into her face till she took her hands away and saw blood on her fingers. Fear and hope knotted tightly together in her belly. She had felt sick with fear since the sombre tones of the newscaster had intoned that the British army had withdrawn to the beaches at Dunkirk. It was a hellish nightmare of retreat against a spitting wall of enemy fire and the soldiers were being taken off the bloody beaches in an armada of pleasure craft.

At sight of the mail boat her heart beat swiftly. There might be a letter from Niall, a wonderful letter to tell her he was safe and coming home in time for the birth of their child. Men were arriving home, straight from the terror and stench of the trenches, still caked with the mud and blood of the lost battle. Niall might be one of them, he had to be.

She got up and was aware that her legs were trembling but she went into the kitchen and began to set the table for lunch. Her father wouldn't be home for another hour yet but she needed something to do to fill her time. She cut cold ham and thick slices of bread. The door was open, with Tot drowsing in the cool draught and the chickens clucking past her, cocking beady eyes to look for crumbs. Shona hadn't the will to chase them so they picked crumbs from the floor and squabbled with each other. A fly buzzed, caught in the muslin curtains, and a spider hung on the sash, busily wrapping a neat parcel of midgies in its web.

It was very peaceful but Shona felt tense and nervous. When Fergus came in she fidgeted and toyed with her food and his stomach tightened with worry which made him irritable.

'Eat your meat, lass! There's no room for waste in this house.'

But she wasn't listening. Erchy was coming up the road faster than was usual for him. He was mopping his brow, his usual jaunty whistle absent as he approached their gate.

Shona held her breath and Fergus too found himself waiting, the very action of chewing a mouthful of food stilled for a moment. But Erchy went on, past their gate and into the Glen. Shona let go her breath and lifted her cup to her lips with trembling hands. She felt the tears brimming in her eyes and desperately tried to stop them spilling over but Fergus saw the swelling gleam drowning the gentian blue eyes and he said quietly, 'No news is good news, mo ghaoil, remember that.' He stood up. 'I must be off! Old Thyme is calving up on the hill. It's a bad one. Bob and Mathew are with her now but,' he smiled ruefully, 'all hands are needed. It's a breach and I think we'll have to use ropes on the poor beast.'

Shona was dozing under the apple tree when the small, dancing presence of Fiona woke her up. The little girl was hopping with impatience. She was a sprite, never still for a minute, every thing about her a complete contrast to calm, unruffled, big brother Niall.

'Mither said can you come?' she imparted quickly, looking past Shona to the swing that hung on a stout branch of the tree. 'She wants to tell you somefing. I think she was greetin', and Elspeth too, the auld Cailleach. She's always that crabbit with me when she's out of temper. I hope St Michael sends her a plook on her bum so's she can't sit down for a week!'

Shona giggled despite herself. She loved Niall's little

imp of a sister with her quick smile and roguish tongue.

The child hesitated. 'Can I have a swing? I'm going up to play with wee Donald and I hear tell Eve is crawling now and goes into the hooses with the hens. I like it fine up there but I'd like a swing before I go.'

'Don't go too high,' Shona warned and went down the track and through the gate with Tot at her heels. Shona was feeling heavy after her nap and Fiona's message hadn't rung any warning bells in her mind. The little girl was inclined to exaggerate and was always wishing some mishap on the unlovable Elspeth.

Slochmhor looked very serene against the green pines and Elspeth, sitting in a chair in the sunshine busily crocheting, completed the picture, though, on closer inspection, the old woman's sharp discontented features detracted somewhat from the illusion.

'He breeah!' cried Shona pleasantly.

Elspeth looked up and there was an odd look in her red-rimmed eyes. 'What's good about it, lassie?' she said huskily. 'Away you go in. Mistress McLachlan's away to meet the doctor. She asked Erchy to send him down from Croynachan. Is your father to hand or is he busy as usual?'

'He's up on the hill with a cow in calf,' said Shona with a puzzled frown.

'Aye weel, he'll need to leave it to the others. He'll be needed down here for a whiley. I'm gey auld to be climbin' up hills though and you're no' much good in your condition. We'd best leave it till the rest get back. Do you think that would be best? Aye, it is, right enough.'

Shona felt a mounting impatience. Elspeth, with all her veiled hints and self-answered questions, could be very exasperating. 'Leave what, Elspeth? Why must my father be here?'

Elspeth gazed into the distance. 'There's that young upstart Angus McKinnon. I'll go and get him to fetch your father. Whereabouts on the hill is he?'

'Just up by Brodie's burn, near the Seanachaidh's Stone. But he's busy, Elspeth, and I wish you'd tell me what you want him for. Has somebody got a sick beast? Is that why you want my father and the doctor?'

There was no vet on Rhanna and Fergus, with his knowledge of the ails of farmyard beasts, was often called upon for his services. If the case was very bad Lachlan's advice was also sought and at the moment no other reason for them both being called upon entered Shona's mind.

'Mercy on us,' was Elspeth's reply, 'is that young Angus comin' or goin'? I canny see in this haze! There's a pot o' tea on the stove. You'd better have a cup for you'll need it.' She shook her wispy head and pursed her lips. 'The Lord has a way wi' Him. I'm no' one to judge but you've made your own bed and it's punished we all are so it is!'

She scurried away, her spindly legs carrying her with surprising rapidity.

Shona wandered into the kitchen but it was warm there and she didn't feel like tea so she drifted into the parlour which was in the shadow of the hill and cool in the late afternoon.

It was a pleasant room, chintzy and homely with pictures of Niall and Fiona smiling from the dresser.

She went to gaze at the boyish features of Niall at fourteen and her hand knocked some letters to the floor. With difficulty she stooped to retrieve them and froze suddenly. One of the envelopes was buff-coloured and would have escaped her attention but the letter inside had partly fallen out and words leapt at her like living things. It was a War Office communication and she snatched it from the floor to read it, her whole body trembling while her eyes devoured the terrible message.

She whispered aloud, 'It is my painful duty to inform you that a report has this day been received from the War Office that Number 206 Private Niall Iain McLachlan has been reported missing, believed to be dead . . .'

She could read no further. The letter fluttered back to the floor and she put her hands to her head, shaking it and groaning over and over, 'No, it's not true! Not Niall! Not Niall!'

She backed away from the piece of paper and knocked over a small table. Unheeding she tottered backwards to stand for a moment against the wall, staring with huge unbelieving eyes at the white scrap of paper on the floor. Then, with a sob, she turned and ran from the house and into the hot sunshine.

She looked round desperately but the only sign of life was Elspeth, a small speck in the distance. A great welling terror rose in her throat and she began to run, as if by the very act of flight she could leave behind the knowledge contained in the letter. The moor shimmered and danced in the haze of heat and it was to its lonely wild stretches her legs took her. Tot, lying in the shade of the porch, whimpered and sat up, looking intently at her mistress's fleeing figure. She got up and walked a few paces but thought better of it and flopped down again, her head in her paws, her brown eyes looking towards the moor.

Shona ran through heather and gorse. Brambles snatched at her, tearing her bare legs but she was unaware of physical pain. Mentally she was in agony and her pumping adrenalin would not let her stop in her flight. Her heart pounded and there was a sharp pain in her side but she went on till she tripped and fell, her face scratched and bleeding by the shaggy moorland heather. She was sobbing, harsh dry sobs, but her eyes were dry.

Sheep, grazing nearby, looked up momentarily at her intrusion into the hush of the day, but she was of no moment to them and they went back to cropping the sparse grass among the bracken.

She lay where she was, stunned by her fall, uncaring that her face rested on sheep's droppings and that her hair and clothes were matted and torn. The only sounds on the unending stretch of moor were her own harsh breathing, the biting of the nearby sheep and a greenshank, startled from its nest in the peat to utter its alarm of 'krji, krji'.

After a time she raised herself on an elbow and saw nestling in the distance the rotting crumbling stones of the old Abbey. She knew now where she was going, the only place in the world it seemed to her, in her numb deep sadness, where she could ever find any peace. Her aching stumbling limbs carried her on to her destination. Was it really possible that less than a year ago she had flown with Niall, on the swift, tireless limbs of youth, to the place where they had woven their child's fantasies; dreamed of magical impossible dreams of their young adulthood and finally, loved with the tender over-riding passion of a love that could never die because it was still at the stage of spring, yet to blossom forth into a summer never yet surpassed.

'He's not dead,' she whispered, stopping to lean against a slender rowan. 'HE'S NOT DEAD!' she shouted in a defiance of her mental torture but the words died quickly away and only the soft sigh of empty spaces answered her. Her ebbing strength forced her to rest again at the walls of the old chapel. Her eyes swept over the gorse-covered hillock where her final footsteps must take her but for a moment she could see no familiar sign to tell her where the cave was. It was so long since she had last been to the lonely windswept spot where it seemed the thin voices of spirits of the past were borne on the breezes of moor and sea. It was a wild forgotten place, inhabited only by sheep and wanderlust cows, but with Niall it had been a happy place and their voices had echoed in the Abbey ruins and their laughter rang in the ancient cloisters of the chapel.

But she wasn't afraid of lonely places, they had always been a balm to her spirits, yet panic now seized her because her wildly searching eyes couldn't find the little birch tree that marked the cave's entrance. Niall had planted the tree and it had grown into a sturdy sapling, twisted by the wild storms of winter, but flourishing despite the moods of the weather.

Then she saw it, almost hidden by the prickly gorse that abounded in the hollow. She walked unsteadily towards her goal till she stumbled through clumps of bracken and heather into the cave. It was cool and dark after the glare of the late afternoon sun. For a moment she could see nothing but blackness but gradually everything that was familiar came into focus. The shelves with Mirabelle's dolls, the kitchen utensils, the little spirit stove, all covered in cobwebs but there just the same, their lovingly gathered possessions.

She dragged herself on to one of the dusty wicker chairs and it was while she struggled to regain her breath that the first pain seized her, like a gripping vice in her belly. She gasped and held on to the arm of the chair and in a few moments the contraction subsided. She lay back, closing her eyes, so exhausted that she fell into a half sleep. But there was to be no rest for her. The second pain was longer and more intense, like something inside tearing her apart. She put her fist to her mouth and even as she endured the pain she knew she was going into the first stages of labour. Sweat broke on her brow, she felt sick with fear and her hands grew clammily cold. She fingered the locket at her neck and fumbled to take it off so that she could gaze at Niall's smiling face, to see the dark honest eyes she loved looking back at her.

'Oh Niall, Niall,' she murmured brokenly, 'if only you were here. Our child's going to be born soon and I need you so.'

She clutched the locket and looked slowly round the cave and all the memories it contained came crowding into her mind. More pains came and in between each one she remembered some incident in time she had shared with Niall. It was their place of dreams and of a love that had conceived the child she was going to have. Slowly, fear was replaced by a new feeling, one of confidence in herself. She knew how to deliver a child, she had all but delivered Tina's daughter, and it hadn't been so difficult. She knew what to do with the birth cord too, she had watched Biddy doing it. A smile slowly lit her small tired face. What more fitting than that her baby should be born in the small haven where it had been conceived?

'Our son will be born here, Niall,' she said gently. 'In time for you coming home.'

Her mind was blotting out the awful message contained in the letter from the War Office and now her whole being was diffused with excruciating pain yet through it all she trembled with joy at the thought of Niall's face when he saw their child for the first time.

She was physically exhausted and suffering from shock but she struggled up to make ready the bed. Everything she needed was in the cave; blankets, cushions, utensils. But something niggled at her. Water! There always had to be plenty of hot water at childbirth. She bent to shake the spirit stove and discovered that it still contained some fuel – but matches, there had to be matches! They had always kept a box on a shelf but they might be too damp to strike. She found the box hidden behind a cobwebby cup and her hand shook so much some spilled out.

She held her breath as she struck one, it flared but died immediately. Several crumbled on contact but another flared and stayed alight. She stared at the small bright flame with tears on her cheeks, realising she should have waited till later to try the matches. She had no water and she didn't want to light the stove too soon and the rest of the matches might not work. Another pain came relentlessly and a dry sob shook her. Then she saw the candle stuck in a cruisie beside one of Mirabelle's dolls. The match was almost spent and the pain in her belly made her want to double up but she reached up to the candle and held the flame to it. The wick smouldered and smoked.

'Oh, please God!' she cried. The match was burning her fingers but quite suddenly the wick robbed the charred remains of its flame and a white oval of light burned steadily.

'Thank you, God! Oh, thank you,' she whispered and sank to the chair to rest for a moment. But not for long. She had to get water from the little mountain stream nearby. She pulled bracken and heather away from the entrance, tied back the gorse bushes then she began the laborious task of going back and forward to the burn for water. She had no bucket; only pots and a kettle. The usually tinkling little outlet was almost dried up and water trickled into the utensils with unhurried tranquillity.

She had left her watch at Laigmhor but she had a vague idea of the time because the sun was setting in a sheet of flame over the Atlantic. The cool night air brought forth the scent of thyme and moss and the sheep cried plaintively over the moor. She was glad of the breeze because it kept away the midges that could hover in dense clouds of torment if the air was too still.

It was very peaceful and the June night would bring no real darkness to Rhanna. She sat by the burn and even in the agony of childbirth breathed in the sweet scents of the moorland with an appreciation of one who had always loved the earth.

Fergus paced the parlour at Slochmhor. 'Where in God's name is she?' he said for the umpteenth time in the long nightmare of a day.

Phebie sat very still and her face had the frozen immobility of one who was in a stupor of grief.

Lachlan cradled his dark head in his fine doctor's hands and Elspeth, her features sharper than ever in her anxiety, said again, 'I shouldny have left her but it was only for a wee whiley. I had to find someone to fetch McKenzie.' She rocked her gaunt frame and a thin wail, which was a mixture of grief and self-pity, escaped her.

Fergus turned on her. 'Will you be quiet, you old yowe! You should be away home for all the good you do here!'

Elspeth gripped her lips together. 'You're a hard man, McKenzie, but for all your fine airs you're no better than the rest o' us. If you'd given your lass more of your iron hert she might not have needed to look so hard elsewhere for a bit o' love!'

Fergus whitened and the muscle in his jaw worked furiously. 'You dried up old baggage! Who are you to . . .'

Lachlan sprang to his feet. His face was deathly white and his brown eyes were dull with the burden of his sadness. 'For pity's sake, the pair of you! Stop it! We'll do no good miscalling each other!' He faced Fergus.

'I'm thinking the time's come to go out and look for Shona. It looks as if she's not coming back tonight. God knows where she'll be nursing her grief. If we could have broken the news to her gently . . . but she saw the letter first and must be in a state of shock.'

Fergus nodded acquiescence. Lachlan turned to put his arm round his wife. 'You go up to bed, mo ghaoil. I'm going to give you something to make you sleep.'

But Phebie shook her head violently. 'No, I'm coming with you! I couldn't sleep – I must be doing something and Shona will be needing a woman to comfort her.'

Elspeth looked up dourly. 'Away you go, I'll bide with the bairn.'

There was a scuffling outside and a murmur of voices. Lachlan went to the door and saw a crowd of Rhanna men outlined against the clear sky in which a pale moon hung like a lantern. Bob and Ranald were at the front of the group, their rough, homely features touched with anxiety. Bob spoke first, his gnarled fingers working nervously on the bone handle of his shepherd's crook. 'We heard about the lass and thought you'd need help to find her. And – we're sorry to hear about young Niall.'

There was a subdued murmur from the men and Lachlan looked at them with swimming eyes. 'Thanks, lads – and you're right – we'll need all the help we can get. We have no idea where the lass might be but if we split into groups our task might be easier.'

Phebie, wrapped in a tartan plaid, joined them. She, together with Fergus, Lachlan, and Bob, were going to comb one section of the Muir of Rhanna, and

Robbie Beag with three others were going over the high rise that led to Nigg. Mathew and Neil Munro went to search the shore round the harbour while the fourth party went overland, south-east, where fields and moors separated them from Portvoynachan.

Bob was well acquainted with the moors; he had roamed them for miles with his sheepdogs, rounding the sheep at various times of the year. Dot, the younger of the sheepdogs, was with him now, keeping just ahead of her master, running in the silent gliding fashion of a good sheepdog.

Nobody noticed the golden, slightly tubby, form of the old spaniel till she pushed her wet nose into Phebie's hand and whined.

'Tot,' said Phebie gently. 'You can't come with us. You're too old to be roaming the moor.' But Tot had waited patiently all day outside Slochmhor. She ran ahead and stopped to look back, a low moan rising deep in her throat.

Bob spat impatiently. 'Ach, get away back girl. You're of no use to us.'

But Tot was a dog with a purpose. To Dot the whole thing was a game, an unexpected outing for a working dog, and she frisked and poked into heather tufts with delight. The old spaniel ran on again on rheumaticky legs and whimpered, her nose testing the wind, one paw raised in the pose typical of the gun dog.

Fergus looked at her and frowned. 'The old girl looks as if she knows what she's about. She seems to know where she's going.'

'Of course,' breathed Phebie. 'Who would know better? She's been all over Rhanna with Shona.'

Bob blew his nose disdainfully. He had time only for sheepdogs; game dogs were all right in their place but not much use on the farm. To his mind they were 'gentry beasts', good for all the useless sport indulged in by useless fowk with little else to occupy them but shooting and fishing.

Tot was well ahead and everyone was running to keep up with her. They covered a mile, then had to pause for breath. The air from the hill was clean and they gulped it in greedily. Tot, tired and panting, had collapsed in a heap and old Bob leaned against a boulder, shaking his head at what seemed an impossible task. They had shouted themselves hoarse and now that they were quiet, the silent, eerie loneliness of the moor enclosed them in a hushed blanket. The sky was clear and everything could be seen quite plainly, with the moor stretching on either side, flanked by the ridges of Sgurr nan Gabhar that separated them from Glen Fallan.

They were on the outskirts of the Burnbreddie estate and a dog howled mournfully. Tot was too tired to even prick her ears but Dot sat on her haunches and, lifting her nose to the June sky, wailed loudly.

'Be quiet, you stupid fool!' ordered Bob sharply. He knocked his pipe against the stone. 'I think we've seen enough o' this part – the lass would never have come so far in her condition. I'm for cutting over to Fallan. Maybe Croynachan or Croft na Beinn would know something of her whereabouts.'

'It might be best,' said Lachlan wearily, getting up stiffly from the heather.

All but Fergus changed direction. He was watching

Tot who, groaning, had roused herself and was heading once more on the course she had set. She disappeared in amongst gorse bushes and Fergus ran forward, his mind and body exhausted, but every fibre of his being urging him onwards.

It was some time before the others realized he wasn't with them. They were plodding over the rough peat bogs to Glen Fallan less than quarter of a mile on.

'He's chasin' that damty dog again,' cursed Bob.

Phebie began to cry, the slow silent tears of despair and grief. 'We'd best go back,' she said, clinging to the rough tweed of Lachlan's jacket.

Lachlan hesitated in an agony of indecision. He felt they were all on a wild goose-chase yet he trusted the strength of Fergus's decisive mind more than any other on the island.

'We'd best,' he said quietly.

'It's daft us all goin' back,' said Bob. 'I'll get along to Croynachan and get Johnston to help me look along the banks o' Loch Sliach. It was a place favoured by the lass and Niall. She might be there.'

He trudged away, his crook helping him over the peaty ground.

Lachlan put his arm round Phebie and they went back to the moor.

Fergus strode after Tot. His breath was harsh and sore in his throat but he was positive the old dog knew where she was going. Her nose was to the ground, her floppy ears hiding her whitening muzzle and intent brown eyes. She was wheezing, her tongue lolling and dry but she kept gamely on.

'Good lass, good lass,' encouraged Fergus at intervals and a memory came to him of a big laughing Highlander handing over the tiny golden pup to a little girl on her fifth birthday.

Dog and child had grown up together, played and romped through youthful years. Now Tot was old, with cysts on her ears and watery eyes; she slept most of the time and romped no more. Yet some force was driving her on over that shaggy unkind moorland, a deep spirit of loyalty for the child she had known all her life was urging her to the very last ounce of strength in her loving old heart.

They had come two and a half miles and now they were breasting a rise. Tot stood looking down, breath rasping and flanks heaving. Fergus looked down also, down into the hollow where the stones of the old Abbey lumped together like the grey stooping figures of old men. His heart sank. Shona would never have come to this eerie place. The islanders avoided it, believing it to be haunted by the 'ghaisties' of the monks that had been slain there hundreds of years before. Peat Hags were said to roam the ruins at night, howling and screeching in glee at the plight of the monks.

People like Fergus knew the screeching to be no more than the wind whistling in and out of cracks and empty windows. Nevertheless even sensible, level-headed people had the seeds of ancient superstitions buried deep, and he shivered at the sight of Dunuaigh and the ruins. But his need to find his daughter was stronger than all else and his deep voice boomed out, echoing over the moor reverberating in the hollow. Over and over he called out but only the plaintive cries of the sheep answered him.

'You were wrong lass! You were wrong!' he scolded the dog. He looked down and saw the old spaniel was lying on her side, her eyes closed. He dropped on his knees and laying his hand on the golden fur felt the flying pulse. Even as he knelt there the faithful old beast drew a shuddering breath and the heart beneath his hand stopped beating.

'Och no,' cried Fergus to the stars. 'Not this above all else!'

He remained where he was for several minutes, the burden of his grief and anxiety stooping his shoulders and bowing his head. His dark eyes stared dully at the lifeless little body lying on the ground, the curling red-gold fur a shade darker than the tough moorland grasses. A cold wind skittered from the sea and he shivered then rose, stiff and cold, with the limp little dog over his shoulder.

He stumbled back the way he had come and in the distance saw Lachlan and Phebie coming towards him. They came closer and Phebie put her hand to her mouth when she saw what he carried.

Like a man drunk he came towards them and wordlessly they all made their way back to Slochmhor little knowing that down in the hollow, among the Abbey ruins, the girl they sought lay drenched in sweat, her belly torn apart by the pains of childbirth. She had heard the faint echoes of her father's voice and had answered, but her voice was a mere whisper in the deep cloisters of the cave.

Dawn was breaking, a faint streak of gold and silver above the dark corries of Glen Fallan. Elspeth was asleep in the rocking chair by the dead embers of the fire. Her face was gaunt in the morning light and she got up slowly at the opening of the door. She looked at the grey hopeless faces before her and her usually edgy voice was soft with pity. 'The men found nothing, though they searched till nigh dawn. They've all gone home save Murdy. It wasny worth his while he says for he'll be out in the fields in an hour or two. He's sleepin' in the kitchen. I'll just go and put the kettle on.' She paused at the door where Fergus stood with Tot draped over his arm. 'Even the old dog,' she murmured quietly and the unfamiliar glimmer of tears shone in her eyes though they were quickly wiped away and she brushed roughly past Fergus.

They were all desperately tired yet unwilling to leave the comfort of each other's presence and the ever flowing cups of whisky-laced tea.

Bob arrived as the sea brightened to a deep gold and the morning chatter of birds drowned the air with song. He looked yellow and old and drew his hand across his nose irritably. 'Croynachan reports nothing unusual,' he said gruffly. 'He's seen nothing up the Glen or by Sliach but sheep and kie. But don't worry, McKenzie, we'll find her but we won't follow the old dog next time, I'm thinkin'. She led us a fine dance.'

'We won't follow her again – she's dead,' said Fergus briefly.

Bob's inscrutable old face softened. 'Ach, but that's a shame, a shame right enough. She took too much upon herself. It was strange, very strange.'

He accepted a glass of whisky then went off muttering, Dot tired and limp at his heels.

Fergus cradled his cup in his hand and stared into

the rekindled fire. 'What are we going to do?' he asked hopelessly.

Lachlan stood up. 'Get a bit of sleep and look again. You'll bide in – in Niall's room.'

'Dammit, man, I can't sleep!' exploded Fergus. 'She could have fallen somewhere, she might be hurt. I must go out again!'

Lachlan's hand came down firmly on Fergus's shoulder. 'Bide a wee, man! You'll do yourself and the lass a lot more good if you do. Heed what I say! Go out now and you'll fumble around and do no good at all.'

Fergus sank back into the chair. 'You're right, Lachlan, but I'll just rest in the chair.' He was asleep even before Lachlan closed the door. In the chair opposite, Elspeth snored softly, her jaw sagging and her lips making little popping noises.

A babble of voices below the window woke Lachlan first. Still dazed with sleep he struggled into his trousers and looked out. Biddy was there, her spectacles falling from the end of her nose as she shooed away the folk who were gathering for morning surgery.'

'Have you no respect?' she shouted severely. 'The doctor's had word his lad's missing and you all crowd round wi' your wee aches and pains like nothing's happened!'

'We didn't know,' said several voices, genuinely shocked and sorrowful. They turned and dispersed slowly, leaving Biddy with a wildly gesticulating, almost hysterical Dodie who was babbling over and over, 'It was ghaisties I'm tellin' you! Moanin' and screamin' like the dead!'

'The dead don't scream,' said Biddy firmly and cuffed him on the ear the way she did with the cheekier of the village children.

Lachlan looked at the clock and was shocked to see that it was nearly ten o'clock. Phebie was struggling to waken and Fiona was singing in her bedroom.

Downstairs Fergus was opening the door to Biddy and a flustered Elspeth was scuttling into the kitchen. It was obvious everyone had just wakened.

Dodie's voice was rising to a higher pitch, his mouth was frothing and he was obviously terrified.

'Johnston told me about poor wee Shona missing,' shouted Biddy above the din. 'I came over quick as I could to see could I help and met this demented cratur shouting about hearing screams over the muir.'

Dodie's nose was dripping on to his saliva-filled lips. 'It was Ealasaid, doctor! I was looking for her last night but she didn't come so I went out again this mornin' – a bit o' cream I wanted for my bread. I went away over the muir and had just got hold of her by the ghaisties' place when they started screamin' at me and Ealasaid run away so bad a fright she got!'

Biddy clucked impatiently but Fergus was looking intently at Dodie. 'Do you means the ruins of the Abbey, Dodie?'

'Aye, Mr McKenzie. Demented spirits screamin' and the Peat Hags moanin'. It was terrible just.'

'How long ago, Dodie?'

'Nigh on an hour! I ran, so I did, it was so skearie. Ealasaid will likely have died o' fright!'

Fergus turned to Lachlan. 'The old dog was right.' His voice was soft but hurried. 'Shona is out there somewhere in the ruins. It was she Dodie heard screaming. It may be the bairn is coming.'

Lachlan was already picking up his bag. 'Let's go,' he said briefly.

Biddy followed though the doctor protested. 'You canny stop me,' she said in a voice that brooked no interference. 'I've walked the island all my life and if I canny walk the moor to deliver the bairn o' the bairn I delivered years ahent then I'm no' worth my worth.'

They met Bob, shamefaced because he had overslept. 'I'm comin' with you,' he said in tones that didn't invite refusal. 'Mathew and the rest can see to things. If the lass is where you say you might need help to bring her back.'

The hollow was a trap of warm sun and honey-laden bees. There was no sound but for those of nature and the men stopped to mop sweat from their faces while Biddy went to the trickling stream to wet her handkerchief so that she could wipe her red exerted old face.

And there in the stillness, they heard a voice singing a Gaelic lullaby, so faint that it could have been the sighing of the wind.

Old Bob, his grizzled head filled with folklore and tales of ancient myths of the Hebrides, looked round the grey silent ruins of the Abbey with fear in his watery blue eyes. He was one of the best Seanachaidhs on the island and proud of it but cosy hearths were very different from this eerie place where souls from the past wandered forever. He gripped his crook tighter and drew a brown hand over dry lips.

'Weesht,' warned Biddy. ''Tis the fairy folk singin' to be sure.'

But Dot, whining and scratching at the gorse of the hill, suddenly disappeared and Fergus and Lachlan ran forward. 'There's nothing here.' Lachlan stared at the huge moss-covered boulder in front of them. 'I don't understand.'

Dot reappeared leaving tufts of hair on the snagging gorse and Fergus ran forward to pull the bushes back.

Shona showed no surprise to see them. She lay on sheepskin rugs and blankets which were saturated with the blood of childbirth. Her copper hair tumbled over her shoulders, framing a face that was pale and strained. But her blue eyes were brilliant and a soft little smile hovered round her lips. 'Hello, Father.' Her voice was low with pride. 'Look now at your grandson. Isn't he the bonniest baby in the world? I did it all by myself, just like I did for Tina. I'm calling him Niall Fergus – it's a grand name I think. I can hardly wait for Niall to see his son.'

She was holding a tiny bundle wrapped in a tartan plaid. Lachlan ran forward while Biddy made a quick examination of the girl. 'The lass is fine,' she murmured thankfully. 'Just a wee clean up and you'll feel lovely, my little one.'

Lachlan had taken the baby over to the light at the door. It was a perfect little boy with downy fair hair. The birth cord was tied as neatly as if Biddy herself had done it and the little waxen body had been wiped clean. Lachlan looked down at the tiny lifeless face and the slow tears burned his eyes. It was the final blow in two nightmare days. The son of his own dear son as dead and cold as a piece of marble.

Fergus was behind him, his tall strong body stooped like an old man. 'Was it – because we never got here in time?'

Lachlan shook his dark head. 'Stillborn – the mite was dead before it came into the world. We'll never know why. She's so young and there was the shock – of – of Niall. Also it was a premature birth – nearly four weeks.'

'But why – why in God's name!' The cry was torn from Fergus in an agony of torment. The cruel irony of the devious twists of life was too much for him and the tears of hurt grief, and pity for his daughter, coursed down his face. He went to her and took her into the fold of his strong right arm, his tears falling on to the bright copper hair under his chin.

She pulled away to look at him with eyes that were unnaturally veiled and dreamy. 'Och Father,' she chided gently, 'don't cry so. Are you not pleased with your grandson?'

'He's dead, Shona,' he sobbed. 'The baby never drew life.'

Lachlan came and pulled Fergus away, shaking his head warningly. 'Don't – she can't take it! Not now, man! She's suffering from shock already. The sooner we get her home and to bed the better.'

They wrapped her in blankets and between them carried her over the warm summer moors. Behind them trailed Bob, his tough weatherbeaten face gaunt and sad and beside him Biddy carried the pitiful little bundle of Niall's dead son.

Chapter Sixteen

When Shona finally accepted the fact that her baby son was dead she withdrew into a lonely shell which nothing seemed to penetrate. She moped around looking like a lost child and Fergus could find no way of reaching the sad, bruised caverns of her mind.

'She'll need time,' said a weary Lachlan, himself struggling to bear his own sorrow. 'She's lost so much – even the very dog she had most of her life. Give her time, Fergus.'

The days stretched into July and four weeks after the tragedy Erchy came whistling up the dusty road from Portcull. He saw Shona, listlessly sitting by an open window and waved cheerily, then went on to Slochmhor where he propped his bicycle at the gate. He clutched a letter in a hand that shook slightly. They had all speculated about the missive at the post office because it was a War Office communication. If he accepted a glass of Phebie's blackcurrant wine he might be able to hang around long enough to find out the contents of the letter.

'A letter, Mistress McLachlan,' he shouted to Phebie who was hanging washing in the sun-drenched garden.

'Leave it on the table, Erchy,' she answered through a mouthful of pegs.

Erchy's heart sank. 'It's a thirsty day,' he said chattily and made exaggerated puffing noises.

'Aye, it is that! Go away ben to the kitchen and take some wine from the larder. I'm too busy to come in now.'

Erchy pulled in his breath. 'It's from the War Office,' he said and exhaled quickly.

Phebie turned slowly and looked at him. Her round sweet face remained immobile but a strange mixture of hope and hopelessness shone in her eyes. She came over the fragrant grass slowly and took the letter with a show of calm. Methodically she opened it with a thumbnail. Erchy watched her, his breath held in his lungs. He saw the slow flush creeping over her face and the slight tremor of her head. She looked up and the glimmer of tears shone in her eyes. 'He's alive, Erchy,' she whispered disbelievingly. 'Niall's alive – wounded but alive.'

Erchy let go his breath once more and grabbing Phebie's plump waist whirled her round and round. The island had mourned with Lachlan and Phebie. The love and respect earned by Lachlan throughout the years went deep. Rhanna loved him and his family and they had wept, the hidden silent tears of the dour, loving Hebridean folk. Phebie was laughing and crying and Erchy whirled and kissed her in an abandonment of spirit.

'Niall's alive!' shouted Phebie and ran on to the road. Clutching the letter she sped with Erchy at her heels to Laigmhor. Shona was still at the window, seeing nothing of the lovely day outside, her thoughts turned inward, on Niall, on the little son who had never known the sweetness of breathing life. She didn't even have the comfort of Tot's head resting on her feet, giving the silent undemanding love she had grown to accept as part of her life. It seemed to Shona she had nothing very much to live for. Nothing was worthwhile any more and not even the strong quiet love of her father could reach into her hopeless world.

She didn't notice Phebie and Erchy wildly gesticulating at her from the garden. Not until they burst into the peaceful dreaming silence of the parlour was she aware of them. Phebie's breath was squeezing from her lungs in short little gasps and for a moment she couldn't speak. She collapsed into a chair and, unable to find the breath to explain, motioned Erchy to break the news.

He ran his hand through his thinning sandy hair and, bursting though he was with emotion, controlled himself enough to say calmly, 'Your lad's alive, my bonny lass. Niall's alive – it's all in the letter I brought to Mistress McLachlan!'

Shona slowly turned her head to look at Phebie. Her dull eyes showed no sign of having interpreted the message, but slowly, like a pale rose opening to the sun, her face diffused with a glow that lit the transparency of her skin.

Phebie nodded and spoke jerkily, the excitement of the past few minutes making her light-headed. 'It's true, mo ghaoil, our Niall's alive.'

Everything about that time had a dreamlike quality. Shona got up and glided over to Phebie. She stared trance-like at the letter, then she was on her knees, her head in Phebie's lap and she cried, all the lonely, tragic tears she had bottled up for so long. Phebie stroked the copper head and let the tears run their course, knowing they would help to wash away some of the agonies endured by such a young heart too many months.

When Shona finally looked up her eyes were red but they contained something that had been missed so much of late – hope and the small beginnings of the joy for living. 'Where is he?' she whispered, drying her eyes on the hem of her dress.

'In a military hospital in England. He was badly wounded in the neck and head and his identity disc got shot off. Just before he was wounded, he'd taken off his jacket to cover another laddie whose clothes had all but been blown off. He was still alive when Niall gave him his jacket with all his papers. But the boy died and they thought he was Niall and Niall couldn't tell anyone who he was because he's had concussion and loss of memory until recently.' Phebie shook her head as if to clear it. 'He's on the mend now and will be home soon, but he'll always be deaf on one side – his ear-drum was damaged very badly.'

Shona's face was wet and swollen but she was smiling the first smile for weeks. 'He's alive – and because of his deafness he won't have to go back to war. I'm so happy I could cry all day.'

'You're happy he's deaf?' asked Erchy.

'Och no, of course not! I'd wish that he was the same as he went away.' Then she paused and continued thoughtfully, 'No – you're right, Erchy, I am glad, if not he'd have been home for a wee while before he went back to war and he might never have come out alive. He mightn't have been so lucky the second time. What's a deaf ear compared to a chance of life?'

Phebie shuddered but she knew Shona was right. To other people it might appear foolish and selfish but to her, at that hour of knowing her son was alive, she would have been lying to herself if she'd wanted him whole and well enough to go back to war, perhaps to get killed in the spring of his life. Far better a deaf ear and a live son than a dead son and memories.

Erchy rubbed his hands together and cocked an eye at Shona. 'I'm thinkin' the occasion calls for a wee dram, does it not?'

Shona nodded. 'You're right, Erchy – and I'm going to have one too. I'm needing it I feel so shaky. Then . . .' She looked at Phebie. 'We'll go and find Lachlan and Father and tell them the news.'

Fergus leaned against the dyke that ran parallel to the road and lit his pipe with the expertise of long practice. He had grown used to only one arm, doing so much with it that he often found himself looking in astonishment at people who could do less with two arms than he could with one.

It was a mild calm morning with a fine mist of rain from the hills and the smoke from the farmhouse chimneys curled lazily.

He puffed contentedly and watched Shona in the garden, gathering flowers and humming a gay little tune. She looked very slim and sweet in her youth with her hair gleaming brightly and it was difficult to believe that her childish form had, until recently, carried a child. He'd never given the child much thought until he'd seen the small features and perfect body of the tiny baby. When he'd realised it was the flesh of his flesh he had known the hopeless longing for the little life that might have been. But his compassion for his daughter had overridden all else and he had suffered with her in her darkest hours. Now Niall was alive and he rejoiced with her yet for reasons he could barely understand he felt that she no longer needed him as desperately as before. She was loving and mindful of his every need, yet he knew that the biggest part of her waited longingly for the time of Niall's return to Rhanna. He was jealous and hated himself for it but was unable to stop from thinking of a future when his house no longer breathed with the life his daughter gave it.

A chestnut mare came cantering along the road. Riding it was the young laird of Burnbreddie, a man now held with respect on the island.

He brought the mare to a stop when he saw Fergus.

'Good day to you, McKenzie,' he nodded. 'Things are a bit more settled now, I hear.' He had glanced towards Shona, and Fergus knew what he meant.

'Aye, the lass is to have her lad back soon.' Fergus didn't want to talk about any of the events that had happened in the last months and people were talking again, saying that he was, 'the dour bugger he was before'.

The young laird dismounted and the mare, her coat polished to the shade of a ripe chestnut, nuzzled delicately at the fragrant clover amongst the long roadside grasses. 'A fine beast,' commented Fergus wishing he'd been left in peace. He liked the laird well enough and could talk easily about the weather and the health of his beasts but it was to Lachlan alone he confided his real feelings.

The laird nodded and brushed a hair from his impeccable tweed jacket. 'I've just come back from the south. Rena was with me and we looked up one or two old friends. We had an invitation from the Campbell-Elliots, people I knew in London years ago. They had gone down to the country for a spell – to get away from all the bombs.'

Fergus shifted impatiently and the laird idly stripped the heads from the knee-high grasses and looked speculatively at the sky. 'Dashed strange coincidence,' he murmured casually. Fergus knocked his pipe on the wall and opened his mouth to make some excuse to escape. 'Couldn't believe my eyes when I saw her,' the laird was continuing absently. 'She's the Campbell-Elliot's governess now. Last time I saw her she was teaching here at Portcull.' He shook his head. 'Funny how things go. The Campbell-Elliots think the world of her. A fine young woman she is. Got a little boy, nice as kids go, not like her at all – black hair and eyes. I only saw her once or twice when I came to Rhanna but I remember thinking what a fine girl she was. I got talking to her, she went a queer colour when she found out who I was and where I came from – and . . .' He looked sideways at Fergus. 'She was asking about you, McKenzie.'

Fergus had frozen, the inside of his stomach felt weak and the laird's voice sounded far away. He stood there, glad of the support of the dyke, unable to speak, yet longing to ask a million questions. Finally he found his voice and looked straight into the laird's pale blue eyes. 'You – know, don't you?'

'Y-es, I knew you were to be married, then you had your accident and I don't know anything after that. Canny the Rhanna folk may be but they've never fathomed what happened between you.' He paused. 'The boy's yours, isn't he?'

'Yes, Goddammit man, he's mine and I've never seen him. Where is she, Balfour? When did you come back to Rhanna? When did you see her last?'

'Hey, hold on, old chap! She's not going to disappear! I saw her a fortnight ago – I got back to Rhanna yesterday. As a matter of fact I rode over specially to tell you. I thought you might be pleased.'

'PLEASED!' Fergus held out his hand and the young laird gripped it.

'Go to her, McKenzie. She still loves you – stupid thing love, isn't it? We botch it up all the time. Anyway – good luck old man. There's a mail boat out of Rhanna tomorrow.'

He mounted and rode away. Fergus felt his innards had turned to jelly. He couldn't believe it. After all the years of waiting and longing he had found Kirsteen at last. No wonder she hadn't seen the notices the lawyers had put into the London papers, she was deep in the English countryside and possibly didn't even know her mother was dead.

Joy washed over him in waves but after the first excitement came fear, fear that she would slip through his fingers again and he couldn't let that happen.

Sweat broke on his brow and his hand felt clammy. He wasn't aware of anything but the great urgency of finding Kirsteen and bringing her back to Rhanna. In his mind it would be as simple as that – it had to be. The laird had slipped a piece of paper into his hand with the address in England written in neat small letters. Fergus stared at the paper as if it were his most precious possession, then he ran to the kitchen where Shona was arranging roses in a bowl.

'Father,' she said on the alert immediately. 'What's wrong?'

He was panting and laughing. 'Everything's *right*, mo ghaoil! I have discovered where Kirsteen is – I'm away on the mail boat tomorrow!'

'Father!' She ran to him and held him close, feeling the trembling of his strong masculine body. 'Oh, my father, I'm so happy I could cry!' she buried her face into his warm neck, feeling his pulse beating swiftly. Her hands caressed the crisp curls at the nape of his neck. At last their world was falling into place. Her happiness was complete now – if she married and left Laigmhor, she wouldn't feel like a betrayer. Her father would have a love of his own and they could stop being so dependent on each other. She sighed deeply and pulled away to look into his deep dark eyes. 'Do you know what, Father?'

'Tell me.'

'I'm looking forward to meeting my wee brother.'

'So am I,' he said softly and climbed the stairs to his bedroom to pack.

He went early to bed, hoping to sleep the hours away. Instead he tossed and turned, sleeping fitfully, wakening just as daybreak crept through the curtains. He lay for a time thinking ahead, trying to visualize what the following days would bring. It was very early, too early to get up, in case he disturbed Shona. He slept again briefly then got up to wash his face and bathe his body with the cold water from the pewter basin on his dresser. He dressed and looked from the window. A white blanket of mist covered the fields and the scent of wet earth was nectar to his nostrils.

He stole down to the kitchen to put kindling on the fire and when Shona came downstairs the kettle was singing and eggs boiling in a big pan. Snap and Ginger had been fed on cream and were washing their faces by the fire.

'You didn't sleep well,' she stated simply when she saw his tired drawn face.

'Not very.'

'Don't worry, Father. Och, I know you must feel all queer and excited. I feel the same about Niall and he's only been gone ten months. You haven't seen Kirsteen in six years. The wee boy will be – what – about five?'

'Aye, he would have been that around January, funny, the same month as yourself, mo ghaoil.'

Her blue eyes were gentle. 'It will be funny having a wee brother here. I wonder what he's like . . . if he's like you at all, Father.'

'Balfour says he's dark so the colouring anyway he's inherited from me. I hope not the temper.'

She laughed. 'He wouldn't be a McKenzie without one. Sit down now and I'll get the eggs. You mustny be late for this boat. Oh, it will be lovely to see you happy, Father, you haven't been in years – not really.'

He squeezed her hand and sitting down forced

himself to eat an egg. His belly was tight with nerves and the food tasted repulsive. He was glad to see Lachlan striding past the window and into the kitchen. It was an excuse to leave the table.

'Good luck,' said Lachlan simply. 'I'm going to Croynachan but wanted to see you first.'

'Thanks,' said Fergus. 'You'll see this lass of mine gets up to no mischief while I'm gone.'

'Father!' chided Shona laughingly. 'How can I with all the work of a farmer's wife to be done. Anyway . . .' she coloured. 'I think I've learned my lesson about mischief-making.'

Lachlan held out his hand and Fergus gripped it briefly. 'Take a good dram before you set out,' recommended Lachlan. 'Doctor's orders.'

He went away quickly and Fergus busied himself with any task that would take his mind from himself. Mathew had been given his instructions but Bob came in with Murdy to go over a few details.

Shona didn't come down to the harbour. She was very emotional these days and didn't want to weep before her father. She hated his going and, though overwhelmed with happiness at the turn of events, felt naturally apprehensive about the great changes there would be at Laigmhor with another woman to run things and a small boy who was her half-brother and a total stranger. But she had always admired Kirsteen and felt excited at the thought of seeing her again, though she couldn't help but retain most of her excitement for Niall.

He had written a letter full of sadness and remorse for all that she had gone through, blaming himself bitterly for everything, even the loss of their son. She had written him letters of reassurance but couldn't wait to see him to prove that her love for him burned even more brightly. They had both known tragedy, each apart from the other, both had grown up and had still to see the changes in each other but she was confident that all they had survived would bring them even closer in the end. She had made up her mind that they wouldn't marry for a while. She would let Niall get over the shock of war and she herself now felt she needed time to let her own scars heal.

She watched the boat leaving the harbour and hoped fervently that her father's journey would be fruitful.

Fergus hadn't left the island in five years and the journey passed in a dream. Glasgow frightened him and he jostled with people in the streets, suddenly conscious that his best suit was drastically out of date. In Rhanna no one bothered about clothes. Suits hung in wardrobes for years, only brought out for funerals or weddings. They never went out of fashion because each man's garb was much the same as the other.

In the city it was different and Fergus felt himself sticking out like a sore thumb, easily picked out as a country farmer. His heart bumped with dismay as he wondered if Kirsteen would see him as such, perhaps be ashamed of him.

On impulse he went into a big store and stared at racks of clothes without seeing them. A sales assistant hovered and he sweated. She came over to offer her help but he muttered something about just looking and she took the dismissal with the smiling mask of a good public servant. He drifted aimlessly and she hovered again. 'Is it a suit or casual wear, sir?'

'Casual – I think.'

'Then might I suggest a nice tweed jacket, a green check would go nicely with your hair and eyes . . . and flannels in a natural shade, plain to offset the jacket.'

He acceded gruffly and was hustled into a cubicle to try the things for size. 'Just right for you, sir,' she enthused when after five minutes of indecisive sweating he finally stepped out of the cubicle. 'Do you want to change back or will you wear them now?'

'I'll keep them on.'

'Right, I'll just put your – er – old things in a bag and we'll go along to the desk.' She smiled and fluttered her eyes at his greatly changed appearance and made polite sounds of approval. 'Now you're more like the thing.' She nodded and he fumed, his black eyes snapping while he waited for change.

Fergus stood in Argyll Street and felt like a tailor's dummy, surely more conspicuous than ever. But no one gave him a second glance.

He ate in the station restaurant and was aware of the uniforms of the armed forces all round him. In Rhanna one was lulled into a sense that the same peace that existed there must surely be in the rest of the world but the cities were full of young uniformed men.

Fergus drifted in and out of slumber while the train rushed him through the night to London.

Before Euston, Fergus splashed his face with cold water but he still felt bleary-eyed and conscious of the dark shadow of stubble on his face. He breakfasted on a greasy egg roll and a watery cup of tea and felt sick on the train to the home counties.

But in a homely country inn at his destination he found solace at last. The innkeeper was unhurried and friendly and guided him to a room with oak beams and a sloping floor. The window looked on to rolling fields and for the first time since leaving Rhanna he felt some of the tension uncoil from his stomach.

'Bathroom's right along the passage,' said Mr Trout showing two aged front teeth. 'We're none fancy here you know, sir. No 'ot water except on Fridays and Mondays for baths but I'll get the missus to bring a pan of 'ot water for you to shave if you want. You look a bit of a gentleman to be stopping 'ere. We're for travellers mostly and locals.'

'I couldn't have wished for a better place,' said Fergus gratefully. 'It suits me fine.'

Mr Trout folded his arms. 'Ah! It's a nice tongue you 'ave there. Where in Scotland do you hail from, sir? Went for a holiday there once and it snowed in May! Would you believe it?'

Fergus smiled. 'It's colder in the north. I'm from the Hebrides, an island called Rhanna.'

'Is that so, is that so? The 'ebrides, eh? Sounds lovely – nice names they 'ave these islands but far, too far they be for the likes of myself. At first I thought you were one of these posh gentlemen from Edinburgh or the like – the clothes you know, I like to dress casual-like myself.'

He looked at his baggy trousers and voluminous cardigan and gave a small apologetic grin. 'Can't be bothered being stuffed up with a tie, the bloody things choke me. Now come down when you're ready, sir. The missus made some nice soup and there's a bit of roast beef if you've a mind. Apple pie for afters – can never resist it myself.'

He went out and Fergus fell on to the big feather bed and laughed with joy. He loved Mr Trout already – Trout, he'd thought that was merely the name of the inn.

Mrs Trout could have been her husband's twin so alike were they in shape and manner. She plied Fergus with platefuls of food and her round face grew quite sad when he refused a second helping of apple pie and cream.

'You're a fine big lad but you need feeding,' she scolded severely. 'Now Mr Trout will eat it and 'im with pounds of blubber already. Ah well, I like 'im that way – we're two of a kind Mr Trout and I.'

'I believe Teesdale House is quite near here?' said Fergus tentatively.

'Bless your 'eart, yes. 'Alf a mile back near Farradale Farm. You know the Campbell-Elliots then?' Her voice was slightly overawed.

'Just someone who is employed there.'

'Nice people they are for the gentry,' Mrs Trout murmured, her voice changed to an unnatural politeness at the very idea of her guest being even remotely connected with Teesdale House. 'Comes in 'ere sometimes, does Mr Leonard. Seems to enjoy an occasional beer with the locals. It's the way he talks, can never understand 'im myself but we're all alike in the eyes of God I say.'

It was a warm evening and the scent of honeysuckle filled the air. The rolling countryside stretched green for miles. It was so different from the wild beauty of Rhanna. There was a gentleness about the fields and the hedgerows and the peacefully grazing, orderly looking cows, so unlike the shaggy self-willed beasts that freely roamed the island. But Fergus felt he would fall off the world at any moment. He needed the strong shoulders of mountains to keep him in place, he was lost without the thunder of the sea and the wild cry of gulls. England was pretty but too fashioned by man, there was none of the sense of freedom of lonely open spaces where one could lose oneself and be alone to think.

He passed Farradale Farm and drew the familiar scent of dung into his lungs. A farmhand nodded at him. 'Nice evenin'. You goin' up to the big 'ouse?'

'How did you know?'

'Gentry clothes you're wearin'.'

Fergus realised how he must appear to a farm worker whose trousers were splattered with mud and whose shirt was patched in sweat. He shook his head, anxious to dispel the illusion his appearance created. 'Forget the clothes. I'm more used to wearing duddies like yourself. It would never do to work a farm wearing tweeds.'

'Wh-at? Duddies?' beamed the farmhand.

'Work clothes.'

'Ah! Isn't that quaint now? You a farmer dressed like a lord?'

'I am going to Teesdale though.'

'Well, just you come with me and I'll show you a

short cut. Not for the likes of everybody mind but seein' as you're a farmer an' all . . .'

He led Fergus through a cobbled yard and opened a gate into an overgrown path. 'Follow it till you come to a copse,' he instructed. 'The 'ouse is on the other side of the copse. Save you a half mile or more goin' this way. Biddin' you goodnight, then.'

The copse was cool with sunlight dappling the grass. Fergus heard the laughter before he saw anyone. His heart hammered into his throat. How many times that same laugh had rung out for him – it was unmistakable, melodious and high.

He stepped into a sunlit clearing and there was Kirsteen standing by a huge oak tree, her hair shining like pale gold in the sun. She didn't see him, she appeared to be hiding from someone and a small peal of laughter was smothered quickly.

He was able to drink in every detail of her, the slim figure in a dress that matched her hair and long brown legs with feet in open sandals. He could hardly believe it, the dream of Kirsteen was now a reality, her living flesh there before him and fate, the force that weaved lives into a pattern, had stepped in once more to fashion a strange twist to their meeting. With woods again as the setting he was about to surprise her as he had done in another time. His heart pumped madly but this time it wasn't desire that made his legs tremble; it was love, pure and naked, the emotions of years culminating in this final moment of nerve-shattering triumph.

A small boy burst into the clearing, a child with crisp dark curls and sturdy limbs. A shout of laughter died in his throat and he stared past Kirsteen to Fergus at the edge of the trees.

Kirsteen turned slowly to look at Fergus, their eyes meeting in a moment when the world held its breath. He saw that she had changed but only by reason that she was more beautiful than he ever remembered. The years had honed the girlish features of his memory to the delicately boned structure of mature young womanhood. Her eyes were very blue in her smooth tanned face and reminded him of the blue of the Atlantic on a summer day. He heard the quick intake of her breath and saw her hands clenching at her sides but her voice when she spoke was calm and held a trace of an English accent.

'I knew you'd come,' she said without emotion.

He stepped forward feeling that such a moment should have been without words. He wanted to gather her to him, declare his love, but their years apart had robbed them of youthful impulses and it was no longer his right to take her intimate responses for granted.

There was so much to say yet he could think of nothing, only the small talk that meant little. 'Balfour told me,' he said, his voice rough with longing.

'I knew he would.'

'And – you didn't run away?'

Her head went up defiantly. 'Why should I? I ran once, now I have no reason to.'

He couldn't believe that the cold toneless words were coming from her lips. Surely, if she'd loved him in the way he'd always believed, she must feel something. The years did not take away the kind of love they had known.

He spread his hand in a gesture of despair and she bit her lip to stop from crying out. The sight of him, bronzed and handsome in his new clothes, despite them, with every lilting word, so endearingly a son of the Hebrides, made her want to run to him, to tell him of the years of her lonely exile away from a love that would not let spirit rest.

Her heart fluttered so fast she was afraid she would faint. She'd counted the days since the laird's departure, waiting and praying for the moment that was now here. She had wondered how she would feel seeing him and had thought that perhaps her mind had magnified her loving memories out of all proportion to what was real in her heart. But it wasn't so; he was here, real and near, and she knew if she touched him that all the resolution and pride she had built round herself would vanish in a puff, leaving her with nothing, no will to deny him anything he asked of her.

'Mother, I found you!' The child's voice broke the silence. 'It's my turn to hide now.'

She looked at Fergus. 'We were playing – it's my day off. I don't get much time to spend with him.'

Fergus bent down to his son. 'What's your name?'

'Grant Fergus Fraser,' said the boy shyly but with pride. 'It's a real Scottish name because although I live in England I'm a Scot really. My father belongs there and he's been living on an island all his life but some day we'll go to Scotland and find him. Who are you, sir?'

Fergus dropped on one knee so that his face was level with that of the little boy. He saw dark, deep eyes with a touch of defiance in them, and a small tanned face with a dimple set in the chin and he felt he was looking at a picture of himself at five years old.

'My name is McKenzie,' he said quietly. 'I come from an island, an island called Rhanna in the Outer Hebrides.'

The boy gasped. 'My *father* lives there! Do you know him? He's big and strong. Mother told me, didn't you, Mother?'

Fergus looked towards Kirsteen. 'You told him the truth. Dear God! Thank you for that!'

Kirsteen struggled to maintain her calm. 'I told him the truth yes, to a certain extent. I saw no point in lying because these things have a habit of rebounding. Ever since he could start asking questions he asked about his father and I told him that you were alive but that was all. He makes things up, that he's going to live some day on Rhanna beside his father. I didn't put the idea in his mind.'

'You're my father!' the boy yelled and a flock of crows rose from the trees in alarm. He held on to Fergus's sleeve and his dark eyes were pleading. 'Have you come to take us back to Scotland? It's terrible not having a father. Other boys are always telling me things they do with their fathers and – and they call me funny names.'

'That's enough, Grant! Come over here!' Kirsteen held out her hand and the boy went reluctantly. 'You mustn't say a word to anyone,' she said severely. 'Promise you won't, please, sweetheart.'

The child scowled. 'Oh all right, but I think it's nasty of you. I've waited a long time for a father and now he's here you won't let me tell anyone!'

'He needs a father's hand,' said Fergus with a faint smile.

'He's needed it for years.'

'Kirsteen, och my Kirsteen, you left me, remember? Please let me talk to you. Could we go somewhere?'

'I'll ask Beatrice to put Grant to bed. She's the housemaid and has been very good to young Grant. Wait . . . here for me.'

Fergus was left in a haze of doubts about everything. His golden dream of carrying Kirsteen and his son back to Rhanna belonged to a fool's paradise. She hadn't even been friendly towards him. He watched her walk towards the big Tudor mansion set in velvet lawns. She had made a good life for herself, she might not want to live on a farm on a wild lonely island. They were worlds apart. She had changed, everything had changed, even his son had grown from a baby to a boy with a mind of his own. They were all strangers to each other and he'd been living in a world of dreams for so long he'd been unable to separate dreams from reality till he'd come face to face with reality and found that it didn't make any sense of his dreams at all.

He felt deflated and uneasy and wanted to walk away from the sun-drenched woods. Instead he sat down on a tree stump and was surprised to find the taste of salt on his lips. He was crying like a lost child, the tears of frustration and sadness, once begun, flowing down his face helplessly. He hid his face in his hand and the sound of his harsh dry sobs made him hate his weakness but he couldn't stop.

Kirsteen's heart was torn in two when she came

back and saw him there, strong, proud Fergus crying like a baby. A sob caught in her own throat and she knew she was going to run to him, to rock him in her arms and tell him how much she loved him. But he looked up and mistaking her look for pity he cried out in anger, 'That's right, look at me damn you! Look at me! It's not the first time, Kirsteen! I've cried for you for years. I cried when I knew you'd left me and I cried when I went to Oban and your mother told me you had gone.'

'She never told me. She wrote – I wrote her – but she never told me you had been to see her, Fergus!'

'Too damned well I know it! She wouldn't tell anyone where you were! Even when she died she had everyone in circles trying to locate you.'

He didn't mean to deliver the blow so hard but the words were out. Her face went pale but she showed no emotion. 'I – didn't know. I haven't written since we came down here last year but she knew this address. She didn't write much so I didn't suspect. I . . . this may sound hard but I can't feel anything very much, pity perhaps and regret that things went the way they did but . . . that's all.'

Fergus stood up and looked deep into her eyes. He made no attempt to touch her. 'Your mother was like me, Kirsteen – too much pride. It's a heavy burden and she died with pride choking her. I've had to swallow mine and the taste of it was bitter and sour. Now I fear I have none left and you've a mite too much. I was too proud at one time to ask a lovely woman like you to be my wife, I drove you away. Now I'd go on my knees to you if you asked me.'

She kept her eyes fixed on the grass at her feet because his nearness was turning her into an unresisting being without control of heart or mind. 'It's not that easy, Fergus. It wasn't easy having a baby in London and finding a place where I could work and keep my son. He was the only thing that kept me sane. That first year away from you I had to fight not to go running back to Rhanna and you. I left the biggest part of myself on that island; the rest of me, the living shell that walked and talked, had to eat and sleep. I went from job to job and hated them all, then I found the Campbell-Elliots and for four years now they've treated me like one of the family. I work for them but they make it a pleasure and it's not many would bother with a single woman and a young child.' She inclined her head towards the house. 'I can't just go off and leave them after all they've done. Try to understand . . . my dear, dear Fergus.'

He looked at her quickly, trying to catch her eye as she whispered the endearments, but she eluded him.

He took a step backwards. 'I'm – glad I saw my son, he's a fine lad – Shona was looking forward to having a wee brother.'

She turned quickly. 'Oh, how is she? I've thought so much about her.'

'She's . . . been my life these years. She's had sad times but they're over now. Niall and she are to be together again when he comes home from military hospital. He was wounded at Dunkirk.'

'Oh, I'm sorry, but glad it's turning out for them. In my heart I always thought they'd end up together, they were so close as children.'

He was turning away from her and a beam of evening sun found the small white hairs among the jet black of his sideburns.

'Oh!' She strangled a cry and moved away. 'I'd better see if Beatrice is managing.'

He nodded, slowly and deliberately signalling his defeat. Then he remembered something and pulled a package from an inner pocket of his jacket. He held it out. 'It's a bit late but these were meant for you. I wrote them four months after you left Rhanna but your mother kept them back from you. I have to thank Mrs Travers for their return – she found them in a drawer after your mother died. They're of little use to me now.'

He pushed the letters into her hand and strode away seeing nothing before him.

She stood where she was, tears coursing down her cheeks, clutching the letters like a drowning person clutches at a straw.

Rhanna was determined to give Niall a hero's welcome. They were all there at the harbour, leaving work behind for the occasion. Todd, with two horses to shoe, had simply taken them to an absent neighbour's barn and let them have a feed of hay. Wullie the carpenter had left some newly cut wood to ripen nicely in the sun and Merry Mary, even Behag Beag, had closed their doors for a whiley.

Canty Tam, with his peculiar leaning stance, grinned aimlessly at the sky and Dodie was lolloping anxiously from Glen Fallan. Biddy, Robbie, Beag, old Joe, Bob and Murdy, all the dour, loving familiar faces were there in the crowd, waiting with a subdued excitement as the boat bringing Niall foamed into the harbour. Hardly a cottage had an empty window, faces peered and the fishermen's wives leaned ample arms on window sills and 'cracked' with each other to fill the time.

Elspeth stood proudly by Phebie and Lachlan, holding the hand of an excited Fiona, and Shona waited quietly with her father. A little behind them stood Alick and Mary with the twins, on Rhanna for their summer holidays.

Shona was wearing her blue dress, the one Niall liked her in best. Her copper hair, tied back with a blue ribbon, tumbled down her back, and her eyes sparkled blue in a face pale with excitement.

Fergus puffed his pipe and the smoke curled in the haze of the autumn day. Behind him the hills were bronzed with bracken and the moor stretched, a sea of purple heather.

The approaching boat brought a swelling tide of green which slopped and swirled against the piles of the pier.

Fergus could sense his daughter's tension and she caught his look and smiled, a quick nervous smile that wakened in him the usual responses of protective love.

'Not long now, mo ghaoil,' he whispered.

'I'm – afraid, Father.'

'I know exactly how you feel, I've been through it too but it's to be sure your meeting will be happier than mine.'

An involuntary little cry broke in her throat and she

gripped his hand tightly. 'I wish – oh how I wish . . .'

'Weesht now, lass, it's all meant for us. Things canny be changed.'

The boat sounded its horn and the pier swayed with the bump. Ropes were thrown and tied. There was quite a crowd of passengers, the last of the summer people visiting relatives. Among them bobbed two heads of bright hair. At first Shona couldn't distinguish Niall then an arm came above one of the heads and she knew it was him.

'Niall,' she whispered, then 'Niall!' in a shout of joy that echoed above the general hubbub.

In a minute he was down the gangplank and in her arms, wordlessly clinging as if he would never let go. A cheer went up and he stared in amazement.

'For you,' she murmured, looking at him, seeing a very pale thin face, so different from the boyish contours she remembered, but still Niall, his brown eyes aglow with joy. 'Why me, sweetheart?' he said. 'I'm no hero, just another soldier who got crocked up in the war.'

'You're a son of Rhanna and to them you're a hero.'

Phebie and Lachlan came over and Niall was smothered with the love of his family. Fiona clung to his neck and he was jostled and welcomed, the tongue of his native Gaelic sweet and dear to him.

Fergus knocked out his pipe and was making his way to the core of the crowd when he stopped frozen, his black eyes looking in disbelief at Kirsteen coming uncertainly towards him, her hand clutching that of their little son.

Fergus was immobile, unable to move while hope

and love churned in his heart. She too had stopped. Grant was looking about him in a wonder of delight. 'Mother, look at the caves!' he cried. 'Look at the mountains! Look at the seagulls!' He broke from his mother's grasp and ran, a sturdy little boy, filled with the magic of his new discoveries, ran to the screeching gulls perched along the harbour and chased them into the sky where they soared in silent majesty of flight.

His parents beheld each other in a daze of longing then the years were bridged in one short moment. She was beside him and he was holding her so tightly she gasped and laughed before their lips joined in a kiss that swept away all doubts in a tide of love.

'Was it the letters?' he whispered in her ear.

'Partly, but mostly because after you left I was so miserable and sad Mrs Campbell-Elliot asked me what was wrong. I told her I had seen you and she said I was to come to you at once. I waited till they had another governess – it was the least I could do. It seemed the longest month I've ever gone through in my life – except when I left Rhanna.' She looked towards the mountains and breathed deeply. 'It's so good to be home . . . do you think it will work for us?'

'My dearest Kirsteen,' he said huskily, 'how could it not? You'll be my wife, tomorrow if possible.'

She laughed. 'Rhanna will be shocked. Fergus McKenzie with a wife and ready-made son.'

'Let them,' he said and kissed her again, uncaring about anyone or what they thought. He caught Lachlan's eye and received a mischievous wink and he raised his hand to the doctor who had devoted himself to the people of Rhanna and who had honoured him with a friendship that was all the stronger the second time round.

Alick and Mary were bearing down on them.

'Welcome aboard,' grinned Alick holding out his hand to Kirsteen. 'Are you all coming along now? It's high time we had a bite to eat. Mary here will thraw a chicken for us.' He put an arm round his wife's waist and they laughed at the look of disgust on her face at the idea of killing a chicken singlehanded.

Shona had just spotted Kirsteen through the crowd and she gasped, 'I can't believe it!'

Niall nodded with quiet satisfaction. 'She came on the boat with me. I knew her but she didn't recognize me – I was only a glaikit wee boy when she went away!'

She smiled at the jibe but continued to look in her father's direction. 'That wee boy – the one with the black curls must be . . .'

'Your brother,' finished Niall before he was lifted to the shoulders of two brawny fishermen. The crowd sang a triumphant Gaelic air and Canty Tam shut his eyes and thanked the Uisga Hags for the return of a Rhanna man.

Phebie and Lachlan each took one of Shona's arms. 'He belongs to the people for a wee while,' said Phebie with a sigh of contentment.

'Then he's ours again,' said Shona.

Lachlan nodded towards Fergus and Kirsteen. 'There will be at least one wedding soon,' he prophesied. 'We'll Ceilidh for days.'

A small boy came running, his face red with exertion. 'Biddy – where's Biddy? Mrs McPherson's started!'

Biddy broke from the crowd. She had lost her hat and her hair straggled over spectacles that were characteristically lopsided. 'Will the folk on this damty island never stop havin' bairns?' she wailed indignantly but as she followed the small boy on legs that were spindly but strong from a lifetime of walking glens and moors, her face was serene and smiling. Nothing gave her more pleasure than seeing a tiny new life come bawling naked into the world.

Dodie, his thoughts already taking him over the moors in a search for Ealasaid and his morning milk, loped after the crowd going into Glen Fallan. 'He breeah!' he shouted dismally to Morag Ruadh who was searching the beach for driftwood, then he wailed to the disappearing crowd, 'Will you wait for me? I have a present for Niall so I have!'

The harbour was quiet once again but for the sound of waves and the cry of gulls. Triumphant in the distance Niall's head bobbed above the rest, a blob of gold against the wild yet dreaming hills of Rhanna.